DEEP RIVER BLUES

DEEP RIVER BLUES

a novel

Tony Ray Morris

NORTHAMPTON HOUSE PRESS

First edition 2020 by Northampton House Press, Franktown, Virginia USA.
Cover by Steve Mousourakis.
"Killing the Blues" by Rowland Salley. © 2002 Telechrome Music, ASCAP. By permission.
"The Second Coming" first published in 1920. Public domain.
ISBN 978-1-950668-01-4
Library of Congress Control Number: 2020900992

10 9 8 7 6 5 4 3 2

Let it rain, let it pour
Let it rain a whole lot more
'Cause I got them deep river blues

~Doc Watson

1
Wading Into Shallows

Cord slid down the bank, catching himself on a few dead shrubs that still held against the drawing cold of winter. The sun had just begun to dip below the high bluffs overlooking the river, the darkening water swirling below. A silvery-white glow reflecting in the eddies and troughs of the river reminded him of the strange serpent-tails of light he'd noticed on the surface of the Pacific when he'd flown home after Desert Storm.

Sam Whatson met him halfway up the bank. "Glad you're here, Cord." The tall, broad-shouldered deputy's sharp, dark eyes set beneath pronounced brows always surprised Cord in their intensity. "Coroner's just getting ready to pull her out."

Cord nodded. "What's to tell?"

"Looks like she took a tumble, f'sure. Hard telling if she had some help. Forensics will have to take a closer look. Pretty nasty bump there on her head. Could be she fell in and cracked it on a boulder." He labored to keep stride with Cord's quick gait over the rocks. A few years junior to him, the six foot, two-hundred-plus pounder was often the butt of Cord's good-natured jabs about his struggles to outpace the more agile sheriff. Now, as they reached the body next to the bridge pilings, he pulled up short behind Cord, breathing heavy. "Wasn't sure whether you'd need to be here, or not."

"Need to borrow some lungs, buddy?"

"Gonna loan me yours?" Sam swiped his forehead with the back of his hand. "Besides, you told me on the first day of spring training I didn't need the speed, long as I had the brawn and the brains."

"First, that was high school baseball. Second, you're still workin' on the brains part of that equation."

"Hey, dickhead. At least I graduated from college."

Cord chuckled. "I'm gettin' there. Just don't have that fancy diploma yet that convinces folks they're equipped to think. Hell. You're the best example I know to prove the converse. Besides, you can learn all there is to know about the science of pitching a curve, but it ain't gonna tell you nothing about the mystery of the moment when you let that ball fly. Now let's get to work."

He stepped into the shallows and panned the light over the body. A slim girl, probably nineteen or twenty, countenance calm, even placid. Long, wavy, red hair floated on the mirrored surface around her head like a flaming halo, shifting in eddies that seemed to circle in, then ripple out again, as if the center of the river's current began and ended at the tangled strands. Folds of her skirt had caught in the overhanging branches of a dead sycamore, the flower-print gingham torn where it had snagged a low-slung branch. Despite the blue-white pallor of her face, and pale green eyes that stared blankly up into nothing, she almost looked alive.

"Got an ID?" He pulled on latex gloves.

"No sir. That there's it. Nothin' but the clothes on her back, and that leather anklet. Way she's dressed, I'm thinking those Glad Earthers down at Hartfield's old place might know her."

Cord studied her face. He'd seen death aplenty. Usually the violent, sudden kind that came from some reckless, vengeful madness brought on by petty envy or overblown pride. But this stranger, with a face so empty of either guile or guilt, struck a chord of pity in him he didn't quite understand. "Damn shame."

2

He reached out his finger and traced a braided leather band tied around her ankle. Something vaguely familiar about it made him briefly pause, trying to place it. Then he lifted a broad, three-fingered, rust-flecked leaf off the top of her bare foot and shined the light on a tattoo. A small, bleeding heart circled in thorns and shot through the center with a blue cross.

Too bad I don't have the faith of Lazurus' sister, Cord thought. He murmured, "And Jesus said to her, I am the resurrection and the life. He who believes in me will live, even though he dies; and whosoever lives and believes in me will never die. Do you believe this?" He dropped the leaf in the current and watched it float away.

"What?" Sam moved closer.

"Nothing. Just a reminder of my feeble faith." He straightened. "You might be right. Sure looks like a Glad Earther."

A few years back, a hundred or so people, young city folk and a few children, had showed up in a caravan of buses, Subarus and SUVs. They'd bought the old Hartfield Farm for a steal and settled into a holler that butted up against the southern shore of the Pigeon River just northeast of Falston, Tennessee, the Acre County town seat. Most locals steered clear of them, and generally the strangers had kept to themselves as well.

Maybe a little too much, Cord now thought. The compound, named Glad Earth Farm, was a poorly tended half-cropped parcel. He'd long suspected it was a cover for not-so-philanthropic activities that fell outside the law. Looking down at the girl, he hoped this wasn't evidence of their cup starting to spill over.

He scanned the rest of the body, then looked more closely at the contusion and deep laceration on her right temple. Purple bruising behind the ear. "Battle's sign," he said over his shoulder. "Probably a cranial fracture. Seen it plenty in Panama and the Gulf." He reached in his jacket, pulled out a pen and used the tip to move her hair for a closer look. "Something about the shape of this bruise. Too uniform. Snap a picture, Sam."

3

As the forensics team moved in and began processing the body, he stood and rubbed an old scar on the side of his own head. A shoot-out years back at Frank Reevers' place had almost left him blind, the bullet grazing just above his right eyebrow, skimming the temple. "Let's find out when and where she went in. I need you to canvass up and down the river, see if anybody saw this poor girl. Hell, we got trout fishers and pleasure boats runnin' the currents regular. Somebody must've seen somethin'. And make a call out to The Farm. See if anyone's missing up there. If there is, get 'em in for a positive ID."

He stared out across the river. High above steep bluffs that rose sharply from the shallow shores, a red-tailed hawk cut through a cornflower blue sky under rippled bands of clouds, shrill whistle echoing off the surface of the chill water. He pictured the girl floating down the river, her loose peasant skirt rippled and spread like dappled yellow leaves floating on the surface of a current that furled and eddied, swirling around legs and torso. Her head and arms would have plunged, submerged, then resurfaced as she dipped and spun into each new trough, or edged around the smoothed slick surface of stones that split the wide, slow course of the river. A slight wind would've breezed across her body as she rolled onto her back, floating for a moment, waves of long, red hair fanning out to frame smooth marbled features. Green eyes staring briefly into the infinite, before rolling face down again to follow the quickening surge of the old, unceasing pull.

"Say a couple of boys found her?"

"Gene and little Freddy Grant. About two hours ago. Said they just came down t' fish the bank. There she was." Sam took off his cap and wiped his forehead with one sleeve.

"Two hours ago? When was it reported?"

"Oh." Sam looked at his watch. "About forty-five minutes ago."

"What the hell were they doing, using her for bait?"

"Said they wanted to show some friends. Johnny Cray's momma called it in when she overheard 'em talking."

4

"One helluva catch for two young'uns." Cord turned and scrambled back over the rocks, up the bank. "See you back at the house," he said over one shoulder. "Looks like we're in for a night."

Cord wheeled Josephine, the Ford Interceptor he'd named after Josephine Humphreys, whose stories never veered far from the mysteries of the ordinary while traveling manifold detours at a good clip, onto the highway. Nothing ever seemed to work out the way he planned. When he'd left home that morning, Lucinda had called after him, warning that this was the last time she would remind him to pick up the new float valve to fix the commode.

"I'm tired of your excuses, Cordell," she'd said. "You've been promising for weeks."

"Sorry. It's just been crazy at the office since the election."

"I know." Her voice had lost some of its edge. "I get it. It's just a busy week here coming up on finals, they're talking about cutting adjunct positions, and I could use a little help."

"I'll take care of it."

"And don't forget to pick up Blu after choir practice."

"On that, too." Their eight-year-old son, had just joined the children's choir at Falston Elementary and was nervous about riding the bus home.

But now, as he made his way back to the office, the radio crackled. "Cord. You there?" said Judy, his dispatch. "We got a 415, local disturbance out at the Rooster."

Judy Hudson had been with the sheriff's department about fourteen years. They'd both hired on around the same time. Seen a lot together over the years. She was single, about ten years Cord's senior, mid-fifties or so, with a full figure and auburn hair she kept swept up in a loose bun. She used to smoke Virginia Slims and kept an ashtray full of the filtered butts ringed with bright red lipstick. Now, with the new non-smoking policy in place, the department's budget for her favorite Pilot V5 extra-fine, rolling ball pens had tripled—oral fixation being the only part of a smoking cessation plan she'd been willing to address.

Smart, sassy, she didn't take herself, or anyone else, too seriously. A good fit for Acre County's small, close-knit sheriff's office.

"Ten-four. I'm on it. Listen, can you do me a favor? I need to pick up Blu from school, but I'm already late as hell. Can you swing by on your way home?"

"Can, and will. And good luck. Sounds like you'll need it. Over and out."

He cradled the handset, flipped the lights and gunned the cruiser north on Highway 73. Ten minutes later he pulled into the gravel lot and slid to a stop in front of the small cinderblock structure, dust billowing behind. He grabbed his hat off the seat, wishing he'd dropped by Goode's Hardware on his lunch break. Might still make it if there ain't too much paperwork after this ruckus, he thought. He took a deep breath, stepped out of the car, settled the hat on and walked to the entrance of Rooster's Bar.

Inside, Webb Rasser, a gangly, tall rounder who worked as a hired hand at old man Grimm's place, was leaning unsteadily against the bar, eyes wide with fear and panic, gripping the handle of a bloody knife. On the floor five paces away, Lou Pollard, a young local who'd recently returned from Afghanistan, lay crumpled next to some overturned chairs. Blood from a gash in his neck soaked his battered brown Carhartt chore coat. Red Slokum, the Rooster's manager, stood behind the bar, back to the shelf of bottles.

Cord settled his right hand on his pistol and nodded at the knife. "So, what's goin' on here, son?"

"Y-you just move on off, now, Sheriff," Webb stuttered. "You know I ain't bad, like some is." He glanced down at Lou. "And I ain't going to jail. Not fer you nor nobody. Gotta make rent this month fer me and Elsie."

Cord eased closer to the bar, keeping his eyes on Webb. "You okay, Red?" He glanced at the big man behind the counter.

"Jus' fine, Cord," Red drawled, toothpick dangling from one corner of his mouth.

"That sonabitch said Elsie were gonna leave me." Webb's voice rose angrily. "Said she probly weren't nothin' but a whore nohow. That she was … just like the rest of 'em."

Cord took another step closer, let go the pistol and slowly raised his right hand, palm out. "Okay, Webb. Steady, boy. I get it." He kept inching forward. "But Lou here is bleedin' bad. It's my job to make sure he don't die so's you don't go to prison." He edged closer, now just an arm's length away from the knife.

"Stay away. Swear I'll cut you." Webb's hand slightly trembled as he raised the blade and shook it like a bloody finger at Cord's face, then lunged.

In one motion, Cord pivoted right and whipped his left arm up, battering Webb's wrist. The knife flew clattering behind the bar. He twisted to the right and sent a quick, hard hook to the side of the man's jaw that knocked him to the floor.

Cord was just this side of medium build. But his training as a middle-weight Golden Gloves boxer often gave him an advantage with scrappers who misjudged the power and speed of a well-placed hook delivered by a 175 pound coiled wire. The boy was in cuffs and getting hauled up and pushed to the corner of the bar before he knew what hit him.

"Get on that phone, Red! Need an ambulance out here. Tell 'em we got a Code 10 trauma." He cuffed Webb to the brass rail then turned and knelt beside Lou. Blood had oozed in a dark puddle on the floor around his shoulders and head.

"Cord. Please." Webb rattled the cuffs. "You know me! I can't get arrested now. I can't."

"Shut up. You oughta thought of that before you tangled with Lou." Cord press a hand against the gash. "Shit! Red, get me a rag. Hurry!" The liquid pulse was oozing against his fingers. Weak, thready. "Goddammit. Where's that—"

Red was already beside him with a soiled rag from behind the counter. "Here." He dropped it carelessly into Cord's hand, shifting the toothpick from one side to the other, then turned to shuffle back behind the bar.

Cord shook his head. "Really?" He folded and pressed the rag to the gash in Lou's throat. "Goddammit, Red. Get back over here, and stuff this jacket under his legs so he doesn't go into shock." He pulled his arms out of the service coat and tossed it. The big man grunted and huffed as he lowered himself to Lou's feet.

"Don't see what difference it'll make." Red bunched the coat under the man's legs and stood again. "Ain't worth the time it'll take to bury him, ye ask me."

Cord ignored him, watching the door. "Dammit-to-hell. Where's that ambulance?"

"Said they was on their way."

Sirens down the road. He glanced at Lou, who was now pale and clammy. Hang on, son, he thought. Hang the fuck on. A minute later, the EMTs pushed through the door.

"Just missed the jugular. Needs fluids." Cord shifted aside, keeping pressure on the wound as Nick Durham, the wiry, energetic ditch doctor squatted next to Lou and flipped open his bag for an IV. Cord had worked a bus with him briefly after coming home from his stint in the service. Nick could save a man with baling wire, pliers, a plastic straw and a shirt-tail, if need be.

"Damn, Cord. What put you out here in this bullshit? Thought you was runnin' with the big dogs now?" He glanced over his shoulder at his partner, Ryanne Brady, a young, dark-haired, half-Cherokee woman just back from the Gulf who was wheeling in the gurney.

"Is that Lou?" Ryanne lowered the gurney. "What the hell happened?"

"That's what I plan to find out. You know him?" Cord stood to let her by.

"We crossed paths over in that hellhole sandpit." She shook her head, dismayed. "Get through that fucked up mission alive only to end up like this." She slung the straps across Lou's body and cinched them. "Guess that bullshit just follows us on home."

"Looks like. Glad *you* made it back. Way things are going around here lately, I could use a few more good corpsman like you in the field. Drop by the office. We'll talk."

"Thanks. I will. Might teach you old dogs a few new tricks." She winked and grabbed a side-rail on the gurney. "Let's get him on the truck, quick."

Nick slipped the IV needle into Lou's arm. "Looks like he just notched the vein. May save him yet." They raised the gurney then wheeled him out the door.

"Hope I don't see you soon, Big Dog." Nick nodded and grinned as the door slammed shut behind them.

"Yeah, right. Big dog." Cord picked up his jacket and started toward the bar. "Outta the fire and into the shit's more like it." He pulled a kerchief from the jacket and picked up the knife from behind the bar. Studied it briefly, then slid it into an evidence bag pulled from his pocket. He stepped over to Webb, unlocked the cuffs, then swiftly turned him and locked his hands behind him, gripping one shoulder hard enough to make the boy wince.

Cord eyed the wide-faced man behind the counter who stood wiping a glass, still chewing on his toothpick. "You're one cold sonofabitch, Red."

The bartender set the tumbler aside, removed the toothpick from his mouth and leaned his belly into the counter. "Look, Cord. I run a business here that sees purt-near as much meanness, greed and lust as yours. Only difference: I ain't paid to care. This ain't no fancy gentleman's club. Folks come in here to forget their troubles. It's called mindin' yer own business."

He leaned back, stuck the toothpick in his mouth again. "That there's Lou's." He folded his arms, cocked his head toward a chair where a small backpack set. "He might need it if he lives."

9

Cord stepped across the room and grabbed the pack. "Fair enough, Red. But this is the fourth time we've had to send out a unit in the last two months." He grabbed Webb by the shoulder and pushed him toward the door. "Something better start changing around here, or I'll shut her down. Then you won't be minding nobody's business. Not even your own." He touched the brim of his hat. "I'll send somebody out for a statement. See you around."

Back on the road into town, Webb started in begging again. "Listen, Cord. This ain't no way to be. You know my daddy. My momma. Your son's in the same school as my brother. Cord, don't do this! M-m-me an' Elsie got a baby on the way."

"Shut up, Webb. You done cut a man's throat back there. You'll be lucky to not spend the rest of your life in Brushy Mountain. Now shut your mouth before you say something that'll put you under the jail."

"I swear to God. If ye just let me out here, I'll...I'll disappear. Go away and never come back. You can do that, right? Just say I got away. You can —"

Cord slammed on the brakes, sending Webb, hands still cuffed behind him, against the back of the front seat. His nose and forehead cracked against the plastic barrier. "Shut the hell up!" He turned to looked him in the eyes. "You just tried to bribe me. That's what I call making things worse. And yes, I know. You and Elsie have had a rough go of it. But now, it's gonna get worse 'cause of what you just did. So, if you want to see that baby of yours, just shut it. Don't say another word 'til you talk to a lawyer. Then I'll forget what you just tried to pull." He scowled. "Understand?"

"Sure. Sure." Webb leaned back against the seat, blood smudged under his nose, face sullen. "I get it."

They rode in silence until he turned onto Main Street and passed the Riverside Inn. Then Webb spoke up again. "I'm sorry, Cord. Real sorry fer what I done."

"I know, son. But there ain't nothin' for it now. I'll get in touch with Elsie. Calm her down a bit 'fore she talks to you. Just don't make it worse by saying how it weren't your fault—or why it happened. That'll all come out soon enough."

"No, sir. I won't."

Cord wheeled into the space in front of the jailhouse.

"What makes it so, Cord?" Webb muttered. "That folks have to hurt so much they start turnin' that hurt back on somebody else?"

"Don't know, Webb. I don't know."

But the truth was, he did.

2

On the Shores of Eden

L evon Gladson turned his head for air, focusing on the rhythm of the long arm stroke, strong legs scissoring head-currents that wrapped his torso, pressed shoulders and chest, pushing him slowly back downstream. It would be easier to just let go and drift. Give himself over to the unceasing pressure of nature's indifferent will. But he'd come too far and sacrificed too much to let go now.

Keep trying. One stroke, one breath, one kick at a time. And though he knew the river would take him in the end, he believed he could gain a bit more time if he just didn't give up. The old girl wasn't going to get the best of him, yet.

He glanced at the shore to get his bearings, then struck out again, bent arms pin-wheeling, cupped hands slicing the surface then pulling hard, long and deep, forcing the water down and back, legs pumping until they burned. Stroke. Stroke. Stroke. Stroke. Until his lungs felt raw and he began to swallow more water than air. He finally rolled onto his back, gasping, and glanced again at the shore. He'd probably gained fifteen or twenty feet.

Not bad, he thought. Stronger every day.

He briefly drifted downstream, eyes closed, inhaling the crisp air before turning back onto his belly. He kicked to the muddy edge and stood in the shallows. Water dripped off his short, thick beard and long dark hair. He waded to the muddy bank, a slight breeze bracing his face and naked body. He looked around at the rolling hills and deep valleys surrounded by the old, worn peaks of the Smokies.

This is it, he thought. Good, fertile land. Fit to make a new start.

He'd worried, after leaving Asheville, that the decision to cross the eastern divide into Tennessee with a handful of idealistic neo-hippies might not have been wise. But they'd been delivered to the land of milk and honey. And once he got hooked up with that distributor out of Nashville, the Lord's work would surely be fulfilled.

"Levon. Levon!" Maya Macauley, slim and blue-eyed, with sandy hair, stood looking down from the bank-top. "Hurry, Levon. They found Zoe!"

He scrambled up the bank, grabbed his clothes and boots and walked briskly towards the main house, dressing as he went. "Where?" He pulled a cinch out of his right pocket and slicked his hair back into a ponytail. "Is she all right?"

"No." Maya scurried to keep up. "They...the deputy said they'd been trying to call since last night. Finally got hold of Sunny in the main house this morning."

"Deputy? You mean she was arrested?" He stopped just outside the door and looked down at Maya.

Her eyes filled with tears. "They found a body on the river." Her voice trembled. "Wanted to know if anybody on The Farm was missing."

"What?" He grabbed her shoulders. "Girl. What're you saying?"

"I'm sorry, Levon. I...I don't know. Don't know what it means." Her voice broke.

The fear in her eyes; was it for him or Zoe?

"Please don't be mad, Levon. I just don't know."

"I'm not mad." He stroked her hair. "Don't be scared, Maya. It's not your fault." He paused as a couple of children ran past, laughing. "Is Sunny inside?"

"Was when I went to look for you."

"Come on." He wiped the tears away. "Stop crying, now. Let's go inside. We'll talk to Sunny. Everything'll be fine."

Sunny was pacing from one side of the room to the other. When he saw them, he rushed to Levon. "Brother, am I glad to see you. This is crazy. A godawful crazy mess."

"I know. I know, Sunny." Levon walked Maya to a beat-up sofa at the side wall closest to the desk and lowered her into the seat. Above her head hung a sign: *For I have chosen him, that he may command his children and his household after him to keep the way of the LORD by doing righteousness and justice, so that the LORD may bring to Abraham what he has promised him.*

Levon strode across the rough boards and leaned against his desk. "Tell me exactly what they said."

"Well, they were pretty pissed off. Been trying to reach us since yesterday. Said a girl's body had washed up under the Collard's Creek Bridge and we might be able to identify her." Sunny was pacing again, swiping the long, blond hair that kept falling in his face behind his ears. "But it don't make sense. Can't be Zoe. Everybody loved her, dude."

"Okay. Okay. You're right. It might not be. But let me think a minute."

Sunny Gregor was a good man. Levon had helped him kick a bad heroin addiction years back in Atlanta. Got him off the streets. Since then, the man's loyalty and love for his "savior" had only blossomed. But his impulsiveness and zeal sometimes tainted his judgment. Levon had been trying hard to keep a low profile with local law enforcement since they'd arrived. He didn't need Sunny's attitude spreading fear and discontent through their community.

The group comprised a hundred-thirty-five young anti-corporate, anti-big-government followers who tended the 400-plus acre farm. Their first year they'd lived in converted travel buses, RVs and a motley collection of camping tents that had dotted the hillsides surrounding the old farmhouse. Conditions had been far from sanitary, resulting in bacterial outbreaks of dysentery and diarrhea. Even an occurrence of hepatitis after three couples had eaten some wild watercress growing downstream of an outhouse. Staph infections, head and body lice were not uncommon.

They'd just finished the eighth of ten planned communal housing units, and their relations with the locals seemed to be warming. Most of the men had been able to secure either day-labor or full-time work in Acre County. But now Zoe, who'd been missing for two days, turns up dead.

"So what's your plan?" Sunny stepped up beside Levon, pleading. "I mean, we got to tell the others. Right? The law's gonna come up here and start poking around. What're we gonna tell them? Ain't cool." He shook his head, emphatic. "It just ain't cool."

Levon sat down behind the small, wood-top desk supported at each end by two oak barrels. He picked up a fifteen-round magazine, slapped it in the Glock 22 he'd just finished cleaning before his swim, leaned back, and slipped the pistol into its tactical holster. "Well," he said, finally, "We gotta make an ID, to be sure. And whether it's Zoe, or whether it isn't, we'll tell them the truth. None of our group would ever do anything to hurt their own. Nor anybody else. Don't need to be ashamed of what we're trying to accomplish here."

He leaned forward and placed his hands flat on the desktop. "This is a spiritual safe-haven for *all* down-and-outers. Folks who don't fit into the global corporate structure, man. We've gotta protect it." He paused and looked at Maya, then back at Sunny. "But truth can be a tricky thing. We have to be careful. Most folks outside the commune already think we're something akin to the Manson Family. Do any of our other members know?"

"No." Sunny swiped another stray strand of hair behind his ear. "Ain't talked to nobody since I sent Maya to get you."

"Good. Where's Lilith?" Lilith Harkin was Levon's primary wife. He'd married her years before Maya. Counted on her support and wisdom more than anyone else's. He needed her here, now.

"I saw her heading over the north slope as I was coming to get you," said Maya.

"Good. Go and fetch her back. She needs to know."

Maya walked briskly out and Levon turned again to Sunny. "Now listen. Before I call the sheriff, we need to gather the cohorts for a quick meeting. Make sure we're all on the same page. Understand? Find out if anybody knows anything about what Zoe was up to the last couple days. But I don't want them freaking out. So don't tell them why. Let them think it's just another Saturday afternoon meditation and prayer meeting. I'll fill them in once we're together. Got it?"

"Sure. Sure, man. I understand." Sunny nervously nodded, then shuffled towards the door.

"And Sunny."

He stopped, hand on the doorknob. "Yeah?"

"Don't worry, brother. I got this."

Sunny smiled, wanly. "Sure, man. Cool." He stepped through and closed the door behind him, leaving Levon alone.

Rays of sun filtered through the high windows, slanting onto an engraved tin box where Levon kept his pot. Sunny had probably left it out after packing the pipe for his morning smoke. Levon reached for the tin, rolled a joint and lit it, then leaned back in the chair. He couldn't completely shake that nagging feeling that he'd somehow missed something. But what? What the fuck was it?

Fuck it, he thought. Whatever, it'll hold for now. He watched smoke rings swirl up through the light. "Poor Zoe. Fuckin' loved that girl." He took another hit, the tension leaving him as he exhaled. "Poor fuckin' stupid Zoe. Now I've got to clean up this mess."

Levon was used to cleaning up messes. He'd spent years working on a hog farm with his alcoholic father, just outside of Carrboro, North Carolina. Plenty to clean up in that shithole. Early on, he'd found a refuge from the daily horror of castration, tail docking, teeth clipping, earmarking, tattooing and slaughter in school, books and long forays into the nearby piney woods around his home.

But after his mother died, his father's anger and bitterness over the loss strangled the last bit of humanity out of the man. His rage and frustration, trying to scrape together a living out of the toxic muck of hogs, all finally spilled over, poisoning him like the lagoons of waste that flooded the local water sources and suffocated every living thing that surrounded the once-fertile grounds. His father's brutal, violent temper and vicious hostility only served to harden in the young man a pugnacious, intense sense that life had visited a savage injustice upon him, and infected him with a like sickness—for which vengeance was its only cure.

So one night, a few weeks before Levon's sixteenth birthday, his father had called him into the living room where he sat in a faded, stained, sap-green recliner. A reality show about swapping wives blared on the television.

"Get me another beer, piss-for-brains." He slung an empty toward the boy, cracking open a split gash just above his right brow.

Levon stumbled back against the wall. "Shit!" He wiped the blood out of his eye with the heel of his hand. "You lazy fuck. Get it yourself."

The man shot up from the recliner, grabbed a 32-inch flexible livestock prod leaning against a side-table, flipped the conduction switch and whipped it at the boy's haunches. The jolt knocked his legs out from under him and he crumbled to the floor.

Then he pinned him, lowering his knee and grinding it into the boy's chest. "So, you think you're ready to take on your old man, eh?" He reached a pack of Marlboros from his pocket, tapped out a cigarette, then clicked open the lid of his Zippo. He lit the cigarette and lowered the lid halfway over the flame. "But you ain't nothin' but a piss-ant, boy. A prissy, book-readin' half-man ain't never gonna be fit fer nothin'. Hell, them goddamned branded pigs out there's worth more'n you." He studied the lid of the Zippo, now glowing orange-red, and sniggered. "Maybe we can put some value on you yet. A little brand of your own."

17

He snapped the lid shut and jammed the glowing top against the boy's neck.

Levon screamed and grabbed at his father's thick wrist trying to break free. But the old man's grip was strong. With his free hand, he held the boy's head down until he stopped struggling, then finally pulled the lighter away and stood up. "There. Now you got a mark show's you're worth somethin'. You belong to me, boy. Ain't no gettin' away from it." He took a deep drag off the cigarette, walked back to the recliner and plopped down. "Now, fetch the hell up and grab me a beer."

Levon pushed himself up and walked to the kitchen. He turned on the cold water, lowered his head under the tap and let it cool the burn. He turned off the tap. Picked up a fifteen-inch black cast iron skillet from the stovetop. Took a deep breath, closed his eyes and tried to slow the heartbeat echoing in his ears.

He exhaled and walked into the next room where his father sat laughing at the wife-swappers. Then, Levon lifted the heavy skillet and brought it down with all the strength his fifteen-year-old body could muster. His father slumped down with a grunt, arms falling limp on either side of the chair. Blood ran from both ears.

Time seemed to stop as he stared down at the old man's bashed skull, waiting for him to move. Finally, he reached out and felt for a pulse on the old man's neck. Nothing. He edged around the chair, looked at the eyes staring blankly at a spot between the floor and the TV screen. He was dead.

He slowly walked back to the kitchen. Washed the skillet and set it on the cluttered counter. Back in the living room, he pulled his father up and heaved him over his shoulder. He carried him outside, certain at every step he'd fall, stumble face-down in the mud and muck. He'd trudge a few paces, stop, catch his breath. Then trudge again until he'd crossed the yard to the hog barn. Once inside, he collapsed against a row of metal feed boxes, dropping the body on the sawdust-layered ground.

He lay in the dark a long time listening to the grunts and squeals of sows and piglets. He breathed in their acrid, sweet stench of filth. His father. The hogs. His own pongy sweat. Then he stripped the clothes off the body, carried them back up the hill to the trash barrel and threw them in. Walked to the shed, grabbed a can of gasoline and the Husqvarna eighteen-inch chainsaw they used for clearing deadfall. That, and a roll of clear six-mil plastic sheeting.

Back at the feed boxes, he cut a strip and rolled the body onto it. Chainsawed into pieces, it filled eight feedboxes. He rolled up the plastic sheet and walked back up the hill. Pulled off his clothes and threw them into the trash barrel along with the plastic. He poured gasoline in and torched it with the Zippo pulled from his father's pants. He rinsed off the chainsaw with the outdoor water hose, then himself. Hung the chainsaw back in the shed. Walked naked back to the fire and waited until everything had burned down to ashes. Then, back in the house, he cleaned up all signs of blood. He dressed, sat down on the couch, and slept.

The next morning, he walked down to the hog barn. They had emptied the feed boxes. He used a rag to wipe a few drops of blood off a couple of boxes, then walked up the hill to the trash barrel, lit the rag and tossed it in. He packed some clothes and food, and left.

Six months later, he'd hooked up with a band of anti-war, people's revolution, occupy-something-or-another types and traveled with them around the country learning the art of what they called "civil disobedience." It was a perfect education for a young man whose life had been shaped by the worst example of a capitalist system run amok. But soon, he grew bored and contemptuous of pansy-ass demonstrators who didn't have the guts to die for radical change. It was going to take something more than protest signs to bring about a new world order. The people needed something powerful enough to move their spirits, not just their minds. They needed a new religion; one for social justice.

So, he headed back to North Carolina and enrolled at Greensboro Community College. Did well enough there to qualify for loans, grants and even a scholarship to enroll at UNC-Greensboro. There, after hooking up with Lilith, he experienced a kind of spiritual awakening.

He'd only been in town a couple of months when he'd seen her at the end of the bar at Natty Green's Brewing Company. Petite, wispy body, curly chestnut hair bobbed at her shoulders, and dark, almost obsidian eyes that seemed to cut right through him. She'd smiled and nodded when he'd raised his glass to her.

Later that night, after making love in her apartment, lying under the heat of her belly as she slowly rocked him inside and he licked the salty sweat from her nipples, she'd leaned down and whispered, "So. If you thought that was good, I've got some shit that'll keep us going for days." And she'd leaned over the side of the bed, pulled up her purse and slipped out a tiny plastic jewel bag she opened and dipped her fingernail into. "Come on, honey. Let's rock this place." She held the white powder to his nose.

His nose burned, his eyes watered and he thought the top of his head was on fire. Then a numbness waved across his face as she rubbed some powder on his gums then bent and deeply kissed him.

Suddenly, he was drifting in waves of pleasure. Arms, legs, hands and lips brushing and mingling together, their separate bodies, now indistinguishable. Every touch, taste, smell and breath lingering, magnified. His body floated into the most beautiful nothingness he'd ever known. He'd found heaven. And the beginning of his new religion.

Over the next few months, he and Lilith developed a system of drugs – marijuana, LSD, cocaine and methamphetamine – combined with sex and sprinkled with bowdlerized sacred verses from various religious sects that would become the liturgical basis of worship for his new transcendental movement. Soon, he began preaching his own form of radical-saviour theology and attracted a following. His charismatic personality, intelligence and ability to communicate across cultural divides made him a natural leader.

His followers were true believers in the new social system he'd developed and preached, including a modified free-love engagement where some marriages were considered communal. He and Lilith shared beds with Maya and Eli.

Maya was the perfect complement to Lilith. Smart enough, but with a certain enduring naiveté that kept her open, curious and trusting. She also had a knack for crafts, and several large weaves and macramé hangings lined the walls inside the cabin. A Lendrum Spinning Wheel and a forty-three-inch Louet Loom sat in the corner of the big room. Levon loved watching her work the heavy wooden shuttles through the weave, the thin, threaded colors combining and blending until the creation slowly revealed itself. Like a God, he imagined, threading the world together each day—knowing how it would all turn out, but just enough room for changes and mistakes along the way.

Maya's husband, Eli Forester, was a young Appalachian State graduate Levon had taken under his wing after he'd donated enough of his trust fund to the Glad Earth Foundation for them to purchase the plot of land in Tennessee that bordered the Cherokee National Forest. He'd hoped that Eli might someday take over the spiritual ministry of their small but growing flock. But Levon soon discovered that despite his good looks, articulate manner and sharp intelligence, the boy had a willful streak. Something in his past Levon could never get to the bottom of. Something dark, but useful if handled properly.

Indeed, his decision to join in marriage with Eli and Maya was partially motivated by his hope that the mature feminine influence of Lilith might help Eli to quiet the demon that rose up from time to time in flashes of hateful anger. Particularly when he felt threatened, or rejected.

It didn't. Despite everything Lilith tried, Eli's black moods would settle on him and he'd lash out at the world again. Only her deep dedication and love for Levon, the strongest bond she'd ever known, kept her from falling into her own deep funk over her failure to change Eli.

Now, as the room filled with the sweet stench of herb, Levon regretted, more than ever, having broken their bond by sleeping with

Zoe. She'd been just seventeen, fifteen years younger than Levon, when he first saw her at a rally in Asheville. She'd come down from Virginia to visit a friend at Montreat College. Only stayed for a few days. But a year later, she was back and attending all of Levon's sermons and lectures, listening with a kind of innocence that only comes with the naiveté of privileged youth.

He'd made love to her six months before they left for Tennessee. It was the closest Levon could imagine to heaven without drugs. But he never told Lilith. Zoe wasn't married to anyone else in the group, and the rules of the disciple-marriage system dictated that only married couples were permitted spousal sharing.

He'd sworn off her after leaving Asheville and they'd all headed to the commune in Tennessee. But her presence at the compound had proved too tempting. One day, he'd gone to the river to bathe, and there she was, stepping out of the water. Venus could not have been more beautiful. They made love again. Then he'd sworn off her once more. That's when he decided to start the Magdalenes, a special designation for the women of the community who'd reached the age of twenty yet unmarried. They, according to Levon, had their own special gifts to contribute to the sacred communal needs.

Zoe had just turned twenty a few weeks ago. Now, as he thought about her body lying on a cold slab at the coroner's office, he remembered the necklace. "Fuck!"

The front door swung open. Lilith stood there for a moment, breathing hard, her pixie-like figure silhouetted in the sunlight, fists clenched at her sides. "Levon. Is it true? Is Zoe dead?"

He opened the tin box and pulled out some rolling papers. "Could be. Come on in and close the door. We need to talk."

3
Liquid Spirits

C ord felt the bitter wash in the back of his throat as he swallowed back the bile. He sat up on the edge of the office cot, cold tile under his feet, gagging back another wave of nausea. What the hell was he thinking, going to Slim's last night?

Slim Johnston owned the Lost Cove Fish Camp on the French Broad River just off Arlen Creek Road. The boys got pretty lively there Friday and Saturday nights. Nothing more serious than a bloodied nose, or a busted knuckle, usually. But Cord liked to swing in ever so often to keep them in check—and to get the latest fishing forecast. Last night, though, he'd needed a nip of the hard stuff Slim sold out back. But he hadn't intended to tie it on so bad.

He'd mostly sworn off the drink a couple years back, a hardpressed promise to Lucinda in another of thier long bids to save the marriage. But despite his best intentions, he'd struggled to keep that pledge. Especially when he got all knotted up. Seeing that young girl under the bridge had reminded him of another he'd known as a young deputy who'd been murdered as payback for an investigation he'd been following. She and Cord had been lovers, and it still pained him every time he thought about her.

So after yesterday's shift had ended, he'd driven to the camp figuring to get a nip or two. Take the edge off. Before he knew it, he'd been two hours shooting the shit with Slim and Joe Collins, a fat, good-natured regular who could talk the tail off an ass. He'd left with a quart jar of Thorn Reevers's mash whiskey, then called Lucinda to apologize, again.

"It's late, Cord. I really don't want to discuss it tonight. We'll talk tomorrow."

"I just need you to know things are gonna change, Luce. The job's just more than I figured when I took on the promotion."

Her chuckle sounded more like a sob. "I don't need things to change, Cord. I need *you* to change. You pour yourself into that job, always trying to live up to some damn ideal about sacrifice and justice. I always admired that about you. But you push it to the point where you lose yourself in that world and forget that you have another life. With us. And things have only gotten worse since we lost the baby. You keep trying to hide it. But that guilt still hangs on you. And when it gets too heavy, you hit the liquor. I loved the man you were when we met. But between the guilt, the drinking, and the job, Cord. Just need to know if what you are now still works with what I need. Okay?"

"All right." He wanted to say more, but his mind was too tangled with the truth of her words. "I might be late."

"It's already late. Goodnight, Cord."

He'd tossed the phone on the seat beside him, watching the yellow lines on the road tick by. The woman had been his anchor for almost twenty years. She'd seen her share of the brutal, destructive criminal element. Vicious, poor and lonely denizens of a job that seemed to follow him home, no matter how hard he tried to separate the two lives. Then four years ago, while investigating a murder case, he'd tangled with Frank Reevers, whose twisted, vengeful hatred of Cord had led him to run Lucinda off the road chashing down into a ravine. She'd lived, but the baby she'd carried didn't. After, she'd needed space to heal. But he wanted to believe they could find their way back to some semblance of the intimacy they'd once known. And for a man who was not known for keeping his counsel, it was a tough custom to simply sit silent by and wait.

So, he'd handled it the only way he knew how—by throwing himself into work. Putting in extra hours on both shifts, especially after the election, trying to clean out the last of the trash and corruption that had collected in the department during the tenure of the past sheriff. If you wanted to find Cord, more than likely it'd be in the cruiser, or at the office.

Still, it had surprised the two deputies at the station when he'd strolled in late last night after leaving Slim's.

"Didn't 'spect to see you here tonight, sir." Clyde "Junior" Dooley, a slim youngster who'd just joined the force, looked up from behind his desk.

"Wanted to check on that drowning."

"No prints. Water took care of that. Doc said he'd know more in the mornin' after the autopsy. Sam talked to Farley McLearen and Jeb Richards who were fishin' down around Mason's Break at 1400. Thought they might've seen something float by off on the opposite bank." He rubbed a palm over his crew-cut, thinking. "And old Darcy Mae said she was shellin' peas on her back deck all day. Said the only thing passed by on that river today was a coon and a day."

Darcy lived about two miles above Mason's Break and five miles north of the bridge. "Make a note to have Sam check the stream flow for yesterday. Might help us narrow down where she went in."

"Yes, sir."

Cord smiled at the Junior's strict routine of maintaining protocol. A new recruit in the Army Reserves, he was all regulation.

"Whadya say, Cord?" Ollie Duncan stepped in from the break room, raising a cup of coffee. "I got my money on that damn clan of hipsters back of ol' Hartfield's." He took a sip and grimaced. "Shit. That's some damn bad joe."

Cord nodded. "It's the bitter keeps you on your toes, not the caffeine." He stepped through the short swinging gate that separated the reception area from the bullpen, cut between the deputy's desks and crossed a short hall leading to his office. "I'll be in here," he said over one shoulder. "If you need me, I'm not in."

"Sheriff," Junior hollered across the hallway. "Webb's been all twitchin' and yellin' back there. Wanting to know if you called his wife."

"Tell him I did. She weren't none too happy, either. I'll stop by her place tomorrow. How's Lou?"

"Hospital says it's not looking good. He lost a lot of blood, but they kept him from bleeding out. Said he'd been on some kind of opiate. Oxycontin or heroin. He's gone into a coma. Until they get a better grip on what he took, it's all wait and see, for now."

"Keep tabs on it, Junior. We got two lives riding on the one."

"Yes, sir."

Cord stepped into his office, shut the door and settled in behind his desk. Strange, he thought. He'd heard Lou had been bad on the hooch for a while, especially after coming back from the desert. But the story he'd gotten from Webb didn't sound like he was acting anything like a sleepwalker or cotton-head. He'd need to follow up tomorrow with the boy. He spun the lid off the mason jar. Swiped out the bottom of his coffee cup, poured it half-full, took a long pull and wiped his lips on one sleeve. Not bad, he thought, rubbing the old scar. Wonder if the damn thing'll ever stop itching. Then he noticed a note from Judy: *Call Bill Crowther.* Gazette News. *Wants a statement about the girl.*

He picked up Friday's reports. Criminal activity in Acre County was normally mundane. Except for a few boys raising hell over on Highway 25 at the Rooster or at Brook's cockfighting pit. Or prostitution busts out at The Thunderbolt Tavern, the occasional bootlegger running whiskey or weed out of Reevers Holler, or, more recently an occasional meth-lab bust, most folks were too busy with the complications of just living. There was the odd domestic quarrel, a local drunk or two to throw in the can. But all in all, life moved along at an easy pace. Now, he might be looking at two homicides in one day.

He thought again about Webb and Lou. Something else itched in his brain he'd wanted to follow up. He took another long swig, closed his eyes and felt the warm numbness spreading out from deep in his belly like a blanket of comfort. The itch was still there, but he'd let it linger for now. He'd remember by morning.

And the girl. What the hell had got her killed? He'd seen plenty of people killing each other over land or money. Domestic squabbles ending in homicide. Vicious barroom murders, like what happened to Lou. And the wars. Heaven knew there was enough death there to last a lifetime. Violence bred the same such back. That was just the way of it. But this. The sheer unforeseen fate of it still startled him. Just as it must've startled the victim.

He sighed, leaned back in the chair and felt the whiskey seeping deeper. The knot in his neck loosened. The tightness in his head slipped away. He wondered now if he was up to the job. He'd just recently been elected sheriff. And though a bigger paycheck made his home life more comfortable, the longer hours and administrative pressures weighed heavily.

His strength had always been an affable, straightforward bond with the people, and his ability to dog out, with manic intensity, the truth of things. Good crime investigators, he'd found, were a bit like good mechanics. Or corpsmen, for that matter: look for a sign or even a clustering of signs that fit a general pattern, narrow the focus down to specific symptoms or clues, then make educated deductions about the best diagnostic procedures to follow. Apply the most obvious solutions first, then work through a process of elimination down the list of other treatments until you hit on the one that worked.

It all seemed straightforward, like living in Falston all his life. The only time he'd ever left was to join the Navy. Wasn't that he hadn't considered college; his GPA was in the top five percent and he liked the subjects well enough. But his family's struggling finances, combined with a natural inclination to study life from the inside out, had sealed his decision to "see the world" as the cliché-spouting recruiter had said.

And after training as a corpsman, he'd returned home thinking he'd find work as a paramedic or sign on as a fire fighter. Neither were hiring, so he'd joined the department and found his skill set suited for the job.

He knew most folks in the county, and everybody knew him— some even liked him. But lately, he'd spent more time behind the desk than in the field. Reading reports, meeting with the mayor, dealing with the press. Much of it PR related, trying to somehow put a fresh face on the crooked cops, corruption and federal indictments that had swept the department the previous year. It made him feel disconnected, out of touch, useless. He didn't think he'd ever get comfortable with the politics. But when the mayor had begged him to step up, being he was one of the few not caught up in the scandal, he'd agreed. Now, with his marriage hitting some rough spots, his struggles with the not-so-fine art of local politics put him on even shakier ground. Today at the Rooster was the first time in months he'd actually been primary on the scene. Felt good.

He picked up the reports and carried them, with the jar of hooch, to the cot in the corner. Settled back under the lamp and started reading. A couple of minutes later, he laid the reports aside and picked up *Michael Robarts And The Dancer,* a book of poems by William Butler Yeats. After finding "The Second Coming" one summer, he'd read everything Yeats had written.

There was something remarkable and terrifying in the poetry. Yeats turned a blue-steeled, honest gaze on the world and acknowledged fate and the frightening role it played in man's problems. For Cord, the poems were almost religious.

He flipped open the book and read:

The blood-dimmed tide is loosed, and everywhere
The ceremony of innocence is drowned;
The best lack all conviction, while the worst
Are full of passionate intensity.

He closed the book, shut his eyes, and dozed off, wondering what passionate intensity, what rough beast could've taken the ceremony of innocence from that young red-headed woman now lying cold in the morgue .

4
Cross-Currents

A slight breeze rustled through the upper branches of scarlet oaks, maples and sweet gums. Yellow, red and gold-tipped spikes of timber carpeted ridges spread like waves across the horizon.

Lucas Monroe rambled north along a trail overlooking the river fifty feet below. His easy, steady gait and even breath belied the steep pitch and rugged surface of the rocky, root-crossed path. He carried a Remington 521 .22 rifle slung in the crook of one arm. And despite the sometimes precipitous trails along which he traveled, he appeared at ease, gazing up into the tops of trees or down on the surging, rolling river below.

Lucas had hiked these trails nearly all his eighteen years. Knew every cut-through, switchback, ravine and crevasse in a fifteen-mile radius of the Nolichucky Basin. From Neddy Mountain to Hall Top, and east to Round Mountain. In some ways he'd been bounded by them, never having traveled farther than the Kill Dee Branch at the North Carolina border or Morristown to the north, let alone Knoxville.

But he didn't much care. He still hadn't gotten his fill of the mountains. The hard, brittle crystalline winters of whiteness that buried the dead branches and leaves left behind after bright, crisp autumns had shed her vibrant colors. The deep greens of summers where all of nature seemed to stretch wide and gather in the warmth through the long, slow days and humming nights. The fertile, river-fed spring soil that urged new shoots and seedpods to take root and grow, sustaining all the creeping, crawling, upright creatures that made this high land their own. This was his home. He figured to probably die here, happy, without ever setting foot outside it.

He stopped as squirrels chittered up ahead and unslung the .22. Moved slowly forward, gazing with narrow eyes into the treetops. About forty yards out, a couple of greys were chasing each other, circling up an red oak, then jumping branch to branch over to a poplar, one fussing at the other from above.

He raised the rifle and sighted in the one perched on the upper branch. Exhaled slowly, and squeezed the trigger. The squirrel dropped, straight down, dead, just off the path ahead.

He kept still, an eye on the other squirrel that shimmied quickly higher and moved around to the backside of the trunk. He squatted on the path and waited. After ten minutes, a plume of tail nervously twitched from behind the trunk, about fifteen feet off the ground. Then the rest of the squirrel, spiraling down, came into view. Lucas quickly took aim and fired. It bumped and grazed down the bark, landing at the tree's base. He collected the kill, smiling. Good, fat catch, he thought. Few more of these and I'll have a fine stew tonight.

He started up the trail again, thinking about the girl, Zoe. A year back, he'd seen her swimming just off the big bend down from Hartfield's place. He'd been hiking the opposite bank, heading back to Thorn's after checking the perimeter, when a flash of her red hair, sparkling in the water like round-leaf sundew stopped him dead in his tracks.

As she floated on her back in the slow current, the girl's skin had looked rosy white, like the veins of sandstone at Crowder's Bluff. Small breasts with light pink nipples just broke the surface. And as she rolled onto her belly, he'd studied the slope of her back, the smooth roundness of hips and the strong kick of shapely legs. He'd sat and watched her dip and surface and dive for almost twenty minutes, until she was joined by a dark-haired fellow.

At once, a jealous ire seethed in his gut. The girl swam to the shallows and stood, waving at the lanky, bearded man of about thirty. In full view, she was even more beautiful, stepping up the thin shoreline to the bank. And as the man stripped and embraced her, lifting her out of the water, spinning round and round, deeper and deeper into the lazy flow where they both fell, laughing and splashing, he couldn't stop the crazy thought that somehow he'd been cuckolded. Cheated. He'd quickly stood and angrily tramped up the trail, breathing hard.

Before the man had arrived, he'd been thinking of ways he might contrive to meet her face to face. Maybe cross the river with a good bunch of wild goldenrod or purple aster, or pale gentian. Or a couple of jars of Carl Dooley's huckleberry honey. If he watched long enough, he might just figure out how often she came down to the river and he'd be there waiting. Maybe fishing off the opposite bank.

He'd smile and wave. She'd wave, smile back, then strip and wade in, motioning him to join her. They'd meet in the center of the current and float, hands held tight, kicking and drifting until they'd come to rest against a large boulder. And there they'd kiss. Her long, white arms wrapping him in her warmth. Her breath sweet and soft against his face. Until, lying back, she'd pull him to her, guiding him inside, both rocking as the water swirled and tumbled around them.

But then the image of the man stepped between them, and a deep, surging violence rose inside him. Fucking hipsters, he'd thought. Thorn had said they weren't nothin' but trouble. He was right. "Reckon I might still get 'er, iffen I tried," he muttered. "Jus' have to find another way t' get there's all."

Now, as he followed the twisting trail leading back to Thorn's compound, bagged squirrels flopping against a thigh, he kept one eye on the trees, and another on the river, hoping to spot her once again, floating down the wide river below.

5

On the Move

Cord sat at the edge of the cot another minute. The blasting headache and dry, metallic aftertaste of the moonshine whiskey stuck in his throat. He looked at the book of poems lying on the floor. Damn, he thought, rubbing his stubbled chin. That shine Thorn's brewin' of late's got a helluva punch. The jar was three-quarters empty now. He lumbered to the desk and stowed it in the bottom drawer, then looked at his watch. Six-thirty. Shit! First shift will be clocking in, soon. He ran a small department, three men on first, three on second, except weekends when he'd sometimes pull in an extra hand. Shift change meant they'd all be here at once.

Dammit. Gotta get cleaned up, he thought. Long day ahead.

He made his way down the short hallway to the head, splashed cold water on his face and rinsed his mouth. His reflection in the mirror reminded him of the old ferryman ready to cross the Styx. He combed his hair, tucked in his shirt, then straightened and stepped back into the hall.

Walter Grey, a tall, old cuss who'd been with the department through two other sheriffs met him before he could reach his office. "Hey, Waddy."

"Cord." He nodded then peered closer. "You look like shit, boy."

"Yeah. Warmed over, too. Long one last night."

Waddy leaned in. "Smells like it." He shook his head. "Ain't good, Cord. You know how that stuff takes hold of ye."

"I know, Waddy. I know." He brushed past into his office, grabbed his hat and turned to leave.

"Can't let it beat ye," Waddy said behind him. "Ye best stay clear of it. Or end up like Sheriff Casey."

Bob Casey, Cord's old boss, along with two other deputies, had been indicted on bribery and conspiracy charges related to a series of prostitution, gambling and drug busts by the TBI and other federal and local agencies. It had put the department under a microscope from which he was still trying to gain some autonomy.

"I'll lay off. You know me. Always takin' the goddamned high road."

Waddy nodded. "Damn straight." He patted Cord's shoulder as he passed. "Ain't too old to still kick your ass. Now get the hell home, clean yerself up. Lucinda ain't gonna take much of this shit from ye."

"Thanks." He snugged the hat on. "I will."

He made it to the cruiser with just a couple of nods to the deputies reporting in, then pulled onto the highway and started towards home. Lucinda'd be finishing breakfast with Blu. Wasn't going to be easy getting by without her noticing the shape he was in. He decided to drop in at Lily's Restaurant first, grab a quick cup of coffee, maybe stomach down some food.

Ten minutes later, he pulled into the lot and parked. He took off his hat and threw it on the seat. Never wore it except on official business. As he stepped through the door, a busy, busty woman, red hair piled on top of her head and skewered with a pencil, looked up. "Howdy, Cord," she boomed. "Ain't seen you here in a couple weeks."

Cord raised a hand, grimacing. "Easy, Lil. Easy."

"All right, Sheriff." Lily chuckled. "A rough'un last night, huh?" She eyed him up and down. "Step on in, darlin'. We got a stool here with your name all over it. Ain't no lie." She stepped behind the counter. "What can I get fer ye today, honey?"

"Coffee. Bla..."

She rattled the cup down in front of him before he'd finished the sentence . "Like ye had to ask."

"Uhm. Right." Cord scratched his head, trying to focus. "Couple eggs, poached. Grits. Plenty of Tabasco."

She sniffed, disappeared into the kitchen, and was back out in a flash, leaning over the counter in front of him. "Headin' in, or headin' home, honey?" Lily was used to serving him all hours.

"Home. For a time." He sipped the coffee and looked around. Old habit. Know your surroundings. Mostly locals heading into work. "Then back in again." He held the cup for a warm-up, still surveying the room.

As Lily filled it, he noticed three long-haired, bearded gruffs eying him from a corner booth. "Or maybe not, I'm afraid." He set the cup on the counter and swiveled around on the stool. "S'cuse me a minute, Lil."

He started toward the booth just as the men began scooting out. "Boys." He nodded, stopping in front of them. "Got a minute?"

A skinny, bearded man in a black and gray Baja hoodie, the one closest to Cord, spoke up. "Sure, man. We're just gettin' ready to head out to work, Sheriff."

"Just got a couple questions. Maybe best step outside."

"What's the problem?" A lean, younger man with sharp, dark eyes and a series of tattoos on his arms depicting the Four Horsemen and the Seven Seals stepped between them. "We didn't do anything." His fists clenched at his side.

"I ain't tryin' to put y'all in a spot." Cord made his accent a bit thicker. "Got a case I'm workin', thought y'all might help me out." He nodded at the other customers who'd begun to gawk and crane their necks. "Might be best to go outside. None of these folks' business."

"We'll step out with you, Sheriff," said a third man, mid-thirties, wearing overalls and black, plastic-rimmed glasses like Cord's Grandpa used to wear. A long goatee reached to his chest.

Cord nodded and followed them outside to an old yellow van parked in the lot. The three gathered in a semi-circle, by now looking a bit squirrely.

"Now, listen." Cord raked his fingers through his hair, trying to loosen the hangover knot still busting his head. "I figure y'all are from the commune. Could be wrong. Just guessin'. But we found the body of a girl washed up on the riverbank last evenin'. Young red-head wearin' a leather anklet, long skirt. Y'all know if anybody matchin' that description might be missing from The Farm?"

"Kinda sounds like Zoe." The man wearing glasses nodded.

"Shut up, Filmore." The one with the tattoos leaned into the others. "We don't gotta tell him nothing."

"What's your name, son?"

"Eli. And I'm not your son."

"Eli." Filmore broke in. "Ease off, man." He turned back to Cord. "Look, Sheriff—"

"You can call me Cord."

"Cord," said Filmore. "Eli here don't mean anything. He's all right. Really, man. Just don't trust the law. Here or anywhere else." Filmore motioned the others to the van. "Get in, Eli. I'll take care of this."

But the young man was shaking his head, eyes locked on Cord.

"Eli!" Filmore reached for his arm.

"Get the fuck off me, man." He knocked Filmore's hand aside. "You're acting like a dog, cowing to the corporate police state." He stepped closer to Cord. "And I already told you, fucker. We haven't done anything. So kiss my ass."

Cord slightly cocked his head, and looked at the man eye-level, half-smile turned up at the corner of his mouth. He'd tried to avoid such confrontations since taking office. No need to elevate the tension that already existed between the locals and the commune. The recent drug busts and corruption scandals in the sheriff's office had only strained the relationship even more. Primarily because not a single member of the Glad Earth community had been implicated, despite common knowledge that they were notorious potheads who grew and sold some of the highest quality marijuana in the border states. Yet they'd somehow come away clean while several locals, with roots sunk deep in the soil, harkening back to a much older and more traditional way of life, had been arrested and sent off to Brushy Mountain Prison.

But this was different. One of theirs had turned up dead in his county. And Cord was ready and willing to plow under the topsoil of their farm to see what kind of worms might be turning under the darkness there. Now was as good a time as any to start.

So as Eli started to turn away, Cord thumbed the crooked bridge of his own twice-broken nose, a boxer's move, and leaned in. "Son. You got daddy issues?"

Eli spun, fist already swinging a wide, wild roundhouse at Cord's head.

He easily dodged the punch. Then lunged and shot a forearm under Eli's chin, bulling him back against the side of the van, pressing the ball of his other hand into Eli's solar plexus just as they thudded into the double-doors. All the breath blasted out of the man's lungs. His raised arms dropped limp to his side.

"Now." Cord's face was inches from Eli's. "There wasn't any reason to arrest you before." He spun the man around and cuffed him. "But this hillbilly don't take kindly to folks ignoring a friendly request. Especially when they top it off by trying to club him." He patted Eli down, pocketing a .38 snub nose he found inside the waistband. "Better hope you got a license for this."

"Sure as fuck do."

Cord looked back at the others. "You two carryin'?"

They shook their heads, mumbled, "No."

He nodded. "All the same. Mind turning around and placing your hands on the van where I can see 'em?" He pushed Eli to the ground. "Now you just rest here a minute." He searched the others. "Okay, relax while I get your partner settled in his new temporary conveyance."

He marched Eli back to the cruiser, stuffed him in the back seat and slammed the door. "Be back in a couple. I'm sure you'll have something to say, then."

"Fuck you." Eli banged his head against the window.

Cord would have to remember to ask, one day, what good they thought it did to bust their heads on the inside glass of a cruiser.

He crossed the lot back to the others. "That's one helluva way to spread the Good Word, eh?"

"Look. Eli's not bad. He just don't always think before acting." Filmore looked across the lot at his friend.

"S'all right." Cord shrugged. "I don't either."

Filmore nodded. "Fair enough. Guess we'll need to get him bail?"

"Unless you want to just let him cool off a bit." He glanced at the cruiser where Eli was still cussing him. "But it probably won't do a feller like him much good."

"Right." Filmore nodded. "So, listen. That woman? Don't know anything for sure. But I haven't seen the girl named Zoe in a day or so. She might've strolled off for a lark in the hills. Lots of land up there. Couples always going into those hollers, man. Ain't unusual for them to stay gone a day or two."

Cord nodded. "Got a last name?"

"Never knew it. We dropped those when we came over the pass. Zoe Magdalene's all I know. Part of an ordination for some of the women members."

Cord arched a brow. Classic cult of personality. "Well. We've already put a call into the main house. Like to get someone down here today, see if they can ID the body. How about it? You can come down with me now. Shouldn't take long."

"Man, I can't miss a shift at the sawmill. They got us on day-labor contract. If we don't show up, I'll lose my spot. Can't afford to get canned."

Cord nodded. "Well, let 'em know when you get back, will you?"

"We won't get in until late."

"Guess that'll have to do. Thanks, Filmore."

"Hey, wait a minute. You sure it was a leather anklet?"

"Yep. Braided."

"Zoe's in the faith, like the rest of us, Sheriff. Don't support products begat from commercialized animal cruelty. Promotes negative consequences. It'll kill ya."

"Right." Cord shrugged at the irony. That's the least of her worries now, he thought. "Thanks again."

"Yeah." Filmore glanced again at the cruiser. "Someone will be down later for him."

They shook hands. Cord headed back into the restaurant as the van sputtered, blasted smoke, then rolled out of the lot.

Back at the counter, he pushed the plate of cold eggs and grits away and laid a ten dollar bill on the counter. "Sorry, Lily. Can't stomach it." He gulped the coffee and held up the cup for a refill. "Some cargo out there I need to get to the station. Any Listerine back there? Need something to wash out the tin in my throat."

"They's a bottle of something Buck uses after all-nighters." Lily pointed to the kitchen. "Welcome to it, darlin'."

"Thanks." Cord took another slug, then stepped through the swinging doors into the kitchen. He was back out in seconds, nodding to Lily as he passed. "See you on the flip side."

"Ain't no flip side here, boy. What ye see is what ye get," she called after him.

He pushed through the door, almost colliding with Ryanne, the new EMT, still in her uniform. "Whoa, now," she backed away, one hand raised, smiling. "Some kinda hurry there, Sheriff?"

"Nope. Just headed home for a shower after a long night. Then back at it." In the light of the morning he now noticed her high cheekbones and wide-set, dark eyes over a strong, straight nose. Standing almost eye-level, he liked the steady, honest gaze she now appraised him with. "How 'bout you?"

"Gotta slug down some coffee and grub before the shift. Pulled a double yesterday. Need some of Lil's strong stuff. You find out what the hell Lou was doin' at Red's yesterday?"

"Nope. But I plan to have a talk with Webb later. Maybe shed some light on it. Said you hung with Lou in Afghanistan?"

"Yeah. We weren't in the same unit, but crossed paths at Camp Losano in Kandahar and Rhino in Garmsir. Two places I ain't ever hopin' to see again." She briefly looked over his shoulder at the river. When she turned to look at him, her eyes met his again, darker now. "Too damn much was lost over there that you can never get back." She shrugged. "Even if you do make it home. Lou was lost in those mountain passes, Sheriff. Never did come back." She stepped past him to the door. "You fill that position, yet?"

"Nope."

"I'll stop by and see you, soon. But now I gotta go. Already late."

"You do that." Cord stepped aside and watched her pass. "And thanks. For everything."

She nodded and disappeared inside.

Back in the cruiser, Eli had finally run out of steam and sat brooding in the back, head lowered, glaring at Cord in the rearview. He stayed that way until they pulled into the parking space in front of the jail.

"So you think because you got a gun and a badge you can run all over us little people, huh?"

Cord shoved the shifter into park listening to the rumble of his Ford Police Interceptor. Nothing like the Polara Pursuit old-timers like Waddy had driven, with 440 cubic inches pushing out 375 horses and turning zero to sixty in 6.3 seconds. But he and Acel, the department's mechanic, had modified Josephine enough to push the factory's 235 horsepower up to 300. On short straightaways on the twisting, mountain roads, he'd taken her to 120 before he'd eased off the pedal, realizing the monster had more power in it than he was willing to try.

He shut her off now and turned to his prisoner, who was leaning close to the Plexiglas partition.

"Look, Eli. This ain't no police state, and we're no goddamned jack-booted thugs. Hell, these people have probably thrown more revenuers and federal agents out of this holler than the KGB have out of Russia. I'm just trying to find out what happened to a girl named Zoe we found dead underneath a bridge."

Eli snorted. "If you're not lying, then you're just one ignorant sonofabitch." He leaned back. "I know the system. And there's going to be an end to it. Soon. The likes of you are gonna wish you'd gotten on board. For hell's coming your way." He paused, staring out the window. "Zoe's just another victim of the fucked up fascist hierarchy. She was a good woman. But who we are, what we do, is none of your fucking business. We'll take care of our own."

"Well." Cord swung around and stepped out of the car, then stuck his head back in. "I'd like it just fine if that were the case. But once her body turned up in my jurisdiction, she became my fucking business, too."

On the road after processing Eli, Cord thought again about the dead girl's anklet. Either she didn't belong to that cult compound they called a farm, or she did and she was breaking with the ways of the tribe. Whatever the case, it felt good to be back in the middle of an investigation. Despite the hangover, his head now felt clearer than it had in months.

As his mind clicked through the day's plans (review the autopsy, interview the boys who'd found the body, talk to Levon and others at The Farm), his pulse quickened, lighting a fire too long smothered under paperwork and "official business." Now, he dipped into another curve in the road, late-morning November sun filtering through the clouds, brisk wind blowing through the side window, focused, alert. Damned good to be back. Damned good.

He pulled the cruiser onto the gravel drive of the old home place, wound down into the valley then up a rise and parked in front of the two-story Victorian that Grandpa Rhys McRae had built on 250 acres in 1917 as a present to his wife, Leanna. A wide, year-round creek fed by two mountain springs flowed through the south end of the property. To the east, a small hunting cabin was surrounded by the hills and mountains full of old-growth spruce, hardwoods and pines. Deer, bear, and coyotes roamed the fields and woods.

The place had wrapped over two hundred years of memories around it. Mostly good. A few, less so. His forbearers, Scots-Irish Presbyterians, had threaded their way over the ridges, through the valleys of the Powell, the Clinch, through Cumberland Gap and on down the Holston. They'd turned east into the Unakas through the water gaps and valleys of the Watauga and the Nolichucky to settle into the coves and hollows of the Great Smokies and the Blue Ridge where winter mornings the red clay glistened in hoarfrost, early spring bloomed laurel, dogwood, wild azalea and rhododendron, and summers, magnolias and gentians grew in the mists of a shimmering waterfall.

The old hunting cabin down behind the barn was the original home place. Still Cord's favorite spot to go when the weight of the shadowy world in which he moved left him feeling cynical and forlorn. There, and the barn where he kept his 1966 Mustang, Roberta, along with his latest restoration project, the 1964 GTO he'd bought off a Vietnam vet who'd stashed the car behind a barn under a tarp. It needed a lot of work, but Cord was happy to get his hands on it.

Lately, a darker thread of recollections had been woven into the fabric of the home in the form of Frank Reevers. Cord had been hard on the drink at the time and in his clouded state of mind had missed some clues that might have stopped Frank and saved the life of Cord's unborn son. He still blamed himself years after, despite Lucinda's insistence it hadn't been his fault. His decision to run for sheriff, with the promise of a big raise and less time in the field, was a kind of amends he'd hoped would repair the damage done. But he still felt, deep down, nothing could ever really make things right again.

Looking up at the green-shingled dormers now, he figured Waddy was right. He'd need to keep a tight lid on the shine or he'd lose it all.

Lucinda was in the back yard hanging clothes. He quickly walked to the sliding doors and stuck his head out. "Hey. It's me. Gotta get back to the jail. Two homicides."

Lucinda, shading her eyes, waved, then turned back to the clothes. After all the years, and all the hell they'd been through, she still possessed a beauty the likes he'd never seen in anyone else. Shoulder-length, brown, loose-curled hair. Almond shaped, bister-brown eyes ringed in apple green set in a heart-shaped face. Lips like a cupid's bow turned sideways. The sunlight shining through her cotton dress outlined her silhouette. Small breasts, shapely hips, and strong legs.

Couldn't do better, he thought as he made his way to the bathroom.

They'd met at UT where she was working as a graduate assistant teaching English composition. After grading an essay he'd written about his experience as a Navy corpsman, she'd tried to talk him into majoring in English. But his academic aspirations were limited to getting the necessary credits and courses for a promotion to sheriff's lieutenant. She had, nevertheless, talked him into submitting the essay for a school-sponsored writing contest after he'd wrangled the promise of a date once the semester ended.

True to her word, they'd grabbed a 14-inch pepperoni and mushroom pie at Pizza Palace, a Greek-owned drive-in and Knoxville low-priced dining institution, after the award's ceremony (the $100 prize for the essay paid for the dinner and filled the tank of his Mustang, which they drove all the way to Falston and back that night).

They'd spent the next two years dating, on and off, while she finished her doctorate at UVA. Then she took an adjunct position at East Tennessee State University and he'd seen his father, Nathan, through twelve months of chemo, ten more of fishing, hunting, and working together to restore his Mustang, followed by two months of hell watching the man waste away and die. He and Lucinda were married six months after they buried Nathan, moving into the old home perched on the bluff overlooking the Pigeon River.

She was in the kitchen making his lunch by the time he'd showered and dressed. "Didn't think you'd be home. Don't suppose you got that valve?

"No. Didn't." He watched her profile for any reaction.

Nothing.

"Say you got a couple of homicides the boys are working?" She sliced a thick wedge off a tomato, licked her thumb and looked up as he moved around the counter for a kiss.

"Yep." He grabbed a pickle out of the jar beside her. "But I might work one of them myself." He leaned on the counter beside her. "Young girl washed up from the river. Maybe from that commune up at Hartfield's old place."

She stopped in the middle of a slice, sighed and set the knife on the counter. "Sure you can handle that with all your other work? You're hardly home as it is. Blu waited an hour before Judy got to school yesterday. You could've called."

"I know, Luce. I should have called. But there ain't anybody else at that office can follow a case like me." He took a bite off the pickle. "Besides. I'd probably just get on your nerves if I were around more."

"No, Cord. You wouldn't." She picked up the paring knife and started to slice another tomato, then turned and wagged the blade under his nose for emphasis. "Now listen. I know you thought getting that promotion was what I wanted, so we could afford more stuff. But it wasn't. I liked it just fine living on less, because you were home more."

She stopped, lowering the knife, brow knitted. "I love you, Cord. Always have. But I'm not going to wait around here while you go to hell chasing down some damn demon of your own making. Now, if you want to keep that job, fine. But do it for yourself. Don't go around thinking you're doing us any favors. I forgave you about Frank Reevers years ago. You're the only one hanging onto that old mess now. Let it go, or you'll be letting *us* go. Soon. Understand?"

He nodded. "You're right." He reached across the counter, clasped her hand and waited. Her eyes studied his face. At last, she took a deep breath. Her features softened as she reached out and pulled him to her. He caught the jasmine perfume of her hair as they kissed. A catch in his lungs made him breath in deeply, sending an almost-forgotten wave of desire to his loins.

"You're right as can be." He pulled away, breathing heavier. Smiled, touching her cheek lightly with a thumb. "And keep that in mind for later. But I have to finish this investigation. The only way I know how to make a difference in this community. And it means finding out what happened to that poor girl on a slab at the morgue."

"I know." She sighed and released his hand, then turned to finish the sandwiches, packing them in a brown bag with an apple and chips, handing it over to him. "But we need to talk about things, soon. They're cutting the budget at ETSU. I might be out of a job. So, I'm thinking of going back to school. Looking into nursing."

He frowned. "Nursing?"

"Don't look so surprised. You know I was pre-med before I switched to English. Pays good. Get a job anywhere." She shrugged. "Just in case. Now go solve your mystery." She stepped back to the sink and gazed out over the yard where a few mitten-shaped sassafras leaves, turning yellow and gold with the coming frost, still tenaciously hung.

Just in case? He hesitated, wondering if he should press the point. Then, deciding it could wait til they talked later, turned and started out the door. "Tell Blu I love him," he called back over one shoulder. "I'll see you both tonight."

"I will. And don't forget that valve!" she yelled after him.

But he was already gone.

6

Take a Shot

As he approached Thorn's compound, Lucas remembered the first time he'd met the owner of the 600-acre plot that had become his responsibility to secure.

He'd just turned sixteen and was living on his own. His father had been killed in an electrical accident down at the Bush's Best Cannery when Lucas was twelve. His mother had recently died of cancer. Lucas was, by nature, a loner, and so had continued to live on in the log house his father had set well off the highway along a ridge near Kildare Knob. He'd maintained the hardscrabble vegetable garden, kept the chickens fed, and hunted the hills for meat to supplement his diet.

One day, traveling out beyond his normal hunting range, he'd ended up following the Little Pigeon River up near Brady's Holler. As he turned a bend overlooking a cove, he came upon a man squatting beside a smoldering fire, poking at the white-gray ash with a forked stick, raking a few glowing coals into a small pile. He threw a couple small chunks of split pine on for tinder, then turned and studied the line of sunlight breaking over the rim of the gorge, slowly pushing back shadows from the sharply looming cliffs that pitched up on the southern bank.

Lucas followed the man's gaze to the crystal reflections bouncing off the tumbling water. That crisp, clear color seemed to make

46

everything vibrate, shimmering with life even in this cool season. Rust and gold-yellow leaves of sugar maples and oaks shifted and spun, defiant in the face of coming winter. Lucas remembered wondering if his own defiance of the inevitable changing winds would someday meet the fate of those leaves.

Just then, the man stood and stretched his lank, lean frame. Took a deep breath, rubbed an unshaven face, and fingered a scar along the edge of his right jaw. "Got this from a bullet from an old friend of my dead pappy."

Lucas started. He hadn't realized the man had even seen him.

"Did leave me a bit wiser, though." He finally turned and looked at the rifle Lucas had slung in the crook of his arm. "Plannin' on baggin' some game?"

"I am." Lucas glanced around. Maybe others were lurking off in the brushy bank.

"Ain't nobody here but me, boy." The man moved across the stretch of gravel, squinting up through the glare of afternoon sun. "You that Monroe boy?"

"Yeah." Lucas watched him approach. He didn't detect any malice, but a life in the hills had taught him to stay wary, or get dead.

"Lucas, right? I heerd about you. My boys say you been livin' up on that ridge all by your lonesome."

"That's right."

The man stopped about five feet away, studying him. Then looked around, pointing with that sharp chin. "This here's my land. I'm Thornton Reevers." He studied Lucas with steady, blue-gray eyes. "Knew your pappy." He nodded. "Good man."

"I heerd of you too." Lucus set his jaw. "But Momma never took a shine if ever your name were mentioned."

Thorn smiled and shoved his hands in his pockets. "Don't 'spect so. Them that don't know me only go by what they hear." He nodded toward the fire. "Come on down and warm yourself. Gonna fry up a couple trout." He sat down by it. "Up to you. But don't forget, you're on my property. Could've shot you when you first come over that ridge. But I didn't."

Lucas was hungry. He hadn't bagged anything that day. "Reckon I could use a rest, Mr. Reevers."

"Thorn." The man looked up over the fire. "Just call me Thorn."

He nodded, slid down the bank and squatted next to the flames, the rifle still in the crook of his arm.

"You don't let that thing get too far afield, eh?"

"No sir." Lucas looked at it. "Not much."

Thorn chuckled. "Don't blame ye." He scratched the scar again. "Was just about your age when I got this. Learned real quick about the ways of my pappy's business back then. Violent turns ended up killing him and my brother, both—but I kilt the sonofabitch who murdered them." He dropped a couple of trout in a black iron skillet over the fire. "Want some juice?" He held up a mason jar. "My own brew."

Lucas shook his head. "Don't touch it. Momma said hit's what kilt Daddy."

Thorn nodded. "Maybe. But what kills us most is life in these here hollers." He turned the fish in the pan, then reached down and picked up a metal dinner plate and a heavy old Colt automatic. He tucked the gun under his belt, behind his back. "Had to grow up fast after Pappy was kilt. Took over the business, outsmarted my competition, even blood-folk in my own clan who'd wanted to take over Pap's operation."

Thorn forked a trout from the pan, plopped it on the plate and offered it to Lucas. "Ain't no side vittles to go with. But she's fresh."

Lucas took the plate, unsheathed his hunting knife and filleted a piece off the side, keeping one eye on the pistol.

Thorn picked up the pan, set it on a flat rock between his feet to cool, and leaned back. "It's this life, son." He spread his hand to gesture around him. "These hills. Does somethin' to a man. I've cajoled, threatened, bartered, bought off, killed and stole enough to turn Pappy's small corn liquor operation into a profit-making enterprise. Three years ago I built a new, two-story, split-level rock and stone house on this-here compound where the damned ol' shitty shack where they reared me used to stand."

He threw a couple more sticks on the fire and watched the flames catch. "I got lawyers. I got guns. And I got money." He reached down, pinched up a chunk of fish, raised it to his lips, blew across the steaming meat, then popped it into his mouth. "Man, don't get no better. Eh, boy?"

Lucas slowly nodded, nervous, scared, but riveted by the story.

"Like I said, already heerd all about you." Thorn tore another piece off the trout and raised it to his mouth. "They tell me you know these mountains like a Cherokee. Said you was a real sharp-shooter, too. Is 'at right?"

"I reckon." Lucas shrugged. "Ain't never really thought about it much."

"No." Thorn chuckled again. "I reckon you ain't." He took another bite of fish and chewed. "So listen here. I'm about to move into a new phase of my operation. I need somebody to take over the security on my property." He studied the sky, then looked straight at Lucas. "I could hire an outsider who was up on all the new high-technology security shit. But I don't trust folks from outside. I need a man who knows the pain 'at's seeped down deep into these stones. Can you read?" he added abruptly.

Lucas flinched, confused. "Yeah."

"Then you can learn." Thorn smiled. "Everthing a body needs to know you can find out on the internet nowadays. Want a job?"

That was eighteen months ago. Now, as he plopped the bushy tails down on the cutting board behind Thorn's house and looked up at the other gutted carcasses, he wondered if he'd end up dead and hanging on a line after Thorn had finished gutting out his soul. He'd just started to dress out the catch when he heard the rumble of a hotrod breaking across the holler.

He quickly skinned and gutted the squirrels, threw the naked carcasses into the chest freezer, then ambled up the hill around the house to the detached four-car garage. Thorn stood leaning over the engine compartment of a souped-up 440 cubic inch V8. He turned and grinned as Lucas approached.

"Lucas, boy." He yelled over the rumble of the turbo headers. "This here's Bill Beloit. Young buck just up from Georgia. Heerd I was lookin' fer runners. Already made a name for himself down at the Dixie Speedway in Woodstock." He winked at Lucas. "Wants to turn big time. Run NASCAR. See his name on the boards with the likes of Jimmy Johnson, Kasey Kane, and Webb Busch. But he's hot-headed. Too many run-ins with other drivers and team owners. Lost his sponsorships. So he needs money."

Beloit sat in the driver's seat revving the engine. "Had to shorten the carburetors just so I could close the hood!" Beloit yelled over the noise.

Lucas admired the clean engine topped with two four-barrel carburetors mounted on an Edelbrock manifold. He figured it could outrun anything the local law could throw at it. Thorn had switched from using runners years before Lucas had come on. Now, he mostly used trucks and vans to haul the meth and heroin he kept stowed under cover of his illegal whiskey. But clearly there was something about this sleek black Plymouth Fury, fitted with heavy duty suspension and low tires, that Thorn liked.

He motioned at Beloit, who shut down the engine.

"So. What d'ya think, Mister Reevers? Purty sweet, huh?"

Thorn nodded and rubbed his chin. "So ye wanna pitch in with the big boys, eh?"

"Yes, sir. I ain't braggin'. But ain't nobody today could outpace me in this-here baby." He opened the door and slid out. "Look. I even got 'er rigged up in the back so's you can pack six crates behind the driver's seat." He stepped to the rear window and pointed.

"That there's some kind of impressive, son." Thorn moved up beside him, placing a hand on his shoulder. "But this ain't no dirt track circle-drivin' we're talkin' 'bout. It's honest-to-goodness fuckin' haulin' ass around two-lane mountain roads with a passle o' police houndin' ye like a fox after a coon."

"Listen, Mister Reevers—"

"Thorn."

"Yes, sir, Thorn. Just so you know, I been turning mountain roads since I was twelve. Come from Dahlonega. They ain't no roads nowhere more twisted. Hop on in and I'll show you."

"That's all right, son. I got some business to attend. We'll take that ride later." He laid a hand on Beloit's shoulder. "I done checked you out. Report's come back good. We'll make a test run in a day or two. Oughter tell the tale on whether you're up fer this."

He pointed down the mountain at the city below. "That there's Falston. Off limits for now. Don't want you gettin' snarled up in trouble 'fore ye get a chance to make us some money. If it all works out, should get you straight enough to buy a whole goddamned racin' team.

"Meanwhile, come on in and meet some of the boys." He nodded at the house. "I'll put you up the next few days and Lucas here'll show you around."

Thorn started towards the house. Beloit shut the hood, then he and Lucas followed close behind. In the kitchen, Thorn washed his hands and pulled a couple glasses from the shelf. He poured the tumblers halfway full of clear liquor and handed a glass to Beloit. Lucas leaned against a doorjamb, watching.

"Drink up. You just got yerself a job." Thorn raised the tumbler.

"Thanks." Beloit tilted the glass, gulped a long swig, then coughed and choked on the gut-burning whiskey.

"Oughter take 'er easy there, son. 'At's the good stuff."

He finally stopped coughing and wiped his watering eyes. "Shit," he gasped. "Reckon I oughter." He shook his head, red-faced. "Ain't that I never drunk 'shine before."

"Aw. Don't worry 'bout it. Takes some gettin' used to. Don't drop the bead like some other shiners. Stronger proof." He crooked a finger for Beloit to follow. "Come on down. Want t' introduce you to my second. Oh, watch out fer the dog," he said over one shoulder. "Won't bite, but he might trip ye."

Lucas and Beloit followed. The click of pool balls cracking together popped in the stairwell as they made their way to the lower floor. Downstairs, several split logs burned fiercely in the big fireplace against the back wall. Sofas and chairs lined two other walls. The third wall faced north, overlooking the valley below and the river to the east. Drizzling rain veiled the panoramic view that normally stretched for miles across ridges that ran like a spine from Hall Top to Neddy Mountain. The heart of Thorn's operation.

"Rad." Thorn nodded to a man leaning against the table.

"Hey, boss," said Radley Sikes, a dark, bearded, hawk-nosed tough. Thorn's only living childhood friend. A kind of captain in his business. Lucas had already witnessed enough to know he'd do anything Thorn asked.

"Winnin' much?"

"Naw." Rad stepped over to the bar, snorted a line of crank, then threw his head back. "God damn!" he gasped. "That's the shit, Boss." He walked back to the pool table, chalked the cue and leaned in for another shot. "Good recipe, but that fuckin' Deputy-dog Sam's puttin' eyes on us. Hurtin' production."

Last year, Thorn had been running one of the biggest meth operations in the southeast region. Profits were pouring in. Enough that he had most county officials in his pocket and it seemed like he'd found the perfect product to leverage his dreams of moving into bigger, more legitimate business initiatives; finance, state-funded road construction projects, shipping and warehousing. But it had all unraveled about six months ago after the Tennessee Bureau of Investigation had turned the screws on one of the local city councilmen. They'd started an undercover sting operation that not only shut down Thorn's gambling and prostitution activities, but busted most of the meth houses he'd set up throughout the county.

And although Thorn had kept himself out of the sweeping arrests made during the operation, most of his trusted subordinates had been imprisoned, including his cousin Mike "Bump" Massey. Bump had been orphaned a couple of years after Thorn took over the business, when his parents were killed in a car accident. No other family would take him in, so Thorn brought him to live in the old shack. Lucas had seen Bump beat a man almost to death with his bare hands, without a blink or a shrug, on Thorn's order, all over the transgression of asking Thorn to front him an eight ball of crank. Bump was probably Thorn's most bitter loss in the whole episode.

Since then, he'd gotten most of his other illicit businesses, including prostitution, online gambling, cock-fighting and moonshining back up and running while the new sheriff settled into his responsibilities and the TBI focused their attention on the "methamphetamine epidemic," as it was now called by the media. But the loss of such a low-cost, high profit product had left him looking for other opportunities to put his long-term plans back on track. And he'd recently found one, in the most unlikely of places: Glad Earth Farm.

"Get that business taken care of at the Rooster?" Thorn went over to a wall rack, grabbed a cue and began chalking it.

"Lou's in the hospital." Rad leaned against his stick. "Coma, last I heerd."

"Good. Heard from the other?"

"No." Rad glanced at Beloit and raised his eyebrows, questioning.

"This here's Bill Beloit." Thorn blew chalk dust off the tip of the stick. "He's all right. Come up from North Georgia. Gonna do some runnin' for us. Reckon we might load him up tomorrow night. See if he's as good as his brags. Right Beloit?" Thorn peered at him over the stick.

"At's right." The boy nodded, shuffling his feet.

Lucas strolled to the fireplace and warmed his hands. Primed by his own experience, he knew what was coming.

"Well, well." Rad laid the stick on the table and approached Beloit. "You that young gunner I heard about from my cousin Rydell? Comes from down yer way. Says yer good. But with a temper. Like two bulls with cinched balls." Rad laid his big claw of a hand on Beloit's left shoulder, and squeezed. "Cain't have no hot-heads in this-here game. You a hot-head?"

Beloit tried to shrug the hand away. "Get off me." Rad held fast. The boy shrugged again.

"Aw. Come on. You ain't s'tough now. Are ye?"

"Get the hell off me, sonofabitch!" Beloit tried to jerk away. When he couldn't, he swung a fist at Rad's head.

"Whoa, now." Rad caught it with his other hand and squeezed until the boy yelped. Then lowered the arm back to Beloit's side. "Ye better figure that one again, bud." Suddenly, he slammed his forehead against Beloit's. The boy flew back against the sofa where he sprawled, dazed. Blood oozed from the split flesh between his brows and dripped down the bridge of his nose.

Thorn casually crossed the room and poked the tip of the stick under Beloit's chin. "Now listen here, son. You're in. But you ain't inside. Ain't runnin' nothin' 'cept that car of your'uns. Understand?"

The boy looked up. He winced as his fingers traced the bloody rise on his forehead. "Yes, sir. Sorry," he mumbled. "Didn't mean t' cause trouble."

"At's right, boy. We don't hanker to have no trouble 'round here." Thorn lifted the boy's chin with the cue. "Got an arrangement with the law. Ain't gonna let some snot-nosed, big-shot driver mess it up." He pulled the stick away and walked back to the table. "Go on upstairs and clean that gash, then come back down here. We got business tonight

54

and I just decided I want you along." He leaned over the table and took aim. "Mind if I take this shot, Rad?"

"Yer the boss."

"'At's right. I am." He pulled the stick back, sighting down the smooth line, then popped the ball solid, but easy. It ran the length of the table and lightly tapped the three-ball, sending it into the corner pocket. "'S'all in the touch," he said. "All in the touch."

Lucas knew that touch, and wondered if Beloit realized his racing skills weren't gonna be enough to save him from the quick pricks and cuts of Thorn's fierce, heavy-handed will.

7
Rising Tide

On the way back to the jailhouse, Cord detoured over to Rocky Top Road and headed to Pine Gulch. Webb and Elsie lived on a hard-chisel patch of land left them by her mother. Not good for much except growing daffodils in the spring, tending a few chickens and raising a cow or two. They were better off than some. But not by much.

Cord pulled onto Pine Gulch, drove about three miles in, and turned onto a steep-pitched graveled drive, rocks pinging the undercarriage as he maneuvered around gulleys and ruts. At the top, a small clapboard house, supported in the back by stilts, hung precariously on the edge of a steep ridge. Roof sagging. Paint peeling from the soffit and sideboards.

A rusted two-door Buick Skylark was parked in front of the porch. Several old tires were laid flat on their sides as flower planters. Tiny triangles cut out from the sidewalls stood up around the inside rim, like over-sized flower petals. The centers of the planters were now empty. Just a few dead brown stems sticking up here and there.

Cord pulled in behind a primer-patched Corolla, parked and stepped out. Elsie stood just behind the screen door, watching. "Hey now, little Elsie." He kicked at the gravel. "In the mood for a talk?"

"Don't know what fer. Webb ain't never been no good." She stepped onto the porch and settled her arms across her chest. She was short, around five-foot-three, with a thin, sallow face, and dark brown hair pulled back in knot. She wore a faded-blue print dress and a thin black sweater tightly pulled around her slightly bulging pregnant belly. "Ain't no use t' worry over the sorry cuss now."

"Aw. Come on now, El." He approached the porch and stopped at the bottom step. "You and Webb's had some rough times. That's f'sure." Cord had known them both all their lives. Hunted and fished with Webb's father, Jesse. Hard working folks. And Cord's own parents had lived just a few miles up the road. He'd watched Elsie growing up. They were both good at heart. But hard times had got Webb on the hooch, which sometimes turned him mean. And Elsie had come out on the hurting end of that meanness, more than once.

"Rough times!" Elsie stepped to the edge of the porch. "I'll tell you rough. Living with a sonofabitch who ain't never cared nothin' about nobody 'cept himself. Lowdown man thinks 'cause it's hard t' get a job he can lay up in here all day tellin' me what to do." Her voice broke. She turned away and paced across the porch. "Slinkin' off to Thorn's t' grab a nip of whiskey and snort crank and callin' it work. And then comin' back down here to beat the shit outta me! Can't even get out and look fer a job. Says nobody 'cept them good fer nothin' hillbilly crackheads got anything fer him. Hell no, Cord." She faced him again, eyes brimming. "I ain't havin' this-here baby growin' up with a tweeker daddy!"

Cord stepped up on the porch and put a hand on her shoulder. She leaned against him and sobbed, face buried in his chest. "I'm sorry, darlin'. I'm sorry." He stroked her hair until her sobs subsided. "How long's he been on the meth?"

Methamphetamine and the rise in criminal activity that came with it had swept into the region about ten years before. More highly addictive than any other drug, except maybe heroin, it was cheap and easy to make and therefore more profitable. The economically-depressed towns along the southeastern slopes created a rich petri dish from which organized crime and the local hillbilly mafia, like that of Thornton Reevers, could develop a deadly contagion. Cord kicked himself now for not noticing the symptoms in Webb at the bar. He'd just figured the boy was jittery and nervous about spending a good chunk of his life in prison after almost killing a man.

Elsie swiped her nose on one sleeve of her sweater. "About four months ago. After he lost his job at old man Grimm's place."

"Why didn't you say somethin', El? You know I'd of helped you."

She sniffed and looked away. "I . . .uh, reckon I figured he'd come around oncet the baby got here. I know it don't make no sense. But I didn't want fer him t' get jailed."

"You and I both know Webb ain't a bad man. You two's been datin' since you were fourteen. Stuck good with you up until now. But that stuff he's on, El. Aint' gonna let go easy. I seen the damage it'll do. But, girl, hold on. He's going t' need you to hold on."

"But I don't know what that means, Cord." Her voice was shrill with fear. "He kilt a man! They'll lock him up fer life!"

"The man ain't dead yet, darlin'." He shrugged. "But you're right. If he dies, Webb might have to go away. Sure might. But look here." He gently pushed her back so they could talk eye-to-eye. "Webb's young. We don't know all the facts about how things went down yesterday. Now you gotta hold onto some hope that he'll be able to get out of this thing sooner than later. You hear me, El?"

She wiped her nose again. "Yessir."

"I'll try to get him some help. If he wants it. But in the meantime, think about this baby. You can't stay here, alone. Didn't your momma have a sister lived up in Knoxville? Pretty close if I remember."

"Yes," she whispered. "Aunt Sophie."

"Good. Get in touch and let her know you'll need to stay for a time. Okay?"

"Yessir." She stepped back. "But what about Webb?"

"I'll do what I can for him." He paused, thinking. "What time did he leave outta here yesterday?"

"'Bout eleven."

"Okay. Did he tell you where he was going?"

"No. But I figured wherever it was, Thorn's bunch would be there. They's the ones been supplyin' him."

"Thanks, darlin'. I'll let him know you're still behind him. He does love you, Elsie. Like nobody else. And he's going to need to know you're still backin' him t' make it through this mess." He looked down at her belly. "And that there baby should know its daddy's a good man at heart. You hear?"

She nodded. "I reckon so. But I'm afeard, Cord. Of what's gonna happen to us."

"Don't worry, Elsie. I'll be around to check up 'til you leave. In the meantime, if ye need anything, you know where I am."

"All right, Cord. Thank ye."

He kissed her on the forehead. Stepped off the porch to the cruiser, slid in and cranked the engine. He glanced her way once more before backing out. The mountains looming up behind made her look even more fragile and insignificant as she stood waving. He'd get Red's statement and talk to Webb again as soon as he got back to the jailhouse. Before he talked to the lawyer. He'd need to get the whole story if he were going to help Webb out of this mess. Not a lawyer standing between him and the truth.

Just past noon, he pulled into his spot at the station. Judy was at her computer, typing out reports as she chewed on a pen. She glanced over her glasses as he pushed through the low gate at the railing that separated the lobby from her desk and the small open patrol room, or bullpen as his deputies liked to call it. Their desks were ranged in two rows down the center of the room. A large county map hung on the back wall beside a dry-erase board containing the names of open cases. On the right, just behind Judy's desk, a doorway opened to a hall that led to Cord's office, the evidence room, and the holding cells at the back.

"What got you draggin' in here so late? You and Lucinda workin' on another package?"

Cord removed his hat and rubbed his head. "Why? You got some pointers?"

"I could tell ye a thing or two, I reckon." She sniffed and resumed typing. "Don't suppose it'd do any good, though. You're too damned hard-headed t' take advice from a fifty-somethin' divorcee." She stopped typing and squinted at him. "You talk to Elsie, yet?"

"Just left her. She was plenty upset. Think I got her calmed, for now." He stepped in behind her and looked at the report. "And I remembered what I forgot to remember this morning. The knife. Webb used a Benchmade 500 SBK Auto on Lou. Not your usual hunting knife. Mostly owned by military personnel, or paramilitary wannabe types. And at $200, a bit too expensive for a rounder like Webb Rasser. Who ain't had a job for four months."

"So where's he gettin' the greenbacks?"

"Thorn Reevers." Cord bit his lip. "I sure hope Thorn's not planning to start kickin' that shit around here again."

"What?"

"Meth. Elsie says Webb's been using, and hanging around with Reevers' bunch. There's no way that boy's got the money to pay for it. I suspect he was getting his fix in trade."

"Time for a little sit-down, huh?"

"Yep. What'd Doc say about that girl we found?"

"Not much. She drowned. Had water in her lungs. Signs of vasoconstriction and blood shift. That blow to the head was concussive. Probably just knocked her unconscious."

"Say what might've caused the concussion?"

"Weren't a rock. Found some wood splinters imbedded in the scalp." Judy tapped a pen on the edge of the ashtray and looked up. "Not a tree limb. Maybe a bat, or ax handle." She chewed on the end of the pen. "What'dya think, Cord."

He turned and looked out the front windows. Across the street the river was rising. Dam locks had opened at the Walter's Powerhouse. Plenty of lost souls had already floated down those waters. Some murdered, others mostly bad luck or carelessness. Nothing new. But it didn't make it any easier. He walked to the break room and poured a cup of coffee, a couple of lines from Emily Bronte popping in his head. *Oh for the time when I shall sleep / without identity.* "I need to find out more about the girl. What else do we have?"

"Nothin', really. No other trace on the clothes. 'Cept fer that anklet."

"Suppose that's already bagged."

"It is."

"Time of death?"

"Somewhere between noon and three."

"Farley and Jeb said they saw something floatin' down the river around two o'clock. About three miles from where we found her. But Darcy was two miles upstream watchin' that water all day, and didn't see a thing. So that puts her going in the water somewhere between three to five miles upstream. I need a crime scene. Did Sam get that stream flow for yesterday?"

"Yep." Judy looked at her notes. "Around 1650 fps. About two miles per hour."

He rubbed at the scar. "That'd put her in the water just under four hours at most since the boys found her at four o'clock. And the Battle's sign I found on her takes four to six hours to develop."

"So, she was knocked in the head between 10 am and 12 pm. Then dumped in the river between three to five miles from where you found her." Judy smiled up, tapping the pen on her temple. Then shrugged.

Cord lowered his hand and rolled his eyes. "Yes, Miss Algebra. You have correctly deduced the timeline and chain of events." He took a sip from the cup and winced. "Damn, that's hot."

"Yep. 'At's the way we drink it 'round here." She twisted the cap off the pen and snapped it onto the other end. "See if I can't rustle up some ice t' keep on hand fer ye." She turned back to the report.

"No ice, darlin'. Remember, I like it hot and bitter. Now, can you get one of the boys out to that river? Tell 'em to start combing the banks in that stretch you so brilliantly delineated, see if we can't pinpoint exactly where she went in." He strode down the hallway to the evidence room without waiting for an answer.

Inside, he found the evidence bag and pulled the anklet. Dark, tanned leather, about one inch wide with long strands at each end tied in a square knot to secure the loop. He'd seen younger folks wearing such. But this one was different. An intricate eight-strand braid instead of the usual three. And midway around the loop, four strands had been strangely knotted together to make a twisted heart-like emblem in the center. *Took some time to piece this one together,* he thought. *Wasn't store-bought. Looks like an item old Circe might know something about.*

Circe Grace was an ninety-year-old mountain woman who'd midwifed most all the children in Falston at one point. Some locals still used her, even with the new hospital just down the road in Newport. She kept to the old ways. Did a pretty fair business at reading signs and making charms and lockets for almost anything that ailed the body or spirit. Cord figured he'd stop over to see if she might help him trace the anklet to the maker.

He stuffed it in his jacket pocket and stepped back into the outer office just as J.T. Swany and Ben Hawkins, two of his deputies, were coming in from patrol.

"Boys." Cord nodded. "Keepin' 'er straight?"

"Aw, hell." Swany pushed his black horned-rimmed glasses back on his sharp nose. "Things're slow as shit today, Cord. Had to stop at the library to check out another Mitch Ralindo book."

Cord chuckled. Mitch Ralindo was an ex-Navy SEAL, turned businessman, turned novelist, who wrote thrillers about a retired SEAL who gets pulled back into service and, well, saves the world and kicks ass in novel after novel. And J.T. Swany, a consistent advocate and campaigner for spending the sheriff's office ever-depleted revenues on developing a tactical unit, was always first in line for the latest Ralindo book as soon as it hit the shelves. He'd come to his position honestly after partially losing the use of his right leg in a shoot-out. He'd been serving a warrant for a dumping violation on a couple of local anti-government survivalist types who'd worn body armor and carried AK-47s.

"It's Falston, Swan. If you want more action, try movin' to New Jersey." Cord tapped the book. "And don't let me catch you reading that stuff on the job." He tried to repress a grin as he read the title: *Operation Sand Storm.* "Don't want people to start thinkin' we got us a real commando in this sheriff's office."

Swany stepped to his desk and tossed the book on the corner. "I'm just sayin', Cord. The real deal's headin' our way. Best get ready."

Despite his somewhat overenthusiastic protect-America-from-its-coming-inevitable-destruction stance, Swany was one of the good guys. That's why Cord had paired him with Ben Hawkins, a ten-year veteran left over from Sheriff Casey's old crew. Hawkins's close connections with Thorn's bunch had motivated Cord to schedule him on first shift to keep an eye on him. Cord didn't trust him any more than he would a bear in a drought. The man's constant niggling sarcasm only made it harder not to send a couple of quick jabs into his ribs followed by a strong uppercut, just to shut him up.

Hawkins now ambled in behind Swany. "Yep. Makin' our pay out there today, Sheriff." He grinned, amused at his own sarcasm, as if the point might get lost on others. "Yes, sir. I'd sure like this-here job better if ever'day was like t'day."

"Bet you would, Hawk. But then I'd have to buy a bigger chair for your lazy ass to sit in. And since there ain't no money in the office equipment budget, reckin' I'd have to fire you instead."

Hawkins mumbled something under his breath, then took a seat at one of the back desks.

"Anybody talk to Webb since last night?" Cord picked up the duty roster and flipped over the sheets.

"No sir." Swany sat down behind his desk. "Ollie booked him in on assault with a deadly weapon and don't know that he's talked to anybody since. 'Cept his lawyer."

"Lawyer? Shit." Cord was already striding toward the doorway that led to lockup. "When?"

"This morning!" Swany yelled after him.

Dammit, Cord thought. Lawyer probably already talked Webb into keeping his mouth shut until they cut a plea with the DA. He'd need to convince the boy to open up if he were going to figure out what the hell really happened in that bar.

He stopped in front of the cell. Webb was lying on the cot, staring up at the ceiling. "You all right, son?"

Webb leaned up on an elbow, groggy but anxious. "Sure, Cord. Lawyer says he might keep me from doin' too much time if I just plead out."

"Son, listen. I just talked to Elsie. She's worried sick."

"You talked to her! What'd she say?"

"Don't worry about that now. I told her I'd do what I could t' see you don't get too twisted up under this one."

"Shit, Cord. I'm already twisted. Ain't nothin' you can do."

"Hold on a minute, Webb. I just need to go over what happened with you."

"But ye said t' keep my mouth shut an' don't talk to nobody 'cept my lawyer." Webb sat up on the edge of the cot, scowling.

64

"I know what I said. But that was then. Now's different. To help you, I need to know everything that happened in that bar. But you'll need to sign over your right to have a lawyer here. Will you do that?"

Webb squinted at him, suspicious. "I don't know."

"Hang on." Cord disappeared from the hallway and quickly returned, sliding a form through the bars. "This here just says it's okay for me to talk to you without a lawyer. You know I ain't gonna throw nothin' on you if I can help it. But I need to get this thing cleared up, pronto."

"But I done told you." He stood and started pacing the small cell, pulling at the bottom of his faded flannel shirt. "That Lou feller started in on calling Elsie a whore and I just plum went crazy! Pulled my knife and swung. Next thing I know, he's layin' on the ground all bloody and gurglin'. And then you. . . ."

"Okay. I know, son. But slow your ass down one damn minute. Sign this form and start again from when you got to the Rooster. And tell me everything."

"Fuck!" Webb grabbed a pen Cord offered and sat back down on the cot, nervously rubbing his hands together. He quickly scribbled his name across the bottom of the form without reading it, then abruptly stood and stuffed the pen and form between the bars to Cord. Pacing again, running fingers through his long, stringy hair. Starting to crash, Cord thought.

"Okay. When I got there, Lou was over at the corner of the bar talkin' to Red. Seemed kindly angry 'bout somethin'. I said 'Hey, Red. What ye pumpin' t'day.' Just like I allers do. They both got real quiet. Looked at me, funny-like. So's I ordered a beer and sat on a stool at the other end."

The words rushed out in a quick stream as if he couldn't stop them. "Red was bein' a smartass, like always. Said, 'Ain't no wonder that gal o' yourn's complainin'. Ye probly ain't even tried t' find work, lazin' round, stayin' fucked up all day.' And I said fer him t' mind his own fuckin' business, finished the beer, and told him t' get me a glass of shine from behind the counter."

"So, Lou and Red were laughing it up when you got there."

"Huh?" Lou stopped pacing and looked at Cord. Scowling. "Well, yeah."

"And what time was that?"

Webb hesitated, gaze searching up to the left. Oh boy, Cord thought. I'm about to hear a whopper.

"Oh, that'd of been around, uh, two, two-thirty."

"Okay. Then what?"

"And that's when that damned Lou opened his big mouth. Said he didn't know how a woman like Elsie put up with a man like me. Said I was s' low-down I couldn't appreciate havin' a gal like Elsie. I'd prob'ly rob food from my baby t' get liquored up. So's I told him to keep his fuckin' mouth shut, t'weren't none of his business neither." Again, the words rushed out without hardly a breath between sentences.

Cord raised his hand. "Hold on now. So when's the last time you or Elsie saw Lou before that day?"

"What? Shit, Cord. What the fuck? I'm trying to remember. To tell you."

"I know." He kept his voice friendly. "I know, buddy. Just gotta do my job and get all the facts, right?"

"Yeah. Sure, right. Whatever the fuck you say."

"So when did y'all last see Lou?"

"Hell. I don't know." He raked his fingers through his hair again. "I swear." He shook his head, voice higher now. "I don't remember!"

"So why do you think he'd say such a thing about Elsie?"

"How the fuck would I know?" He sat back down on the edge of the cot and rocked, confounded.

"Okay, son. 'At's all right." He needed to keep him talking. "So you told him to keep his mouth shut . . ." He waited, the silence building.

Webb finally spoke. "Yeah. So then, he walks across the bar to where I'm standin' and leans in real close." Webb shook his head in disbelief. "Then he whispered: 'But you ain't gotta worry 'bout that, little man. That baby ain't even yourn. Hell, that woman ain't even yourn.' He called me a fuckin' stupid ass that ever'body's laughin' at!" Webb bolted from the cot, crossed the floor, grabbed the steel bars and pressed his face between them. "And then he . . . then he spit on my boots, and that's when I reared back and swung. But he moved quick-like, and tripped me onto the floor. And that's when Red tossed him that there bar bat. So I jumped up and reached for my knife, told him t' back the hell off. But he just come on swinging."

"Ho, ho. Hold on, now. There weren't a bat when I got to the bar. What happened to it?"

"Well." Webb was looking at his feet now. "So, like I was sayin', when he come at me, I ducked and swung out too, automatic-like. Swiped that blade 'cross his neck and he went down. Didn't even know I'd cut him 'til I saw the blood. Jus' stood there, froze. Scared as shit, Cord. Reckon that must've been when Red came around the bar and fetched up the bat. Said since Lou never hit me with it, weren't gonna be no defense since I was usin' a knife. Said it'd just get him in trouble and I didn't want that, did I?"

"So Red took the bat?"

"Yessir."

Cord nodded and paced in front of the cell. "So. That's it?"

Webb nodded. "That's all there is." He wiped the sweat off his face and rubbed his hand against the front of his shirt.

Cord thumbed the crook on his nose. He leaned in closer. "Look at me, Webb."

He looked up. Eyes wide. Sweating.

"Why are you lying to me?"

"What! I ain't lyin'."

Before he could shove away, Cord grabbed him hard by the collar and pulled his face back to the bars.

"Oww. Watch the nose, Cord."

"Gonna be more than a nose bleedin' if you don't come clean with me." He clinched him tighter against the bars. "Elsie said you left the house around eleven. So if you didn't go straight to the Rooster, where were you?"

Webb glared, struggling to break loose. "Fuckin' Elsie! Goddamnit, girl." He gripped the bars so tight his knuckles turned white, still trying to push away. "Look, Cord. I can't tell ye!"

"Can't, or won't?"

"You don't understand." He shook his head. "I got mixed up in some bad stuff. Please. I can't say no more."

"Look, son. I know you been getting' amped on crank. It's done messed with your head so bad you don't know which way's up. You've even gone off on Elsie. Your momma and daddy'd be rollin' in their graves if they knew. I ought to just climb in that cell right now and knock the shit outta you for what you done to her. And if you don't get yourself clear of that poison, you're gonna end up hurtin' the baby too, just like Elsie. Understand?" He loosened his grip. "Look at me."

Webb slowly raised his eyes. "I know. I know, Cord. But that shit's eatin' in me now. Spinning around in my brain and my veins and all over. I . . . I don't see no goin' back. I just need t'get outta here."

"Listen. I promised Elsie I'd do what I could to get you outta this mess and find some help for your addiction. You ain't been tweekin' long. You can still whip this shit. But you gotta get outta this legal mess you're in, first. I can help. If you give me something. Who're you gettin' this shit from? Thorn?"

Webb's eyes looked wild. "I, I didn't say no such. Don't you put that on me. He'd kill me fer sure."

Cord nodded. "You might be dead anyway." His voice was flat, hard. "You think Thorn's gonna let you slide just 'cause you're in jail? You're the link that connects him to this. They know you ain't got it in you to do the time. Without my help, you don't got long, in *or* out of prison." He let go of Webb's collar. "But it's your life. Do with it what you will." He turned to leave, then stopped and looked back. "One more thing. Who gave you that knife?"

"Knife?" His eyes shifted away. "Uh, I bought it."

"Sure you want to throw that bullshit out there for me to step in, son? Ain't no way you could ever afford one like that." He stepped back to the cell. "Now take your time and think hard before you open that mouth and let fly. I can help you. Turn this around. I can protect you, Elsie *and* that baby. Or, I can walk away and let you fry." He paused to let the last sink in. "Oh, didn't you know? Lou is in a coma. If he dies, charge won't be assault with a deadly weapon. It'll be murder. And we ain't in no death-by-injection state anymore. Governor signed the bill. We're back on the electric chair."

"What! Cord, please. Don't do this to me."

"I ain't doin nothin'. This shit's all on you, son. Least if you ain't talkin'." He waited, fixing Webb with a sharp gaze.

After a moment, the boy sighed, stumbled back to the cot and dropped onto it, face in his hands. "All right, all right. It was Rad. Radley Sikes. I was into the crank for two grand. He told me if I'd put a scare on this feller Lou, he'd wipe the debt clean. Gave me the knife. Said I'd need somethin' besides some rusted ol' saw-blade to get the job done right. But I swear, Cord. I never meant to kill him. It'us like he knowed I was comin' fer him. Jumpin' me like he did soon as I come in that bar. But I never meant to kill him! I swear."

"Maybe not." Cord nodded. "He still might live. Either way, I'll make sure the judge knows you cooperated. That'll help. Now, write out everything you just said. Including that stuff about the bat. Understand?"

"Sure, Cord."

"I'll send one of the deputies back to get your statement. Write it out just like you told me. Hear?"

"Yes, sir." Webb plopped down on his back, hugging himself, shivering. "I know it's bad, Cord. Real bad." He gripped his head between his hands. "But ye gotta tell Elsie I love her. And I'm real sorry fer what I done."

"I will, son. Don't worry. Do what I can. Meantime, you sit tight."

Webb stared up at the ceiling, hugging himself tight. "Ain't nothin' else."

Cord walked quickly back to the front office. "Hawkins. Get your damn feet off that desk and call up Red. Tell him t' get the hell down here for a statement."

"What fer? He already talked t' Junior last night."

"'Cause I need to talk to him."

He ain't gonna like it," Hawkins drawled.

"Don't give a shit what he likes. Call him, now. How about Lou's daddy—anybody contact him yet?"

"Ain't been able to find him," said Swany. "Ollie tried last night. Even went by his place. Nobody home."

"Gotta head up that way myself. Probably better comin' from me anyhow. I'll drop in this afternoon. Meantime, stay on the horn. If ye get hold of him, call me. Ever get in touch with the folks up at Glad Earth Farm?"

"Talked to that Sunny feller, this morning. Said Levon'll be down this afternoon to ID the body and bail out that Eli feller."

"This afternoon? What the hell! Ain't in much of a hurry to find out if that girl belonged to their bunch. Not much on social charity. Did Sunny say if anyone was missing?"

"No sir. But he sounded a little confused."

"Confused my ass. Probably so fogged up on pot he don't even know what day it is."

Sam walked in carrying lunch from Jimmy's Drive-Thru. "Supper, boys?" He sidled through the gate.

"Drop that, grab your grub and follow me. Gotta take a ride out to Circe's, then drop by Fred Pollard's place. Let him know his Lou's in the hospital. Be rough on the old man since Katie just passed last year."

Sam deposited the bags on the corner of Hawkin's desk, fisted out three cheeseburgers and followed him out the door.

Cord tossed his hat in the back seat to make room for Sam, cranked the engine and jumped on Highway 73, edging along the east bank of the river, headed towards Sweetwater Road. Circe lived in a little two-room cabin up around Piney Mountain. Figured he'd head there first, then truck up to Garretville and check on Fred.

"So what d'you think, Sam? Damn Levon hasn't even called back."

"Maybe nobody's missin' up there."

"They'd of said so if that were true." He idly fingered the scar at his scalp. "No. That girl's from up The Farm, all right. Ran into some of his boys out at Lily's. Locked one up this morning after he tried to clock me. Some of 'em are awful jumpy."

"You lookin' at this for a homicide?"

"Maybe. But ain't had any problems from them folks at The Farm before. Sure like to keep it that way."

He skidded onto Sweetwater. Rain clouds were gathering. A sharp, chill wind blew from the north. Leaves whipped through the air, collecting in clumps along the shoulder, clogging the shallow creek-bed below. Rain'll knock a bunch of them off, he thought. Soon be nothin' but bare sticks angling at the sky. Damn, winter's almost here.

As far as Cord was concerned, winters were only good the first couple months. After that, the cold and darkness and heaps of dirty snow, the low-lying clouds blocking out the sun, and the shortened gray days always made him feel hemmed in. Bundled up, tramping everywhere, head pressed down to fend off the biting winds that stripped away the green knobs and ridge lines exposing the hard, sharp-angled granite underneath. Too much like the hard, harsh life most folks around these parts lived every day. And trying to change them was about as likely as changing the dull, muted season. "They race, they wither worse," he muttered.

"What?" Sam mumbled past the cheeseburger he was wolfing. He wiped the corner of his mouth with his big mitt and looked over quizzically.

"'Winter Winds.' Hopkins. Listen, had a little conversation with Webb. He'd been getting' tweaked on crank. Into Radley Sikes for a couple grand."

"Damn. Thought that boy had more sense. Ain't no way he could ever come up with that much. Hell, he can't hardly keep him and Elsie fed."

"Yeah. That's not all. Said Rad would go his debt if he'd put a slice on Lou."

"You believe him?"

Cord nodded. "Do."

"Rad ain't gonna do anything without Thorn's okay." Sam wadded up the wrapper and tossed it in the bag.

"That's the way I figure it." He wheeled around another turn. He smelled the rain almost on top of them. "But I can't figure Lou's connection. You've been keeping tabs on that bunch. Ever catch sight of Lou hanging around?"

"No. What I understand, he's pretty much kept to himself since he got back from the desert."

"We'll pay a visit to Thorn. See if we can't get some clarity on the subject." Cord broke hard at a hairpin curve, then accelerated.

"They got a new driver." Sam unwrapped the second burger and bolted it too. "Figure they might be plannin' some kinda run soon."

The old days of running moonshine in specially-modified Fords, their flathead V-8s replaced with Cadillac ambulance engines and suspensions fitted with ultra-stiff shocks and springs to carry their hundred-gallon loads, had ended in the 60s. Thorn mostly used pickups, vans or SUVs to haul his mash whiskey and drugs. But there were a couple of younger drivers still out there who liked the thrill and reputation of outrunning lawmen over the twisting back roads of the mountains.

"Is'at so?" Cord pocketed the anklet, whipped the cruiser onto Piney Mountain Rd. and gunned it. "Let me know if you catch wind of that run. Ain't blown out the pipes on Josephine here in a while."

The previous sheriff and Thorn had observed a kind of truce over the corn liquor operation. As long as the 'shiner steered clear of local violence and stayed out of other criminal activity, Sheriff Casey pretty much turned a blind eye. But over the years, Thorn had expanded his enterprise to include running whores after buying the Thunderbird Hotel, gambling operations both online and in various mobile cock-fighting pits, and, until the recent busts, cooking and distributing meth. Cord needed to put a clamp on the operation, but had hoped for a little more time to build a trustworthy team of deputies. To settle into his new role at the sheriff's office. And on the practical side, there wasn't much he could do to stop it. He was out-gunned, out-manned and out-financed by Thorn.

And then there was the community. The recession had brought even more pressures to bear on an already-depressed economy. Several of Thorn's enterprises, in fact, brought much-needed revenue into the local economy. Particularly for younger men like Webb. It was not going to be easy to knock it out completely. But as that great intellect and social commentator Mike Tyson once said, "Everybody's got plans . . . until they get hit."

Reckon the time's come to get in the ring. Training days are over.

"Want one of these?" Sam offered the last burger.

"Naw. Could use some coffee. Maybe Circe's made some fresh." He pulled the anklet from his pocket and tossed it to Sam. "Reckon she can tell us somethin' about this?"

"The girl's anklet?" Sam turned it over squinting. "Ain't seen one exactly like this before. Funny kind of braid." He looked out the window, as if thinking. "But it does look familiar."

"That's what I thought, too. Just couldn't place it."

They pulled onto Greer's Gap, a dirt and gravel road that cut up between some steep ridges, then slowed and turned on a thin spit of a

73

driveway. Their progress was slow as they bumped and bucked up the steep pitch to the top, undercarriage scraping bottom along the gouges and troughs. At the top, Cord parked and blew the horn.

A pack of mangy dogs came boiling out from behind the house, barking and snapping, surrounding the car. A couple seconds later, she stood on the edge of the porch whistling them down.

"Jasper! Ye ol' devil." Get on down, now. Leave off them boys." She tapped her cane several times against the porch boards. "Get on, Huck. Get on, Bailey. Get back yonder and behave."

The dogs dispersed, running behind the house snapping and growling at one another as they went. The men cautiously stepped out of the car. Cord nodded and waved. "Afternoon, Miss Circe. Been well?"

"Far to middlin', I suppose. Rheumatiz kickin' up some. Ain't nothin' age won't cure." She chuckled at her own bad humor. "You, Cord. How's that purty wife of yourn—and young Blu? They still hainted?"

News of Blu's kidnapping and Lucinda losing the baby was common knowledge in Falston. Circe was one of the only people Cord didn't mind asking about it. "Maybe a little. But we're workin' through it."

Circe nodded, pulling a thin green shawl tighter around her shoulders. "Well. T'was some evil, 'sure. Tell 'em come see me. Got some herbs and roots here do 'em good." She started into the house. "Come on in. Freezin' out."

They followed her inside the cabin just as the first drops of rain fell. A potbellied stove burned warmly from the center of the room. The walls were roughed in, the pine flooring smoothed with wear and age. Plants and roots hung from the bare rafters along the south wall where rain now pattered against the small window overlooking the hollow. An oil lamp, hung low from a hook, flickered over the pine kitchen table. She hobbled over to a rocker between the stove and table, cane tapping the floor, and motioned them to sit in a couple of straight-back chairs.

"Coffee?" She grabbed a blue enameled pot off the stovetop, poured two cups and set them on the table before they could answer. "Now, then. What're you fellers needing' from ol' Circe? Know ye ain't here fer the comp'ny, or my radiant looks."

Cord lifted the cup in salute, took a sip, then pulled the braided anklet from his jacket. "Got somethin' I need ye to look at."

As he handed it across, she cocked her head and frowned. "This thing got some death on it, boy. Lord, Lord. Why you bring this in here to ol' Circe?" She turned it over, fingers rubbing the braids. "Um. Lord, Cord. Ain't good. No good at'all."

"I'm real sorry, Miss Circe. Found the girl what wore it drowned under Collard Creek Bridge. Need to find out what happened to her. Ever seen a braid the likes of that one?"

She leaned closer over the table and studied the band under the lamp. "Uh-hum…I see'd this a'fore. Ida Monroe used to turn a braid purty as you ever did see." She leaned back, thinking. "Learnt to weave six and eight strand braids. Even turn these mystery binds in 'em." She fingered the raised knot. "But this ain't hers. Knot's too hard. Real tight. Strong, fevered fingers bound this, Cord." She handed it back to him. "They's a sharp, tough love bound up in that'un."

"I'm obliged, Miss Circe. Anybody else still weavin' 'em?"

"He ain't no bad boy."

"Who?"

"One 'at's done that." She pointed at the band.

Who's that, Miss Circe?"

"Onliest one she had 'fore she died. Name's Lucas."

"Lucas Monroe?"

Cord and Lucinda had helped raise the boy after his father died a few years back. Always kind to Blu. Had a way with the animals he'd tended over the weekends and summers on Cord's farm. Then a couple years back, after his mother died of cancer, he'd dropped out of school and took up with Thorn. His roots seeped in the backwoods and mountain trails like his own blood. Good tracker. Good shot. Good woodsman. Cord liked the boy.

"I know he ain't bad, Miss Circe. But I still gotta talk to him."

"I reckon so. Jes' don't push too hard. He'll talk, iffen ye let him get there on his own."

"I'll sure try, ma'am. 'At's a promise." He and Sam stood to leave. "You take care, now. And I'll send Luce up soon for some of them herbs."

"You do that, afore ye lose her."

"What do you mean?"

"Just pay a mind to her's all. Got a good heart. But it's heavy, of late. If nothing changes, everything changes. Now get on." She waved as they pushed out into the drizzling rain and dashed to the cruiser.

Once inside, Cord thought a second about Circe's riddle. A warning best heeded if he wanted to save the marriage. As soon as this case is solved, he thought. Take some time off. Maybe a vacation. Then he laid the anklet on the seat beside Sam. "That there's our best evidence, so far. Unravel the Gordian knot, and maybe we find out who killed our gal."

"I'd rather just use the sword." Sam nodded, his straight, muscled jawline set.

" That history degree didn't do you a bit of good. Did it?"

"Hell of a lot more 'n your ain't-got-none-yet degree. Hell, you'd try to talk it loose."

Cord smiled. "Diplomacy does have its advantages. How do you think I've kept this face so unblemished?

"Unblemished like a catfish head caught in a treble-hook." Sam chuckled, grinning. "Hell, that nose of yours needs to be broke twice more just to set it back straight."

"Either way, Thorn's due for a visit, on two counts, now. Let's go, Josephine." He cranked the car and drove on down the slick, muddy, gulley-washed track. "But first we gotta go tell a good man his son is in a coma."

He turned onto the highway just as the sky opened up and fat drops of rain pattered hard against windshield. As he squinted to see through the sudden wash, a shiver ran up his back. Something out in the darkness ahead he couldn't quite make out loomed, and for a second, he was lost in the flood of his past.

8

The Far Shore

The rain had eased off by the time they got to Fred Pollard's farm. No one answered the door, so Cord sent Sam around back to check the barn. He knocked again and peered through a crack in the curtains. Nothing. He knocked again and checked the doorknob. It was unlocked, so he turned it and stepped inside. "Fred Pollard! It's Cord McRae, Fred. You here?"

He edged into the living room. The television was blaring out a local commercial for Bills Bedding and Sofa Company. An ashtray lay on the floor beside a broken coffee table, cigarette butts strewn over the floor. Cushions on the sofa and chairs had been slashed. Picture frames and glass lay broken and crushed on the floor. He stepped around an overturned chair, clicked off the TV, unbuttoned his holster and crossed to the kitchen.

A few dirty dishes lined the counter. A pone of cornbread and a glass of buttermilk sat on the table. Flies buzzed the food. He traced his steps back through the living room and checked both bedrooms. Mattresses were pushed off the box springs and slashed. Drawers hung open, rifled. Overturned boxes, a flurry of clothes pulled out of the closets.

"Ain't in the barn." Sam called, stepping into the house. "Damn, Cord. What the hell happened here?" He fetched up the chair and looked around.

Cord came back to the front room, shaking his head. "Can't say." He pulled a latex glove from one pocket and stepped to the couch. "Got some blood here." He knelt beside the coffee table. The front of the couch was stained. A small pool had puddled on the floor beneath. He pulled his phone, took a picture, then carefully lifted a heavy glass ash tray. "Could be the weapon?"

"Think Lou and Fred got in a tussle?"

Cord set the ashtray back down and scanned the room. "Don't think so. Somebody was looking for something." He pointed along the unscuffed outline of pine flooring in front of the coffee table. "A rug's missing."

"Not good." Sam stepped into the kitchen. "Cornbread and buttermilk. Never could get a taste for buttermilk. Don't look like it's been out more than a day."

"No, it don't." Cord shook his head. "And Lou was over in the hospital by 1800 last night." He stood and studied the room. "Whoever did this wasn't interested in talkin' things out. I'm startin' to think Lou might've got called to a rigged match. Fred got caught up in the fight."

"Webb told me Lou was acting funny in the bar. Like he already knew Webb was there to do him harm." Cord looked through the window out at the hay field. Uneven yellow-brown stubble poked out of the ground like bristled quills, hard and stripped against an empty gray sky. A bad feeling clenched his gut.

"We'll need to get the boys up here to CI the place."

"Should they bring the dogs?"

"Sure as hell hope we don't need 'em." He started out the door, stopped and snapped a picture of a crumpled piece of paper lying on the floor next to the television, then bent to pick it up.

"What you got there?"

"Letter to Lou from the Veteran's Administration." Cord smoothed out the wrinkles "Test results for cancer. Dated back three months ago." He studied the numbers. "Ain't good."

"Didn't even know the boy was sick." Sam stepped to the edge of the porch, took off his hat and fiddled with the brim. "Spend all that time avoiding snipers, IED's and fellers who'd just as soon strap on a passle of explosives and blow themselves to hell to take out a few others." Sam spat off the edge of the porch and followed Cord's gaze across the fields. "Make it back after all that bullshit over there and then find out you got cancer? Don't make a fuckin' bit of sense."

Cord thought about his own father. He'd watched Nathan wither and shrink down from a sturdy 185 to 135 pounds over a six-month period. The memory of his hollow, vacant eyes, the bony wrinkled hands that gripped his son's fingers with a strength surprising Cord at the time, still haunted him. He hadn't always agreed with his father's flinty Presbyterian ways, but he'd loved and admired the man who'd taught him just about everything he knew of the value of the mountains. Of the respect due a man who could work with his hands using the tools and machinery necessary to carve out and cultivate a small space on which to live under the mountains' shadow. It was why he'd never leave. And also why he had to do whatever he could to save those mountains from the not-so-civilized world, from both inside and outside these hollows, that threatened to strip everything good and beautiful away.

"Hell, Sam. Lightning strikes. Floods. Boulders cut loose above a stretch of highway crushing every living thing below. Life don't always make sense. But this letter might explain why Lou's in a coma. Oxycontin or dilaudid is prescribed for cancer patients. If he was loaded up on scripts when he went into shock, could of knocked him so far down, he just didn't make it back up."

He sighed and folded the letter. Stuffed it in his shirt pocket and stepped out the door to the car. Sam followed, shutting the door behind him, a pane of glass loosely rattling in the frame.

Back on the road, Cord picked up the mic. "Judy. You there?"

"I'm here, Cord."

"Heard anything from them folks at The Farm?"

"Did. Said Levon'd be here by three. Where are you?"

"Just leavin' Fred Pollard's. Need to send a couple boys up here with the crime scene kit. Possible 211. And tell 'em to do a thorough search on the property."

"Is Fred okay?"

"Don't know. Looks like there was a struggle. Can't find him. Could be visiting his sister over at Hard Hill. We'll see. How 'bout Red? Hawkins get hold of him yet?"

"Just got in. Hawkins is takin' his statement now."

"Tell Hawk to hold him there until I get back. Got a couple of stops to make. Shouldn't be long."

"I'll tell him. Red's gonna be mad as hell. Already come in here cussin' up a storm 'bout how he was losin' business."

"You tell Hawk I said keep his ass there. He's witness to an attempted murder, and I need to ask a couple of questions. He can tell Red if he don't stay put I'll be stickin' to his bar like molasses on a biscuit. He won't have nothing but sober customers comin' or goin' for weeks."

"I'll get that to him just as soon as we're off."

"At's my girl. We're headed to Glad Earth now, then swingin' by Thorn's. Anything else?"

"Yep. Bill Crowther's called two times today. What do you want us t' tell him?"

Shit. Forgot ol' Bill, he thought. "Tell him I'll call for a comment just as soon as I get in."

"Will do. Out."

Sam nudged his hat back on his head. "Thought we were goin' to see Thorn."

"We are. After we drop by Glad Earth."

"Why stop there? Judy said Levon was comin' in."

"He is. That's why we're goin' to the commune. Eyewitness accounts, along with TOD, indication of Battle's sign, and the river-stream flow information you pulled up put that girl going in the water at least two hours after her attack. Got the boys searching the banks three to five miles upstream from where we found her. So happens Glad Earth's property backs up to that section on the river. Figure we'll stir the pot, see what rises."

They caught Highway 340 to Fair Chapel Rd., then wheeled onto a muddy track. About 200 yards in, they stopped at a cow gate with a sign reading **GLAD EARTH FARM.**

Sam shook his head and chuckled. "Don't know how glad the earth is, but they sure as hell some happy campers when the crops come in. I'll get the gate."

He stepped out, walked to the gate and pushed the button on the intercom. "Deputy Sam Whatson, here. Just need to ask a few question about a young woman who might be missing from your community." The residents had recently installed the new gate and security system, although there were plenty of other places to gain access to the property, since only about half the land was fenced.

"Do you have a warrant?" A male voice crackled from the speaker.

"No, sir. This is just a friendly call hoping you folks might shed some light on the poor girl's identity. I can go back for the warrant—or haul every single one of you back to the station to talk, then grab a warrant and search every barn, privy, shed and stall on the property." Sam paused. "But that'd be a lot of work and trouble. So, what about it? We're not here to search. Just talk."

There was a long silence from the box, then a buzz as the mechanism on the gate unlatched.

82

Cord pulled through, stopped to pick up Sam then drove another hundred yards to the old farm house, a long, low-built log cabin, smoke rising from the chimney. A few travel-buses still dotted the surrounding hillsides, but most of the disarray Cord had seen right after the community arrived had been replaced with a graded gravel road lined with eight long structures. They reminded him of the pictures of old Cherokee long-houses that used to dot these hills and hollows three hundred years ago. A few men wearing coveralls or jeans and flannel shirts or tattered sweaters and jackets looked at them as they passed, eyes narrowed. Some mixed-breed dogs barked and sniffed the cruiser when it stopped. A passel of kids ran up as they stepped out of the car, mostly ignoring their mothers' entreaties to stay away. Instead, they rapidly fired questions at Cord and Sam.

"Hey. Are you the po-leese?"

"Say, mister. That a badge? Can I hold it?"

"Guns kill people."

"You gonna stop our worship?"

"You don't look like a devil."

"My daddy said you don't have any right to tell us what to do!"

Cord waded through the children, smiling. Thing he hated most about this place was the their strangely elitist attitude. A clear belief in their own intellectual superiority over the locals, whose ignorance of the real world wasn't any less than the Glad Earthers themselves. Bad enough he had to deal with the closed-off ways some of the poor, isolated, undereducated locals displayed. But to purposely bring children up here to raise, then keep them fenced in—cut off from every real-world difficulty and opportunity? He just couldn't figure it.

Nevertheless, he'd tried to respect the life they'd chosen. Even toned down the mountain dialect when he talked to them. He didn't want the Appalachian patois, as distinctly beautiful and interesting as any he'd heard, to unnecessarily add to the long-standing prejudices mountain folk already endured.

As he and Sam approached the main house, Sunny Gregor stepped out, a 1911 holstered at his side. "Sheriff." He crossed his arms. "You just missed Levon. Already left. Said you wanted to see him."

"Nope." Cord shook his head. "Not him in particular. Just wanted an ID on a body we found. Never did hear if anybody from here was missing." He pointed his chin at Sunny. "You know?"

The other pursed his lips. "Levon's gone down to check things out. You need to talk to him. So why not get the fuck off this property. We ain't done nothing."

Cord raised a hand. "Hold on there, Sunny. Didn't Sam already tell you? We're here investigating a possible suicide. Maybe even a homicide. Sure, I can leave and come back with a warrant from the judge. Won't take long. But if I do, then I'm not just going to be asking questions. We'll go on ahead with a search, too. Sam said he smelled a peculiar odor as he stepped out of the car. Maybe we'd come back and find a little contraband hereabouts. And since none of these structures have a separate address, I can search 'em all—and the entire premises." Cord kicked at a rock. "But I'd rather just talk to a few folks while I'm already here, and then leave you be." He paused. "What do you say?"

Sunny scowled and studied Cord a moment before nodding. "Okay, man. Just be cool. These are good people. No use bustin' 'em over nothin'."

"Yeah, Sunny. I got it."

Cord looked around at the crowd that had started to form. "Gather round, folks." He waved them in and stepped to the center, raising his voice to carry over them. "Deputy Whatson. Please get the names of these good folks while I inquire whether any of them might have information about, or knowledge of, the girl we found drowned under Collard's Creek Bridge."

He slowly walked across the opening that had formed into a semi-circular picket of bodies, mostly young and fresh-faced. Cord figured most knew nothing of the drowning. But if he shook them up a bit, it might break some information loose.

He surveyed the group. They gazed back, quiet. And sincere. No one spoke. He smiled and stepped up to a women with deep green eyes and straight, oily, brown hair. "I'm trying to find out how a woman died, ma'am. Do you recognize this picture?" He pulled the morgue photo from his pocket and held it in front of her.

She stared at him, silent, defiant.

He shook his head and sighed. Why the hell were they so dead set against finding out if the missing girl was one of their own? "Did you know, ma'am, that this woman was found in the river? We thought it might be suicide. But there are very few suicides by drowning. About two percent. A painful death, and the person usually shows signs of severe depression beforehand. Did you know her, ma'am? Was she depressed?"

The woman backed away, glancing at the others as if for support.

"Hey! What the fuck?" Sunny quickly crossed the open space to Cord. "I said be cool!"

"I am cool, Sunny. But I've already talked to a couple of men from the community who recognized my description, and since I pretty much know most the other women living in these parts, I'm guessin' this woman is one of yours. Did you know her?" He held up the picture.

"I ain't sayin' nothin', Sheriff."

Cord took a deep breath and wondered if there might be a profit in setting up a school of diplomacy for all the Jim Jones, David Karesh, cultist-leader-wannabes, like Levon. Or at least a crash course in public relations. Then turned back to the group and slowly worked his way around the arc. He stopped in front of another woman, dark, curly hair pulled back with a macraméd band, wearing sandals that exposed the tops of her feet. A small heart with a crucifix driven through it and droplets of blood dripping off the cross tattooed the top of her foot.

"Do you know this girl?" He pointed at her feet. "I think her name's Zoe. She has a tattoo like yours. You get that done in town?"

"No. I'm a Magdalene."

"A Magdalene?"

85

"Yes. One who serves the Lord." She lowered her head and turned away into the crowd.

Cord tapped the photo on the back of his thumb. "Look. I know you folks don't trust the law. But if you're good people, and if she's one of your own." He held the picture up. "Are you just going to let her death go unaccounted?"

He glanced at a blond woman, medium height, full-bodied, wearing a peasant dress similar to Zoe's. He'd seen her with Levon before. Maya was her name. "You're one of Levon's, right?"

"I'm not 'one of' anybody's. I share myself in marriage with Levon and Eli."

Cord cocked one eyebrow. "Okay with me." He shrugged. "Not trying to offend. Did you know this girl?"

"You wouldn't understand." She paused. "Levon's got the sight. He knows the truth of things. You're all blind and lost."

So sincere and naïve. Cord was almost willing to let it go. Almost. "Can you tell me what kind of sight he's got? Because I really don't know what that means."

She balled her fists at her side and shook her head.

"Oh. Right." He started to walk away. "Maybe you were talking about the kind of sight that can get a young girl in trouble. Maybe a young girl who ends up dead underneath a bridge. And maybe you knew her. What do you think, ma'am?"

He looked around at the others when she didn't answer. "Now listen, folks. Here's the girl we're trying to identify." He held it above his head and slowly turned around so they all could see. "I know somebody here can tell me something to help figure out who she is and how she died. But there's no need for us to keep bumping heads like a bunch of billygoats all day. So me and the deputy are heading back to the jailhouse now. In the meantime, if you can help, give me a call."

He reached in his pocket, pulled out a business card and handed it to Sunny. "Don't lose this." He stepped closer and whispered. "It's your get-out-of-jail-free card if you come up with some good information.

Understand? I'm not trying to set a trap. Just want justice for a dead girl lying on a cold slab in the morgue without a name."

"It's Zoe." A slender woman, with short, bobbed hair stepped forward. "Zoe Chandler. She's from Virginia. Came with us from Asheville."

"Well, well." Cord removed his hat. "Hey now, Miss Lilith. Wondering where you were hiding. Good to see you. Been a while." Cord liked Lilith. She was straight-up honest, not as starry-eyed over her husband as the rest.

"It has, Cord. But now you need to leave. You got your answer."

"Whoa." Cord scratched his brow. "We'll take our leave. But just one more question, please."

"Just lay off us, man!" Sunny stepped up beside Lilith. Several of the other men also moved in. Protectively.

"We're going, Sunny. After I ask Lilith one more thing." He leaned in closer so the others wouldn't hear. "You know women are twelve times more likely to be killed by a man they know than by a stranger? And three out of four rapes are committed by men the women already know? And I don't believe Zoe's death was a suicide or an accident. She was murdered. So you need to be asking yourself, how well do you know your men around here?"

"Stop it, Cord!" She shouldered him aside and started toward the cabin. "I trust these men more than I trust you. Now get. You've worn out your welcome."

Cord nodded. Might've hit a nerve there. "Okay." He turned to Sunny. "Next time you see Levon, tell him we need to talk." He tipped his hat. "We'll leave you folks for now. Like I said, anyone knows anything, Sunny has the number."

He wove through the crowd to the cruiser. "Come on, Sam."

Sam was squatting next to a small boy, talking. He stood and rubbed the youngster's head. "Right behind you."

Cord circled Josephine around the small clearing, then bumped and slid back down the mud-slick track to the road. Levon was just entering from the highway as Cord emerged. He yanked his orange and black GMC dually to the shoulder, watching as they passed. Cord checked the rearview and saw Levon gun the truck up the spit, slinging mud and rocks behind.

"Think we got him on edge, Sam. Might shake somethin' outta there, yet."

"That little boy I was talkin' to. Beam's his name."

"Beam?"

"Yeah. Sunbeam, Moonbeam, Headlightbeam. Who knows. He had this braided strap he was using for a toy whip. Looked an awful lot like the weave of that anklet."

"Say where he got it?"

"Some young local. Said he didn't know his name. That he never saw him but oncet or twice."

Cord whipped Josephine onto the main highway. "Could be Lucas. And we need to get more on this Magdalene thing. Sounds like some kind of religious order. Our girl, Zoe, had the same tattoo. And one of the fellers this morning said her last name was Magdalene—a surname Levon gives 'em as some kind of religious designation. Damned if it ain't startin' to look like our gal weren't any Ophelia. Mayhaps we're lookin' for a Desdemona instead."

"Damn, Cord. Talk English. Don't start throwin' that literary shit around again."

"Can't help it. My wife leaves them books layin' around. Besides, wouldn't kill you to read a little Shakespeare, Samuel." He wheeled onto the junction at Route 9 and headed toward Little Trout Road. "You might even like something a little earlier. Maybe *The Iliad*."

"*Iliad*? Good example of poor siege tactics. But I liked that feller Odysseus. Wily character. Reminded me of Homer Caldwell up around Baker Ridge. Damn fine boilermaker and a helluva storyteller t' boot."

Cord smiled. "He is at that. Speakin' of boilermakers, reckon we oughter head on up to Thorn's. See if we can't track down young

Lucas." He caught the turn-off to Little Trout then slowed into the curve onto Foggy Top Pass.

"He ain't gonna be none too happy. You dropping in on him like this."

"Hell, Sam. He ain't ever none too happy 'bout nothin'. Needs a woman to civilize him."

"Don't you start on that civilizin' shit. Feller don't need a woman to keep him. Look at me."

"I do. And it's poor sight, f'sure."

"Least I ain't tryin' to avoid goin' home at night so's I can sneak around and have a nip." Sam raised his brows.

"Aw shit, Sam." He pulled the cruiser into the paved drive that led up to Thorn's house and stopped at the gate. "What the hell you know about marriage?" He shifted in his seat, grabbed his hat from the back and smoothed the brim. "Marriage ain't so bad, really. Like Socrates said, at best you'll be happy, at worst you'll be a philosopher."

"Yeah? Then I'd say you're livin' proof that feller weren't so smart after all."

Cord opened the side window. "I'll get back to you on that. Now let me talk to this damn speaker so's Thorn'll open this stupid-ass iron gate."

A couple years back Thorn had installed a state-of-the-art security system and fencing around the entire six hundred acres of his property—what he called his "living space"—complete with intercom, cameras and remote controlled gate-locks. "Never can be too safe, Sheriff," he'd said. "Specially since we got all them hipster liberal-types movin' in. Things could get dangerous."

Cord eyed the gate again and pressed the button. The easy part was getting in, he thought. With Thorn, it was always the getting out that counted.

"Well, hey boys." Thorn's voice sounded thin as a wire over the intercom. "What're y'all doin' in Reevers Holler t'day?"

89

"Just come to have a word." Cord wasn't in the mood for Thorn's infernal insouciance. "How 'bout openin' up? Won't take long."

"Sure. Sure, Sheriff." The saccharine disembodied voice was even more grating digitally than in person. "Always happy t' help out the local constabulary. Just leave the car and walk on up. I'll meet you outside."

The gate swung open. Cord snugged on his hat and started up the hill beside Sam.

He'd known Thorn all his life. Watched him grow up under the hard hand of his father, Frank Reevers, a rigid, mean, coal-chiseled cut of hillbilly as flinty as the mountains from whence he came. For a time, after Frank had married Darla Mae, he'd leveled out some. But after she died giving birth to their third, he'd lost his only anchor to humanity. Ended up dead, killed by the hand of violence he'd lived and cultivated around him.

His only living son, Thorn, had avenged that death. And in a strange twist, by doing so had saved Cord's life. For that, he was grateful. And though Thorn didn't possess the same low-down meanness of his father, there was still a streak of the old violence in him. A deep-seated tendency Cord feared. Not so much for himself, but for Thorn, and those he gathered into his vicious circle of rapacious ways. Any goodness in his soul was buried under the weight of a desperate fate Cord had seen time and again in the jungles of Latin America, the deserts in the Middle East, and the flinty, dark hills of Appalachia. Over time, that burden could crush a body's spirit. And when that happened, there was nothing to stop such a man from tearing down everything around him.

When they got to the top of the hill, Thorn was standing on the front steps of what folks around Falston would call a mansion. Five thousand square feet of carved stone, like some old college hall down at Sewanee University, or like a fort laying for siege. He'd only been inside once, but figured it probably housed more than furniture and appliances.

"Thorn." Cord touched a finger to his hat. "Keepin' them boys straight?"

"Why, Cord. You know my associates stay in line 'round here, keeping a close eye on my legitimate business enterprises. They're a fine bunch of law-abidin' citizens."

Thorn had "diversified" as he called it, into property management, including a couple of seedy motels off Highway 321 and a trailer park down near Cosby. He also owned a scrap metal yard and had strong-armed a fifty/fifty partnership of the Red Rooster Bar. The properties served as covers for prostitution, illegal liquor sales, money laundering, and illicit drug distribution and meth operations.

"I know." Cord took his hat off and scratched his head. "Don't suppose you heard anything 'bout that girl drownin' down Collard Creek yesterday?"

"Matter fact, did." Thorn crossed his arms and raised his brows. Looked surprised at the question. "Heard might be one of those girls from The Farm."

"Believe so." Cord looked up from his hat. "Ain't seen Lucas 'round, have you?"

He scratched his head. "No, sir. Luke lit out this mornin'. Ain't seen him since."

Even when Thorn was a boy, whenever Cord caught him in a lie, he'd cock his head slightly to the left. It was cocked now. "All right, then. When you see him, tell him to ring me. Got a few questions need to run by him."

"I'll do that, Sheriff. So what's it about I should tell him?"

Sam picked up a stone off the drive. "Funny how something so little can put a hurtin' on a fender or windshield, Thorn." He coiled his tall, lean body and whipped his long arm around, sending the stone flying over the pasture fence a hundred yards out. "Tell him it's about a little braided leather."

Thorn shook his head, like he hadn't heard right. "What? Braided leather?"

Cord pressed the hat back on and pulled down the brim. "That's all. Would you tell him?"

"Why, sure." Thorn nodded, brows furrowed. "I'll sure do that."

"Good." Cord turned to go, then stopped. "Oh, just one more thing," he said, facing him again. "Why is Rad giving knives away and putting the squeeze on poor saps like Webb Rasser to do his dirty work?"

Thorn paused, gaze shifting away like a cornered coyote's. "I ain't Rad's keeper, Cord. He manages some of my businesses. What he does in the off time's his business."

"Buddy, we both know that man don't shit without you givin' him leave." Cord lowered his chin and thumbed the side of his nose. "You and I know the day's comin'. Could be soon. But we don't need to get into that ring before warmin' up. So why don't you send them boys down to see me and maybe we can get this straightened out gentleman-like before the title match. What d'ya say?"

Thorn glared, eyes as shiny as two black onyx marbles. "See ye round." He turned his back and started back to the house. "And don't expect to get in here without a warrant, next time."

Cord smiled. "See you 'round, Thorn."

Sam joined him and they started down the drive. "Got that crafty sonofabitch thinkin', f' sure," Cord muttered.

Sam whistled. "You did. No doubt."

"Reckon we kicked over a couple of hornet's nests today. Might be a busy one tomorrow."

"Hell, Cord. Tomorrow's Sunday. My day off."

"Not now it ain't. We got work to do, Hammer."

"Shit. And I was gonna catch up on some reading. Just started on a book by Shelby Foote. Civil War, Volume 2."

"Civil War can wait on our own battles here the next few days. Meanwhile, let's get back to the house. Almost five. Red's probably madder'n two bloodied cocks at The Pit."

When they reached the cruiser, he threw Sam the keys. "Show Josephine how a rookie drives. I gotta figure out what lie I'm gonna tell Lucinda. Forgot the ball valve for the damned commode again."

On the way to the station, he watched the sun lowering behind the mountain rise. The rain had cleared. A hazy mist settled into the valley and hugged the sides of the mountain slopes, swirling and gauzy, like the smoke for which the ranges where named. Some folks believed ghosts haunted those clouds. Especially the souls of those who'd been taken before their time. Those whose fate had been sealed in some malicious encounter with evil. Cord wasn't sure God worked that way. But wasn't sure he didn't either. He did believe, however, that it was his job to answer how they died—and deliver some justice for their untimely death. Give 'em some peace their memories deserve I reckon, he thought.

He flipped the receiver and picked up the handset. "Judy. We're 10-19. You still there?"

"I'm here, Cord."

"How 'bout put a call to Lucinda. Tell her I'm comin' home late. Still gotta interview Red."

"I might. What's in it for me?"

"Breakfast from Lily's tomorrow."

He paused, listening to static. "What do ye say?"

"All right. Is that all?"

"Did Levon show up to ID that gal?"

"Did. In and out in less than ten minutes. Said her name was. . . ."

"Zoe Chandler."

"That's right. How'd ye know?"

"Me and Sam just left Glad Earth. Friendly visit."

"Bet it was. Well, he skedaddled outta here. Said they'd be down to get her soon as we release the body."

"Okay, girl. Get on home now. And don't forget to call Lucinda."

"Hold on. One more thing. Get yer ass here quick 'fore Red busts a vein and has a heart attack at the house. Ain't nobody here t' get his fat ass to the doctor."

"Be there in ten."

Sam came off the mountain and barreled down Bridgeport running the super-charged Interceptor eighty miles an hour.

"What's your hurry, son?"

"If I gotta work tomorrow, gonna get in some reading tonight. Keep a level on your damned flights of fancy. Balance the feather with the anvil."

Cord sighed. "See, that's what I'm talking about. Historians can't put an analogy together worth a shit."

"At least I don't try turning everything into one. Gettin' in the way of hard, cold facts."

"Reckon that's right." Cord watched the trees flash by. Could Zoe Chandler's short life be summed up with an analogy? "You did put on some real detective work today."

Sam stopped at the junction and turned south on Highway 73. "Might catch on to this detective shit if I keep hangin' out with you, Sherlock."

"Don't push your luck. Might hurt yourself. And me along with you."

The radio crackled just before they pulled onto Main Street. "Sheriff, this is S.O. Come in. Over."

He grabbed the handset. "Cord here."

"Better get back out to the Pollards'. They found Fred. Looks like a 11-44. Over." Junior's young voice was shaky. "Found the body down by the pond."

"Okay, son. Put a call in for an ambulance. And get Doc out there. Were on our way."

"Yes, sir. Done dispatched the ambulance. I'll run over to Doc's. They don't answer after hours."

"10-4. We're headin' up there now. Anything else?"

94

"Got some prints off the ashtray."

"Good. Who's out there?"

"Swany and Hawkins."

"Tell them we're on our way."

Cord racked the mic, shaking his head. "Who'd want to kill Fred?"

Sam shrugged, frowning. "Don't make much sense. Can't believe Lou would do such. Him and Fred were always close. 'Specially after Katie died. He never disrespected his momma or daddy. But who knows what he might've got mixed up in. That boy just wasn't the same when he got back. That Middle East sand trap sure messed up his head."

"Maybe we'll get some answers at the farm. Let's run out there."

Sam spun Josephine around, flicked on the lights and gunned it. The cloud cover had cleared. The rapidly-setting sun glared across the Pigeon River, now swollen, muddy and angry. Saplings and low brush along the bank bleached to dull slate. The breeze was cold. It felt somehow like snow. It'd been a while since a November snowfall It'd be just his luck for it to come early this year.

9
Stirring the Sediment

L evon wrapped his parka tighter, watching the sun disappear behind the ragged edge of the ridge. After passing Cord and Sam on the way to the compound, he'd pulled the pickup off the graveled trace and hiked up the rise just south of the commune. He needed time to think.

Seeing Zoe's face—blotchy gray, and bloated—as the coroner had lifted the sheet was unnerving. Despite his past vicious, ugly experiences with death, this was different. Other than his father, he'd never wanted to kill anybody. And seeing her there today had reminded him of the strange twists of fate that could take a man like himself and place him in a position of relative success, while a privileged person like Zoe could start out with everything and end up laid out on cold metal by the time she was twenty.

He studied her: the fiery red hair, the long, thick ringlets that still seemed full of the same vitality that only two days ago he'd seen in her eyes. Guilt and shame rose in him like a bile. He'd reached out and touched the strands briefly before turning to the deputy and giving a terse nod. "That's her. Zoe Chandler."

He'd given her date of birth, her parent's contact information and assured them he'd make arrangements for the burial, then left. He didn't ask about the necklace. That was what he couldn't remember earlier. But he didn't want to raise suspicions now. He'd get it when he came back to collect her personal belongings.

The afternoon rain had carried a windy chill that struck and held in the crooks and crevasses of the hollow. Fog lay heavy in the bottoms, pressing up against the hunkering bellies of the surrounding mountains. Wet leaves dropped. Bare limbs, mottled-brown and ashy, shook and rattled, rotted ends snapping. The dead, brown grass clinging to the stony banks of the hillside hugged the ground, a bent and soggy carpet over the cold, red clay.

Darkness settled on the compound below as he watched his people gather around the central bonfire in small clusters. They'd be scared and worried, wondering why he hadn't returned yet. He'd reassured them earlier during the morning meditation meeting that even if it was Zoe who'd been drowned, they'd carry on their work. That despite the tragic loss of a life so vibrant and brilliant, her loving and kind spirit would remain with them. Her deep devotion to their cause should be even more of a catalyst to move ahead and make their dreams of turning Glad Earth Farm into a heaven on earth come to full fruition. And that of all the people he'd ever known, she'd be the last to want them to mourn her death. Because she knew, beyond all doubt, that this earthly journey was merely a passing phase into the next transition towards cosmic transcendence. Someday they'd all be there, together.

But sitting now on the ridge overlooking his flock, he wasn't feeling so self-assured. Even after talking with Lilith, he'd felt a kind of impending doom. A dark apprehension of something just outside his line of vision. He'd always been good at figuring options, able to look five or six steps ahead. But Zoe's death coming just as he was getting ready to make a play on Thorn Reevers' operation brought in variables he hadn't anticipated. He didn't like the feeling that there were other players operating outside his control; players he still couldn't read well enough to calculate their next move.

Foremost, the damned hillbillies. While generally poorly educated, they possessed a kind of world-weary wisdom that kept their ways especially closed off to strangers. Rarely could he get a good read on their true disposition. Especially the sheriff, McRae. Like today, showing up unannounced. Pretty sneaky, knowing Levon would be off in town identifying the body. He'd told everyone in the compound, "Don't talk to the authorities. Leave this in my hands. I've got a good relationship with the lawman." But he now wondered what Cord had picked up today from the visit. And if it could somehow lead the investigation back to him.

He finally stood, made his way back down to the truck and drove through the gate to the main house. He stepped out of the truck and walked over to a group of men closest to the big house.

"Zippy. Quentin. Sebastian. Good to see you." He clasped their hands in turn, then took a deep breath. "I'm sorry to say, it was Zoe."

"Fuck, Levon! That ain't right." Quentin, one of Zoe's friends who'd joined the group a few months back, bowed his head. "I fuckin' loved that girl. You sure?"

Levon nodded. "I know you did, Quentin. We all did." He started to lay a hand on the man's shoulder, but Quentin shrugged it off.

"What do you know?" Quentin backed away. "She wasn't nothing to you but another adoring piece of ass. Fuckin' prick."

"What the hell?" Quentin's anger surprised Levon. He'd thought he had a solid grip on the pulse of the members. "I've never looked at Zoe like that, brother. We were close, but that was all. Just friends."

Quentin nodded. "Yeah. That's what I heard. Just fuckin' friends. Like all the rest of the Magdalenes." He turned and stomped away into the darkness.

"Don't pay him any attention, Levon. He's been strung out about Zoe all day." Zippy squatted and pulled up a handful of wet grass. "Said he knew it was her soon as he heard a body'd been found." He rolled the grass between his palms then let it drop to the ground. "Sheriff's visit kinda fucked with him. Took him over the edge."

"What do you think, Sebastian. Can we count on him?"

"Sure, dude. Quentin's just worried. We're about get into some pretty heavy shit. And the way Lilith's been acting today isn't making it easier." Sebastian shook his head. "She ain't hardly come out of the main house, except when the sheriff was here. Then just got more pissed and wouldn't talk to anyone. Not even Sunny."

"Damn it!" Levon paced a few steps towards the house then back again. "I really don't need this shit, now. Making the ID on Zoe was bad enough. Broke my heart seein' her that way. Didn't anyone listen this morning? We've got to pull together like family to make this thing work. That's what Zoe wanted. Dissent and petty jealousy won't do anything but tear us apart!"

"I hear you, dude. Just give it time. Zoe's the first death here on The Farm. Hard to take in." Sabastian stood and clasped Levon's hand. "But we're here for you, brother. Don't worry."

"But you better smooth it out with Lilith," Zippy added and shrugged. "Don't know how long we can keep things together if she's on the outside of it."

Levon nodded. "I'm going to talk to her now. I need you both on your toes. Shit's coming down in two days. We ready for the meeting?"

"Yeah. I got the hardware. We've set up a good spot to keep an eye out. We got your back. Zippy here's a sharp-shooter, man. Seen him hit Pronghorn out in Montana at four hundred yards. No worries."

"Good. So, go tell the others about Zoe. We have to arrange a funeral. Take up a collection. I'm going to contact her parents tomorrow. See if they want to come for the burial. She wanted to live and die on this mountain. Said so in a will she left with me a few months back. We can give her that, anyway. Now, I need to get in and see what's eatin' Lilith." He turned and hurried to the house.

Inside, Sunny was asleep on the couch. Lilith sat behind his desk smoking a joint.

"Hey." He stepped across the room and leaned over to kiss her.

She pulled away. "Was it her?" She took a long drag, held it for a moment and exhaled, smoke drifting up in thick ribbons.

"It was." He sat on the edge of the desk. "Where's Eli and Maya?"

"Sleeping in Lodge Three tonight."

"What? Why?"

"Said until you and I worked things out, they didn't want to be around." She studied the red glow of the hotbox at the end of the joint as if to avoid looking him in the eyes, then took another drag.

"What the fuck, Lilith. The others need to see us unified, not divided. This is our dream. We've got to hold it together through this rough time, Lil. If we don't, it can go all to hell." He stepped in front of her. "Look at me! Why didn't you try to stop them?"

Lilith shot up from the chair, her speed and quickness surprising Levon, and slapped him. Sunny rolled over on the couch, rubbing his eyes, confused. "What the fuck, y'all?"

Lilith pointed a finger. "Shut the fuck up, Sunny." She turned back to Levon. "Listen, you lying bastard. I've stood by you through all the god-damned shit you've spun out for everyone else to follow. I've sacrificed everything, including our baby, so you could pursue a dream. This impossible dream of a life not sucked up by the capitalist killing machine. One we could build without being sell-outs to that system. I did it because I believed, truly believed. Then you had to go and fuck it all up. You and your fucking dick-pleasing ego!"

"Lilith. It wasn't like that. I—"

"And now you want me to stand by while you use a poor innocent like Zoe—another fucking pawn in your game. That sermon this morning was disgusting. If I wasn't stoned off my ass right now, I'd be sick just looking at you." She glanced at Sunny, who fidgeted, awkward and silent. "Bet you felt the same, huh?"

She sat down heavily, leaned her head back and sighed. "But I *am* stoned," she said finally. "Because on one count at least, you're right. These people have trusted and followed you all the way to the fucking hillbilly hollows of hard work, shitty, hard-scrabble soil, ignorant neighbors and unsanitary living. All because they believe in that same dream you've stuck in their heads. They've sacrificed everything. And don't deserve to lose it all because you're a selfish prick."

She pulled herself up straighter and took a last drag off the roach. "So yes, I'll play the part. I may even get over it someday. But don't even think about preaching to me about obligations. I know mine better than you. The plan is in place. I'll keep the girls in line. You get the money from those militia fucks in Nashville so we can follow through. Then, maybe Zoe's death won't be in vain."

He stood staring at her, silent for a moment, bemused. Then, in a low voice, said to Sunny, "Looks like I'll be sleeping there tonight." He nodded at the couch. "You go on now." He jerked his chin toward the door. "Bunk up in Lodge Three. See you in the morning. Okay, man?"

"Sure, sure. I can crash with Breezy tonight." He stood. "I'll be here first thing in the morning." Sunny stepped out into the cold air and shut the door.

As soon as the latch clicked, Levon spun, took two long strides across the room, grabbed Lilith by the throat with his right hand and shoved her back against the wall. "Okay, bitch." He pushed face up into hers. "I deserved that. And I'll do everything I can to earn your trust again. In the meantime, if you ever go off on me in front of a subordinate again, I'll gut you—just like those filthy fuckin' pigs on my daddy's farm. Understand?"

She nodded, her gaze steady, afraid but defiant still.

He held her there a moment before loosening his grip and stepping back. "You know there isn't anyone I love more than you, woman—but don't pull that shit on me. Not here. Not now. One little misstep and we're done. Maybe even dead. These new partners are tied into some bad motherfuckers. Play this right, or we're all gonna pay."

She rubbed her throat. "Okay, Levon. I get it. I'll go along." Her eyes burned like polished melanite. "But if you ever lay hands on me like that again—you better kill me." She took a deep breath. "Now, I'm fucking going to bed. Long days ahead. Burying the first of our family, and it—" Her voice broke. "Won't be easy. I'll see you in the morning." She strode down the hall to the back bedroom and slammed the door.

Levon gritted his teeth and punched the desktop. "Goddammit, Zoe!" That one little piece of ass threatened to bring the whole house down. He was angrier at himself than at any time he could remember. "What the fuck?"

He dropped into the desk chair, opened the tin, rolled a joint and lit it. As the hit filled his lungs, he felt the light-headed rush, the familiar palpitation in the heart. He exhaled, feeling all the tension leaving his body. The trouble with Lilith was bad. But in the end, she'd do the right thing. Not for him. But for the others. Bigger problem was the uncontrolled variables: McRae. Thorn. With Lou now in the hospital, he hoped Eli would come through for him, or the meeting with his connection would be a bust. And without that connection, he'd never make the kind of cash needed to pay for the arms shipment from his contacts at Ft. Bragg.

He took another toke, kicked his feet up on the desk and closed his eyes, thinking of the Magdalenes. Other than Zoe, the website had been a huge success. Over 50,000 hits a day. PayPal money pouring in. He'd never dreamed it would be so successful. But why not? Hadn't that always been the way of man? Drugs, whores and money. And to pay for the keys to a heavenly kingdom, you sometimes had to do time in the Devil's playground.

He leaned back, took another toke. Dreaming of shopping malls, sporting events, parades—the whole damned world on fire.

10
Crossing Over Jordan

Hawkins sat leaning against a post on the front porch whittling a stick when Cord and Sam pulled up the drive. He threw the stick aside. Then stood and folded the blade, slipping it in one pocket and crossing his arms.

"He ain't none too happy." Cord grabbed his hat and the coffees they'd picked up at Lily's on the way. "We need to talk about replacing him, Sam."

"You're telling me. Can't trust him enough to put on drug surveillance detail. Let alone any other assignment with a whiff of Thorn." Sam cracked the door and got out. "Ain't done nothing' but sit on his ass since you took over."

"That, and twisting up Thorn's whores for a free ride." Cord grabbed his hat and followed him to the porch.

"'Bout time," Hawkins grumbled. "Startin' t' think y'all was gonna leave me up here t' starve." He spat tobacco juice off the edge of the porch and wiped his lips on one sleeve.

Cord climbed the porch. "If I'm gonna pay you for doin' nothin', might as well know which nothin' you're doin'. Coffee?"

Hawkins grabbed the cup. "Aw, shit, Cord. Why you always bustin' my balls? I ain't no rookie. Waitin' here with that gung-ho SWAT-team wannabe Swany and a fuckin' bloated, stinkin' dead man."

Cord took a deep breath, then leveled his gaze on him. "Hawkins. If you were half the deputy Swan was, I'd get you in line for a promotion so fast your head would turn. But, lately you ain't been nothin' but a body in uniform I put on the streets for appearances. Lazy, shiftless, not enough sense to stay away from the low-lifes and misfits whose crimes and misdeeds my good men risk gettin' killed over. Let alone the common courtesy to know how to treat the dead."

He took a deep breath to calm himself. "I'm sick and tired of keepin' tabs on you all the damn time, Hawk. You gotta change, or you're gone." He flicked dust off the hat brim and snugged it on his head. "So shut the hell up, slink on down to that cruiser and head back to the house before I decide today's the day."

Hawkins stared back for a moment before stepping off the porch and slouching out to his car. Nick and Ryanne pulled up in the ambulance. Sam watched Hawk spin out, then looked back at Cord. "Sure you want t' let that dog off the leash? Might be more trouble off the force than on."

"Might be. But at least then it'll be clear which side he's on."

"Hey, Cord." Nick stepped up to the porch. Pinched brows had deepened the normally-mischievous wrinkles around his pale blue eyes. "What the hell happened?"

"Don't know, Nick." Cord bumped a fist on the porch rail. "But we're sure as hell gonna get on it now."

Ryanne came up beside Nick. "If Lou makes it through, this'll hit him hard. All he talked about was getting back home. Sure loved his daddy."

Cord nodded and looked toward the pond where Swany waited. "Y'all stick here until we CI the scene."

"Hold up, Sheriff." Ryanne stepped closer. "Can I stop by after my shift? Got a few things I need to run by you. About Lou. But not here."

"Sure. I'll be in and out all day. Just call before."

"Will do." She nodded once, then turned as he and Sam cut out across the stubbled corn field, careful not to step on old tracks.

Swany was down a sloping bank, about ten yards up from the pond, taking pictures. The body lay about three feet away, covered with a sheet to keep the buzzards at bay.

"Ain't doin' much good." Swany scowled at the vultures.

Cord pulled his service SIG Sauer and fired a round into the pond. The black, tatter-winged scavengers flapped and hopped and finally took to the air, circling overhead.

The body had been buried in a grave hardly deep enough to cover it. Once it had started to bloat, Swany had spotted it.

"Godalmighty." Sam squatted and pulled the cover back. "Never get used to that smell."

Fred's face was in bad shape, pecked and torn. Cord took a knee beside Sam, squinting against the stench.

"Damn. Had the hell beat out of him first. Nose broke. Cheekbones busted in. Turn him so I can see the back of his head."

Sam clicked a couple of photos with his phone, pulled latex gloves on and gently rolled the battered head to the side. A green and rust braided rug lay underneath him. Cord leaned down for a closer look.

"Back here, too. If it was Lou done this, sure had some rage in it."

"More than a fight about hayin' the back forty." Sam lowered the head back into its muddy indention.

Cord nodded. "Reckon that rug was used to carry him here." He looked around at the purr of a car. The coroner's van. He got up and waved as it stopped at the top of the drive.

Doc Kirby operated a small clinic in downtown Falston where he took care of almost anything that didn't require major surgery. A tall, serious man who lived in an apartment above the clinic where he spent most of his time. Cord often saw him at odd hours, silhouetted by lamplight, as he sat reading in the window overlooking Main and the river he loved so much. Doc also served as the county coroner.

Kirby met them halfway and shook hands. "Cord. Sam. Helluva thing. What happened?"

"Don't rightly know." Cord looked over one shoulder at the house as they trudged back to the pond. "Somebody clobbered him. Beat the hell outta him. Then half buried the body down by the pond." He pointed.

Doc pulled a briar pipe out of his jacket pocket, clenched it between his teeth and torched the bowl with a butane lighter. "But who'd want to hurt ol' Fred?" He let the smoke and words seep out together around the stem of the pipe.

Cord shook his head. "Maybe Lou? Found a letter from the V.A. Seems the boy had cancer. But his ailments might've been more than physical. I'll check around inside, see what I turn up. Sam and Swany here'll help process the scene and load the body."

"Damn, son. I ain't had to care for so many stiffs since the Crowders tangled with those Lowden Timber boys, back in ninety-three." He took his pipe out and pointed it at Cord. "Better slow down. I'll be runnin' out of space in the cooler soon. Ain't kiddin'." He flirted ash from the pipe, slipped it back in, then motioned to Sam and Swany. "Come on, boys. Got work t' do."

Cord walked back to the house, ducked under the yellow tape and through the screen door. His men had bagged the ashtray and the cushions from the couch and dusted for prints. Everything else was the same. He walked through the living room into the hallway. The first door on the right was Fred and Katie's. He found her old hairbrush and hand mirror, keys, a little silver tray, and shattered glass from their busted wedding picture frame lying around their dresser. The mattress was shoved off the box springs, the hand-stitched quilt now wadded and rumpled on the floor. What the hell was this character looking for, Cord wondered.

He moved into the next room, Lou's. Dirty clothes were strewn here and there. Sheets and blankets tangled and wadded up at the foot of the bed. Again, the mattress was pushed off. A 30-06 Remington 700 leaned in one corner. Clothes had been pulled off hangers, drawers opened; some smashed. Cord pulled on latex and rummaged through the clothes, scraps of papers and old receipts scattered across the floor. He found a picture of Lou with four other young-faced men in camo fatigues, standing in front of a green banner that read *OK CORRAL*, arms over one another's shoulders, smiling.

In the nightstand, he found a batch of old letters. Mostly sent by Lou's mother, addressed to military bases in Afghanistan. News about the farm and folks at church. Also some medals, ribbons, and other military gewgaws. The bottom drawer hung half open. He reached down and pulled it the rest of the way out. A black Moleskin notebook dropped to the floor inside the cabinet frame.

Must've gotten lodged in there as drawers were getting yanked, Cord thought. He lifted it from the floor. Inside, written in tiny, careful print, were short, dated journal entries—observations and thoughts about the land, people, culture Lou'd been to the other side of the world to protect, save, and kill. But as he flipped through the pages, Cord found several other odd entries toward the back. Columns of coded numbers and symbols were written next to dates, names, and email addresses. Each entry was bulleted with a letter:

$k3161694\gamma0\lambda \wedge 6571694439\eta0\delta$

$kswk3211191170\lambda \wedge 6604642990\zeta20\delta$

$h3136364740\lambda \wedge 639586110999999850\gamma$

$hcbn301345228\lambda \wedge 622626626999999640\gamma$

Maybe it was nothing, he thought. But he needed to spend more time with this little book. He secured it with the elastic band, slid it into a plastic bag and slipped that inside the pocket of his jacket.

As he turned to leave, he noticed a power cord for a laptop plugged into an outlet behind the bed. Where was the computer? He swept the room again, then checked the others. No laptop. Made sense they'd had one. Most military families used them to stay in touch nowadays. But why wouldn't it still be here?

He stepped into the bathroom on his way out and checked the medicine cabinet. The usual over-the-counter stuff. Aspirin, Tums, eye drops, razors. But on the top shelf, a bottle of dextroamphetamine pills. Black Beauties. Cord had seen them lately on the streets, here and there, as a party drug. The drug had also been used by special forces to stay alert on long missions. The biggest drawback was they could be extremely addictive. These had been prescribed to Lou. He also found an empty bottle of Oxycontin. Both were from the V.A. pharmacy. But why the hell would they be prescribing him uppers and downers both? He bagged the bottles and left the house.

Outside, Sam and Doc pulled up in the van. Nick and Ryanne slid the body into the wagon. He stepped off the porch and met them at the cruiser.

"Got some pills here, Doc. Black Beauties." He handed over the bottles. "Any idea why the V.A. would be prescribin' these to Lou?"

Doc pulled out reading glasses and read the label. "Sure. Read somewhere they use these to treat depression, and other psychiatric syndromes. Obsessional illness and such." He handed the bottle back. "Dangerous stuff to be givin' a soldier just home from a war zone, you ask me. Not that anybody is. And the Oxycontin. Not sure. For pain relief? I'd have to know more about his condition to say."

"Letter we found earlier said Lou had cancer."

Doc nodded and tapped the bottle with the pipe stem. "Well, that might explain these, I suppose."

"What about Fred?"

"He sure took a whuppin' before they shot him."

Cord frowned. "Shot him? All I saw was that bump on the back of his head."

Doc smiled at the look of doubt. "Easy to miss an entry wound. Left side, under the ribs. Or notice the blood on his lips."

"Dammit." Cord grimaced, annoyed at having missed such an obvious detail. First rule, don't assume. "Saw the blood. But I was focused on that contusion and the facial wounds. I figured the blood was residual from a busted lip or nose. Didn't think to check beyond that."

"I'd say he took that knock on the head first. Then whoever did this beat the hell outta him, shot him, then hauled the body down there." He pointed with his pipe. "Must've bled out somewhere else. Only a couple of small stains on that there rug."

"Caliber?"

"Maybe .38? Have to get it out t' see for sure. But close up. Powder burns on the shirt."

"TOD?"

"Way he's bloated, the rigor set in pretty good, along with body temp—somewhere between twelve to eighteen hours."

Sam glanced at Cord. "That'd put Lou off the list. He was laid up at the hospital last night after his tussle with Webb."

Cord nodded. "Strange place to shoot a man; up under the ribs. Unless you had the barrel planted in his side. Okay. Thanks, Doc. We'll see you back in town."

"See ye, boys." Sam stepped out of the van and Doc placed the pipe between his teeth, then pulled down the rutted drive, the ambulance following.

Swany joined them walking toward the cars. "What can you tell me, Swan?" Cord asked him.

"Tracked drag marks leading from the back door. About halfway to the equipment shed, come across some blood. Inside the shed, next to his tractor—looks like that's where they beat the hell outta him. Lots of blood. Didn't find no casings, but it's more than likely the murder scene. Took photos of footprints. Three sets. Two others besides Fred's. Square-toed boots on one. Not much to make out on the other. Pretty big, maybe size twelve."

Cord scratched his chin, watching a crow fly in over a wire and land on a fencepost, fluttering its wings. "Maybe they were trying to get something out of the old man. Like that missing computer. Dammit, Lou," he muttered. "What'd you get your daddy into?" He turned to Swan. "Let's wrap it up here and head back in. I got two dead bodies and one in a coma 'tween me and a good night's sleep. Like to get this solved before my wife divorces me over a toilet plunger, or whatever the hell it is."

"Hate to say it, boss. Especially after that up-an-down you put on Hawk. But I could use some grub."

"We'll stop off at Lily's. I could use some chow myself."

As he cranked up Josephine, Waddy's voice broke over the radio. "Cord. You there?"

"We're here, Waddy. What's up?"

"Just thought I should let you know, Red's about to walk outta here, thanks mostly to Hawk. Who's done nothin' but cuss and bitch about you and this office since he got back."

"On our way. Use your old-timer wisdom and expertise to keep Red planted 'til we get there."

"He'll be here. Count on it. Over and out."

Sam sighed. "What did I say about getting some reading in tonight?" He pulled out his phone and hit the contact for Lily's. "Hell, I ain't even gonna sleep tonight, way things are going." He held the phone to his ear. "Lily. Sam here. Need some take-out." He turned to Cord. "What'll it be? Saturday night special?"

Cord pressed the pedal to the floor and blasted onto the highway. "Ain't good for nothin' but put a man six foot in the hole. Do I have a choice?"

"Not really."

They parked in the reserved space and walked into the jailhouse, Sam and Swany were loaded down with white paper bags and drinks.

Red stood as soon as he saw them. "What the hell you makin' me wait here for? I'm losin' business every hour I'm stuck here."

"Sit down, Red. I ain't in no mood for your shit right now." Cord pushed through the wooden gate and tossed his hat, brim up, on Judy's desk. "Got a few questions about the conversation you were havin' with Lou before Webb came in yesterday. But that'll hold."

In four quick strides he was in front of Hawkins' desk. "In my office," he said, low, but sharp. "Now!" He spun and stalked across the room. Behind him, Hawkins scraped his desk chair back and slowly ambled to the office door.

Cord went to stand behind the desk, arms crossed. "Come in. Have a seat."

"Damn, Cord." Hawkins shook his head in disbelief. "I just don't get it with you."

"Shut up, Hawk. I'm not in the mood for any feigned vexations. You know exactly what I'm talking about. Now sit."

He waited until Hawkins had settled, then continued. "When I took over this office after the election, I said you'd have to make some changes to stay on here. Your attitude, for one. I could've used your experience to help put this office back on course after the shit-wreck your pal Conley left us. You had a choice then. Could've put your skills and connections to good use binding things together and steering us back on a true course. Instead, your presence here has constantly worn at this crew. Your disrespect and loud-mouthed comments corroding whatever trust we've been able to build."

"Now, hold on a fuckin' minute, Cord. I reckon I got a right to my own opinions about—"

"Shut it, Hawk." Cord slapped the desktop. "I ain't finished. Second thing I asked was that you cut the ties you'd kept with several criminal associations outside this office. Particularly Thorn and his crew. And those whores you can't seem to leave be."

"I ain't gotta sit here and listen to this shit." Hawkins pushed himself out of his chair. "An' I reckon I can associate, as you put it, with whoever I damn-well please, I'm off the fucking clock."

"No, Hawk. You can't!" Cord banged a fist down, boiling on the inside. A couple quick jabs and an uppercut would feel even better. But not here. Not now. He spoke slowly now. Voice low. "If you go out that door, leave the gun and badge on my desk and keep on walkin'. Next time we meet, it won't be as professionals."

Hawkins glared, brows furrowed, for just a moment before lowering himself down and back into the chair. "All right, then. I'm listenin'."

"This office is a twenty-four-hour a day gig." He pointed to the lobby. "And you're a deputy everywhere. On or off the clock. What people see out there is what they believe about us in here. Bad enough they've seen you bettin' the cocks and pickin' up whores at Thunderbird. Now you come here, into our house, and badmouth us in front of the likes of Red? You got no idea what this job's about anymore." He shook his head in disgust. "Maybe you used to. Maybe that's why I kept you on. But I'm done."

He walked around the desk and stood beside Hawkins' chair. "Now, go on home. And when you get there, take a good look at that cute little ranch house. Your wife of twenty years, who's stuck with you through the kind of shit only men like you and me know. Hug your two little girls. Then, think about what you want out of life. 'Cause this is my last warning. Pull your head out of your ass long enough to see what's up, or look somewhere else to hang that attitude."

Cord circled back behind the desk, dropped into his chair and started shuffling through reports. "Go on, now. Get out of my sight."

He didn't look up as Hawkins left.

Waddy knocked and stuck his head in. "Anything else you'll be needin' me for?"

"You done all I need tonight. Thanks for keepin' Red at bay."

"Ain't no problem, pardner." He stepped into the office and shut the door behind him. "I just reminded him about how my buddies know a few things about illegal liquor sales and prostitution comin' out of the Rooster and seein' as how I hadn't recorded a bust in a while, that place might be a good first stop." He hitched up his belt with its holstered, long-barreled Smith and Wesson .38. "Say ol' Fred took a good beatin' 'fore they did him in?"

"Did." Cord leaned back, thinking about the jar of whiskey tucked in the lower drawer. A long pull right now would hit just the right spot. "He sure didn't deserve that. Any of it." Outside the window, he caught the shine of the river pushing its way north, one of only a handful in the world that moved in the wrong direction. Was his term as sheriff headed the same way?

"Waddy, I got two murders and another, maybe, if Lou don't make it. We're one of the smallest counties of Tennessee, normally averaging three murders a year. I'm just six months into a four-year term. I got a wife and son who both think I spend too much time away from home. I might've made one of the worst choices I could've when I took this job."

Waddy wasn't quite as tall as Cord, but still solid and tough for a man pushing seventy. Now, he pulled himself up a little bit straighter and rubbed the neatly clipped beard that always reminded Cord of some Civil War general. "Way I figure it, Cord. You knowed 'xactly what you was gettin' into when ye ran fer office. Damn, boy, you worked here fifteen years. Lived in town purt' near all yer life. Seen all what's changed in this county over the past few years. That's why ye ran. 'Cause ye didn't want to see what's left gone to hell. Blue Ridge is in yer blood. Ye won't be happy anywhere's else. So get off yer ass and do what the folks hired ye t' do. Arrest the damned sonsofbitches who done kilt them people."

Cord chuckled. "Can always count on you to cut through the bullshit, Waddy." He stood and walked to the door, clapping his dputy's shoulder. "So let me get back to it. Go on. Get some rest. Got a feelin' I'm going to need you to keep me squared away the next few days. Oh, and tell Red to come on in here."

"Will do. And don't forget to keep 'er straight."

"Always." He waited at the door until Red came grumbling down the hall.

"Come in. Have a seat."

Red dropped into the recently-vacated chair, thighs bulging over the sides. "Now what the hell you talkin' 'bout, Cord? Me and Lou never had no talk."

Cord slapped the back of the publican's head as he walked past, then turned and leaned against his desk.

Red winced. "Shit, Cord. What's 'at for?"

Cord reached back and jabbed the button on the intercom. "Junior! Got time to bring me a cup of coffee?"

"Yes, sir."

He turned back to Red. "For lyin'. Now I'll ask one more time. And you're gonna answer, or you ain't gettin' out of here the rest of the night. And how do you think that's gonna make your partner, Thorn, feel?"

Junior knocked on the door and sidled by with the coffee. "Junior," Cord told him, "Can you pull our records on Mr. Red Slokum here? I might want to go back and review what all he's been up to. Seein' as I've only recently taken over and need to have a good idea about all our most upstanding citizens."

"Yes, sir. I'll get on it."

"Listen, Cord." Red pleaded as Junior turned to go. "I don't know what Lou was talkin' about. Somethin' 'bout a woman leavin'. Said it'us killin' him. But he was drunk. Hell. Probly didn't even know what he was sayin' hisself."

"Yeah. And when Webb pulled out that knife, you just stood there and watched?" He nodded for Junior to go on out.

"At's right."

114

Cord stood and kicked Red's chair leg, almost tipping it out from under the big man. He leaned down and slapped one fat thigh. "You forget that bar bat you got hid behind the counter? And how you tossed it to Lou when you saw Webb's knife. And then put it up behind the counter again before calling us?"

"Cord. Listen. I . . . I didn't think it would matter."

"I'll be goddamned if it doesn't! Could be Lou will die. And could be a jury might see your actions as contributing to his death. Could be they'll wonder why you didn't make the phone call to us sooner. Could be you should be locked up in that cell alongside Webb."

"I swear. I didn't think it'd matter." Red's bulbous face grew redder as his fat haunches squirmed against the arms of the chair he was squeezed into. "Hell, I liked ol' Lou. A little crazy, sure. But I liked him jus' fine."

"Well enough to tell him Webb was coming for him?"

"What? No. I—"

Cord planted one boot on the chair's edge, between Red's legs, and leaned the toe into his crotch. "I told you no more lyin'."

"Oww! Goddammit, Cord. Okay! Okay!"

He eased off. "Talk to me, Red."

"Listen." He raised a hand, pleading. "I was just tryin' to get back what's mine. Lou'd been talkin' 'bout a new game in town—said Thorn and his bunch were gonna have some competition, soon. He knew how Thorn had got holt of my place. Said if I wanted to get out from under, just pass on to him or his associates anything I might hear."

"What associates?"

"Don't know. Said we'd meet up with 'em after I had somethin' t' trade."

"So, when you heard Rad was strong-arming Webb to do a little dirty work, you passed that on to Lou."

"That's right." He nodded, nervously glancing down at Cord's boot. "But I swear, I didn't want no real harm t' come to either of them boys."

"What else did you hear."

"Nothing."

Cord pressed the boot down again.

"All right. All right," Red wheezed. "I did hear Rad talkin' about makin' a big run in the next couple days. Somethin' 'bout hooking up with an outfit outta Nashville. I swear, that's all."

Cord dropped his boot to the floor. "Here's what you're gonna do." He yanked open a desk drawer, pulled out paper and pen and slammed them on the desk beside Red. "Take this pad and write down exactly what happened in that bar. Everything. And once you're done, get the hell out of here."

He moved to the other side of the desk and sat down. "And next time I need help, ye better give it quick. 'Cause the onliest place you're even half a king is that little bar of yours. Anywhere else in this county, I rule. Got it?"

"Sure, Sheriff." He looked up, sullen.

Cord watched, sipping coffee as Red wrote out the statement. When he'd finished, Cord followed him out into the squad room, escorting him to the door. Halfway there, Red turned and spat on the floor. "That badge don't give you no right to treat folks like shit. Ye don't have cause t' act all high and mighty with me."

Shit, Cord thought. Didn't even make it out the door before turning surly. Apparently, following the law was now an act of the "high and mighty." He glanced back at Sam, who was standing on the other side of the rails, and nodded toward the door. Sam stepped to block the entrance.

Red pulled up short. "Get the hell outta my way, you fuckin' bootlicker."

"Red." Cord set the coffee cup on the desk and clapped his arms across his chest, studying the man.

"What?" He scowled.

"I used to think you were just dumb. Closin' the family hardware store when your pappy died. Buyin' The Rooster, then losin' it to Thorn

116

in a damn card game. But now, I know it's something deeper. Plain ol' low-down meanness. And for that, one day I'm gonna kick your ass up your throat. I swear. You and your low-life friends don't run this town anymore. Old sheriff's gone. Want me to show you high and mighty? Be happy to oblige." Cord paused, half-grinned and tipped his chin up.

Red studied him briefly, took a deep breath, then shook his head. "Naw." He looked around. "Not today."

Cord read disdain and hatred in his stare. "Let me know, buddy. Anytime. But for now?" He stepped closer, pulling a kerchief from his back pocket, tossing it in Red's face. "You're gonna wipe up that mess you made on my floor."

Red's face bulged as he bent down, grunting, and wiped the floor. He straightened, red-faced, outstretched hand gripping the damp kerchief.

"Keep it," Cord said. "Now get the hell out of my sight. And I better not get any calls out to that bar again this month. For anything. Understand?"

"Yeah. I understand."

Sam stepped aside and held the door open. Red stomped out.

"That's what I call sheriffin'," the deputy said after he shut the door. "This job just might get fun again."

Cord lifted his cup and swigged the last shot. "Or it just might not. Talk to me about Thorn?"

"Okay. Why?"

"Red just gave me a lead they might be setting up a meet with some Nashville outfit. Want you to shake the tree, see if we can't flush somethin' out. And I guess I need to put a call in to Beth. Looks like we may have some gang action to deal with. And two murders."

Beth Trulan was a field officer with the TBI in Nashville. Unlike Cord's own mostly unplanned entry into law enforcement, Beth had decided her career path long before graduating high school. She'd earned a bachelor's degree in criminology, graduating first in her class, followed by extensive training at the state academy, outranking ninety

117

percent of her male peers in both physical fitness and mental acuity. She'd gone on to become one of the most highly successful field agents in the state, recently leading the investigation that had shut down the biggest meth operation in Tennessee history. She was also Cord's first cousin and adored spending time with both with his wife and son—which he played on heavily sometimes, when he needed a professional favor.

"Sir." Junior held up a phone. "Hospital."

Cord took the call at Judy's desk. "Sheriff McRae here. Yes. Yes. I see. Okay. I'll send someone over to pick up his personals." He hung up the phone and sighed. "Make that three murders, now. Lou just died. Where's Ollie?"

"Went to check out an accident down on Turner's Gap, sir."

"Okay. Sam, can you stick here until Junior gets back?"

"No problem, boss."

"Junior, I need you to get to the hospital and pick up Lou's personal effects. Maybe something in 'em will help us understand what the hell he was doing that got him and his daddy both killed."

He strolled to his office and closed the door behind him. Pushed the uneaten carton of food to the edge of the desk and opened the window. The cold breeze reminded him it was time to wrap water pipes at the house before the first hard freeze of winter. Four notes from Judy reminded him to call *The Gazette*. He picked up the receiver. It was only eight o'clock. They'd still be in, working on tomorrow's edition.

"Bill? Cord here. Yeah. Sorry for taking so long to get back. Yeah, I know. Yes, she is from the Glad Earth Farm. Zoe Chandler, twenty. No, she drowned, but we're still lookin' into how it happened. That's right, holding off on a cause of death for now. Yes, I'll contact you as soon as we know something more. And listen, Bill. Do me a favor. Don't release the name yet. Give us a chance to inform her family. Right. Okay, buddy."

He hung up, thankful for the small-town media consideration. Then opened the bottom drawer, pulled out the mason jar and studied the clear liquor. One good pull would relieve the pressure building behind his eyes and clear his head. He glanced out the window over Main. Lights were still on at Doc's. The hotel's sign wagged in the breeze. Across the river, the bluffs rose sharply into darkness. He pictured his house settled like a rugged ship in the hollow just behind that ridge. He set the jar back inside, shut the drawer.

Not now, he thought. Not yet. He called Lucinda. After three rings, she answered.

"Hey. Just wanted to say I'll be home in a bit."

"I heard about Fred." She paused. "I'm sorry, Cord. He was a good friend."

"Yeah. A good man to have around. Reminded me of Pops."

"Do what you gotta do. I'll see you when you get here."

"Okay. And thanks, Luce."

He laid the phone in the cradle, sighed. Outside, the music of the Long Branch Bluegrass Pickers down at the Humdinger Bar & Grill floated out over the hills.

Let the rain drive right on
Let the waves sweep along
'Cause I got them deep river blues. . . .

11
Smoke on the Water

Wind battered the side of the Plymouth as the uprated Fury dove into another turn. The rear end fishtailed, then caught on the water-slick blacktop, engine revving higher as Beloit downshifted, then floored it before braking for the next turn.

Thorn sat shotgun, gripping the handrail, smiling. It'd been years since he'd ridden in a runner. Brute horse power and stiff suspension under the agile handling of a tested driver was a thrill he'd missed. This boy'll be worth keeping around even if he never hauls an ounce of meth for me, Thorn thought. A wild ride on a night like this every so often makes for a mighty good time.

The car raced along back roads, skirting two-hundred foot drops off the north side of Neddy Mountain. Lucas and Rad sat in the back. Rad snorted crank and hooted out the window. Quick accelerations, followed by sudden decelerations and hard turns, sent the two of them sliding and bouncing against the seats, the side doors, and each other.

The plan was simple. Slip onto the Glad Earth Farm at the darkest hour, set fire to a couple of lodges, and skedaddle out before the freaks knew what'd hit them. Several cans of kerosene were riding in the trunk, and the boys in back carried some Louisville Sluggers just in case. Thorn's old 1911 was holstered on his hip.

"Cord and Sam stopped in today." He glanced over his shoulder at Lucas. "Said they needed to talk to you."

"Me? What the hell for?"

"Somethin' 'bout that girl what drowned."

Lucas frowned. "What girl?"

"Not sure. Young red-head in a long skirt. Maybe from The Farm."

They stared at each other for a moment, until the car shimmied into another curve and they both grabbed for something to keep upright in their seats.

Thorn swiveled around again as they came out of the turn. "Wanted me to give you a message. 'Braided leather,' he said. Strange, huh?"

Lucas didn't answer.

"Said, come and look 'em up. Wanted to ask ye about braided leather." Thorn paused. When he spoke again, his voice was sharp, hard. "I 'spect somethin' like those goddamned braided leather key chains ye been passin' out to the boys! Fuckin' dumbass. What the hell, Lucas? Told ye not t' fuck with them damn hipsters."

"But I didn't, Thorn. I swear."

"Oh shit, boy. I don't wanna hear it. Don't even care. All's I want is to be rid of McRae askin' questions. Last thing we need. Law snoopin' around right when we're gettin' ready to make a big hit. So get your ass to town tomorrow and clear it up. Lie. Tell the truth. I don't give a damn what ye tell 'em. Just don't let it come back around to my business. Understand?"

"Yeah. You know I'd never put you in a spot. I'd go to jail first."

"I know. But I can't use you in jail. Stay out, if ye can."

Lucas nodded fervently. "Yessir. I will."

They rode in silence the rest of the way, pulling into a cow track about a quarter mile from The Farm to stop, around four A.M. Beloit stayed in the car. Thorn and the others got out, fetched the kerosene from the trunk, then huddled.

"All right, boys. We gonna traipse on up there, real quiet-like, and check things out. If it's clear, we'll move on in, pick out two or three places down at the south end, close to the road. Once we get the kerosene poured, we'll need to light 'er up, quick. Then haul ass outta there." Thorn pulled his pistol, chambered a round, and lowered the hammer carefully. "Beloit!" He looked back at the driver. "Pull back out on that highway and mosey back down to the end of the drive we passed 'bout a quarter-mile back. We'll meet you there."

"Uh, Mr. Reevers?"

"Goddammit, boy! Name's Thorn."

Beloit didn't meet his eye. "Thorn. I'm not so sure this here's what I signed on for."

Thorn walked over to the driver's side window and leaned down. "Son, this ain't no time to be getting the jitters. Now pull on down the road an' get your ass where I told ye."

"But, Thorn. I . . ."

Thorn raised the .45 and leveled it at the boy's face until the end of the cold, round barrel touched his cheek. He clicked the hammer back. "Now listen up, fuckhead. I hired you to work for me. An' that means anything I say, you do. Anything. Understand?"

"Ye-yes, sir." His face drained of color, his Adam's apple bobbed. "I do."

"Good. An' if you're thinkin' of haulin' ass outta here in this souped-up deathmobile, think again. 'Cause I'll hunt you down, haul ye off to where ain't nobody ever goes, and shoot you dead. Got it?"

"Yes, sir."

Thorn lowered the gun and stepped back. "Go on, then." He waved the pistol toward the highway.

Beloit cranked the engine and slowly pulled back down the soggy track into the darkness.

"Okay, boys. Let's light 'er up." Thorn tramped up the hillside, the others close behind.

Ten minutes later, they stood on a low ridge overlooking the compound. Just to the east sat the old log house and barn. Eight other longhouses lined a paved track leading away from the main house. Large tents dotted the hillside here and there. All was quiet.

"Them's the ones." Thorn pointed to two houses on the south end. "Yell out when ye light 'em up. Don't want any of 'em dying. Just throw a good scare into the fuckin' pricks."

They scrambled down the steep bank, sliding on mud and slick grass to the bottom. Then scurried over to the lodges closest to the road. Rad and Lucas poured kerosene around the back edges of each while Thorn kept watch. Rad had just lit his when suddenly the door flew open on the lodge closest to Lucas. A tall, blond-haired man in longjohns stepped out and stretched, then saw the seething blaze and yelled, "Fire! Fire!"

Lucas edged around the corner of the house behind the man and lifted his bat. The first swing cracked against the man's head. He crumpled against the door, then started to rise. People were stirring inside the lodge. Lucas raised the bat again, swung, and with a solid thump cracked the man's right arm.

"Come on, boy!" Thorn waved at Lucas, then jogged off down the drive.

Lucas grabbed the kerosene can and sprinted after the others just as a bullet whizzed past his ear.

At the bottom of the drive, Beloit waited, engine idling. Rad had already piled in the back. Lucas and Thorn jumped in and they wheeled off down the highway.

"Shit, Thorn. That was close." Rad leaned over the front seat, grinning. "Fuckin' guy came outta nowheres." He chuckled. "You got him good, Luke." He clapped him hard on the shoulder. "Thought you was gonna kill him."

Thorn turned to glare at him. "Shut up, goddammit! Shut the fuck up. He could've seen us, ye dumb fuck. Good thing Lucas was there. Might've been a real mess."

Rad mumbled, "Fuck, Thorn. Just funnin' is all."

"And while we're at it, Rad," Thorn added. "I got a message for you, too. McRae fingered you on the goddamned knife you give Webb."

Rad gaped. "What?"

"That's right. Told him I'd send you his way to answer questions— but that'll have to wait until after the meeting tomorrow night. That is, if there's anything left after I finish with you!"

"Ain't got a problem, 'lessin' someone talks." Lucas leaned up and punched a finger in the side of Beloit's head. "Ain't none of us gonna talk, is they, Beloit?"

Beloit shifted down and blasted through another curve, sending them all hard against the left side of the interior, then gunned it down a straightaway. "Ain't sayin' nuthin' t' nobody. Not a word." He stayed focused on the blacktop ahead.

They rode in silence the rest of the way back, headlights reflecting off bare dark pines that rose like stakes beside the highway. The wind picked up, howling through the hollow. Somewhere in the hills, a bobcat screamed out into the night.

12
Baptized in Fire

Cord woke the next morning only a little worse for wear. He'd left the jailhouse just before midnight. When he got home, Lucinda and Blu were both asleep. He'd sat outside for a time watching the dark house. He liked knowing they were safe, curled in blankets, drifting in the gauzy mists of slumber. A thin wisp of smoke rose from the chimney. The temperature, already dipping down into the twenties, augured more ill weather to come.

Stars against a blue-black night sky blinked though the patches of clouds floating above. He pulled the jar of whiskey out of the glove box and swigged a long pull. As the liquid warmth settled, he thought of the old spirits still floating restless in the hills. So much brutality. So much useless damned cruelty blanketed these hills. Like snow drifts that covered dead grasses, smothering the earth with its quiet stillness, the weight of those souls sometimes seemed to choke the living. People bore up under the day-to-day hardships. But it was the memories that broke them down. Too long living with a past that seemed never to change.

Once this community had thrived. A direct route between Knoxville and big cities like Washington, DC to the northeast and Atlanta to the south. At the apex of two wide rivers, French Broad and

Pigeon, which had brought coal companies, tanneries, timber mills, textile industries to the area. But they'd all come and gone, leaving the locals hopeful one day, in despair the next. No way to see how one generation would ever get ahead of the last. Only way up was out. Move to one of the cities and leave the old ways behind. Cord knew he was seeing an old breed dying. The kind of folks who still held to the beauty of the hills as a kind of solace for their other hardships. But he was pretty sure the generation coming up wouldn't give a damn about such things as natural beauty—let alone a sense of history that would somehow keep that beauty from disappearing.

He'd finally let himself in and made his way to bed without waking Lucinda.

Now, squinting against the light from the bedside lamp, he heard water pattering against the tiles in their shower. He glanced at the clock. Six-forty-five. That'd be Lucinda. Sundays, Blu would wake just in time to dress, grab a slice of toast or a biscuit, and then they'd rush out the door to church for an early choir practice.

He thought about years past when he'd take an opportunity like this to slide into the shower and make love to Luce. Water warming their bodies against the autumn chill. Long kisses. Frantic hands reaching and pulling. The slow, relaxed descent after that left them both smiling. Furtive glances and winks across the table as Blu ate his breakfast and chattered about school or a new friend in class.

But lately, those days were fewer. Wasn't that they'd stopped loving each other. Probably put more care and thought to one another's needs than any time before. But after she'd lost the baby, and he'd spent the past few years trying to get over the guilt of it, they'd just never been able to spark that desperate urge of desire that had been such a natural and easy part of their marriage before.

She stepped into the room wearing a Chinese silk robe and drying her hair. "Glad to see you're finally up." She glanced in the mirror. "What time you get in last night?"

"'Round midnight." He threw his legs over the edge and stood. "Lot of running yesterday. More today."

"Find out anything about that girl?" She laid the towel across a chair, slipped out of the robe and began to dress.

He studied her for a moment, feeling the old urge rise. Then he pushed the thought aside, the taste of whiskey lying like nickel on his tongue. "Zoe Chandler. From Virginia. Twenty."

"Twenty! Cord, that's awful. So young." She looked at him in the mirror, eyebrows knit in worry.

"I know. Barely out of childhood."

"Hush. Don't even want to think about it." She finished dressing and started to the door. She stopped and kissed him on top of the head. The scent of lavender shampoo in her hair made him want to pull her down on top of him.

"Hurry up. Don't want you eating cold grits." She walked out the door, glancing back, smiling over one shoulder.

"Right behind you." He showered and dressed, then started down the hall to the kitchen. Blu was just coming out of his room. "Hey, Daddy." He jumped up, grinning, arms extended.

Cord caught him in mid-air, lifting and tossing him over his shoulder. That sleepy voice reminded him of the days when his son would come into the bedroom in the early morning hours and ask to sleep with them. As Blu would lie in the crook of his arm, Cord was always amazed at the child's complete and total giving-over to sleep. As if the world outside, with all its dangers and hardships, would never touch him. As if there wasn't a speck of evil anywhere that could spoil such innocence. But it had. And Cord knew the boy had never slept that way again, not since the kidnapping.

"Gonna give me a hug, son?"

He squirmed around and squeezed Cord's neck.

"Hey now." He swung him down and held him in the crook of his arms. "Everything all right? You mindin' your mother?"

"Yeah. Got a big singin' at school. Miss Dover says I got the best soprano in the choir."

Cord set him back on the floor and straightened. "Good. Sorry I haven't seen you in a couple days."

"That's all right." He walked toward the bathroom. "I know you're busy." He shut the door behind him leaving Cord standing in the hall, alone.

"I love you," he said, to the door. Then turned and headed to the kitchen.

"Sleep okay?" Lucinda set a bowl of scrambled eggs on the table.

He poured coffee, sat down, grabbed some bacon and a biscuit off the platter then scooped a spoonful of grits and eggs onto his plate. "Okay, I reckon. The cases are just piling up. Lou died last night." He buttered a biscuit and took a bite.

She grabbed a cup of coffee off the counter and sat down beside him. "Talk to me."

He swallowed down some eggs and took a sip from his cup. "Well. Got a lead of sorts on the girl's case. Little piece of evidence may link up to her murder."

"So, she was murdered?"

"Can't prove it yet. But ain't no doubt. Just got to sniff out a motive. Probably head back over to the commune for more interviews."

"What about Webb? You going to charge him with murder?"

"Don't see how I can't. But there's somethin' else. Whoever killed Fred was lookin' for somethin'. I found a notebook Lou'd hidden under a drawer. I'll go through it today. And his computer's missing. Anyhow, Webb's mixed up in the mess. No motive for him beyond tryin' to get out from under a drug debt. He's just a tool for whatever Thorn's cookin' up next."

"Thorn? I thought he was laying low after all those meth busts."

"But he was never out of it. Rumor is there's some new competition trying to muscle in." He took the last bite of eggs and wiped the plate clean with his biscuit.

"Poor Fred. I've worried about them both since Katie died."

"I know."

Blu rushed in, hopping on one foot, still putting on his shoes. He was short for his age, like his grandmother, but with the same compact and athletic shape as Cord. Kids made fun of him, calling him Minion and Little Boy Blu. But he was smart, creative, already one of the best players on the Little League baseball team. And although his quiet, solitary ways might keep him from ever becoming a prom king, he had a generous heart and a sense of humor that always surprised Cord, knowing what he'd been through.

"Gotta go, Momma." He ran to the counter and opened the bread keeper.

"Breakfast is on the table, baby." Lucinda brushed past, carrying dishes to the sink.

"Choir starts in ten minutes." He reached over Cord, grabbed a biscuit and split it open. "Can you slap some jam and a couple slices of bacon between there?" He held the two halves open.

Cord screwed the lid off, scooped a dollop of strawberry jelly and spooned it onto one half, then broke a couple of bacon slices in two and laid them on top.

"Thanks." Blu pressed the biscuit together and licked his finger.

Just like his momma, Cord thought.

His son took one bite, then dashed out into the living room. "Seen my tie, Momma?"

"Thought I saw it—"

"Found it!" He rushed back in holding the tie in one hand, the jellied biscuit clamped in his mouth.

"What're you so blamed busy about, son?" Cord took the tie, clipped it to the top button and smoothed the collar. "Slow it down."

Blu took another bite of biscuit sandwich and jumped up into the the chair opposite. "Got to get there early so's I can warm up." He took another bite and grinned. "That's what Miss Dover said."

"You're not going anywhere in one piece the way you run around like a chicken with its head cut off." Lucinda set a glass of milk on the table. "Now finish that biscuit and drink your milk."

Blu looked at Cord. "You should come, Daddy."

"Not today. Too much work."

"Aw. You never come with us anymore."

"I know, son. But I will, soon. I promise."

Lucinda sat down next to him. "Your daddy's real busy now, Blu. But he'll get back to us real soon." She raised her eyebrows at Cord.

He nodded. "That's right. Now finish that biscuit, like your momma says." He turned back to Lucinda. "Listen. Before you leave, heard anything lately about Lucas Monroe? Doesn't Janet Shaffer's son, Joe, still kept up with him a bit."

"Not really. She did say Joe went deer hunting with him a few weeks back, but she didn't mention anything new. Except Lucas was thinking of trying for a new job. Or maybe going back to school. Why—is he all right?"

"Don't know. Why I'm asking." He paused. "What about you? Thought any more about your future plans?"

"I have. And we need to talk—"

The phone rang and Blu rushed to pick it up. "Hello? Hey, Ollie. Yessir, he's here. Hold on." He handed the phone to Cord.

"Ollie. What's up?" Cord stood, wiping his mouth with a napkin. "What? Okay, I'm headin' in now." He threw the napkin on the table and handed the phone back to Blu. "Have a good day, little man." He kissed his head. "Gotta get."

"What's wrong?" Lucinda stood and dropped her napkin on the table.

"Trouble out at the Glad Earth Farm. Somebody set a couple houses on fire. Clobbered one of the men over the head. Hurt pretty bad. I'll be back later and we'll talk. I promise." He grabbed his hat and holster, kissed Lucinda, and rushed out.

On the highway, he flipped on the lights and grabbed the receiver. "Base. This is Cord. You there?"

"I'm here."

"What the hell's goin' on?" When did we get the call?"

"Six fifteen."

"Six fifteen! Why didn't you call then?"

"Didn't know it were serious, at first. Girl called in screaming 'bout a fire. Somebody hurt. Thought they'd started it themselves. Didn't know 'til we got out there and called it in that it was an arson."

Cord swung onto Route 9 and gunned it. "Who got hurt?"

"Sunny Gregor."

"Anybody see anything?"

"No. Too busy tryin' to put out the flames. If Sunny hadn't stepped out for a piss, might be talkin' somethin' a lot worse."

"Where's he now?"

"Took him t' Kirby's. Hurt pretty good. Concussion. Smashed arm. If Doc thinks it's bad enough, they'll send him to Newport."

"All right." Cord caught the Mannings Chapel turn-off and headed to the track leading up to the farm. "I'm almost there. Thanks, Ollie. And call Judy. We're going to need her to come in today. Out."

He pulled up the muddy trace through the gates of the compound and stopped next to one of the half-burned houses. Swany and Hawkins were talking to a group of people fifteen yards off. He got out and saw Levon striding toward him across the field.

"What the fuck, Cord. Some of your local hillbilly assholes almost killed Sunny!" He spun and pointed back at the lodges. "Could've killed a lot more if it weren't for the warning he gave before they battered him."

"I know, Levon. I know. We're gonna do everything we can to find out who did this."

Levon rounded back on him. "What the fuck are you bunch of Barney Fifes gonna do, Sheriff? You come up here and hassle my people. Talk to the women like they're trash. Stirring up suspicions. And now this!"

Cord sighed and kicked at the dirt. "Levon. I know you're angry. But I'm just doing my job."

"I'd like to see that job description."

Cord held up a hand. "You need to calm down. Your folks here. They're scared. Some hurt. They don't need to see you like this. And I need you to cooperate while I investigate this arson. But remember. This ain't the only investigation I'm working. Zoe's still lying dead down at the morgue. So I'm goin' to investigate that crime, too. And if we're lucky, us hillbilly Barney Fifes may just solve 'em both. But what I'm not gonna do is stand here and put up with your bullshit right now. So go on back over to your folks and help them settle down. They need you to lead. So lead."

Levon shook his head, lips a tight line, then finally walked away.

Cord surveyed the black patches of grass and debris where houses had once stood. The volunteer fire squad and EMT's were packing up. "What d'ye got, Swan?" He walked up behind the deputy, who'd just finished talking to a woman.

"Me and Hawk interviewed just about everybody. They didn't see nothin'." He pointed to the houses. "Some barely got out 'fore they went up in flames. Strong smell of kerosene." He walked with Cord to the closest house. "Got a list of the people stayin' in each." He handed the pad over. "All present and accounted for."

Cord looked down the list of names and raised a brow. "Says here Zoe Chandler stayed in one of the burned lodges."

"Yessir. Where she kept her belongings."

Cord looked over the burned lodges. "Which one?"

"That'un there." Swany pointed.

132

Cord walked over and squatted next to the site. "Tape this off, Swan. Don't want folks traipsin' through here." He whistled to Hawkins. "Get over here, Hawk."

"I'm comin'." The lanky deputy sauntered up the small rise to the site.

"Get any information?"

"Just that folks was up late last night. Some kinda special meeting." He reached in a shirt pocket and pulled out a pouch of Redman. "Everybody's shook up." He opened the pouch, nailed off a plug and tucked it into his mouth. "Some even talkin' 'bout leavin'."

"Probably what the low-lifes that did this figured." He squinted up at Hawk. "You know whose work this looks like, don't you?"

"Naw." He shrugged and stuffed the pouch back in his pocket. "Couldn't say."

"Wouldn't say is more like it." Cord shook his head. You duplicitous prick, he thought. "If this ain't Thorn Reevers's doin', I'll promote you to captain."

He turned at Sam's voice. "Did I just hear the name 'Thorn' associated with arson?" He trotted up and stopped, a little out of breath.

"Glad you made it, Sam. Rough night on the Rappahannock?"

"Shit, buddy. Weren't any bureaucratic delays like General Burnside had, but movin' traffic over at Cole's Knob this morning was about as slow as floatin' Union pontoon bridges in place. Timber truck overturned. Had to wait' until HP showed up. Got here soon as I heard. Think this is Thorn's doin'?"

"I do." Cord picked up a stick and stirred the smoldering, charred bits of plastic, broken dishes and ash. "One of Pappy Frank's favorite tactics for gettin' rid of the competition."

"Think it's about competition?"

"Come on, Sam. You know these folks are growin' more than beans and 'maters up in here. Nickels to a dollar you go sniffin' round the hills you'll find marijuana tucked into creases all over this holler."

133

"True that." Sam smiled, reminding Cord of his younger day with his blond buzz haircut and sky-blue eyes. But underneath the calm, slow manner, Cord knew he was one of the smartest deputies you could ever want. And a great wingman in a jam. "Backed up like they are to the national forest, it's a wonder the DEA hasn't put its foot on their necks already." Sam walked around the edge of the burned-out structure and picked up a charred book and turned it over. *Aesop's Fables*. "Folks lost about ever-damn thing. Heard these lodges hold about twelve people in each. That'd make twenty-four without homes. Guess they'll pull out the tents again. It'll be a cold winter." He threw the book back down in the ashes, shaking his head, dismayed.

Cord joined him, poking through the ashes with the stick. "We'll see if we can't get some folks from town to help out. The second lodge didn't burn too bad. Looks like they put it out before any structural damage got done."

"First time I been up here." Jess Hambrick, the volunteer fire chief walked up behind Cord, slapping his legs with heavy leather gloves. "Got some purty interestin' security, eh?"

What's that, Jess?"

"Me and the others was just noticing, in that first house." He pointed with his chin. "Lot of electronics. Wired up for video cameras and such. Almost every room had its own security camera set up. Like they was keepin' watch on their own."

"Show me."

They followed him to the first building. The roof had collapsed, and almost everything inside, except for appliances, had melted down or burned. But as they walked along the exposed, charred 2 x 4's, they saw the distinct outlines of twelve separate bedrooms. Six on each side of the house, containing burned and singed bedframes, sodden mattresses and dressers. Jess pointed. "In the corners of each room, as we dug into the debris we found exposed wiring and connectors for what looked like video hardware."

"What the hell." Cord stood for a moment scratching the scar above his brow. "Find any cameras?"

"Nope. But computer power cords still plugged into outlets."

"Swan."

"Yeah, Boss."

"Let me see that list again." He grabbed it out of the deputy's hand and glanced down at the names. "This is Lodge One?"

"Yessir."

All female. Including Zoe. But she was listed as living in the other house, too. "I need to talk to every woman who lived in this house. Now."

"I'll round 'em up."

"Sam. Check on Lodge Two. Let me know if you find anything of interest. And get pictures." He turned and considered the burn site again. "Can you help him out, Jess?"

"Sure."

"Hey." Levon's voice was sharp and loud. "What's going on here?"

Cord looked over at Hawk. "Tape it off."

"You got it."

"Goddammit, McRae. What're you doing?"

"This is a crime scene, Levon. So back up now and let us do our work."

"A crime scene? Look, I thank you and your men for getting up here and helping put out the fire. But you can leave now. I'm not giving you permission to cordon this off."

"Maybe you didn't hear. We're not leaving. Arson and assault are crimes. We have statements from your folks as to what happened. And you got a man in the hospital."

"I don't give a fuck." Levon quickly closed the space between them. "I want you off my fucking property. We're not pressing charges—so no need to investigate anything. Now get the fuck off my land."

Cord slowly nodded. "Okay, Levon. At this point we'll be happy to leave. But the fire department came at your request. They'll need to make sure everything's safe before they go—a liability issue. They will also determine whether this was arson, for their report and for any current or future insurance purposes. We're here in the capacity of keeping peace and helping out where we can. Understand?"

"I don't care why you're here. I just want you gone."

"I get it." His voice was hard-edged. "And the quickest way to get gone is for you to let us do our job. As soon as they finish, we're out of here." He looked over his shoulder. "Hawk!"

"Yeah, boss."

"Escort Mr. Gladson outside the investigation scene."

"Yep." Hawk nodded and motioned toward the main house. "This way, Mr. Gladson?"

Levon reluctantly started away, muttering. "I sure as fuck do."

Cord watched them leave, then looked down the list of occupants again. Sarah, Rebecca, Ruth, Abigail, Delilah, Lydia, Rachel, Ariel, Chloe, Myra, Phoebe, and Zoe. All twelve carried the last name: Magdalene.

"Cord. Here they are." Swany walked up behind him followed by eleven women.

"Hello, ladies." Cord tipped his hat. "Just wanted to let you know how sorry I am you lost your things today. If there anything we can do, please let us know."

They stood silent, looking down at their feet. Cord followed their gaze and noticed several weren't wearing shoes. On their insteps were the same tattoo: Cross, heart, drops of blood.

"Look, ladies. I'm not trying to get anybody in trouble. But we'd like to find out who might've set the fire. Sunny was badly hurt. Can you tell me anything about what happened this morning?"

A tall, full-bodied blonde raised her eyes. "We're the daughters of Magdalene. We shouldn't even be talking to you. We serve a higher calling."

136

"What's your name, ma'am?"

"Abigail."

Okay, Abigail. When you say 'higher calling,' do you mean Levon?" Cord tilted his head.

"Levon's an apostle. He teaches us how best to serve." Her raised, defiant chin was reminiscent of his son's childish imperiousness.

Cord nodded. "All right. I get it. But I still need to ask some questions which I hope will not intrude on your oaths. Did any of you keep computers in your rooms?"

The women glanced at one another, but didn't answer.

He waited a few seconds before continuing. "Okay, listen. It's none of my business, but looks like somebody might have been videotaping you. If you knew that already—some kind of security measure, say. Fine. But if not, and you're bothered that your activities in private may have been monitored or recorded, give me a call." He handed the tall one his card. "That's all."

Abigail looked around at the others who were all shaking their heads as if in warning. "I don't know anything about that," she finally said, looking less certain. "The men handle security." She took a deep breath, hesitantly glancing back at the others. Finally, they all turned to leave.

"Wait. Are you the only women here with those tattoos?"

The blonde turned back, frowning. "I thought you said that was all."

"Sorry. Your sister Zoe wore the same tattoo."

"She wasn't our sister." Abigail paused, looking like she wanted to say something more, but turned away again and slowly followed the others up the hill, flicking his card into the mud alongside the path. Sam and Jess passed her coming back down from Lodge Two.

Sam stopped beside the leaning corner of Lodge One. "Don't seem like the other house is wired for video like this one."

"Think the fire's about done too." Jess eyed the burned eaves. "Sending the guys home. But I'm going to stick around until I'm sure we're safe."

"Okay, Jess. Thanks." Cord looked up the hill towards the back of the property. "Let's poke around some more, Sam. See what else we might turn up. Swan, you and Hawk can head back."

"See you there." Swany waved and stepped off to the cruiser, Hawk following.

"So if you were plannin' to come in here at zero-dark-thirty, where would you pick as your entrance point, Sam?"

"Reckon I'd skirt in on the east end. Lots of open fencing."

"Me too. Let's start there."

"Get anything from the women?"

"You mean beyond the veiled silence of a quasi-oath supported by pseudo-apostolic apologetics? No."

"Maybe they'll come around." Sam brushed ash from the sleeves of his jacket. "That video equipment may hold more than they're willing to let on."

"Maybe. Ain't holdin' my breath. Them lambs are hooked hard in their shepard's crook."

Before long, they found footprints leading up the slope to a ridge overlooking the compound. They followed the trail back to a cow trace and the spot where a car had obviously been parked.

"Looks like this is where they got in." Sam walked the tire tracks leading from the road.

"Some interesting treading here." Cord was kneeling where the car had been parked. "Got a feeling ain't too many folk 'round here drivin' on such tires."

He stood, looked around. "Got some footprints here. Looks like they're only headed in one direction. The Farm. Must've come out down below. Let's check it out when we leave."

They followed the tracks to the commune, and Cord paused at the top of a ridge where it looked like they'd stopped. "I count three of 'em."

"Yep. And one's a pretty big feller by the look of this print." Sam pointed to a deep imprint at the edge of the rise.

"Get a photo." Cord was about to start down the hill when he noticed something shiny in the grass. He pulled on gloves, bent and picked up a knife. "I'll be damned. Second Benchmade in three days. Reckon they buy 'em in bulk at Sam's Club?"

"Maybe Cabela's over in Nashville." Sam grinned his pearly whites.

"If this don't have Rad's fingerprints on it, I'll buy you dinner at The Lodge." He dropped it in a bag and slipped it in his jacket. "We got enough here, for now. Let's get on back to Doc's. Need to talk to Sunny."

Sam followed him down the ridge to the cars. Levon was waiting. Cord noticed the Glock snugged in a Kydex tactical holster.

"I don't want trouble here, Cord. But have a warrant next time you show up."

Cord had seen that gaze before. Dark, reflective. Like the narco sociopaths he'd come across in Central America. Violence lay behind such eyes. "That's fine, Levon. Just take care of your folks. You can pull that yellow tape now. But we'll need to talk later."

"Call first. I'll bring my lawyer."

Cord tipped his hat, stepped into the car and pulled away down the track, Sam following. At the main road, they stopped and found tire tracks matching those they'd spotted earlier.

"Same tread." Cord looked up the road. "Got an exit point. Grab the camera out of the back seat."

Sam took a couple of shots from different angles, then walked back up to where Cord waited. "That oughter do it."

"Good. Now head up the road and get some snaps of those tracks and the footprints on that ridge. I'll slide over to Falston, talk to Sunny and meet you back at the house. We'll ride out to Thorn's. This time, do more than just stand in a driveway shootin' the shit."

"Sounds good, boss. See you there."

Sam trotted back to his cruiser and Cord pulled onto the highway.

It was pushing nine-thirty as he crossed the J.T. Huff Bridge over the French Broad heading west. He passed the jailhouse and pulled up in front of a small, two-story brick building. The sign above the door read: Dr. Daniel Kirby, General Practitioner. But the large storefront window still displayed the peeling letters of the old occupants: "Griffin's Feed and Seed: We Pack It, You Plant It." When he'd moved in, twenty-three years back, Doc said, "It'll wear off soon enough. No need to pay somebody for what nature'll do for free." Over time, Cord had come to believe the decision had less to do with economy than with the man's tragicomic sense of life's fatal twists. But you'd never get Doc to admit it.

The bell tinkled overhead as he pushed through the door into the waiting area. "Hey now, Sheila." He took his hat off and nodded at a woman sitting behind a counter watching a screen.

"Hello, Cord." She briefly glanced up then went back to work.

Doc had hired Sheila Bird after moving his practice to Falston. One of just forty-two Cherokee Indians living in the county, she'd graduated high school with honors despite the desperate poverty and violent environment in which she'd been raised. Even got into University of Tennessee on a special scholarship with full tuition. But after completing three years, family troubles brought her back to the mountains, so Doc had hired her on as an assistant. Since then, his clinic was one of the only places in the county where Cherokees could go for honest-to-goodness medical treatment.

A woman holding a small child wrapped in a blanket sat against the side wall, rocking. "Well. Hello, Millie. That little Jen you got there?"

"Hey, Mr. Cord." Jennifer Potts peeked over the blanket.

"What're you doing here, Jen. Ain't feelin' good?"

"No, sir." She laid her head back against her mother's arms and coughed, phlegm rattling deep in her chest.

"Been coughin' fer a month now." Jennifer pulled her closer. "Ain't runnin' a fever. I s'pect ain't much t' worry about." She brushed a stray strand of the child's hair behind one ear. "Just thought I'd see Doc about it. Acel picked up some work down in Atlanta. Said t' bring her in."

Millie and Acel Potts lived up near Sinking Branch. Acel was a good mechanic, but there were plenty of good ones in these parts. And most folks too poor to hire one practiced their own shade-tree tinkering. Like many locals, Acel had moved to a city to find work, sending what he could back home.

Cord leaned down and stroked Jen's head. "You just hang on, girl. Ol' Doc'll have ye up and playin' with your dollies before ye know it." He straightened and breathed a deep sigh against the tightness in his chest. "Take care, Millie. Call if ye need anything."

"I will. Thanks, Cord."

He walked to the counter and looked down at Sheila. "So, I hear you got a feller here that's got a nasty knock on his noggin?"

Sheila looked up, face tranquil. No smile or other acknowledgment. "Nothing Doc cannot fix. Back there wrapping his arm in a cast now." She stood and walked into the back office, leaving Cord at the counter. In a couple minutes, she returned, sat and resumed working on her Medicaid reimbursements.

Cord waited. "So? You think I can go on back?" He looked at the top of her head, his eyebrows raised.

"You need to see Doc? Why didn't you say so? Step on in."

Cord held back a smile. Sheila never assumed anything. Not a bad trait for a small medical clinic that served mostly poor folk for what little the government paid out.

She waved him to the door and turned back to her paperwork. He strolled down the hallway. Doc's office was first on the right, across from two examination rooms. A doorway in the back led to a small X-ray facility, a lab, and what passed for the town morgue. He found Kirby in the first exam room sitting on a rolling stool beside a bed, wrapping Sunny's left arm in a cast.

"Doc." He laid his hat on the corner of a medicine cabinet. "Sunny. You all right?"

Sunny rested against pillows, head wrapped in gauze and bandages. He squinted up at Cord. "Hey, man." He winced and touched the bandage. "Splittin' headache. But I'm okay."

"He'll live." Doc sat back and dipped another bandage into the casting solution. "X-rays didn't show anything worth worryin' about." He started the next wrap. "This damn arm was splintered all t' hell, though. Gonna take some time t' heal." He put the last wraps on and pushed away. "Reckon that head's harder than the devil thought." He chuckled and walked to the sink to rinse his hands.

"All right if I talk to him a minute?"

"If he feels up to it." Dirby dried his hands and left.

"Listen, Sunny." Cord rolled the stool over and sat down beside him. He'd always liked Sunny. He was hard-edged and short-tempered. But had an earnest, straight-forward way about him that led Cord to believe that he truly cared about the people on The Farm. No need to go at him hard, he thought.

"I know you think I don't get what y'all are tryin' to do up there, Sunny. But I do. Hell, this whole Blue Ridge community, from one end of the Smokies to the other, is filled with people who were outsiders once. Folks who wanted nothin' to do with people tellin' them how to live. We have a history of runnin' them types out on a rail."

"Like y'all are trying to do to us?"

"Ain't the same." He pointed at Sunny's arm. "Boys done that are after something else. Don't know what yet. But I'll find out. No, what I'm talking about has to do with a deep-down suspicion of authority we both share. Especially authority that comes through here with the word 'help' attached to it. Like coal mining companies, logging and timber operations, railroads and such. All backed by the government and promising the world. Then in a year, or ten, they all turn tail, pull up stakes and skedaddle when the profits get too lean. Leave the locals to cut and tumble-wrestle out a livin' on their own. It's the same reason you and Levon and the rest settled here. Get leave of a world that's all mixed up and turned around. Have a place where you could live on the land in peace. Hell, you got a dream, just like everyone else around here. I get it."

"So why don't you just leave us be?"

"Because it's my job to keep that peace. Sometimes, all those independent dreams and aspirations butt heads. Then people get hurt. That's when I got an obligation to bring justice to bear on them that caused the harm. And I also got an obligation to show the folks who bore the brunt of that harm that there's an answer as to why. Folks like Zoe's parents." He paused. "They deserve to know what happened to their daughter, Sunny."

He leaned his head back against the pillows. "Cord, please. I don't need this shit right now."

"Just listen, then. I'm not tryin' to tear down The Farm. But if you know anything that might help explain what happened to that girl, I'd appreciate it."

"What about the fuckers did this to me?"

"I'll get 'em. I swear. But don't you or your people care about what happened to Zoe?"

Sunny grimaced as he pulled himself up and slowly shook his head. "Look. Levon's like a brother, man. He saved me from the streets. Got as big a heart as any I've known. He'd never do anything to hurt Zoe. He loved her."

"I reckon he loves all the women at The Farm."

"No. I mean," Sunny hesitated. "They had something special goin' on for a time, man. Pretty serious, I think. Saw them together. Down at the river." He shook his head again. "Fuck, Cord, I don't like this."

"It's okay, Sunny. So, they were lovers? That don't bother me. Just need to understand what's what."

"Yeah." He hesitated. "I guess they were. I know he gave her a necklace. A wooden heart strung on a purple ribbon."

"Wait a minute. A purple ribbon?" Cord felt a spark of recognition fire off in his brain, behind all the other questions punched into his head over the last two days.

"I found it on a table back when we were still living in the tents. Asked her about it. Said her momma had give it to her. But I think she was lying."

"Why?"

"Because there was an inscription carved on it. *My hope, my light, my desire.* Come from one of Levon's favorite sermons."

"But I thought Zoe was a Magdalene."

"No, man. Not yet. She was still an initiate. Levon was going to perform her naming sacrament today. They would have finished the inking last Friday."

"Inking?"

"All the Magdalenes are tattooed. You saw it. The heart, the cross, the three drops of blood. A sign they've given their lives to the service of The Trinity. She was supposed to get her blood drops inked. That comes last."

"So, they're like nuns?"

"Yeah, man. Serving the community, helping with children. Teaching, caring for the sick."

"Can anyone become a Magdalene?"

"No. Only women who are still unmarried by the age of twenty. But they can leave the sisterhood if Levon consents to it. Say, if another man shows interest in marrying one of them."

"And all the Magdalenes stay in Lodge One?"

"That's right."

"I see. So, why do you need to keep them under observation?"

"What?" He turned his head to look at Cord and winced. "Ouch. Shit, that hurts."

"Well, we found evidence of surveillance equipment in Lodge One."

Sunny looked down, frowning, as if confused. "I . . . don't know. Don't know what you're talking about." He leaned back against the pillow, shook his head and sighed. "I really don't. Levon, Lilith and Eli manage those girls. Tried to tell Levon the Magdalenes was a bad idea when Eli suggested it." He waved his hand, resigned. "He wouldn't listen. Never has much. But it's got worse. At least since Eli came into the picture." He paused, thinking. "If what you say is true, I need to get myself back into the middle of things again."

"Maybe." Cord patted his leg. "You've been a big help." He stood to leave.

"Hold on." Sunny popped up on one elbow, wincing again. "One other thing. I saw a young dude a few weeks back hiding up on a low ridge behind some trees. Watching Zoe. I ran him off. Didn't think much of it until yesterday, after you left."

"Remember what he looked like?"

"Yeah. A little taller than you. Blond hair. Athletic. Carried a rifle."

"Thanks, Sunny. That might help."

"I love that farm, Sheriff. It's got good people on it. I don't want bad stuff happening out there. If you find out anything else, I want to know."

"I can't reveal the details of our investigation, Sunny."

"I know. But take my number and call if there's anything I can do. Please."

Cord briefly studied him. He seemed sincere. "Okay. But the best thing you can do, Sunny, is to let all your people out there know what's happening. Don't wait for me to fix it."

"Right. I won't." He leaned his head back against the pillow, and stared up at the ceiling.

Cord knew that look. The same dejection he'd seen on the faces of guerrilla militiamen on both sides of a conflict who'd realized their leaders were actually power-driven madmen who had no real consideration for the people they claimed to serve. And that service to those very same leaders had only furthered the destruction of the very people they'd hoped to save.

On the way out, Cord stuck his head in Kirby's office. "Thanks for takin' care of him."

"It's what I do." Doc looked up over his glasses. "Sure as hell wasn't gonna let him die. Then I'd have to do an autopsy. Hate to waste valuable time."

"Cord smiled. "Anything else you can tell me about that dead girl?"

"Took another look at her head. Real nasty blow. Didn't kill her, but probably did more damage than I first thought. Still can't figure out what weapon. But I know it weren't a stick or a limb nor a rock. Impression was too clean. Weren't a bat nor a board neither. Impact of a bat leaves a rounded imprint; a board'll often leave a v-line. This was done with something smooth, but tapered down to a rounded point. It's almost like a large puncture wound." He pushed his glasses up on his nose. "I also pulled a good-sized splinter from the scalp. Hardwood of some kind. Not maple or oak. More like a fruit wood, maybe."

"Thanks, Doc." He turned to leave.

"One other thing. She was pregnant. Couple of months, I'd say."

"Pregnant?" Cord paced to the other side of the room. If what he'd just heard from Sunny was true, a pregnant Magdalene wouldn't fit too well in Levon's plans. *I'll string that bastard up by his balls if it's Levon's,* he thought. "Okay. We'll need to get the DNA out to the lab, then."

"Already sent." Doc looked at him again over his glasses. "That's about it. Sorry to deliver more bad news. Oh, and those folks from The Farm called. I'm releasing the body so they can prep her for burial."

Cord nodded. "Thanks, Doc. When do you think you'll get to Fred?"

"Should have something by tonight."

"As soon as you can. I know I'm pushing it, but the boys from Knoxville are probably going to want to move in as soon as they get a whiff of this in the morning. Sure like to keep it local as long as I can."

"Just plan on dropping off a bottle of Chivas when we get this cleared up."

"Will do."

On the way out Cord passed Sheila, who was still working on reports, or applications, or whatever was on her screen. "If you don't take a break, it'll cramp your hand," he told her

"Nope." She glanced up with a barely-perceptible smile. "Won't cramp. Strong hands." Then bent over her keyboard again.

Outside, he walked a couple of blocks to the station. Judy was at the switchboard. Sam was filling out a report. Robert Crayton, the local public defense attorney, was waiting on the wooden bench along the wall in front of the railing. "Hey, Bob," Cord said.

"Sheriff. We need to talk."

"About what?" He passed through the gate, winking at Judy on the way to the coffee pot. Joke was, if you wanted to end up in Brushy Mountain Prison for jaywalking, just get Crayton to defend you. The son of a respectable lawyer from up near Sevierville, he was generally disorganized and late to court, which never went over well with the judge. Probably spent too much time hittin' the hooch. Or it could be he was just dumb.

Now Crayton stepped to the rail. "I came in here this morning to talk to my client and discover you've been interrogating him. That won't stand. No sir. It won't."

Cord ambled back to the front, cup in hand. When he reached the rail, he raised it in salute. "Here's to you, Mr. Crayton, Esquire, consummate lawyer. Who'd let a young buck like Webb go to prison, twenty-five to life, on a guilty plea of first degree murder, instead of tryin' to get him reduced to a lesser charge. Say second degree? Or even justifiable homicide." He took a sip, set the cup on the corner of Judy's desk and picked up a form from a pile she'd been working on.

"Or didn't you even talk to your client long enough to get the full story?" He waved the paper in Crayton's face. "Why don't you read this-here confession?" Cord slapped it against his chest. "Hell, might even get him off on a self-defense or malignant heart argument. Lucky for him, he decided to talk to my deputies without you around. Signed the damn release form and everything."

"What is this?" Crayton frowned as he studied the forms.

Cord shook his head. "What the hell, son. You want me to try the case too?" He stepped to the gate and came around the rail where Crayton stood. "It's the beginning of a defense for your client, if you'll take it. Now, here's what you do: take these back to your office." He tapped the files. "Draft up the rest of a respectable defense. One that'd make Atticus Finch proud. And if you'd like to bring it back and let Judy here look it over, that'd be fine too. But you're not gonna let Webb plead out on this. Understand?"

"Yeah." He nodded. "I understand."

"Good." Cord patted his shoulder. "Tell your daddy I said 'hey,' and I'll see you in court next week."

"I will."

As soon as he was gone, Judy and Sam both burst out laughing.

"Damn, Cord. You ain't cuttin' nobody slack today." Sam met him at the rail as he came through the gate. "And what was that reference you made? Hell, that boy probably ain't read enough to know an Atticus Finch from a house finch."

"Reckon he'll put together anything worth reading?" Judy reached for a new pen and dangled it between her fingers.

"He might. I'll mosey over to his office in a couple days. See if he'll show me the draft." Cord started to his office, but the phone rang.

"For you, Sheriff. It's Ms. Trulan, from Nashville."

"Send it in here." He stepped into his office, picked up the phone, and pushed the blinking button. "Beth. I was just gettin' ready to call."

"What the hell you got going on down there, Cord? The DEA and ATF burning up my answering machine this Sunday morning. Don't like to get caught off guard."

"Hell. You tell me. A couple of unrelated homicides just popped up down here. I got a boy killed in a bar whose father was also found dead in his home today. And a girl from the local commune drowned. Possible homicide. Wanted to see if you could put a rush on DNA evidence, maybe run some prints. So, what's got all the big boys a'flutter?"

"Apparently, that compound down there's been under surveillance for a while. They popped up on the radar after multiple gun, ammo, and powder purchases. Then the fire out there last night, and the state boys were worried you might get in there and put a wrench in their operation."

"An operation beyond surveillance?"

"You know I can't say. But don't be surprised if the Ray-Bans drop in asking you to tread lightly."

"Would it have to do with some drug running out of Nashville?"

"Dammit, Cord. Told you I can't say." The line was silent for a few seconds. "But I picked up some unofficial chatter about new gang activity, ex-military out of Berry Field Air Base. Guns. Explosives. Drugs. You name it. But you didn't hear it from me."

"Well, I consider this my official call informing the TBI of these homicides. I'm following up on other leads to see if I can't shake something out on my own. I'll let you know if I need more in the next day or so."

"I can send a CI team if you need it. And I'll push through that DNA and fingerprint analysis quick as I can. Anything else?"

"Yeah. Any information on the leader of that commune, Levon Gladson, would be a help."

"I'll get you something by tomorrow. And tell Lucinda I'm looking forward to seeing her and Blu again. There's a great new Thai restaurant over on Woodland. I got box seats for the Vanderbilt game and a new VU hoodie that's a perfect fit for a seven-year-old."

Cord hesitated. "Luce's coming up for a visit?"

"You didn't know?"

"Too damned busy around here. Ain't had much time to talk. But I'll tell her. And thanks again for the heads up."

"You bet. Later, Cord."

He hung up and leaned back. Strange, he thought. Maybe Lucinda just didn't have time to tell me this morning the way I rushed out.

Sam knocked. "Ready for some grub? I'm sending out."

"Just got off the phone with Beth. Looks like Levon's building a little arsenal on The Farm. No wonder we spooked him this morning. More than just some weed he's planting and harvesting out there."

Sam nodded. "Fits with all his anti-government leanings. But what does the girl have to do with it all?"

Cord rose and grabbed his coat. "Need to get out and clear my head. We'll take Josephine and you can give me a refresher about John Brown's revolt. We might have our very own will-o'-God insurrectionists right here in Acre. Levon Gadson's no John Brown, but he might could be just as dangerous."

13

Running the Rill

L ucas stood over the young racing driver, shaking his shoulder. "Wake up. Wake up, Beloit. Gotta go."

"What're you talkin' about?" Beloit rubbed his eyes and squinted against the noon sun slanting through the curtains. They'd only been asleep a few hours.

"Get up. I need ye to take me into town. Got some business t' tend to."

"Thorn said I ain't supposed to go there." He sat up on the edge of the bed. "No fuckin' way I'm goin' against him after last night!"

"Shh. Keep it down, dammit. Wanna wake the whole damn house?" Lucas paced to the other side of the room and back. "I know what Thorn said. But I need you to help me out." He sat on the bed next to Beloit. "They's a girl killed a couple days back. She had somethin' of mine. Give it to her as a present."

"So what the hell's the problem with that?"

"Sheriff come 'round askin' about it. Wants to see me. And law don't take kindly t' my kind ignorin' their requests. Can't have 'em comin' up in here lookin' fer me. Ye heerd what Thorn said last night."

"That's all fine and well." Beloit started to climb back under the covers. "But I don't see what it has to do with me."

Lucas grabbed his shirt and yanked him up by the collar. "I'll tell ye what." His voice was raspy, desperate. "Has to do with me stayin' alive and out of jail. Cause if I don't, ye ain't got a chance around here." He pushed Beloit back onto the bed and stood glaring down at him, fist clenched at his side. "Listen. I know ye just fell into this shit. And prob'ly wonderin' by now why the hell ye even came up here. But ye did. And now yer stuck. Fer better or worse. But I can help, if ye want to get leave of it." He paused, his voice calmer. "Understand?"

Beloit straightened his T-shirt and looked up skeptically. "Reckon if you can figure a way outta here, and guarantee Thorn won't cut me from gut t' gizzard when we get back, I can drive you." He stood and pulled his jeans on. "But you gotta swear to get me outta this mess 'fore I end up deader 'n hell. This here's one goddamned dangerous business. Rather take my chances on a track any day."

The house was quiet as they made their way to the front door. Outside, they jogged to the car parked at the top of the circle drive.

"Kick that thing into neutral and roll her down to the gate. I'll meet you there." Lucas sprinted down the hill.

When Beloit got to the gate, Lucas punched in the security code. He waited until the Fury was through, then shut the gate behind them and entered the locking code. They rolled down Foggy Top another hundred yards before Beloit fired up the engine and drove the rest of the way down the mountain.

"When ye get to Bainport, turn right."

"What? I thought we was goin' t' town."

"Never you mind. Just drive."

At Route 9, they headed east. When they got to Mannings Chapel, Beloit pulled over.

"What the fuck you thinking, Lucas. Are we goin' back to The Farm? Shit! You're crazy!"

"I know what I'm doin'. Just gotta check on somethin' before I talk to the sheriff." He nodded up the road. "Now slap 'er into gear and get movin'. If we're lucky, might make it back 'fore they's awake at the house."

"Fuck!" Beloit slammed the gear shift and spun the tires back onto the blacktop. "I ain't feelin' much luck right about now."

They passed the lower track leading to the compound and the cow trace further up. About a quarter mile farther, they turned onto Larks Road.

Lucas pointed to a cutoff on the left. "Pull in there."

Beloit drove down the spit about thirty yards and parked behind a tree. Lucas jumped out and ran around to the driver's side. "Just give me fifteen minutes."

He took off running across the ridge of a foothill that hemmed in the eastern side of the compound. He hoped to find the little boy quickly. If he was playing in the usual spot next to the cow stream that cut through the compound, Lucas would be fine. He loved the feel of his legs pumping, long strides punctuated with leaps over boulders and deadfall. Lungs filling to capacity. He was alive, and wanted to stay that way.

At the stream, the kid was poking sticks in the mud and lining a pretend-fort with pebbles. He was alone. Lucas slid down the shallow bank and walked up behind him.

"Hey now, Beam. Playin' fort again?"

The boy looked up, brow creased. "Hey, Lucas."

"What's wrong, buddy?"

"Somebody burned our house last night. Mommy says it was hillbillies." He looked up at Lucas. "Are you a hillbilly?"

Lucas smiled. A name outsiders liked to paste on people they'd never spoken to. Let alone understood. Made him the backwards, ignorant outsider. Turned him into a cipher. Figured that was probably the way she'd seen him, too.

"I am, Beam. But yer momma's wrong. Was bad people burned them houses, not hillbillies. Just plain ol' bad people."

Beam nodded. "You wanna play?"

"Ain't got time, today. But I need to ask if you talked to anybody about me. Remember, you promised to keep our secret if I'd show ye how to catch tadpoles in the spring."

Beam looked up, sheepish. "I told a deputy man yesterday when they were here. He was asking about my whip." He reached in his pocket and pulled out the short strap of leather.

Lucas shook his head. "Damn."

"I'm sorry, Lucas. I know you said to keep it hid, but I wanted to show my friends, so I took it home." He sniffled, about to cry. "When Zoe disappeared, the Sheriff come up here and started askin' a bunch of questions. I was nervous cause Momma was scared, so I had it out swingin' it around. And that's when the deputy came up and asked about it. Said I could hold his badge if I'd let him look at it. I'm sorry."

Lucas knelt beside him. "'At's all right, buddy. Don't you fret. I ain't mad at ye."

"Really?"

"Neary a bit. But can you remember what all ye told that deputy?"

"Yes." He nodded, looking serious now. "I never told him your name. Just that you were fun, for an adult. Said I only seen you a couple times." He was smiling now, proud of his lie.

"That's good, Beam. Real good." He stood and looked down toward The Farm. "Anybody hurt in the fire?"

"Just Sunny. But they said he'd be back tonight. Everybody else is okay."

"Good." Lucas thought about the rage that had risen in him when he'd seen the man come out of the house. Same sonofabitch who'd spotted him watching the girl and chased him off. Called him a sick-ass pervert and a sister-fuckin' hillbilly. Lucas felt the wrath seething again as he thought about it. He reached down, cupped some stream water and splashed it on his face.

"Listen, Beam. You been keepin' watch on that girl, Zoe, like I asked?"

"Sure, Lucas. But she's gone now." The boy dug some mud out of the ground with his hands and tossed it away. "She was nice to me and Momma. When that man came up here the other day, I got scared."

"What man?" Lucas knelt and grabbed the boy by the shoulders. "What man, Beam?"

"I don't know. Zoe called him Lou." He wiped some snot off his lip. "I seen him a couple of times before, with Levon and Eli. He was Zoe's boyfriend." He leaned in and whispered. "Zoe said they was going to run off and get married." He grinned, happy for sharing a secret. Then turned serious. "But last time I saw 'em together, they was fightin'. She was cryin', tellin' him not to leave. Then he pulled at somethin' on her neck. A ribbon necklace. Yelled at her about stayin' true and shoved her down. Then I ran away 'cause I was scared he'd see me."

"When did this happen?"

"Early Friday morning."

Lucas took a deep breath and looked down the ridge at the river below. "Okay, Beam. Okay. You done real good." He ruffled the boy's hair and stood. "I best get goin'. But I'll be back to play with ye soon. Thanks fer bein' a friend."

"You're welcome." Beam stood and hugged his legs. "Bye, Lucas."

He patted the boy's shoulder then struck out back to the car. In a few minutes he was sitting beside Beloit again. "All right. We're done here. Let's go on into town and get this over with."

Beloit cranked the engine. In twenty minutes they were riding down Main.

"Just to drop me off, then head on back t' the house. Ain't a good idea you hangin' round here. I'll find my own way back."

"Hell I will! Ain't goin' back to face Thorn alone! You're the only assurance I got of stayin' alive." He stopped in front of the jailhouse. "Ain't lettin' you outta my sight."

"Goddammit, Beloit." Lucas looked around nervously. "Ye can't sit out here in front of a fuckin' jailhouse in the getaway car used in an arson last night! Just drop me off, then go park up the road a piece. Meet me at the BP station in an hour."

"All right. But if you ain't there in an hour, I'm blastin' outta here and won't stop 'til I get west of the Mississippi."

Lucas nodded, slid out and walked to the sidewalk. He turned at the door and pointed up the street. Beloit backed out and headed north. Lucas watched until he'd turned the corner at the end of Main, then stepped inside.

14
On the Muddy Banks

On the drive to Lily's, Cord studied the cirrus clouds settling onto the ridge peaks. The air felt heavier and had warmed a bit since morning. But the iron taste of winter chill coming through the open window still struck the back of his throat.

"Cord. You there?"

"I'm here, Judy. What's up?"

"Y'all picked a bad time for lunch. That boy, Lucas Monroe. He's here. Said you was lookin' fer him."

"That's right. Tell him sit tight. We'll be there in about thirty minutes."

"Will do. Out."

"Well. Looks like we'll get the chance to line up another piece, Sam. Don't even know what round we're in, but I believe we're gettin' in a rhythm here."

"So, he's mixed up in all of this. Reckon he knows about the fire?"

Cord shrugged. "That leather anklet ties him to Zoe's death, and I aim to figure out exactly how."

Sam tapped a hand on the doorframe. "Damn sure is odd, the video cameras. Think any of those girls knew?"

"If their reaction is any indication, no. And neither did Sunny. So Levon must keep a pretty select group on this little project." He pulled the cruiser into Lily's parking lot, which was already full with the Sunday lunch crowd. "Let's grab some grub. Might be all we get the rest of the day if it keeps up like it started."

As they walked to the entrance, Cord nudged Sam and pointed. "How about it, bud! Ever seen that baby round here before?"

Sam glanced at the low-slung coupe parked in the shade of a large Ram pickup and smiled. "Sure haven't. And would you look at them tires. Road-racin' treads if I ain't mistaken."

Cord nodded. "Damn. Sometimes a feller just gets lucky. Let's mosey on in here see what's on the menu."

They strolled in and sat at the counter. Lily brought two cups of coffee almost before they'd gotten seated. "My two favorite lawmen." She pulled a pencil from the bun of hair. "Want the usual, or ye interested in the special?"

Cord looked around the room and saw a young white man he didn't recognize in a back booth, alone. "What's special today?"

"Shit, Cord. Same as always. Country fried steak on Monday, chicken on Tuesday, pork chops—"

"I know, Lil." He swiveled on the stool to face her. "Sorry. Just give me the usual."

"Same here, Lil." Sam pulled off his cap and set it on the counter. "You still seein' that feller from over at Dandridge?"

"Hell no. Second date he tried to split the dinner bill with me. I told him go to hell and lose my number." She disappeared in the back and returned with a fresh pot of coffee. Served another customer, then came back. "Why? You interested?"

He raised an eyebrow at her, smiling, then leaned back. "Maybe."

"Aw. Shit, Sam." She brushed by him, frowning. "If you wanna date me, ye gotta do better 'n 'at." She moved down the line of tables, refilling cups.

Cord laughed. "You want to take on that woman, Sam? Better be ready to prove somethin'. She's a firecracker."

Lily returned, placed the carafe on the warmer and pushed through the swinging doors to the kitchen. In a minute she was back with their plates. "Here ye go. Double-burger, fries, extra mayo." She sat the plate in front of Sam. "Pork chops, mashed taters, black-eyed peas fer you, Cord."

"Thank ye, darlin'. I was just telling Sam here he needs a good woman to keep him from sitting on his brain all the time. Start takin' to life as it should be."

Sam nearly choked on his burger, then spilled his coffee reaching for a napkin. Lily guffawed so loud everybody in the restaurant craned to see the commotion. Including the young man, who only now seemed to notice the officers sitting at the counter, which made him slide lower in the booth.

They quickly finished their lunches. Sam followed Lily to the register while Cord strolled to the back, toothpick dangling out of the corner of his mouth. "That your Fury out there?" He pointed the toothpick out the window.

"Yes, sir." The lanky, sharp-eyed boy squirmed.

"Nice ride." He placed the toothpick back in his mouth and tongued it over to the side. "See you got Georgia plates. Passin' through?"

The young man nodded. "Stayin' with a friend a couple of days." He stammered. "Uh, Lucas. Lucas Monroe."

"Is 'at right?" Cord nodded and removed the toothpick again. "Now that's interestin'. Cause I'm headed to the jailhouse right now to see Lucas. Ain't that somethin'. Small world, eh?"

"Yes sir. It is. I . . . I brought him there to see you." He looked nervously around.

"And where is it you're stayin'? Up at his place over on Neddy?"

"That's right." He nodded, swallowing.

"What's your name, son?"

"Bill, sir. Bill Beloit. You might've seen me on TV, driving the—"

"Well, Mister Beloit. We finished up here?" Cord pointed to the half-eaten burger.

"I am."

"Good. 'Cause I'd like for you to come on down to the station."

Beloit gasped. "What?"

"That's right. Were doin' good 'til you lied about where you were stayin'. Lucas ain't been to his old home for almost a year now. Stays up at Thorn's. And I suspect that's where you're at too. Am I right?"

"I ain't done nothin'. I swear."

"Ain't said ye had, son. Or that you're in trouble. But since your friend Lucas is already there, and you gotta get him when he's done, I don't see any reason not to come on in with us. Do you?"

"Uh, no sir. I don't suppose."

"All right, then. I'm Sheriff McRae." He reached out and shook Beloit's hand, pulling him to his feet. "Most folks 'round here just call me Cord. That's fine with me." He led Beloit to the register. "We'll just square up with Lily here. Then Deputy Whatson will ride with you into town. He loves a hotrod 'bout as good as any I know. Ain't that right, Sam?"

"I do. I sure do, Sheriff." Sam turned to Lily. "What's the young feller here owe, Lil?"

"Five dollars, twenty-five cent." She winked, amused, then rung the tiller open.

"Here ye go." Cord nudged Beloit. "This one's on us. Now, let's take a ride in that there fine automobile." He clapped the boy on the back and pushed him out the door.

They left the restaurant lot, Cord following the black Fury until they pulled side-by-side into the spaces fronting the jail. Sam got out and stroked the hood as Cord stepped around the front. "Mister Beloit tells me he's got two four-barrels sitting atop a high-rise manifold underneath here. Needs that special scoop there just to fit it all in."

"Damn, son. That thing sounded purty going down the road. Not all noisy like some street rods." Cord kicked a front tire. "Don't seem like it's set up for street racin' though."

"Oh. No, Cord." Sam stepped up beside him. "This here's built for them speedways down in North Georgia. Says he wants to run NASCAR one day."

"Yeah? Well, you might get there, if you keep your nose clean, son. Can't do much drivin' if you're locked up." Cord narrowed his eyes at Beloit. "Right?"

"No sir." The boy shook his head. "I'm just here to see Lucas. Then I'm headin' back home to try and get on with a sponsor."

"Speakin' of Lucas. We better get inside and have our little talk, so y'all can get back to your visit. What d'ye say?"

"I reckon."

"Grab that satchel out of my car, Sam." He laid a hand on Beloit's shoulder. "Welcome to my house, son."

When they stepped through the door, Lucas shot up out of the chair he'd been waiting in, blinking first at Cord, then Beloit, then back at Cord again.

"Hey now, Lucas! Look who we ran across over at Lily's. Your buddy, Bill. Been havin' a good conversation. Ain't we?"

Beloit looked anxiously at Lucas. "Told 'em I come up here to see you for a spell. But I'm leavin' soon. Goin' home."

Lucas shook his head. "Come on, Cord. Don't do this. He brought me here to see you, like ye asked. Leave him out of it. He don't even know what fer. About me, nor Thorn, nor anything else. I swear."

"Have a seat, Bill." Cord jerked a thumb at the row of wooden chairs lining the lobby. "Judy. What's the update on that girl?"

"Levon called. Said if we're ready to release the body they'd like to come on down and ready her fer buryin'. Sloan's Funeral Home's fixing up a closed casket. Parents flyin' in on Tuesday."

"Ain't getting her until we're finished with the investigation. Damn it. I shoulda called the parents already. Give me their number, I'll get in touch. Anything from Waddy and Hawkins?"

"Think they found the place where the girl went in the river. Up at Cecil's place, just this side of the Glad Earth Farm."

"Footprints?"

"Couple of different prints. One set's probably from a woman. Sandals, maybe. The other boots, Merrell's, Waddy said. Took pictures and measurements. And they found a trail. Follered it up to the old barbed wire borderin' The Farm. Said they couldn't find any evidence of a struggle."

"Okay." He nodded. "Where's Swan?"

"He took a call out to Joe Lee's place." Judy raised her eyebrows. "Cow fell in a ditch, broke her leg. Backhoe they're usin' to pull her out is holdin' up traffic on Route 9."

Cord shook his head, amused. "Don't say it, Sam."

"What?"

"Udder jokes."

"Catastophe?"

Cord rolled his eyes. "Okay. Guess it'll hold until tomorrow. We'll get a warrant for The Farm and run an honest-to-goodness investigation." He stepped through the gate and held it open. "Come on back to my office, Lucas. We'll talk."

Lucas glanced at Beloit. "Don't say nothin' more."

"But I ain't said. . . ."

"Lucas." Cord sighed. "He's all right. You got bigger worries, partner. Let's see if we can't dig down to the truth of it."

Cord followed him into the office, shut the door. "Lucas, boy." He stepped around the desk and laid his hat on the cot, brim up. "I've known you since you were a nipper." He studied him for a moment, then sat in his chair and leaned back until it creaked. "Watched ye comin' up. Was friends with your pappy. There for your momma after

162

he passed. Me and Lucinda came up to your place and helped clear that scrabby patch of land enough to grow a little vegetable garden.

"And I 'preciate it. But—"

"Please." Cord pointed to a chair. "Park it and hear me out. It weren't out of pity. We thought the world of y'all. Stopped by just to visit. Lucinda and Ida sitting on the porch shellin' peas while you and Blu played in the yard. Planted flowers that first spring so Ida would have some color in her life.

"And you, son." He leaned forward, resting his elbows on the desk. "Showed ye how to kill and butcher your first hog. Taught ye to swim, and fish. Followed your football games before ye dropped outta school.

"I know it ain't been easy. Not since your momma died. And I'm real sorry for that." He shook his head. "But why the hell get mixed up with the likes of Thorn and that bunch? You're smarter than that, Luke." He studied the boy's face, imagining he saw the pale blue eyes briefly brim with tears. But he wasn't sure.

"Look, Cord. I ain't never fergot it. I was too young t' know all it meant when Pappy died. Guess I figured it were normal fer y'all t' come around. But I knew oncet I got up in school an' the other kids had pappys and I didn't." He took a deep breath and looked away blinking. "I never got made fun of, on account you was there. And everbody knew you was." He looked out the window towards the river. "For me.

"But when momma died, somethin' broke." Now he looked back at Cord, eyes truly shining now. "Can't explain it. Too much like all the other reason's fer doin' all the things I ever done. Got sucked down and pulled away. Like one of them cross-currents in the river. I reckon I just did what ye told me. Let go and left the currents t' tug and tow me downstream, holdin' my breath, hopin' I wouldn't drown 'fore I hit the shallows. But I ain't sure they's any smooth waters left down this stream."

Cord stood and walked to the window. The high, wispy clouds seemed lower now, had started to condense. The afternoon light grayer. A red-tailed hawk swooped down over the river, dived into a clump of tall grass above the bank and rose quickly again, clutching something Cord couldn't identify from the distance. But it struggled in the claws. "You're in the calm now, Lucas. But ye gotta swim to the bank." He went back to the desk and perched on a corner. "I'm here."

Lucas peered up. "That girl you was askin' Thorn about?" He hesitated, flushing. "I didn't kill her. We never did really even talk. Last summer, I saw her in the river. Swimming. She was beautiful. Ain't never seen a girl so purty. I just watched her from the banks, at first." He looked away, ashamed. "Too scared t' speak to her. But I started hikin' over to that farm ever week or so after that. Studyin' up on 'em. Tryin' t' figure a way get to know her.

"A couple months back, I came across one of their kids. A little 'un, name of Beam, playin' over by the east stream. Figured maybe he could get us introduced. Made him a little braided strap. Asked him t' give it to her. Made me happy when she started wearin' it." He shook his head. "But I never talked to her. Then, last week, I saw her again in a clearin' down behind the cabin at The Farm. Talkin' to a man I'd seen her with before. Think his name's Levon."

Cord frowned. "You hear what they were sayin'?"

"Looked like she was beggin' him to stop talkin'. She got all mad and started yellin'. Couldn't hear exactly. But there was something she didn't want to give up. Said she couldn't get rid of it. Then she turned and stomped away, crying." He looked up at Cord, eyes hard. "I was gonna beat the hell outta him for makin' her cry, Cord. But another feller, Sunny I think they call him, come up and chased me off." He paused as if just realizing something. "Guess that's why I broke his arm last night."

"You're the one beat on Sunny?"

"I did." He nodded.

Cord stood and paced to the other side of the office. "Goddammit, Lucas. You got yourself in one helluva mess here." He rubbed the scar on his head. "Who else was with you?"

Lucas shook his head. "Can't say."

Cord rolled his eyes, stepped across the floor and leaned down, thrusting his face inches from the boy's. "Now listen here, son. I might believe you didn't have anything to do with what happened to that girl. But you just admitted to another crime. You could've killed somebody last night! Lucky Sunny got out a warning and saved them folks or you mighta been lookin' at something worse than prison."

Lucas slumped in his chair. "I know it."

"Now, this ain't no time for petty loyalties. I'm the only good and loyal friend workin' your side now. Better tell me everything if you want to keep that trust alive. I already know there was three of y'all up there. That Thorn was behind it. This ain't the first time the Reevers clan's used barn burnin' to run folks off. So you might as well talk."

Lucas looked up, steady, determined. "Can't do it Cord. Thorn's been good t' me. And fer all his meanness, they's somethin' good about him. He has my word. I ain't got much left but that now."

Cord straightened, raking a hand through his hair. "How about if it ain't Thorn. What about Rad?"

Lucas thought. "Depends on what else ye got. But I ain't givin' 'em up on my word alone."

"All right, then. That's somethin'." He walked to the interior window that looked onto the outer offices and cracked the blinds. "And what about Speed Racer out there? He in on it?"

"He just come up yesterday. Kinda got hisself in too deep, too fast. Couldn't figure a way out. Ought not fault him fer that."

Cord took a deep breath and sighed. "I need more if I'm gonna cut you any kind of deal." He looked around. "So?"

Lucas hesitated, then nodded. "They're plannin' a big meeting t'night. Keep talkin' about some Nashville connection. Think it has to do with distributing new product. But that's not all. Thorn and Rad been meeting with a feller named Eli from over to The Farm."

"Eli?"

"Yep. Don't know what's stirrin'. But he's in it with 'em."

Cord sat down and looked at the boy across the desk. "Now that puts a whole different spin on things."

Lucas leaned forward. "Cord. The girl? I asked little Beam to keep an eye on her. Talked to him just before I come to see you. He said he saw her with somebody on Friday. He'd seen the man before, talkin' to Levon and Eli. Said the girl called him Lou." He paused and looked away, swallowing. "He said Zoe told him they was gonna get married."

"Lou and Zoe, married?"

"That's what Beam said. That she told him they was runnin' off to do it. But last Friday they started fightin' about a necklace. Said Lou shoved her down. Scared Beam pretty bad."

"What the hell?" Cord leaned back in his chair. "What kind of damn necklace?"

"Somethin' hangin' on a purple ribbon."

Now he remembered. In the clutter of Lou's nightstand, a purple ribbon. Among the various medals and ribbons he'd figured were commendations from Lou's service with the Army. He made a mental note to revisit the crime scene. Could be more hard evidence there linking Levon to the girl's murder.

"Right." Cord stood and stretched, looking through the blinds again. "Here's what we're gonna do. I'll cut you and Beloit loose. Thorn'll know something's up if I hold you. You high-tail it back up to Thorn's and hang tight. If things get dicey tonight, keep your head down. Don't do anything stupid. Keep yourself alive. And that boy too." He nodded out the window at Beloit, who sat drumming his fingers on the chair rail.

"Yes, sir."

"Tell him keep his cool if he wants to live to see another NASCAR race, let alone drive in one. Besides. Doc says he's runnin' out of room in the morgue."

15
Rocky Shoals

Goddamn little pricks, Thorn thought as he stood at the sink looking out over the valley, sipping on his coffee. What the hell Lucas thinkin' takin' Beloit along with him? And he'd told that Beloit sonofabitch t' stay away from town. Fuckin' young'uns never listened.

The night before hadn't gone well. He'd expected it to be easy. Start a couple of fires. Rattle his competition. Get a good blood-rushing ride in a dual-quad road machine and check out the new driver all in one. Instead, they'd almost been caught. Might well have killed a man. And to top it off, he'd woken with a blasting hangover and a premonition that plans for picking up a new distribution and a new product line might be in trouble. And after finally stumbling downstairs to put some coffee on and grab a nip of whiskey, he'd checked the security tapes and realized the trouble might just be getting started.

He didn't like it. They'd left before the boss got up. Not saying a word to anybody. He looked at the clock above the stove. Plenty of time to adjust his plans in case they got tied up in some mess in town.

He decided to re-route the drivers. Take the decoy haul into Damascus instead of Abington. The ride was more hazardous, distribution lines more complicated. But at this point he didn't know what the boys might've given up, so he couldn't take any chances.

"If it ain't one thing, it's your mother." He stepped over Homer, an old coon dog he'd taken in years back. The mangy stray had seen Thorn through more tussles and territorial battles than any of his men had.

"Them two'll be lucky t' survive the night if they mess up this run, buddy." The dog followed him outside onto a raised deck, hobbling on an arthritic hip. "Come on, Homer. Ain't got all day."

Thorn stood for a couple of minutes studying the sky. From here, he could see all the way to Bull's Gap. Sometimes Rogersville, on a clear day. He often wondered what his pappy, Frank, would think about the changes he'd made to the operation. Not just the business, but the whole new approach with the land and the treatment of the people living on it. For Thorn, buying and distributing meth (or weed or moonshine like his pappy had) was just the simplest, most profitable way to change the poverty and suffering he'd grown up in. There wasn't any other option he could see. He'd watched plenty of law-abiding folk suffer along trying to bring home a fair and honest wage. Folks who'd rather die than take a handout. They'd been crushed by the bureaucracy, the companies, and the wrong-headed intentions of do-gooders.

Way he figured, he had the means to provide a product that caused no more harm than thousands of other goods sold on the open market. Along the way, he provided jobs to men and women who desperately needed to feel they were worth more than dirt. More than the aw-shucks actors that the rest of the country laughed at on television and in movies, as if they were real.

Sure, what he did was illegal. Didn't measure up to the morals of some. No matter that he'd never stripped a mountain of timber, nor dug out its guts, releasing deadly poisons into the mountain creeks like those big-money corporations. Never dammed a river, like the government. They could care less about the people, the land, or wildlife that roamed the hills. The tender affections at the very heart of all those who truly loved these mountains.

Not that he'd ever fooled himself that there weren't some terrible consequences, too, that came from all he'd done. The whorehouses, the bar, and the scrap metal yard he used to launder money carried with them the seeds of bloody violence, loss, and heartache. That was just the way of things. But it wasn't like those problems would disappear if he closed shop. Somebody else always filled the need for such vices. Besides, way he saw it, he kept the corruption from spreading by running out the competition. And until recently, the town leaders had all agreed, tacitly approving what he did by encouraging the law to turn a blind eye as long as the violence was kept to a minimum.

But things had gotten a little more dicey since Cord had taken over.

Even before Pappy Frank had died, Cord had tried to convince Thorn there was a way to use his talents outside the family business. He wasn't quite a do-gooder, like some. But Cord had seemed to spot something in Thorn that gave hope he could be brought over to the other side.

He was wrong. Thorn loved this life like he loved his family. He'd been born to it and wanted nothing more than to live this way until it killed him. As, of course, it probably would. Someday.

But not today, he thought, draining the cup, turning to get back in the house.

"So ye think I oughter let them boys live, Homer?" He held the door for the dog, then closed it to shut out the cold. "I ain't quite made up my mind. Reckon I'll at least hear their story." He glanced down and patted Homer's boxy head. "I always did fancy a good story."

"Get 'em up now, Rad!" he yelled from the bottom of the stairs. "Loadin' and haulin' t' get done today."

He poured another cup of coffee, then ambled downstairs to his office. Needed to call his distributors in Abington to let them know the shipment wouldn't be making it in tonight. They'd be mad as hell, but he'd promise to send an extra load next run, no charge. Ought to keep them happy. Next he'd call contacts in Damascus to make sure they had the capacity to store and distribute the large quantity of product he'd be sending up their way. Finally, he'd call his suppliers and let them know they'd need to switch their schedules and routes to include a stop in Damascus instead of Abington.

He'd just finished the first call when someone knocked. Rad opened the door and leaned in. "Lucas and Beloit ain't here." He scratched his head. "Want me t' go lookin fer 'em?"

Thorn leaned back in his chair. "They'll show up soon enough. Told Lucas t' talk to the sheriff. Probably just took Beloit along since he still ain't got a driver's license." He didn't really believe it himself. Lucas preferred walking to driving. Loved hiking the hills, regularly crossing over the ridge several times a week to visit folks in town.

Rad nodded. "All right. So, reckon I'll ride out and make sure the boys is gettin' everthing packed an' ready fer t'night."

"Load up an extra truck. Make sure we have enough decoys. Don't want any tails on us. I still ain't so sure Beloit's ready. If we get the law on our ass, he might outrun 'em, but he might not. Did Eli ever get back to us on a location for the meeting?"

"Supposed to call this afternoon."

"He damn well better come through. After last night, we need to drive some nails into that coffin. Tired of outsiders comin' in here, thinkin' they can muscle in on my territory." He frowned at Rad. "You find that computer?"

"No."

"Damn it. Well, won't matter after tonight. We'll get what we need one way or another."

Rad perked up. "Eli might still come through for us."

Thorn snorted. "Hell, I ain't countin' on it. Never did trust a man with divided loyalties." He waved a hand. "Go on now. And top off them tanks. I'm changing the decoy run to Damascus."

"Damascus? What the hell, Thorn. Those twistin', hilly roads add an hour to the drive and near empty a tank. And that's if the weather holds. Thought you had it all lined out."

"I do. And we're sendin' our boys to Damascus." His voice was hard, impatient. "Got a problem here?"

"No." Rad shook his head. "Just wonderin's all."

"Then get to it. Run starts at midnight."

Thorn turned back to the phone as Rad clomped up the steps. Fifteen minutes later, he heard the front door open.

"See ye, Thorn," Rad hollered down from the top of the stairs.

"Load 'em right. I'll see ye back here tonight."

He made the last call, then walked upstairs to refill his cup. Homer lay down at his feet, groaning as he settled.

"Wisht but I could trust 'em, ol' boy." Homer gazed up as Thorn patted him on the head. "Onliest thing I don't like about the business. Can't never trust nobody. Not really."

At least not since Jesse Ellen, he thought.

Jesse Ellen had moved to Falston to live with her aunt and uncle fifteen years ago. Her father had been sent to prison for murdering Jesse Ellen's mother. She'd been sixteen at the time. Took a job at her uncle's hardware store, working at Asa's after school and on weekends. Thorn had driven over to pick up a fifty-pound sack of rye meal one Saturday and saw her there behind the register.

He hadn't fallen for the kid right away, though she was pretty enough. Medium height, not too slim. Short, dark, wavy brown hair. But it was her eyes, so dark and deep they glistened, that he'd noticed right away. It was those eyes he still remembered most.

Eventually, he'd asked her out. Thorn had been slow to press her for more than she was willing to give. Over the next year, his patience paid off in Jesse Ellen's growing trust. She never judged him, nor the life he'd chosen to make a living at. Instead, her own experience with poverty and violence had somehow helped her understand how he was trying to build something to benefit more than just rich folks. She saw the good in him. Had trusted he'd never do anything, if he could help it, to hurt anyone who didn't deserve hurting.

After a year, she'd consented to marry him. But a month before the wedding, a late March snow-storm socked in the mountains. And that weekend, as she was riding to work with her Aunt Dory, a local drunk named Caddis Colby ran a stop-sign and T-boned their car. Dory was laid up in the hospital for a month with broken ribs and a cracked wrist. Jesse Ellen had been ejected from the car, flung like a broken doll out into the cold, dark morning. She'd landed twenty yards away and slammed against an oak, breaking her neck instantly. She was pronounced dead at the scene.

Thorn had paid for the funeral and services, but was shaken so badly he could barely remain on his feet through the burial. He'd never loved anyone so deeply. Had never known a love like that of Jesse Ellen. He'd decided then, looking down into that dark, wet hole slowly filling with snow melt and mud, that he'd never trust that kind of love again. It was too dangerous.

Caddis Colby was found a week later hung from the rafters in his barn, a beer bottle stuffed down his throat. Since then, Thorn had believed in only one kind of justice. Quick, and violent.

Now, he heard the low rumble of the Fury outside and gulped down the last swallow of his lukewarm coffee. "Better keep yer head down, Homer. Could get rough."

He marched through the front door to the driveway before the car had a chance to stop. As Beloit shut down, Thorn yanked open the door and pulled him out by his collar. "You little fuckin' shithead, you." He threw him on the ground and kicked him in the ribs.

Beloit curled and covered his head, holding one hand up. "Please, Thorn. Wait. Please."

Thorn bent, grabbed him by the front of his shirt and yanked him back to his feet. "I told you t'stay here!" He slapped him before Lucas made it around from the other side of the car and grabbed his arm.

"Stop, Thorn! Stop it! It were my fault, not his!"

Thorn flung Beloit to the ground and turned on Lucas, driving him back against the doorframe, forearm pressed against his throat. "And

172

you. Knew I didn't want that boy t' show hisself in town and you took him anyways! I oughter kill you right now. But a beatin'll do." He swung his right fist and bone cracked as blood spewed from the boy's nose.

He stepped back as Lucas crumpled, soaking up the blood with one sleeve. Thorn stabbed a finger a him. "You stay right there, or I'll shoot you."

He turned and stepped over to Beloit, who'd risen to his knees. Drew the pistol, pressed it against the top of his head and cocked the hammer. "Beloit, I gave direct orders that you disobeyed. Don't know how I could've been more clear than I was, last night."

The boy looked up, shaking his head. "Please, Thorn. I didn't do anything. Didn't talk to nobody. I swear. Just don't kill me. Please."

Thorn laid the hammer down again, slowly, with his thumb. Then raised the pistol and brought the butt down hard against the side of Beloit's head. He collapsed in a heap on pavement, blood oozing onto the asphalt drive, and didn't move.

"Now pick up that sorry sonofabitch and bring him inside," he barked at Lucas. "We need t' talk."

Lucas stood, staggered over, picked up the unconscious boy and carried him to the house. Inside, he followed Thorn downstairs and laid Beloit on a couch. The boy shook his head against the cushions and blinked his eyes open, wincing against the pain and light.

"Get him a cold rag. Then step into my office."

In a couple of minutes, Lucas was standing in the doorway, watching Thorn wipe the blood off his knuckles. "Grab some ice outta the freezer, then sit down." Lucas stepped out to the bar to grab a couple ice cubes, then returned and sat in the chair next to the desk.

Thorn stood up over him and placed his thumbs on either side of the boy's nose. "Gonna hurt," he said, then quickly pressed the thumbs together, crunching bones of the broken, crooked nose back into place.

"Shit! God dammit, Thorn!" Lucas jerked his head away, tears swelling, cupping his nose.

173

Thorn handed him the bloody rag. "Wrap them cubes up and lay it 'twixt yer eyes. You'll be all right." He sat down and studied the boy's face. Finally he said, "When ye first come t' work for me, I didn't know how you'd fit in. Figured to use ye like the others, fetchin' supplies and such. But you studied them websites and learned how to put in a fine security system. Not only that, set up other systems for the stills and meth labs. Probably saved my ass last year when all those busts were goin' down.

"So I come to trust ye, Lucas. You was straight with me. Carried more sense than most. This is the first time y'ever done somethin' made me unhappy. So, I'm gonna give ye a chance t' explain why." He leaned forward, eyes narrowing. "Just the one chance. So get it right." He leaned back and waited.

Lucas held the rag to his nose for a moment then dropped it in his lap. "Ye want fer me t' explain how I was skeered? Skeered 'cause that girl what drowned was the same I'd been watchin' and follerin' over at that farm fer months. And when she showed up dead, wearin' a braided anklet I'd made, figured the sheriff'd arrest me fer sure.

"Then when Cord come round here, pullin' you into my mess, I got more skeered." He paused. "But not of you. Hell, Thorn. You've done more fer me than anybody since Momma died. I'd do anything t' keep from bringin' trouble yer way. And that's what skeered me. Thinkin' I'd brought the cops snoopin' around.

"So this mornin' I just wanted to get into town, quick. Get things straightened out, like you tole me to. That's why I took Beloit. That, and I didn't want t' try and explain to you and Rad how I'd fallen fer a dead girl I ain't never even spoke to." He hung his head and fell silent.

Thorn had to admit, the boy could tell a story straight. "Okay, Lucas-boy. I believe ye. But tell me this: how come they didn't arrest you?"

"Cause I didn't do it, Thorn! I didn't kill Zoe. Just gave her a braided band, is all." He looked up, hesitant. Thorn caught a glimpse of deep sadness behind the boy's eyes. "That's as close as I got t' knowin' her." He shook his head, grimacing. "Just don't seem right, Thorn. It ain't right."

Thorn sighed and patted him on the knee. "It never is, boy. Never is."

16
Hell or High Water

The smell of charred wood, burned grass, paper, plastic, and fabric still lingered as Levon visited the families in the other six lodges. Each of them now trying to make room for ten to fifteen new occupants. He'd spent the first hours after the fire trying to reassure everyone they'd be safe now. To quell the panic that had started to spread. Some of the men had expressed a desire to pack it up and pull out, fearing that other attacks might end in more casualties, or even death.

Carl Gleason, at forty-two an elder, had approached him with a group of five other men. "Look, Levon. We're all believers. You know that." He pulled on his beard. "But we got families here. Kids. Didn't sign up for this." He tilted his chin toward the charred lodge, then glanced at the others, who nodded agreement. "Me and the wife just wanted a place to raise our kids off the grid. Give 'em a safe upbringin'. Didn't know we were movin' to a war zone."

"Carl. Listen." Levon kept his gaze steady, voice even. "I get it. But please. Don't quit. Not now. We've already come so far. We can make this work. Can't you see?" He spread his arms. "Your leaving is exactly what these damned backwards, ignorant hillbilly arsonists want. Put a scare on you all and send you packing." He gestured across the hallow. "But look around. This is the promised land. The place you and your wife dreamed of. A brave new world we're building for your children and grandchildren." He sighed. "It's here. But you and the others gotta brace yourselves up."

Carl took a deep breath, turned and gazed across the hollow at the men, women and children struggling to pull debris and salvage from the ashes of the burned out lodges. "We're scared, Levon."

He nodded. "I know. But it sometimes takes sacrifices to make paradise, Carl. You knew that when you joined up." He stepped forward and placed a hand on his shoulder. "We'll protect our people. I promise. I've already talked to Eli. We're installing more cameras on the perimeter and closing off gaps in the fencing. Breezy's setting up to post watches. In the meantime, I need you to stay. Please. And pray for courage. Like Moses battling the Canaanites, call upon him to gird your soul and smite those who would move against his chosen people."

Carl glanced at the other men, biting his lip. "All right," he said, finally. "I'll stay. But I don't speak for the others. They'll have to make their own choices."

Levon shook his hand and watched as the group moved off, talking amongst themselves. He'd probably lose a few of them, but for now, he'd kept the largest contingent of the community intact.

Next he began to organize clean-up details, finding and salvaging the video equipment, making arrangements for new housing assignments. The old system had come about gradually, naturally, the young folks taking up with cliques of friends and relatives. The people with whom they felt most comfortable. But now, with twenty-five extra bodies to shelter, Levon thought it would be easier if he worked out the logistics himself. They'd have time to switch to more comfortable arrangements after everything settled down and they'd raised funds to build new longhouses. Problem was, the farm had already started to feel more like an army base than an open village of loving brothers and sisters.

No helping that, he thought. Not yet. But he wanted revenge. Thorn was probably behind the arson, and as soon as they connected with their contacts in Nashville, he'd show the fucking inbred hillbilly some real low-country vengeance.

Two good things, however, had come of the arson. First, he and Lilith were again on speaking terms—at least for the interim. She'd immediately jumped in and organized the women to care for those injured trying to put out the fires. She also started a sort of relief warehouse, collecting household items and clothes from those who could spare so the folks who'd lost everything could at least have the essentials.

And just as important, she'd been there beside Levon, convincing others to stay. Commiserating, giving solace and comfort to those who felt their dreams of a better world had gone up with the blaze and smoke—assuring them it was all still there, if they'd only keep the faith. That she did, and more as the day wore on. Reminding Levon, once again, why he loved her so much in the first place.

Second, Eli had stepped up into a leadership role, without the normal rancor and ill-will toward the perpetrators of the crime Levon would've expected from him. Instead he focused on organizing the men and women for clean-up efforts, contacted the mill owner and arranged to have a load of salvage lumber picked up that could be used to build temporary shelters, and set up teams of skilled and unskilled carpenters to start clearing out and leveling land to build on. In the process, he'd stayed on a positive note, helping reassure the others, encouraging them to stay on.

But through it all, Levon couldn't stop worrying about the damned necklace. He hadn't found it in Zoe's lodge, which he'd searched the day before the fire. It wasn't in her personal belongings. He'd even asked about it when he'd called the morgue to find out when the body would be released. He couldn't believe she'd have gotten rid of it, no matter how mad she was at him. And it wasn't in her nature to destroy a gift, even one given under less-than-appropriate circumstances.

Now, sitting in the office, he wondered how he could've let the chance to get it back when she was alive slip through his fingers. If it turned up and Cord found out about it, he'd be in real trouble.

The door opened and Lilith walked in, followed by Eli and Maya. "Hey." Lilith stepped behind the desk and placed a hand on his shoulder. "You okay?"

"Yeah. Just beat is all. And worried about Sunny."

"Didn't anybody tell you?" Maya stepped to the side of the desk opposite Lilith. "The doctor called half an hour ago. Said he was all stitched and bandaged and we could pick him up anytime." She sat on the corner of the desk and swiped a stray hank of hair behind his ear. "Want me to go get him?"

"Might not be a bad idea. I'm still waiting for a call from Zoe's parents. We'll need someone at the airport to pick them up if they decide to travel in."

"I'll talk to the boys and get a volunteer." Eli grabbed the doorknob to leave. "We'll clean out a van."

"Hold up, Eli." Levon brushed Maya's lingering hand away and leaned forward on his elbows. "That'll wait, man. Sit down a minute. Let's talk."

"Sure." Eli crossed to sit on the couch and pulled off his hat. "Been a busy one, man." He ran fingers through his hair. "Probably need to start thinkin' about dinner."

"Slow down, brother. We got time. I need to let you know how much I appreciate your work today. You really made me proud, man. No shit."

Eli fiddled with the brim of the hat. "Just tryin' to do what's needed."

"Look at me, Eli. You did. But you helped them even more by the way you acted. If ever there was a time to lose your cool, today was the day. Instead, you looked after everyone. Kept their needs upmost in your words and actions. You went beyond today. You started to act like a shepherd. Guided the flock and kept them calm. Didn't let your own feelings get in the way of doing the right thing for the people."

Eli smiled and nodded. "Thanks, Levon. Well, I don't know . . . something happened out there this morning when I saw everybody running around, all panicked and scared. Guess I saw not only those homes going up in flames, but our whole commune." He paused, reflecting. "So I knew, for the first time, how important it was. Not just for me, but for everyone here."

Levon leaned back. "I know, Eli. I know. And thanks again."

He nodded and stood to leave.

"Hang on, Eli." Maya reached in front of Levon and pulled the top drawer open. "Pass me the papers." She grabbed the dope tin and pointed.

"Not sure that's the best idea if you're driving into town." Levon raised his brows.

"What do you think they're going to do, old man? Stop me for driving too slow?" She sprinkled sticky weed into the crease, licked the paper, rolled it and reached for the lighter. Levon picked it up and lit the end. She drew a deep toke, then passed it over.

"Definitely need it after a morning like this one." He hit it long, held the smoke in his lungs for a moment and exhaled, coughing. "Damn." He passed it to Lilith. "We're starting to get some good crop."

"No doubt about that." She squeezed out the words, trying to hold back the hit. "And it sounds terrible to say." She exhaled and shook her head. "But Zoe was one of our best breeders. Really knew her cannabis."

Eli stepped up behind her. "She's not even buried yet. Show some respect."

Lilith laid a palm on his cheek. "Didn't mean anything by it, Eli. I loved her like a mother. You know that." She offered the joint.

He waved it away. "Still a lot to do. I'll catch some later, when I can relax." He walked across the room to the loom, studying the patterns in the weave. "I know you cared about her. Didn't mean nothing."

Levon took the joint and pulled another toke. "He's had a hard day, Lilith." The smoke rolled out of his mouth as he spoke. "And just trying to remind us she was so much more to this group. Had a spirit of justice, generosity. She reminded me of you." He looked at her through the haze.

"Well, I still love ya, Eli." She stood and walked to the door. "I'm going to pick up Sunny." She cocked her head at Maya. "You coming, girl? Levon's got work to do. The folks could probably use a good sermon tonight. Maybe something from The Mount."

Maya kissed Levon, then followed Lilith.

"Any news on the computer, Eli?"

"No. But I heard Lou died last night."

"Fuck!" Levon shot up and paced behind the desk. "What the hell are we gonna do? Those badass minuteman wannabes gonna be madder 'n hell if we show up without Lou. All the coordinates and contacts were in that computer."

"I know. I'm worried too. Maybe now's not the time to make this move. We've got a good crop of sensemilla bud back on the south slope. Enough to get us through winter."

"No, goddammit. Now is the time." Levon leaned against the desk and closed his eyes, thinking. "Okay. Here's the deal. Those fuckheads will be happy as hogs in shit to have a chance to get out from under the Mexican cartels. We'll toss them an ounce of that Afghani Smack for a sample, let them know we're open for business. Those fucks won't know from shit if we can deliver. Right?"

Eli nodded, looking skeptical. "But they'll be expecting more. And soon."

"We got the beginning and end of the supply and distribution line. All we'll need to do is fill in the gaps. I got my Fort Bragg and Fort Benning connections. More coming online all the time. It'd be nice to have all Lou's contacts, but let's work with what we got, for now. We need to fill out our arsenal."

"Okay." Eli pulled on his hat. "So where and when?"

"Caggle Knob. Tonight. One A.M.. I'm posting Sebastian and Zippy on the west ridge for cover in case it gets ugly. You'll be with me. Should go just fine. How are the girls?"

"We've got them settled into Lodge Three, but it'll take time to get us back online. Pretty much all the equipment was lost in the fire. I can pick up new webcams tomorrow or Tuesday, but it'll take several days to get everything installed. Lilith said we're losing a couple thousand a week."

"Fuck me! When it rains it sure as hell fuckin' pours. I was counting on that cash. We'll need it more than ever if this deal goes through."

"Look, Levon. Maybe I haven't always been the most level-headed of the group, but I've got a bad feeling about rolling on that deal tonight. Our plan to build more lodges and another barn for an arsenal has to be moved back months now because of the fire. And we still need to get the rest of the men on board to beef up our security. Not to mention we need more electronic surveillance, and a better fence around the whole perimeter down to the river. I'm just not sure we're ready for a move like this. Hell, you think the cartels aren't going to be pissed off when we take their business?"

"Goddammit, Eli! You think I don't fuckin' know that already? But if we don't move now, we may lose those Afghan contacts forever. Can't afford that. The profits on just four kilos of uncut heroin could turn this farm into a fortress. Buy the resources we need to complete our plans. Won't fuckin' argue anymore. It's a risk. But one I'm damn well ready to take. It'll buy what we need to move into final phase of chaos we're gonna rain down on this system. Keep your eye on the game, Eli."

"Okay." His voice was flat. "You're the boss. I'll get the boys ready."

Levon held up a hand. "Eli. I ain't your 'boss.' Just need you to understand this is our chance. The opportunity we've been working toward for three years now, like I said. You done good today. Just hang in a little longer. Can I count on you?"

"Yeah." He nodded. "You can count on me."

"Good. See you at the service."

Eli stepped out the door. Levon leaned his head back and stared up at the rough beams crossing the ceiling. Took another toke, closed his eyes, and reviewed the words of The Sermon:

And seeing the multitudes, he went up into a mountain: and when he was set, his disciples came unto him:

And he opened his mouth, and taught them, saying,

Blessed are the poor in spirit: for theirs is the kingdom of heaven.

Blessed are they that mourn: for they shall be comforted.

Blessed are the meek: for they shall inherit the earth.

Blessed are they which do hunger and thirst after righteousness: for they shall be filled.

Blessed are the merciful: for they shall obtain mercy.

Blessed are the pure in heart: for they shall see God.

Blessed are the peacemakers: for they shall be called the children of God.

Blessed are they which are persecuted for righteousness' sake: for theirs is the kingdom of heaven.

Blessed are ye, when men shall revile you, and persecute you, and shall say all manner of evil against you falsely, for my sake.

"And these were the words he spake," Levon said out loud. "And every one that heareth these sayings and doeth them not, shall be likened unto a foolish man, which built his house upon the sand: and the rain descended, and the floods came, and the winds blew, and beat upon that house; and it fell: and great was the fall of it."

183

He pinched the roach off into the ashtray and leaned back in his chair. This whole damned fucked up world is gonna fall, he thought. Bound to happen. A dream built on sand. All I need to do is pour on some water and wash it away.

He shook his head, and got up stretching. "Well, fuck." He muttered. "Better get out there and calm the sheep."

17

The Distant Shore

Cord had just started reading through Lou's Moleskin notebook when Sam knocked on the door. "It's open." He tossed the notebook on the office cot.

Sam stepped in. "Thought you'd like to know. Waddy and Junior have been going through Lou's personals. Got his cell phone, and found a Chromebook in his backpack."

"I'll be damned. He had it with him the whole time. Whoever ransacked Fred's place was probably looking for it."

"Junior's going through it now. No hidden files. Looks like he mostly used it for email and surfing the web. But there's one site he'd browsed recently called Magdalenes4U.com. Looks like Levon's taking his religious order right into hell. You should take a look."

Cord swiveled in his chair, grabbed the computer mouse, clicked open the browser and punched in the address. He quickly clicked through the eighteen-or-over permission screen, then leaned back. Just beneath the pink and purple bubble-font web name, GLAD MAGDALENES—ALL NUDE VIRGINS—LIGHT YOUR WICK!, the faces of eleven young women were tiled. A caption beneath each contained their name and the story of each woman's conversion experiences. Underneath the photos, a blinking header read: "Cum to us, dear Lord," followed by a brief site introduction:

There is only one God. Each man is made in His image. From the beginning of time, God has given man dominion over woman. On this site, you will find the true followers of Christ. The thirteenth disciple, Mary Magdalene's devotion to Jesus set the example for all Christian women to follow. If you would see the world restored to its original sinless beauty, follow us to a heaven on earth. The cost for maintaining this site is considerable. We allow a one-time free tour. Thereafter, you will be asked to pay a small tithe to support our work.

Cord clicked on the photo of a woman he recognized from The Farm, name of Ruth. A page popped up with an "Under Construction" message stating that the site was down due to server problems. The background wallpaper was a rose circled with thorns, shot through with a crucifix. Other information on the page listed a one-year subscription to the full site, live shots and live sex included, for just ten dollars a month. Nothing strictly illegal, unless the women being used hadn't given permission. But Cord had a hunch they hadn't.

"Shit. A porn site. Levon's got these women turned into virtual whores."

"And according to Junior, Lou was on this site last week. Nothing before that." Sam raised an eyebrow. "Welcome to the new world religion."

"Yeah, right. Unless these women didn't know they were being filmed. And Levon's got 'em so under his spell won't none of them talk to us."

Cord sighed. "Let's see if we can't take another run at them tomorrow. I've already ordered a warrant to check out Zoe's death. Bet one or two wouldn't be none too happy if they knew what was really going on. Sunny sure didn't act like he knew anything about the video equipment when I mentioned it."

"Sounds good. And on Lou's phone, we found recent calls out to The Farm. A few more to a cell we're trying to trace. Don't know why he'd be callin'." Sam sat on the edge of the desk. "But I don't think he was trying to join the congregation."

"Probably calling Zoe."

"The dead girl?"

"Yup. When I interviewed Lucas, he said that little boy, Beam, had seen the two of them arguing. Complicates things. Got two suspects now. Levon Gladson has a motive for murder if Zoe found out about the website and didn't want any part of it. On the other hand, Lou and Zoe were having some kind of lover's spat. Beam said Lou pushed her down. Happened last Friday." Cord leaned back and rubbed the scar. "But we still haven't found anything on Lou's computer or phone that'd explain why anyone would kill Fred. This is all connected, somehow. I want to head back out to his place tomorrow and take another look around." He clicked the window shut on the browser. "Nothing more we can do tonight. So, let's talk about the meeting Lucas told us about."

Sam walked over to the map hanging on the side wall. "Waddy and Swan been keeping tabs on Thorn's boys for the past month. No pinpoint on the stills or labs, but we got a pretty good idea where they roll the hauls in and out. Waddy called in an hour ago. Rad left out this afternoon and made stops at several of those locations. Vans and trucks goin' in, but not comin' back out. Probably loading a haul. I think Thorn's plannin' to make a delivery, soon. Maybe tonight." He pointed at the map. "Problem is, the locations under surveillance probably aren't the only places they got labs hidden. I'd guess there's two or three more I haven't been able to get a line on yet."

"Show me the five you think are most likely. We'll bring in all the boys and put a car on each of 'em. They'll have to ride solo. Except for Hawkins." He winked. "He can double up with you."

"Don't make me ride with that sonofabitch. He'll be more ornery than a bear woke in the winter."

Cord chuckled. "No doubt. But I can't afford to have him on his own tonight. He'll run straight up to Thorn's and tip him off."

"What about you? Why not take him for a little Josephine ride-along."

"Won't do, buddy. I'm chasing Thorn's ride tonight. He didn't bring that hot-shot driver up here just so he could sit up in that safe, secure mansion on the hill. He's moving with them. I think this run is just a cover. Tonight's about that meeting."

He hiked a thigh on top of the desk and crossed his arms. "That man's got a bug for excitement. Ain't done nothin' risky since those meth labs got busted last year. He's gettin' flabby and knows it. Saw it in his face yesterday. That's why he brought that souped-up Fury here. For the thrill." Cord smiled, thinking about his own heightened vitality the past few days as well. "And I'm gonna be there to pump some blood into it."

"Well. I wouldn't get too cocksure. That Beloit? He can drive. And that car's a flat-ass runnin' sonofabitch. Ain't no lie."

"I've got an advantage. I know these roads like a coon dog knows scent. And, I won't have a mean-ass, cold-blooded, gun-tottin' bastard like Thorn sittin' beside me hollerin' in my ear."

"Got a point." Sam stood to leave. "Reckon I'll get out there and tell the boys to get ready for a long one tonight."

"Call Ollie in. When he gets here, send him up to relieve Waddy."

Sam nodded and stepped out to the bullpen.

Cord took a deep breath to suppress the familiar tightening in his gut, the pressure behind his eyes that made it hard to focus. Damn, but he needed a drink. He pulled open the drawer, slugged down the shot left in the jar, then screwed the lid on and tossed the empty back in the drawer. Grabbed his hat and marched out. "I'll be right back," he called to Judy as he pushed through the gate.

He pointed Josephine towards Arlen Creek Road. It was still early enough on a Sunday to hope he wouldn't run into anyone but Slim. Just a quick nip and he'd be gone.

He pulled down the dirt and gravel cut-off of Arlen Creek and stopped in front of the Lost Cove shack. Harp Lincoln was leaning back in a chair propped against the outside wall, cap tipped over his eyes. When Cord stepped up on the porch, Harp nodded awake and tilted up the brim of his cap.

"Cord." He squinted through the light of the late-afternoon setting sun. "Didn't 'spect t' see ye here t'day." He pushed away from the wall and let the front legs of the chair drop to the floor. "Slim's down checkin' the dock. Few fellers got out there last night fightin'. Tore down a rail." Harp chuckled, pulled out a can of snuff and dug a pinch out. "Almost drownded the both of 'em. Weren't fer Bo Callum throwin' out an inner-tube, reckon they might've."

"That's fine, Harp." He looked past him. "Anybody else here?"

"Hell no." He stuck the dip in his mouth. "Slim run 'em off this mornin'. Said they didn't need t' be lazin' round here all day fer nuthin'."

Cord nodded. "Well I'm kind of in a hurry. So I'm gonna step inside and grab me a nip. Tell Slim when he makes it back up."

"All right then." Harp balanced the chair back against the wall and tugged the bill of the cap down over his eyes again.

Cord pulled the screen door open and hurried to the back where Slim kept the cooler and a couple cases of shine. The boxes weren't there. He quickly looked behind the counter, rummaging under shelves and through containers of assorted fishing tackle. Then he heard the screen door squeak and looked up.

"Hey, Cord. What ye lookin' fer?" Slim strolled into the room, ambled over to a cabinet behind the counter and put away the hammer and nails he'd been using to repair the rail.

"Just thought I get a quick nip. Couldn't find none in the back."

Slim wiped his nose with the back of one big hand and snickered. "Shit, Cord. Ran out last night. First time in months." He walked to the cooler, pulled out a beer and popped the cap, letting the lid drop on the floor. "Ain't been able to restock fer a couple weeks now. Thorn's been having problems with a couple of his black pots. Weren't able to get me the usual order." He took a long swig, wiped his mouth and held the bottle up. "Got plenty of these if ye want."

Cord shook his head. "Hell no. Need some of that mash I know you got stashed." He strode from behind the counter, grabbed the bottle from Slim and slammed it back down on the table next to them. "So get your ass back there and bring me out a quart 'fore I decide to shut this place down for public nuisance."

Slim backed through the door leading to a storage room. Cord heard boxes being moved, the tinkle of glass on glass. Then Slim reappeared carrying two mason jars. "Here ye go, buddy. Ye know I always take care of ye, Cord. Ye just ain't been around as much of late. These here Thorn dropped off a few days back. Showed up with Rad and some long-haired, tattooed feller." He handed over the jars.

"Tattoos. Seen him before?"

"Naw. Figured Thorn was just showin' some new buyer the product."

"Catch a name?"

"Think it was Eli." He chuckled. "Membered it 'cause of that 'ol Three Dog Night song."

"Thanks, Slim." He nodded. "You helped me more than you know." He held up the jars. "Only said one."

"At's all right. No charge. Atter all ye done fer me, keepin' the boys straight whenever things get outta hand. Take 'em both. You'll need 'em again sooner or later."

"All right, Slim. I appreciate it." He turned to leave then stopped. "A word of advice. Stock up on that beer. Never know when things might get dry around here."

On the way out, Harp leaned forward and spat, then brushed the tobacco juice from his bushy moustache. "Ye keep 'er straight now, Cord. I'll see ye 'round the next bend." He smiled and leaned back against the wall.

"See ye 'round, Harp."

He flopped down in the front seat and put one jar in the glove box beside a little .380 Kel-Tec he carried for emergencies. He twisted the lid off the other and swigged a gulp. It went down easy this time, his body starting to remember the bite of it.

Now that's some strange bedfellows, he thought. Thorn and Eli. What the hell those two cookin' up? Wonder if Levon knows his right-hand man may be pulling some left-handed shakes. He twisted on the lid, cranked the engine, backed up the drive and spun the car around, slinging rock and pebbles as he powered to the road.

The radio crackled just as he turned onto Bainport. "Cord."

He snatched up the mic. "Yeah, Judy."

"Waddy called in. Said Rad showed up at Thorn's driving a van."

"Thanks. Be there in fifteen. Out."

Thorn must be planning to use a couple vehicles, the car and the van. Maybe a little diversion in the works. The warmth of the liquor rose to his head, and the tension eased. "Got to keep it steady, boy," he muttered. "The game's afoot."

He pulled up at the station just as Judy was leaving. She bent down and stuck her head through the passenger window. "You call the wife?"

"Did."

"Cord. I can smell it on you, honey." She put her hand on his cheek. "Be careful tonight."

"Sure. Sure I will." He patted her hand and smiled. "Now get on home, and I'll see you in the morning. I promise."

She straightened, pulled her coat closer against the cold and took a deep breath. "All right, then. G'night."

Cord watched her walk to her car, admiring those round, shapely hips and long legs stretching out beneath her short coat, and even shorter dress. The woman sure knew how to dress. Even if she was just a hillbilly, he thought, smiling.

Inside, the second shift had arrived. Ollie and Junior were cutting up in the break room with Swany. Sam stood studying the pins stuck in the large map at the back wall. Hawkins sat with boots propped on top of his desk, snoring.

Cord stepped into his office, pulled the jar from his jacket and stowed it in the bottom drawer. He walked quickly to the bathroom, gargled, then went back out into the patrol room.

"Hey, boss. Wondered where you'd wandered off to." Sam pointed at the map. "Been going over my notes. Picked out the most likely sites Thorn might use."

Cord looked it over and glanced at Sam. "You sure?"

"Hell. If I were sure, wouldn't be workin' here." He grinned.

Cord tilted his chin at Hawkins. "Think I'm gonna jail him."

"What? Shit, Cord. You can't do that."

"Hell I can't. I don't trust him, Sam. Having him out on the line would put these other boys in even more danger." He peered in the break room at the others. "Besides you, Waddy's the only one I trust to handle him. But hell, it's gonna be hard enough for Waddy just to stay awake. And I don't want Hawk backing your ass." He sighed. "Can't send him home. Don't see no other choice. Gotta lock him up. And you're gonna help me."

Sam sighed. "Let's get it done, then."

They walked to Hawkins' desk, Sam taking up a post behind his chair. "Come on back with me, Hawk." Cord hitched a thumb over his shoulder.

The deputy shook himself awake and dropped his feet to the floor. "Huh? What the hell, Cord. We movin'?"

"Come on back. We need t' talk."

He looked around at Sam. "About what?"

"Stand up." Cord's tone was sharp, but even. The others stopped talking and gathered at the break room doorway, watching.

Hawkins glanced around, nervous now. "What fer? Hell no!"

He shoved hard away from the desk. Sam moved in and grabbed his arms from behind. Cord quickly stepped close, laying one hand on Hawkin's chest, the other under his right arm. "Stand up, slow."

"Ye goddamned, fuckin' pricks. Get yer damn hands off me." He tried to swing at Cord, and Sam pulled his arms up, torqueing them in their sockets.

"Quiet down, Hawk. I'm puttin' you in the freeze, just for tonight. We'll let you out when we get back from our little proceedings. Don't want you gettin' mixed up in the skirmish."

"I'll be a sonofabitch if you will." He started to struggle again.

Cord pulled out his leather slap-jack. "Calm it down, Hawk, or I swear I'll thump your head so hard you'll feel it next week."

Hawkins ceased struggling and glared, face red. "You fuckin' prick. I'll get you fer this. I swear I will."

"Maybe. But not today. Now let's go."

They walked him to lockup, and in a minute were back in the bullpen with the others.

"Gather round, boys." They slowly shuffled over in front of the map. He studied each man's face. Swany looked bemused, nodding. The others, except for Junior, who looked confused, held his gaze, steady. He nodded toward the cells. "Sorry that had to go down the way it did. But I can't run this department the way it needs if there's even one man on the team I can't trust. I'm not putting you, or the people we're sworn to protect, at the mercy of the likes of Hawk anymore. He was the only one left of the old bunch. Kept him on 'cause I figured I might be able to turn him around. But it just ain't workin' out."

"Hell, Cord." Swany tapped the desk he was leaning on. "Wonderin' why it took so long."

"Man deserves a second chance, Swan. And I know some of you are friendly with ol' Hawk. And that's fine." His brows furrowed as he looked again at each of them. "But this here department has got to be your first loyalty. Understand?"

"Ain't we gonna be short tonight without him, Cord?" Ollie pulled a chair up to prop his boot on. "I mean, he still trucks with Thorn's bunch some. But do we gotta lock him up?"

"Ollie, this operation's going down tonight. But we don't know exactly what we're getting into, and I can't chance losing any of you because one of our own may not be trustworthy. I'd trust any damn one of you with my life. You all need to feel the same about me and everyone else on this operation. Is that clear?"

They nodded and murmured assent.

"Good. 'Cause if anybody don't feel like what I did was right, or don't want t' be on this team anymore, say it now."

He waited.

Junior raised his hand. "Sir. Does this mean we'll be hirin'? I'm 'bout ready for another proby t' take my place."

The men laughed.

"Hell, boy." Ollie clapped him on the shoulder. "You the best coffee-getter we had here in years. Ain't never gonna stop bein' the proby I can help it."

Cord smiled. "We'll worry about that later, Junior. In the meantime. We've got a big night ahead. Sam here's been working with Waddy and Swan on stake-outs to get a line on Thorn's stillhouses and labs. We got a tipoff they're planning some kind of meeting tonight and runnin' a haul, maybe up into Virginia. We're gonna try to stop every ounce of crank they been cookin' and every damn gallon of whiskey they brewed from makin' it out of this county." He pointed to the map. "Sam's pinpointed five locations— here, here, here, here, and here—we think are the most likely departure points and supply routes he'll use tonight."

Ollie stepped up to the map. "What makes you think ol' Hawk didn't already tip his buddies?"

"Ain't nobody but Swan, Waddy, Sam and me knew about this surveillance operation. And Swan's been keepin' tabs on Hawk the whole time." He turned and faced the map again. "I think we got a good chance of pulling this off. Most his drivers'll probably just cut and run when you flip the lights on. Since Thorn don't pay 'em much, ten or twenty cases of 'shine or a few pounds of meth ain't worth goin t' jail over. Nor getting' killed over. So, easy does it."

"That means you, Mister tactical hotshot." Ollie elbowed Swan, grinning.

"Don't worry. No low-life tweeker's worth my spit. Let alone another leg. But that don't mean I won't be sportin' Kevlar 2-layer sleeves and medium-duty gloves tonight."

"Wouldn't expect any less." Cord patted his shoulder. "Now I'm assigning each of you a route. Ollie, you'll take the junction at Sapp's Holler. Junior, cover Cray's Trail. Swany, Pig Trot Run. Sam will cover Silas Road, and we'll send Waddy over to Cove Branch. I'll be watchin' Thorn's place."

"But, Boss." Swany raised a hand. "Thorn ain't personally run no whiskey in years."

"I know, Swan. But he ain't hired a runner in years either—yet he did last week. I got a pretty good hunch we'll see ol' Thorn out there tonight. That's another reason I locked Hawk up. With the big man on the towline, he might feel bound to send out a warning. We don't want Thorn to slither away like he did with the Conley bust last year. Let's cut off the head of this snake and shut him down."

Swany and the others nodded, looking grim and determined.

"They won't move 'til late, so y'all get in position by 2100 hours. Could be a long night, so get some rest. Any questions? None. Good."

He pointed his chin at Ollie. "Go on up and relieve Waddy. Fill him in and send him back here. Okay—that's all, men. Stay sharp. Let's not get hurt out there."

He walked back to his office with Sam. "We've got a couple of hours yet." He sat on the edge of the cot. "I'm gonna see how much of this little book I can get through. Make sure they're all fed and ready to go by 2030."

"I'll do it." Sam started to leave, then hesitated. "And, Cord? That's good what ye said out there. Boys needed to hear it. Been wonderin' when you'd finally get around to it."

"Shut the hell up and get outta here, before I lock you up too."

After Sam closed the door, Cord sat on the edge of the cot, moving papers aside to make room. He flipped on the lamp. Leaned over and opened the bottom drawer of the desk, grabbed the mason jar. Then relaxed against the wall and picked up the Moleskin. Outside, cloud cover was thick and low, darkness closing in fast. It'd be a starless sky. The kind of inky-black mountain night that wasn't open to any understanding beyond staying closed up, safe and sound behind locked doors. He spun the lid off the jar and was pouring a trickle into his cup when someone knocked. He chuckled, shaking his head, screwed the cap back on, and set the jar back in the drawer. "Come in."

"Hey, Sheriff. Sorry to bother you." Ryanne Brady stepped in and stood in front of his desk, body at ease, but eyes alert, knit cap held between her hands. Her raven-black hair was tousled. Her deep fern-green gaze was steady, direct. "Can we talk about Lou?"

"Come on in. Have a seat." He gestured to the chair.

"If you don't mind, no thanks. Been sitting most of the day. I'd rather stand."

"Go right ahead." Cord liked her directness. Military training was still in her DNA. "So what d'ya got?"

"I heard Lou died. And, well, sir. I didn't want to say anything earlier in front of the others. But like I said, I saw Lou a few times over in that desert shithole. Never got to spend a lot of time with him. But enough to see a change. Started hangin' with some rough crudes. Reminded me of Thorn's bunch, but even worse. Cruel. Stupid.

Vicious. Military service was just gang initiation far as they were concerned. They used their time over there to develop contacts and resources they could leverage for their homies when they got back stateside."

Cord stood, nodding. "I've heard these deployments have become a boon for gangland recruitment."

"Wouldn't know, sir." She shrugged. "But Lou got mighty close to some of the Afghani tribesman and other internationals up in the Kandahar and Helmand Provinces. The Golden Crescent opium production and distribution types. Afghans, Syrians, Greeks, Russians, Kurdistans, Dutch, French. A real UN of shitheads. Plus the growers. Same farmers we were trying to convert to legitimate agricultural production. And there he was, smack dab in the middle of that shit. And worse, the last two months over there he was in a stupor most the time. Slammin' the brown tar regular. I tried to talk to him. He wouldn't listen. Said it was just a way to keep from going crazy. Said he'd quit when he got back stateside."

"Did he?"

"Well, when I got back home, I visited him a few times. He seemed better. Cleaned up. Even said he'd found a girl. But when we tried to talk about the war. . . ." She paused, looking down at her cap, then looked up. "I never understood that. So I guess I'd hoped . . . well, there aren't a lot of people around here we can talk to about things we saw over there." She paused, shook her head.

"I know." Cord leaned forward on the desk. "Not much stomach in regular folks for the shit we've seen and done."

She nodded. "I've noticed. Anyhow, after we got the call today and I saw Fred, I remembered Lou also told me he'd found a way to pay off his daddy's farm debt. He was excited. Said everything was gonna be all right. He'd be clean, they'd be able to live without the worry and fret. But he was secretive about the details. I couldn't help but connect his new scheme to the Afghani skag-chasers he'd been hanging with." She shrugged. "Now that he's dead and seein' his daddy died the way he did, thought I better let you know. Hope it'll help."

Cord scratched his head, thinking, then slapped the desk. "Ryanne, you may have just helped more than you know. That's some good thinking. Listen, do you like working as an EMT?"

"What?" She frowned, confused.

"I think I have an opening coming up in this office soon. I could use a perceptive, smart woman like you on the team."

She raised a brow skeptically. "I . . . hadn't ever thought about it. But I'll let you know."

Cord extended a hand. "Good. I'll be in touch. And thanks for the info."

He shook her hand, followed her to the door and called Sam into his office. By the time the deputy reached the door, he'd already grabbed the Moleskin off the cot and was behind his desk flipping through it.

"Shit, Sam. Don't know why I didn't see this before. Get on that computer. Do a search. Just give me a minute." He leaned over the notebook, then grabbed a yellow pad and began scribbling. Finally, he scratched his head, looked up and smiled. "Type this in the search engine: 31.616944400000000000 Latitude and 65.716944399999990000 Longitude."

Sam typed in the numbers, squinted at the screen. "Comes up Kandahar."

"I'll be damned. Look here. See these entries. I knew they looked familiar somehow. But the Greek symbols threw me off.

k3161694440λ ^ 6571694439η0δ.
kswk3211191170λ ^ 6604642990ζ20δ
h3136364740λ ^ 6395861109ζ850γ
hcbn3013452280λ ^ 6226266269ζ640γ

"You see, it's not uncommon to shorten up latitude/longitude coordinates for the sake of convenience. 29.3286 and 48.0034 is the latitude and longitude of Kuwait City. Had that shit slammed in my head during Gulf One. But if you're trying to record an exact lat/long location, you need 16 places after the decimal."

Sam leaned over and studied the book, then tapped the map on the computer screen. "Makes sense if Lou didn't want anyone to figure out what he was recording here. He dropped the decimal point and turned the coordinates into a ten digit string, substituting the Greek symbols after the first ten digits to represent repeating numbers."

"That's right." Cord nodded, biting his lip. "So, in this first number set, 3161694440λ, the last digit, zero, is followed by the Greek letter symbol for lambda, the eleventh letter. Eleven zeroes at the end of the number string."

Sam scribbled the numbers on a pad. "If we add the decimal back in and the zeroes at the end, we get: 31.616944400000000000. And the second number set has the number nine followed by the Greek letter symbol for Eta, the seventh letter. So we have seven nines, and a zero followed by the Greek letter symbol for Delta the fourth letter. We get four zeroes at the end of the string. Or, 65.716944399999990000."

Cord nodded, smiling. "Not bad for a hillbilly."

"But why the hell record this, Cord? So, he has coordinates for Kandahar. Who gives a shit?"

"Maybe somebody who's trying to set up supply and distribution lines for heroin."

"Heroin?"

"Smugglers and dealers are thick as ticks in July in that godforsaken place. That's why Ryanne came in. To tell me Lou had gotten hooked up over there. Wouldn't be hard to make contacts. Problem is distribution. Most of our heroin comes from Mexico or South America. Easier than moving it from half-way around the world. But if a man could figure a way to smuggle junk from the Golden Crescent."

Sam drummed his fingers on the desk. "Using military connections like Lou had."

Cord nodded. "He could make a fortune. I think those coordinates pinpoint some of the highest opium production sites in Afghanistan."

Sam leaned back. "And the recent crackdown on meth and even pharmaceutical opiates has made heroin a profitable enterprise again." He shook his head. "Could be its what got Lou and his daddy killed."

"These email addresses and phone numbers were probably his contacts." Cord paced to the other side of the room. "Doubt they're any good by now. Disposable phones and email addresses linked to ISPs that are no longer active." He watched the treetops above the opposite riverbank swaying as the north winds picked up. "This might be too big for our little office. I'll see if Beth wants to come in. Help us coordinate with the other bureaus."

He stepped around the desk, mind racing. Thorn's meeting tonight was taking on even more significance. "Look at this." He pointed at the numbers beneath the ledger. "Today's date is beside this phone number." He paced to the door and back, rubbing his scar. Then halted, and whistled through his teeth. "Damn, Sam. That's it!"

Sam looked up from the monitor. "What?"

"Lucas said Thorn was trying to set up a new distribution for product tonight. It ain't for meth, but *heroin*. And it's not Thorn's meeting. It's *Lou's*. Thorn's makin' a play to take it over. Or shut it down."

Sam leaned forward. "Thorn somehow got wind of it and ain't none too happy about Lou tryin' to muscle in on his business. So why not just kill him and call it done?"

"Because he likes the idea. Knowing Thorn's prideful nature, his self-image as local hero, he probably tried to convince Lou to join his operation. Maybe got him to reveal enough to persuade Thorn it'd be profitable. Let's say Lou refused. According to Red, he already had another backer. So Thorn decides to let him know that shit's not gonna fly. He gets Rad to lean on Webb to put a scare on Lou."

Sam nodded. "'Problem is, Lou ends up dead. Meantime, Thorn knows Lou must have a record, somewhere, of his contacts and such. On a computer. In a notebook."

Cord held up the Moleskin. "That's why they broke into Lou's house, then tortured and killed Fred. Looking for this."

Sam nodded. "But they didn't find the book. We did. So how would Thorn know about this meeting tonight?"

Cord shrugged. "My gut's telling me we'll get answers when we show up unannounced, and they'll all point to Thorn's avaricious foolishness." He stepped to the door and stuck his head out. "Got coffee out there, Junior?"

"Yeah, boss. Want me to bring you a cup?"

"Bring two." He scanned the room. Waddy was back, at the switchboard up front talking to Swan. "Hangin' in there, Waddy?"

"Yep." He leaned back, looking across the hallway separating the bullpen and Cord's office. "Just shootin' the shit with Swany-boy. I'll be fine. Ain't the first time I pulled a double."

Cord chuckled. "Just holler if ye get to feelin' old and decide to take the long sleep out there t'night."

"Hell. Way yer pushin' it, be seein' ol' Death long 'fore I get a ticket fer that train." Waddell slapped the other man's knee, grinning. "Right, Swan?"

Junior stepped into the hall. "Here ye go, sir."

"Thanks. You ready for t'night."

He scratched his buzz-cut head. "Yessir. Little nervous. Ain't been on an operation this big before."

"Relax, son. You'll do fine. Last thing these boys want is to get arrested. Just stay on your toes. Don't try to be a hero."

"Yessir."

"One hour, boys. Check your gear." He went back inside his office and handed a cup to Sam. Then picked up the Moleskin and sat at the desk, fingering the pages. "Who'd have thought a little black book could cause so much heartache?"

Sam blew across the steaming coffee, took a sip, then raised the cup in salute. "Only in your world, boss. Only in yours."

The intercom buzzed and Waddy's voice crackled out of the box. "Call coming your way, boss. The wife. Line one."

He punched the blinking button. "Hey—Lucinda?"

"So where are you? Thought we were going to talk."

Oh shit. He grimaced. "Can't tonight, honey. New developments in the cases. Don't know how late it'll be. Maybe an all-nighter. Sorry . . . can it hold?"

"Sure." She sounded tired, resigned. "As always." The phone clicked dead.

"Damn, boy." Sam tapped the book. "Sounds like you got problems need fixin' outside this-here black book."

Cord nodded. "Yeah. And way beyond a damn broken toilet."

18
River's Bounty

Rad ducked his head under a low-hanging Budweiser sign Thorn had commandeered from the Red Rooster when he took it over. "Got 'em loaded and ready to roll, Boss. Five of our best drivers. George Tate's in the Ford pick-up, Slim's runnin' the blue van, Ottie and Dale's runnin' the two white vans, and ol' Caster's takin' the Chevy. Told 'em t' wait 'til after midnight t' get on the road." He grabbed a cue stick and started chalking the tip. "All of 'em 'cept fer Caster was fine with changin' routes. He's just s'old and cantankerous, prob'ly be complainin' even iffen we didn't change a thing."

Thorn leaned in, popped a seven ball into the side pocket and straightened. "Then this'll be his last run. A man too old t' run or fight's not good for us out there. From here on out keep him at the pots or in the labs."

Rad set the chalk on the table-edge and rested against the stick, shaking his head. "Gonna kill the ol' man, boss. Ye know he lives fer these-here runs."

"I know." Thorn moved around the other side, aimed and tapped the eight ball into a corner pocket. "He's been with the family since the beginning. But we're growin'. I just can't take the chance he'll get caught

203

and end up locked away in some damned cell." He shot and dropped the nine ball at the other end. "Bring the other van?"

"Did. Seems t' be runnin' all right. Been a while since we used her. Missin' on one cylinder. But oughter work fer what yer needin'."

Thorn nodded, eying down the stick, then banked the cue ball around the fifteen and dropped the ten in the corner. "Reckon it'll be tough to foller the two of us if we get a tail. More 'n likely go fer the car if they figure it's carryin'. You done good t'day. I'm fixin' dinner t'night, so get cleaned up and be at the table around eight. Want'er finish this off fer me?" He pointed at the table.

Rad grinned. "Sure." Thorn handed over the stick and he leaned in and popped the cue ball. It tapped the eleven. Too much English. Clipped the shoulder of the corner pocket, missing. "Damn."

"Keep practicin'." Thorn started up the stairs. "Ye'll get there one day."

"Hey, boss. Them boys get back all right?" Rad cut his eyes upstairs.

Thorn nodded. "Jus' don't ask where they got them bumps on their heads. May be a little sore." He whistled. "Come on, Homer." The dog thumped his tail against the couch leg then labored up and limped after.

In the kitchen, Thorn pulled out pots and a cast-iron frying pan. He mixed flour, salt, pepper and paprika in a large bowl for the fried chicken. In another, he beat two eggs and poured in some milk, mixing. Then lit the stove, set the skillet on the burner and dropped in some shortening. As it melted, he opened a can of green beans, poured them in a pot, dropped in bacon fat and salt, then put that on the burner to simmer. He held a hand over the skillet. When the heat felt right, he picked up a chicken leg, dipped it in batter, rolled it in the flour mixture, and carefully dropped it into the hot oil. It's all in the temperature, he thought, watching the leg start to sizzle and brown.

He'd been the youngest. After his momma'd died, Frank had put him on kitchen duty where he'd learned to cook. Mostly through hit-and-miss, including some real smoking disasters. But he also gathered some hints and tips from his aunts over the years. He liked being in the kitchen. Something about handling the raw food and spices, the good smells that filled the whole house as a dish simmered or baked, the scents lingering in the air made everything somehow seem better. And Frank had always been easier to handle when he'd eaten.

He dropped the other chicken pieces in the pan, pulled a jar each of canned okra and tomatoes from the shelf, poured them in a pot and started it simmering too. Then he turned to the old marble pastry board to roll out the biscuits. In a few minutes, he had everything cooking. "That there's how it's done, buddy." He patted Homer's head, then tossed him a couple chicken skins.

Thorn walked to the bottom of the stairs. "Dinner's on in twenty, boys!"

He turned the chicken over, and lifted the pot lids. "Just right. Let's step outside fer a minute, boy."

He grabbed his coat and they walked out to the deck. A deep chill had settled over the hollow. The sky was winter dark. Hard, cold air that settled inky-black against the mountain crests. Could snow f'sure, he thought, shutting the door behind him. The wind coming in from the north shook tree limbs, that clattered and creaked.

"Hard and cold as bones." He reached down and patted Homer's head. "Pull this run off, and we could break into some big money. Might build that pool I been wantin'. Huh, bud?" He looked out into the darkness, thinking about the opportunities arising with a bigger market. "Shit, Homer. It's colder 'n a witch's tit out here. Let's get the hell inside."

Back at the stove, he checked the biscuits, pulled out the first batch of golden-brown chicken and started another. Rad walked in, opened the refrigerator, grabbed a couple of beers and tossed one to Thorn "Smellin' good, boss." He twisted off the cap, flipped it in the trash and took a swig. "Shew." He wiped his mouth with the back of a sleeve.

Thorn turned off the oven, lifted the sheet of biscuits out and slid them into a bowl. Then turned off the burners, carried the pots of beans and okra to the table, and returned to the stove. Then he forked the last of the chicken onto the platter, grabbed it and the biscuits and handed them across to Rad. Lucas and Beloit came around the corner.

"Pull up a chair, boys. Got some fixin's here to brace ye fer anything." He took the head chair and motioned them to sit.

Rad started snickering as he eyed the two under the dining table light. Purpled-blue splotches ringed Lucas's eyes. A dark line of dried blood cut across his nose where it'd split. Beloit's head was thinly wrapped in gauze. A red blotch had bled through the bandage.

Thorn scowled. "Leave 'em be, Rad."

"Yessir." Rad snorted and clapped a hand over his mouth to cover a smile. "But it ain't easy."

The corner of Thorn's lip rose almost imperceptibly to a half-grin. "Hey. That's enough."

"Yessir."

"Now, as these boys know, Beloit." He gestured at Lucas and Rad. "I like t' take what we work hard for and use it to live a better life." He waved his hand to encompass the room. "All this I got from hard work, self-sacrifice, and the smarts t' go along. Took a lot of years, and we've lost a few battles along the way. But without the whiskey and hillbilly crack we're getting' ready to haul t'night, wouldn't none us be here livin' on this fine land, in this fine house, eatin' such fine food. And so, whenever I can, I like to celebrate. That's what this here is. A celebration of this new line that's gonna make us all richer and happier." He lifted his beer. "So raise your bottles, boys. Here's to a successful run, and a more successful ambush."

After the clink of the glasses, they all took a sip. Thorn forked some chicken off the platter and passed it to Rad. As the food filled the plates, they began to eat.

Thorn looked around the small group. They're a good bunch, he thought. Even Beloit. Don't know if he'll last, though. A little green around the ears. But at least not a weasel, like some. The combination of the food and the beer and the good prospects of tonight's success made him feel better than he had earlier.

As they finished, he gulped down his second beer and stood. "So, here's how it's goin' down. We're gonna start this little two-car caravan just before midnight. Rad in the van, me, Lucas and Beloit in the Fury. We're ridin' light though." He looked at Beloit. "Ain't that I don't trust yer drivin', boy. But with the extra passenger, just ain't gonna have room. We'll load up the trunk and pile about ten gallons in the back with Lucas.

"The van Rad's drivin' is gonna be empty. If we get tailed, we'll split up. Then the deputy's gonna have to decide which of us to foller. We want 'em to go after the van. And they probably will, thinkin' the bigger catch is there. If they don't, then it'll be on you, young feller."

He walked to Beloit's chair and stood behind him. "And I'll just tell ye this, son. I ain't goin' t jail. Not for nothin' or nobody. So ye better be ready to drive t'night like it was the Daytona 500. Get me caught, and you'll never drive again. I promise ye that."

19
Still the Waters

B y the time the girls returned with Sunny, Levon and Eli had the community almost back to normal. Families and friends had worked together to make space for the added occupants in their tents and buses. Food had been distributed after Filmore and Breezy had run to town for more groceries. All around, Levon could see folks gathered for dinner, children laughing and playing together, husbands and wives hugging each other and talking with other couples around the table. And despite temperatures that seemed to be dropping lower every minute, here and there small groups, mostly men, gathered to pass pipes or joints around, laughing and happy.

He'd called a meeting for the evening, so Eli'd started a large bonfire in the middle of the field, not far from the raised platform built last summer as a stage for Levon to preach from, and for concerts held every week by musicians in the group. The two now stood just outside the shimmering heat of the fire, watching the flames catch and jump, flakes of glowing ash floating into the sky. He'd need to hit the notes right tonight to convince some of the holdouts to stay. Three or four families were still not totally committed.

"Lilith thinks I should do the Mount sermon." Levon lifted a hand from the pocket of his coat and wiped his nose. "What d'ya think, man?"

"That you're better off thinkin' for yourself." Eli picked up a twig, broke it and threw it in the fire.

"So. We ready?"

"The boys got all the gear packed, and we're set to roll in the van. Zippy and Sebastian already hiked out over the mountain to set up. It's only a fifteen minute drive to Caggle's Knob. Are *you* ready?"

"Damn, Eli. I was born that way. My daddy, sorry sonofabitch he was, taught me one good thing. Ain't nothing can't be whipped. These boys we're meeting with probably never seen the hard end of life. I can talk the side off a barn. Once they're on board, we'll just need to finish setting up that supply. Nothing to worry about. Besides, we got some pretty fucking badasses on our side. And plenty firepower to back them up."

Eli nodded. "So, do the Mount sermon. They need hope." He glanced around the field at the scattered lodges and tents. "Hell, we could all use some tonight."

"That'll do." Levon stood for a moment more staring into the flames, then turned and walked to the cabin. Inside, Maya and Lilith sat in chairs they'd pulled up in front of Sunny, who was lying on the couch.

Levon shook his hand. "How you doin', brother." He sat down beside him. "They banged you up pretty good, huh?"

Sunny lifted his left arm with his right and slowly sat up, grimacing. "I'm okay. Had worse on the streets before you came along."

"Fuck, Sunny. You're a super-savior, man. Fourteen people you kept from burning alive this morning. You're a fuckin' hero, dude!"

"Levon, I…" He winced as he turned his head to speak. "I appreciate it. But I just got up to piss and ran into a couple guys lighting up the lodges."

"Well. Those people out there think you are." Levon walked over to the loom and looked at the patterns. "What's this, Maya?"

She joined him, putting an arm through his. "A tapestry called 'Le Vin Et La Vigne.' I copied it out of a book. See?" She lifted a volume from a side table. "I've always loved it. Reminded me of what we're trying to create here. A garden of united workers using gifts of the earth to bring pleasure. Do you like it?"

"Hell, yeah. It's beautiful." He ran a hand over the glossy page. "And you're right. It is what we're doing here." He turned to the others. "We're the workers in this vineyard. These men and women have come together, like us, to turn God's garden into a paradise of peace and pleasure. They labor together in harmony sharing toils and triumphs." He hugged Maya closer and kissed her. "Thanks, darling. We'll hang this up as a symbol of what we're trying to create."

"Shouldn't you be getting back out there, Levon?" Lilith got up, cracked the door and looked out.

"Come on over and look at this. It's beautiful."

"I've seen it." She glanced at the loom. "It's pretty. But since the community is waiting to hear how you think we should proceed, I thought you'd want to talk to them. They need you, Levon."

He nodded. "Okay. You're right. Let me help you up, Sunny. You've got to say a few words." He pulled Sunny up. The other man leaned unsteadily against him. "You gonna be all right?"

"Sure." Sunny nodded. "Just so I'm not standing too long."

"Let's go, then."

They all left the cabin and the crowd outside broke out in applause as soon as they saw Sunny. Hoots and whistles rose from the hollow. Several men came forward to help him climb the steps to the stage. Levon joined him while Maya, Lilith and Eli stood at the back of the stage.

Levon held up his hands. "Okay. Okay. Quiet down, now." When the hoots and whistles finally died down, he spoke again. "Now, listen

210

folks. Sunny here's going to say a few words. Can't be up here too long. For some reason, he's feeling a little sore tonight."

The crowd laughed and yelled out jokes and compliments.

"Yay, Sunny."

"We love you, Sunny."

"Sunny! You're our hero, dude. God bless you."

Sunny stepped up to the front and raised a hand. "I just want to say, I'm not a hero. Only did what any of you would've done. But I will say—" His voice cracked. "I will say *you* are *my* heroes. If it weren't for all of you, I'd have died a long time ago. And I'll do anything I have to, anything, to make sure this farm stays around for your children and your children's children. I swear."

The crowd cheered. Sunny backed up to sit in a chair Eli brought out to the edge of the stage.

Levon approached the front of the stage again and raised his hand. "Brothers and sisters. I'll make this short because it's cold, and dark, and the day's been long. And we all have another long day tomorrow, getting ready for the funeral." He paused and bowed his head. "We thank you. Lord, for bringing us through these trials, and for the opportunity to carry your love into another day. Please help me, Lord, to say what you would have me say, and no more. Amen." He raised his head and looked out over the crowd.

"We have come through much over the last twelve months. This journey started out as a dream many years ago. The same dream humans have had since the beginning of time. To live free from the shackles of tyranny and violence. To find a place where each person could walk in peace and harmony. A dream that's traveled across time and lands and has always, always manifested itself in arts and music and literature.

"This same immortal, eternal dream was mine, too. And yours. We shared a desire to make that dream real. And that great desire pushed us across this continent to where we now stand. Brought together in the hope we might succeed where others had failed."

He paused and looked around. "We knew there would be hardships. That people would jeer and shun us. We also knew there was a chance violence would come to us. Because it always does when people try to live outside the strictures of materialism. Because once you step outside that world, it no longer controls you. Can't get its grubby, capitalist hands on you. That makes them mad. As for what happened here last night, those people will be brought to justice. Justice, I say. For vengeance is the Lord's. And they shall know His vengeance. In this world, or the next.

"Because we are the righteous. Blessed. Tonight, we may be poor in spirit, but we know our kingdom awaits. Blessed, because even though we mourn our dear sister, Zoe, we will be comforted. Blessed, because we are the meek who shall inherit the earth. Blessed because we are they which do hunger and thirst after righteousness.

"And here, from this land, we will spread the fire of righteousness over the earth. Blessed, because we are merciful to those who surrender to our ways, and shall therefore obtain mercy. Blessed because we are the pure in heart, who shall see the face of God shining through the light of the mountains. Blessed, because we are the peacemakers, and shall be called the children of God. Blessed, because though we are persecuted for righteousness' sake, ours will be the kingdom of heaven. For we shall fight and our persecutors shall be vanquished. For when men come and revile, and persecute, and do evil against you, the blessed give over to universal love. Whatever it calls us to do.

"We thank you once again for all your blessings. Give us the strength to carry your will throughout the days of our lives. You are the love, the power, and the way. Amen."

He lifted his head and saw their faces open, receiving his words. "Now go home. Hug your children. Your wives and husbands. Your friends. And remember, this is the way. The righteous will persevere. Persevere, brothers and sisters. Persevere. Goodnight."

Levon watched the crowd disperse to their makeshift homes, then turned back to the others. "It's fuckin' cold out here. Let's get inside."

They helped Sunny into bed. Then Zoe, Blu and Lilith joined Levon in the great room.

He sank down behind his desk. "Well. I think it went well."

"You were great, Levon." Maya knelt down next to him, placing a hand on his thigh.

"That's sweet, girl." He stroked his hair as she laid her head in his lap.

"You did well, Levon." Eli nodded. "Now, I need to check on the boys and take a walk on the fences. They might try another attack tonight. See you in a couple hours?"

"Sounds good. 'Til then."

After Eli stepped out into the night, Lilith slipped behind the desk opposite Maya and kissed Levon. "I'd better get a little rest. Already been a long day. And tomorrow's not going to get any easier. I love you, Levon. Good luck, tonight."

"Goodnight, woman."

She disappeared down the hallway.

Levon sat for a moment before opening the tin.

Maya stood. "Let me, honey." She quickly rolled a joint, lit and passed it to Levon.

He pulled a long toke, handed it back and pulled her closer. She leaned down and kissed him, her hand sliding to his crotch.

They made love, Maya climbing on top and rocking above him. Her breasts swayed inches from his face as she leaned forward and cradled his head in both hands. She smiled and pressed her hips down, moving in a circular motion. His fingers traced the small of her back and he pulled her close, burying his face between her breasts. He turned her around and lifted her skirt, entering her as she pressed back against him. He pushed her head down on the desk and rode her trying to hold back the soul-wrenching rush that built, strong and deep until the

213

pressure burst, emptying him of all the pent-up anxiety and frustration he'd held onto over the past week.

After, lying in front of the fireplace, Maya in the crook of one arm, he stared up at the rough-hewn boards of the ceiling. Soon the world would know the force of a love bright and powerful enough to wash away all its sordid, dark, filthy stink. He closed his eyes and recalled how his followers had stood tonight looking up to him. Trusting. Faithful. Ready to follow without reservation. Soon, he'd have an entire country of people just like them.

He grinned. And a whole harem of Magdalenes.

20
Solitary Watch

Cord pushed his chair back and walked to the interior office window that looked out over the patrol room. His men were huddled around the map again, listening as Sam reviewed the plan. He had a pretty good feeling about the operation. But his stomach still tightened as he thought about the chase. Might be biting off more than they could chew. He grabbed his hat and coat and stepped out into the bullpen.

"All right, boys. Get your noses out of that map and circle up." He waited until they'd gathered around him. "Now, remember. We got two objectives. First, put a hurtin' on Thorn's operation by confiscating as much meth and illegal whiskey as we can. Normally we'd be limited to settin' up road blocks and looking for some traffic violation that'd give us a reason for pulling over one of Thorn's runners. If not, we'd go home empty-handed. But tonight, we got some good intel that might allow us to arrest the fools almost before they get started. Unless our stake-out crew was made, we have an even chance to bag three or four of these haulers tonight.

"But remember. We still haven't pinned down the exact location of their stills and meth labs, just the tracks and roads they use gettin' to and from the sites. So let's not show our hand too quick. We want to continue monitoring their operation after tonight. Stay out of sight until they're rolling, then keep your distance for a mile or so before you flip the lights and pull 'em over. Understand?"

Junior looked nervously around and raised his hand. "Sir. What if they don't roll?"

"Then I'll be taking the extra overtime pay for y'all out of Sam's wages for the next three months. How's that sound, Sam?"

"Not worth a shit." He pointed a finger at Junior. "So you damn-well better make an arrest tonight, even if you have to go in there and drag them runners out."

The other men laughed and nodded agreement.

Cord rapped a knuckle on the closest desk. "If there's no other questions, second thing I need you to remember is to stay safe out there. Keep in radio contact, and if things start going sideways, call for back-up." He looked at each of them in turn. "Any questions?"

He nodded when there were none. "All right. Let's go."

They followed one another out of the station. Sam shadowed Cord and waited outside the cruiser as he got in and rolled the window down. "Sure you don't want some company out there? Don't need any dead heroes tonight. And you're tailin' the only runner who'll be willing to shoot."

"I know. But I'm willing to fire back. And I'm a better shot." Cord smiled and cranked the engine. "Now get going. And good hunting."

"The blind's set. Now we wait."

"Ten-four, buddy. See you after midnight." He backed out, turned onto Main and gassed it towards Foggy Top. About a quarter mile from Thorn's place, he pulled onto a cutoff behind some pines and parked behind Ollie.

"How you hangin', buddy?" He slid in the passenger side of the deputy's car.

"Pretty good. Just cold as hell, t'night." Ollie rubbed his hands together. "Should've brought some hot coffee."

"Hang on." Cord trotted back to the car and returned with a dented metal thermos. "Junior fixed us up." He opened the top and poured a cupful in the lid. "Here ye go."

"Thanks." He held it with both hands, taking in the warmth. Finally, he took a long sip. "Man. 'At's the stuff." They sat watching the house for a minute before he looked at Cord again. "Reckon this'll work?"

"If it don't, I'm gonna have a passel of mean, tired deputies tomorrow. And that ain't good." He paused. "Yeah. It'll work. Just get your ass down there to Sapp's Holler and see if it don't."

Ollie gulped down the last of the coffee, twisted the top back on the thermos and started the engine. "See ye later, Cord."

"Later for sure, Ollie." He stepped out and watched him turn around, then head back to the road. Then he walked back in his cruiser and pulled the patrol jacket tighter against the chill, watching the house as the first light snowflakes began to fall.

21
Over Thin Ice

Red-orange embers floated up the flue as Thorn poked the short-cut, split oak, watching the fire slowly come back to life. Snow had begun to fall two hours ago. So far it was a light dusting, hardly sticking to the ground. Bound to get worse as the night chill seeped deeper into the already damp ground. Not a good omen, he thought as he slid the poker into the flames, so it heated to white hot.

Behind him, pool balls clacked as Rad played a solitary game of Nineball. Lucas sat at the bar, detached but watchful. Beloit silently paced at the back of the room, chewing on a thumbnail and shooting glances at the clock.

Thorn finally stood, pushing Homer away. "Saw ye drive on some slick roads last night, Beloit. How well ye do in snow?"

"All right, I reckon. Tennessee ain't the only place it snows."

Thorn crossed the room so quickly Beloit staggered backward against the wall. He grabbed the boy's collar and held the poker next to his cheek. "Open that fuckin' mouth again with a smart-ass answer and I'll burn your goddamned tongue out." He lowered the tip to hover near the corner of Beloit's lips and held it there, waiting.

Beloit stared wide-eyed at the red iron until Thorn finally released his grip and lowered the glowing iron.

"I asked ye a fuckin' question 'cause I wanted a fuckin' answer. Can ye drive in this here snow? Or not?"

"Yes sir. I've driven plenty in this kind of weather."

"Yeah? Well why don't ye tell me about it. 'Cause I ain't in no mood to slide off the side of the road and down a ravine somewhere's between here and there."

Beloit pushed up and settled on the couch. "Last year, me an' my daddy were comin' over from Mineral Bluff to Dahlonega. We'd been fightin' about racin'. He thought I ought t' quit and get a job down in Atlanta workin' in a factory, or an auto repair shop. So I made him a bet. If I could get us home in forty minutes he'd leave off the jawin' and let me drive." He glanced over Thorn's head, as if reflecting on the day.

"It's a forty-mile drive on the tightest turns and steepest rises and drops in those North Georgia mountains. Wasn't sure I could do it, but I meant to prove myself to Daddy and get some peace from all the tongue-waggin'. So I gunned it. Everything was going just fine until ten miles from home. Big flakes started ploppin' against the windshield. I turned the wipers on and tried to push 'er harder, to beat the storm. But it was just comin' down too quick.

"About five miles out, the road got so slick it felt like the wheels weren't even rolling anymore, just slidin' along like sled-runners. Daddy was yellin', 'Slow down. Slow down!' But I just kept slidin' through them curves and pushin' on to the next." He smiled. "When we finally pulled up in the drive, I couldn't stop and ran right into the side of the house." A slight smile touched a corner of his mouth. "Two months' worth of work to pay for the repairs. But Daddy never again scolded me about drivin'."

"So. You actually won the bet?"

"Shit no." Beloit shook his head and looked him straight in the eye. "Took us an hour and five minutes. But we didn't die. That impressed the hell outta Daddy."

Thorn chuckled and patted the boy's shoulder. "Okay, son. Okay. Reckon yer startin' t' grow on me."

He walked back to the hearth and racked the poker in the stand. "All right, then." He clapped to roust them. "Let's ride." As they all walked out the door, Thorn patted Homer's bony head. "Wish me luck, old faithful."

Beloit cranked the engine, backed up, then pulled ahead of the van. At the bottom of the drive, both turned left and started down the mountain. Ten minutes later, they stopped at the intersection of Cross Cut Road and turned right. Thorn figured the longer the little caravan stayed on the back roads, the less chance of coming across a checkpoint stop. But a quarter mile farther, the van blinked its lights. The signal that they were being followed.

"Get on it, boy."

Beloit pressed the accelerator down, pushing the speedometer up to sixty. The snow was just starting to stick in patches. Here and there, Thorn could feel the tires break loose, floating over the black-ice slicks briefly, sluicing back to center-line then catching asphalt again with a chirp as the stench of burned rubber filled the car. He looked back for another sign from the van as they pulled up to the Bainport Road. The van's headlights blinked again, the signal that Rad would roll across the intersection while the Fury broke off, turning right onto Bainport. Thorn watched through the rear window as they turned.

The van pulled across the intersection, but the tail didn't take the bait. Instead it turned right, following the Fury, then started gaining on them.

"Shake him loose, boy. Or ye'll be losin' more'n a bet this time."

Beloit maneuvered through a couple curves, then floored it across the bridge, tires thumping over expansion seams. The tail's headlights dwindled in the distance and Thorn relaxed, momentarily. But soon the lights began to shimmer more brightly again as the cruiser reclosed the gap.

"Road ahead cuts off to the left. Make that turn!" Thorn shifted around in the seat, holding tight to the armrest.

Beloit turned hard, engine screaming, onto Scratch Road, a thin snake of blacktop leading up into the foothills. The car slewed sideways as he shifted down and fish-tailed around a curve. Back tires slid off the road's shoulder, rear-end shuddering, sending a hail of rocks and gravel rattling over the edge of the thirty-foot drop.

This is it, thought Thorn, gritting his teeth in joy. This is why I do it. He reached into his coat pocket to caress the smoothworn ivory grips of his daddy's old Colt. Might need this after all.

22
Hung Up On the Shoals

Snow, stuck here and there to tufts of brown grass, crunched beneath his boots as Cord walked to the edge of the ditch and pulled his zipper down. Too much damned coffee, he thought, shuddering as a chill moved up his spine. Then voices carried faintly across the distance as the door to Thorn's house slammed shut. He zipped up and trotted back to the cruiser as the van's headlights flashed on. The low rumble of the Fury rolled out across the hollow.

He cranked the cruiser, watching the van and car progress down the drive. Waited a minute before backing up the cut to the road, then shifted into drive and followed, picking up speed down the hill.

He let the caravan roll ahead until they hit the bottom. He eased his boot down against the gas pedal, the extra-heavy spring pressing back against the leather sole. "Easy, Josephine. Ea-sy." The van began to speed up as the cruiser slowly gained on the rear vehicle. Typical move for a runner. If a tail fell back as you accelerated, you were being followed by a civilian. If not, it was probably a cop following. He pressed the accelerator down and started to gain on the van again.

A call broke over the radio. "Cord. Waddy. Got a 10-15, prisoner in custody out here. Just picked up Jim Broker over at Cove Branch. Pulled right over when I flipped the lights." He chuckled. "He were plum surprised when I walked up, opened the back panel of that van without ever sayin' a word, and pointed my pistol at that whiskey. Don't look like any meth, though. Gonna foller him back t' the house. See ye there. Over and out."

"10-4, Waddy. Good work." Cord grinned. Well, the night's started right, he thought. Let's see how it ends.

At the Bainport intersection, they coasted to a stop, then the Fury turned right. The van didn't move. He watched the runner's tail lights growing smaller in the distance. After a few more seconds, the van finally rolled across the intersection. "Come on, Josey." He gunned it, rear tires spinning and squealing on the blacktop as he turned east and picked up speed. Two tiny red specks were just disappearing.

By the time he hit the same curve, he'd cut the distance in half. He flipped the lights and siren as the Fury sped up, pushing eighty as it skidded onto Route 9 and flew across the Huff Bridge over the French Broad. Cord stomped the pedal down in hot pursuit. He'd just started to gain again when they slewed onto Old Scratch Road, infamous for numerous fatal crashes over the years.

On this stretch, young hotrod bucks liked to play a hillbilly version of chicken, racing side-by-side down the narrow, two-lane pass. Often they just barely avoided head-on collisions with other drivers who encountered the hot-rodders diving two abreast around the treacherous hairpin curves. Too often, someone didn't make it. Cord had been called out to more horrific smash-ups than he cared to remember on Old Scratch. Head-on collisions. Multi-car pile-ups. Guardrail-jumping rolls that spun cars out over the edge for a hundred-foot vertical drop to land crumpled and crushed at the bottom of the ravine.

The boy's smart, he thought. Or maybe it's Thorn. Whichever one's at the wheel, he knows he can't outrun me. Gonna see if he can out-drive me instead. Cord pulled the shifter down into second and floored it up the twisting asphalt ribbon.

The snow was coming harder. Now, as they dove into each new curve, the tires under the heavy chassis of the Interceptor began to float and spin, then grab again. And as he watched the Fury slide into each curve ahead, Cord couldn't help but smile. The Beloit kid showed some real talent. The car ahead seemed to float and glide smoothly around curves. He seemed to be working the slick surface, angling the car and slowing at just the right moment, allowing it to spin almost sideways before catching the road again and turning steadily into the next curve.

In fact, Cord was losing him. He gunned into the next tight curve, then geared down, lifting his foot off the brake, trying to avoid a slide out into the abyss beyond the low steel rails. Suddenly, the left-side rear tire lost traction and dropped off the shoulder, sledding towards the edge of a deep drop. He gunned it hard and the right tire grabbed pavement, just pulling her back onto the road.

Ahead, the Plymouth's tail lights were disappearing around the next turn.

He punched the pedal and bulleted down the dip to the next hairpin curve. He tapped the brakes a couple times, then cranked the wheel. The back end begin to skid, then slip, and finally slide as it hit a patch of ice, aiming straight for the ravine. He jammed the shifter back into third to lower the torque, lifted his foot and tried to steer off the line enough to keep from skating over the brink into darkness. The car shuddered as it hit a dry patch, slowing just enough to let the rear end swing around, the fender and chromed bumper striking sparks off the metal guardrail as the car ground to a stop.

He sat gripping the wheel so hard his hands grew numb, then breathed a sigh of relief. The car sat almost parallel to the road now, so he turned the wheel and pulled back onto the pavement.

Suddenly a set of headlights blinded him. Damn. Didn't expect that, he thought, blinking, squinting down the road at the approaching glare. Got us a little standoff; a game of chicken. He could let them pass, then turn and pursue. Or try to block them by pulling across their path. But in these conditions, it'd be easy enough for the boy to bulldoze the cruiser out of the way. Or worse, over the side into the ravine.

His old boxing coach, Rory Shenahagn, used to tell him when he was against the ropes, Punch it on out, boy. Body, body, body. Head. Drive 'em back.

As the Fury picked up speed, heading right for him, he pressed the accelerator slowly, steadily to the floor. Angling straight at the oncoming car. He figured with the snow and ice coating the road, neither could get up enough speed to cause any great damage to the other. Even if they collided head-on. The greatest danger was the possibility of losing control after impact, then one or both tumbling down the precipitous drop into the rocky ravine behind him.

As the distance closed, someone stuck a gun out the passenger-side window and fired. Cord flinched as the bullet burst through the windshield. Something sharp bit his left shoulder. He yanked the wheel hard right and stomped the brakes, sending the rear end skidding sideways into the front bumper of the Fury.

A sickening crunch of metal slamming metal, of fenders and frames crumpling and folding. Cord throttled the wheel as both cars spun off in opposite directions, tires screaming like demons into the darkness. For a moment, he got that strange, slow-motion sensation that sometimes happens in moments of intense danger. When every detail snaps into clear focus and, instead of confusion, there comes a sense of calm awareness, a feeling everything is happening exactly as it should. The glove box flies open. His pistol spins out to strike the backrest of the passenger seat and bounce off onto the floorboard. The jar of shine rolls from one side of the box to the other. His paperwork shifted, fell, and spilled between the passenger door and the edge of the seat, the sheets like winged creatures seeking cover. Outside, the sheer vertical face of the mountain flashed by.

Cord gripped the wheel a moment longer, waiting. Then the right rear end shifted and dropped. It slowly began to slip backward, toward the ravine.

He looked over a shoulder as the car edged closer and closer to a death-drop. He grabbed the emergency brake and pulled so hard a burning shot through his deltoid muscle. He winced at the tearing pain, but the backward slide of the cruiser stopped. He couldn't see his shoulder in the dark, but he figured the bullet had left a deep flesh wound. He still could move the arm, it just hurt like hell. He pushed the shifter into park and shut down the engine, wondering how long the brakes and tires would hold. Grabbing the handle, he carefully pushed the door open with his right hand. Pulled himself up out of the seat and onto solid ground, then looked around.

The cruiser seemed stable for now, its lower frame just in front of the right-rear wheel wedged on a rock outcropping at the edge of the drop. The Fury, however, lay forty yards away up-ended on its passenger side, front tire slowly spinning, roof leaning against the face of the mountain, trunk popped open. Cord pulled his Maglite and scanned the wreck. At this distance he couldn't tell if anyone was hurt, or armed. But he needed to radio in and get help.

He reached inside the cruiser and lifted the receiver. "Anyone there? Over."

"Yeah, Cord. This is Sam."

"I'm two miles up Scratch Road. Got a nasty wreck. Might need an ambulance. Could be injuries."

"On my way. Ambulance too."

"And call in a tow truck. Might save Josephine if it gets here afore she slides into the ravine."

"Will do. And Cord? Junior, Swany and Ollie all made busts tonight. I'm the only one comin' up empty."

"Good job, buddy. Those stake-outs paid off. Now get your ass out here. I'm freezin'."

"10-4. Out."

As Cord tossed the receiver onto the front seat, he noticed the pistol and jar of whiskey again. Now that's a combination, he thought, reaching in to grab them both. He flung the jar into the ravine and picked up the gun. Then headed across the icy asphalt to the Fury, shining the Maglight over the car as he approached.

Holding the pistol down by his side, he walked slowly around the front. The windshield lay on the ground still in one piece, but crumpled and shattered, looking like some old, bleached leather hide. Lucas was hanging upside-down in his seatbelt, like a fly in a web, a huge gray automatic dangling loose in one hand. Cord holstered his own gun, laid the light on the ground pointed inside the car, then edged his body through the small gap between the hood of the car and the sheer rock face of the mountain. He crawled through the opening left by the missing windshield and reached the boy. He slid the pistol out of Lucas's hand, decocked it, and tossed it aside. Cord supported his weight as he unlatched the belt, then lowered him. Lucas seemed only partially conscious, or partially unconscious. Cord helped him over the seats and through the opening, then led him crawling and stumbling away from the wreck and sat him down on a slight rise beside the road to rest. He still looked stunned and disoriented, but Cord saw no blood and he didn't seem to have broken anything.

"Lucas? Lucas, boy. Where the hell's Thorn?"

The boy looked up, confused. "What? I . . . I don't know." He rubbed his head and looked around. "Beloit. Is Beloit okay?"

"Sit tight. I'll be right back." Cord squeezed around the bumper and hood again, boots crunching over shattered windshield glass, and crawled back through the opening.

The driver lay crumpled against the driver-side window. Cord carefully hooked both hands under his arms and pulled him up between the seat and steering wheel. Then hauled him through the windshield opening and dragged him clear of the car.

"Beloit. Beloit." He gently lowered him to the ground on his back. A veil of blood covered his eyes from a deep gash on his forehead. Cord checked his pulse. Weak. Probably in shock. He removed his coat and covered him the best he could. Need that ambulance bad, he thought, checking the rest of him for injuries. Left shin was busted up pretty good. Beloit's right arm flopped broken just above the wrist.

227

"Is he all right?" Lucas stumbled over to stand unsteadily next to Cord. "Is he gonna live?"

"Don't know. Think so. But we need that ambulance." He pulled Lucas down. "Hold his head up. Keep talkin'. See if you can get him to come around."

Cord ran over to the cruiser, found the first aid kit lying on the floor. He carried it back, folded some gauze and pressed it against the gash to staunch the bleeding from Beloit's forehead. Then told Lucas, "Hold this here. I gotta look for Thorn." He grabbed the flashlight and started up the road.

"He ain't here," said Lucas dully.

Cord stopped and turned back. "What? What do you mean?"

"Can't say, Sheriff." Lucas shook his head.

"What the hell you talkin' about?"

"He'd kill me fer puttin' his name anywhere close to this." The boy jerked his chin at the wreck. "Far as yer concerned, we're just a couple young'uns tryin' t' get ourselves killed racin' on this-here mountain. He put that gun in my hand so's it'd seem I was the one shot at you. Ain't even got no 'shine, Sheriff."

Cord walked around to the back of the car. The boy was right. Not a drop of liquor or meth anywhere. "I'll be damned."

But the trunk wasn't empty. Wedged up behind the spare tire was a two-gallon kerosene can under some rags. He wrapped one of the cloths around the handle and carried it back around to the boys. Lucas was talking low and earnestly to Beloit who was still unresponsive. He looked up as Cord approached.

"What's this?" Cord held up the can.

"I hid it in there after we got back the other day before we come t' see you. Thought it might help."

Cord looked down at him and nodded. "Sure might at that."

"And listen." Lucas brushed Beloit's hair back from his face. "That van weren't just a decoy. And we didn't take this road by accident. It were all planned." He glanced back down the mountain.

Cord trudged over the snow some yards back. There he found a third set of tire tracks leading back down the mountain toward Route 9.

"Goddammit!" Rad had backtracked and followed them up Scratch Road. Thorn had had him tail the tail. Then he must've jumped and run while Cord was making the call on the radio. "Shit." Cord shook his head. "Good move, you devious prick," he muttered.

He glanced down the mountain again. The flashing red and blue lights of Sam's F250 and the ambulance were headed their way. He walked back over to Lucas and knelt beside Beloit, who was blinking back to consciousness.

"Shit, Sheriff," he said as his eyes fluttered open. "Tryin' t' kill us?"

"No, son." He pulled a kerchief out of his back pocket and wiped more blood out of Beloit's eyes. "You'll be all right."

"Sure. Sure." He leaned back and closed his eyes again. "Sorry about Thorn," he whispered.

"I know where they're goin'." Lucas leaned down close to Cord's ear. "Caggle Knob. Heard him talkin' to Rad." He glanced up the mountain. "Other side of this-here pass. I know a trail that'll get us there in fifteen minutes. Quicker than drivin'."

Cord squinted up. "Why you tellin' me this, Lucas?"

The boy shook his head. "Thorn's been good t' me. But only as far as it's good fer him. He's a slow poison that blackens and kills everything it touches. I don't wanna die, Cord. But that's what'll happen if I don't get leave of him. And that ain't gonna happen 'less he's locked up, or dead."

"All right, then. Let me grab my shotgun." He looked back down at Beloit, who was unresponsive again. "You done good, son. We'll get that sonofabitch. We'll get him. You hang in there."

Tires crunched over frozen gravel. The pickup pulled in and shined a spotlight on the scene. "Damn, Cord. Thought you knew how to drive." Sam jumped out and ran toward them. "What we got here? You hurt?"

"A scratch. Beloit's gonna need some attention, though." Cord looked to Lucas. "We're going after them."

Sam frowned. "Who?"

"Thorn and Rad. The bastard put a tail on the tail. Rad must've circled back to pick up Thorn. They're meeting over at Caggle Knob. Lucas says we can cross over there in fifteen minutes on foot."

"I'm goin' too."

"No, you ain't. Stay here with Beloit until the EMTs come. Then get on the horn to Ollie and hightail it up to the Knob soon as you can."

"Shit, Cord. Sure you didn't get your head busted in that wreck? That's just plain-ass stupid."

"We can't let Thorn beat us. If this meeting was important enough for him to use a knotty ruse as this, it must be mighty damned important." He stood and started toward the wrecked cruiser. "And I aim to be there for it. But don't worry," he yelled over one shoulder. "Won't start nothing if I don't have to." At the car, he unracked the Remington 870, grabbed his Steiner Nighthunter binoculars, then marched back. "Still carry that Browning 30-06 in your truck?"

"I do."

"Grab it and a box of ammo. Give it to Lucas. And if you got 'em, extra shells for this." He held up the shotgun.

Sam trotted to the truck, grabbed the rifle off the rack and rummaged in the compartment between the seats, then returned as red lights strobed and the ambulance rounded the switchback.

"I'll be on the two-way, so keep the channel open." Cord grabbed the shells, passed the rifle to the boy, and shrugged. "We better hump it, Lucas. We got a date with the devil, and I don't want to keep that black angel waitin'."

23

Twisted Currents

The van bounced across a pothole and turned onto Fair Pond Road, headed east. The snow had eased off. Only a few flakes fluttered and swirled across the windshield. Thorn sat in the passenger seat watching the fence posts fly by. His plan had worked. When he saw the tail gaining on Lucas so quickly, he'd figured it was Cord. Sheriff drove the only cruiser in these parts that might could stay with Beloit's Fury. But Thorn had wanted to test the boy's skill. So he'd turned him up Scratch Road and held on as Beloit shifted and snaked around the tight curves and hilly dips up the mountain.

He'd kept an eye out the back window, watching as Cord tried to keep up. And when the cruiser almost careened into the ravine on the last turn, he'd told Beloit to stop and turn around. As soon as they faced the cruiser, he'd drawn his pistol and rolled down the window. "Run that sonofabitch off the road," he'd said. "Now!"

He knew Cord would never back down. And as the boy pointed the Fury at the cruiser and gunned it, he also figured he might lose this gambit. But it was sure as hell worth a try.

He'd aimed and fired just before Cord suddenly braked and swung the rear end of the cruiser into the oncoming sedan, sending both cars spinning and skidding in opposite directions across the narrow road.

Thorn had lifted one hand above his head, bracing the other against the dashboard as the Fury flipped and spun onto its side. Beloit lost his grip on the steering wheel when his head bashed into the windshield. Finally, as they'd come to a stop, the car smashing and rocking up on its side next to the mountain, Thorn realized he hadn't felt so alive in years. Heart pumping strong. Breathing steady and even. Mind clear as a high-mountain trout stream.

He'd glanced back at Lucas hanging strapped in the seat belt, half-conscious. Thorn ejected the magazine from the pistol, thumbed out the unspent rounds, and racked the slide to empty the chamber. Then twisted in his seat to place the gun in the boy's hand, wrapping his unresisting fingers around the grip.

"Thorn?" Lucas' eyelids fluttered.

"Thorn's not here, boy. Never was. Just you and Beloit havin' some fun, gettin' chased by the local law. Think I'd risk hauling a load with a couple of greenhorns the likes of y'all? No, I was over at Caggle Knob with some associates tonight." He glanced at Beloit. "Hope he makes it. Kinda liked the ornery bastard." He looked back at Lucas and winked. "Shouldn't be shootin' at the sheriff, boy. Could land a body in jail."

Then he'd kicked out the front window, crawled across the pavement and peered around the front end of the car. Cord stood next to the cruiser talking on the radio. Thorn grinned, remembering how the patrol car had tottered on the edge of the ravine. Then he scurried across the road to the bend and trotted down the incline to meet the van.

And now, as they wound up the northeast side of Caggle Knob, fence posts flying by, he felt easy and comfortable. If tonight's hit worked out, he could expand the operation. Have to get more protection, though. Hawkins and a couple of county commissioners were already in his pocket. But he'd need to pull in others along the routes into Virginia, North Carolina, Georgia and Alabama. But that shouldn't be a problem once they got the supply contacts from Eli.

Thorn leaned back in the seat, watching the road stretch out in front of him, knowing now all would be well.

Rad stopped and then backed the van down into a shortout behind a thick stand of spruce pine five hundred yards below the lookout pull off. Caggle Knob was a low mountain rise, sandwiched between Slope Mountain to the south and Breen Ridge to the north. About fifty yards from the top was a little lookout area. Tourists stopped there for a panoramic view of the valley stretching east into the Smoky Mountain National Park, where Eli had said the meeting would take place. Thorn looked at his watch. 12:50. "Come on, boys. Don't want to miss the party."

Jake Harkell, a lean, sharp-nosed stomper whose pappy had worked for Frank, grabbed his Savage .308 lever rifle as they all now piled out of the van. Thorn and Rad took along AR15 carbines, racking the charging handles to load the chambers.

Thorn slung his carbine over one shoulder. "If we cut up this rise here, should be able to ease around and catch 'em in a crossfire."

Rad and Jake followed him up the hill until they'd almost reached the top. They cut east along a thin ridge until they were standing just above a group of men huddled below. The clouds had broken. Wan moonlight reflected silhouettes off the thinning snow. Thorn counted seven men down there. Four stood not far from a black Hummer parked next to the drop-off. Three others had their backs to a green van. Eli wore what looked like some kind of army cap.

"Okay. Jake, you stay put," said Thorn. "Me and Rad gonna move on across this-here ridge, plant ourselves behind them boulders. Wait 'til I take the first shot, then let loose on them sonsabitches. But don't shoot the one in the funny hat. He's our man." He clapped Jake on the shoulder. "Least, he will be if he lives." Thorn chuckled and turned away to disappear into the trees.

24
Into the Swirl

Lucas trotted ahead, that long liquid gait reminding Cord how much closer forty-eight years was to sixty than twenty. They followed the road for half a mile, then Lucas jumped the rail and slid, bent-legged and half-hopping, down a cut to the bottom of a deep gulley. The moon broke between low-rolling clouds, illuminating the dense, snow-dusted path ahead as they crossed a shallow, frozen stream and clambered up the backside of Caggle Knob. He stayed close behind Lucas, watching his footing, grabbing saplings and chinks in the granite to leverage himself up the steep incline.

Two-thirds of the way up, breathing hard, he stumbled over a root, almost falling face-first on frozen scrabble rock, barely catching a spindly rhododendron branch with his free hand, gripping the shotgun tighter. When he looked up, Lucas had disappeared behind a sharp outcropping ten yards above. He scrambled up, skidded over a loose bed of gravel and swiveled around the jutting boulder where the boy waited.

"There's a trail just ahead that loops around above the lookout." Lucas pointed with the rifle. "Shouldn't take us more 'n five minutes."

Cord leaned against the boulder, catching his breath. "Don't know what we're goin' to find, so ease on in there nice and quiet-like. Check that Browning, make sure you got one chambered."

Lucas pulled the magazine. "Five in the box and one set to fire." He smacked the magazine back in place.

Cord slapped the slide back on his pistol, re-holstered, then pumped a round into the shotgun. "Reckon I should deputize you, but I'm just not sure how to write it up in the report. Seeing as you're intimately involved with the crimes I'm currently pursuing."

"Write it up however fits best, Cord. I done lost my stomach for anything to do with Thorn. Don't much care what much all happens to me later. But I sure as hell don't want that shithead footloose and free while I'm doin' time at Brushy Mountain."

"Consider yourself deputized and lead the way then, son."

Cord edged along the ridge behind Lucas until they stepped off on a narrow trail. They picked up the pace, hit a switchback that angled up about thirty degrees, then came around a bend.

Some forty feet below two groups stood talking. Lucas motioned Cord behind a boulder just off the trail. Cord drew his binoculars. He counted seven. Thorn wasn't among them. Instead, Cord was surprised to see Levon and a couple others who seemed to be arguing with a group of four other men standing alongside a dark Hummer. Their brush-cuts and upright bearing somehow struck Cord as military, or maybe militia-types. What the hell? He swung the binoculars, scanning the mountain for Thorn. Nothing.

Then, just above them and slightly to the left, something glinted in the moonlight. He started to focus, but was distracted by a commotion below.

He swung the binoculars around. Two black SUVs had wheeled up onto the lookout. Seven or eight people, all wearing dark caps, piled out, pistols drawn. He could just make out DEA logos on their jackets. They advanced on the first group. "Get down, down on your knees!" one agent yelled. Then a rifle report came from above and one of the

DEA agents dropped to the ground, head blossoming red against the white snow.

All hell broke loose. Men retreated in all directions, firing pistols and automatic rifles in a melee like Cord hadn't seen since his days in South America. Then another rifle cracked from just below them and to the right. Another ATF agent yelped and went down, then started crawling to the SUV for cover.

"Lucas! Got a couple of snipers knocking out the good guys down there." He pointed up to the left. "One's about three hundred yards across this crescent, forty feet up. Can you take care of him?"

"Don't see why not." Lucas lowered his rifle and leveled it against the boulder.

"He's got a scope. Look for a reflection or a muzzle flash, then take him out. I'm going to circle on down, see if I can't knock out the shooter below us."

Cord crossed behind Lucas and cut out over the ridgeline. Below, the DEA team, taking cover behind their vehicles, fired volleys at Levon and the others; who fired back from behind the van and some boulders hemmed up against the mountain. Cord worked his way around just above the shooter, a dark hulk in silhouette squatting beside a tall spruce. He popped another round off. But this time, one of the men with Levon went down.

The thought that he'd stepped into something bigger than he'd bargained for flashed through Cord's mind just as he hit a patch of slick leaves and lost his footing. He landed on his ass, slid down the bank, and came to rest six feet behind the shooter, watching his shotgun rattle down the hillside.

The man spun around to gape at him. Cord saw first the distinctive white scar running down the forehead and across the nose, then the look of disbelief in Jake Harkell's eyes as the man took a step back and started to raise the muzzle of his AR15. Cord used the forward momentum of the fall to roll up and lunge him across the few yards between them. He slammed into Jake's chest, sending them both rolling and tumbling down the mountainside.

As they plunged down the scrabble slope, Cord's head banged against a jagged outcropping, slashing cheek and temple. A searing red explosion burst behind his right eye, blinding him momentarily. Then Jake's grip loosened as they plummeted off a ledge, freefalling ten feet before slamming down onto a granite slab below. Cord landed atop Jake and heard the other's ribs crack under him.

He shook his head, dazed, and looked around to catch his bearings. They'd landed on a short outcropping twenty feet above the DEA trucks. But the agents were too busy returning gunfire and keeping their own asses covered to notice any ruckus overhead. Cord pushed up and leaned over Harkell. "Well, howdy, Jake." He glanced at the rifle lying within reach. "What the hell, you tryin' to kill me?"

"Ow. Goddammit, Cord. You fuckin' prick." Jake winced, groping for the AR.

Cord kicked it away. "I think you're the one's fucked here, buddy." He rolled Jake onto his side and cuffed him just as the slight but distinct whisper of air puffed close to one ear. Then a whine as a bullet ricocheted off the stone behind him.

Cord rolled to the downhill side of Jake, using him as a shield as he pulled his pistol, aiming up the mountainside. He caught movement to his right twenty yards above and fired off two rounds. A shadowy figure took off running across the ridge. Cord calculated his lead and squeezed off three more rounds slow. The third found its mark. The figure stumbled, collapsed, and rolled down the hill, landing like a heavy sack of grain against an old pitch pine. Radley Sikes' eyes rolled over to white.

"Goddammit, Rad." Cord shook his head, frustrated at yet another senseless death. It'd been a long time since he'd had to fire on a man. Let alone kill one. And he'd never found any truly satisfactory reason to account for the men he'd had to kill.

No time to ponder that now . . . His gut churned as he turned back to focus on the firefight, ears ringing from the rounds he'd just fired. A report from above drew his attention as the bullet plinked into the side of one of the SUVs. Surprised to find the binoculars, one lens busted, still hanging around his neck, he rolled onto his belly and lifted them.

Below, an ATF agent and one of the militia-types lay dead in the center of the fray. Another militiaman lay on his back, wounded, next to the Hummer. Twenty yards behind it, Levon and a man whose face Cord couldn't make out, hidden as it was beneath the brim of a Castro army cap, were firing from the cover of boulders. At the distinctive boom of the .30-06, Cord glanced up just in time to see the body of the second sniper fall from his mountain perch and land with a dull thud on the asphalt. He swung the binoculars back to the boulders, but Levon and the other seemed to be gone.

Must've taken off down the old forest road on the backside of the Lookout, he thought. He rolled onto his side and punched the button on his two-way. "Got a real party jumpin' here, Samuel. Honest-to-god shit-storm. What the hell's takin' so long. Over."

"We're a minute out, Cord. You okay?"

"I'll give a blow-by-blow later. You're coming up on a crew of DEA agents who might be a tad trigger-happy. Just found themselves in a firefight I don't think they expected. Better let them know I'm up here on the ridge above, with Lucas."

A pause. "DEA?"

"Yeah. We've been trackin' the wrong buck, buddy. This here's Levon's party, not Thorn's. Meeting must have been some kind of important to set up this sting. Guess they didn't know Thorn and his crew had their own plans to crash the festivities."

Below, the two militiamen, apparently realizing they were outgunned and outmanned, had ceased firing. They tossed weapons from behind the Hummer, waving their hands, yelling for the agents to stop shooting.

"Looks like it's winding down here, buddy. Just tell them agents to keep their powder dry. Don't want to get my head blown off by friendlies."

"We're pulling in behind them now. You stay safe."

But before he could answer, three quick shots barked across the hollow from forty yards to his right, from up on the ridge.

"Lucas!" He scrambled up the slick incline to the trail and sprinted to the hump of rock.

The boy lay on his back between two boulders, bleeding from his shoulder and chest. Blinking as he tried to lift his head.

"Heard him comin'." Lucas grabbed Cord's hand. "Got one shot off."

"Don't talk, boy." Cord leaned over, pulling his flashlight to inspect the wounds. One bullet had entered the chest, center-left. The other had ripped through the deltoid of his shoulder. Gripping the flashlight in his teeth, Cord unzipped the boy's jacket and tore the shirt away from the wound. He pulled a pair of rubber gloves from his pocket and applied pressure with the heel of one hand to seal the opening, to keep the lung from collapsing. He punched the button on the two-way with the other. "Sam, call in an 11-41. Need medics up here, now! Lucas is down. One shot to the chest, another to the shoulder. Grab a first aid kit and shag-ass to my position on the flashlight." He positioned the light on top of the boulder to shine down towards the SUVs. Then turned back to Lucas. "Hang in there, partner. Help's coming."

Lucas reached for his hand, breathing shallow now, eyes wide in panic. "That girl. Zoe." He paused and closed his eyes. "She liked my braided heart."

"Don't you fade out on me, Lucas. Don't you fade." But he could feel the boy slipping, the pulse thready beneath his fingers. He slammed the button on the two-way again. "Sam! I need that fucking kit, now!"

25
Away from Stormy Waters

Thorn ran along the edge of the ridgeline until he picked up the trail heading back down to the road. Stumbling off the trailhead at the raised blacktop shoulder, he pulled up short to watch from behind a leafless maple as an ambulance shot by strobing and wailing. He crossed the road, dashed to his van and jumped in, pausing just long enough to catch his breath before firing up the engine.

He kept the headlights off and nosed the vehicle up the shortcut back to the road. Despite the cold, sweat trickled down his neck, and the pungent odor of gunpowder rising from the steam off his body filled the cab. He worked his jaw to try to clear the ringing in his ears, then rolled onto the blacktop, flipped the headlights on and headed down the mountain, slow and steady. Snow had only dusted the roads with a powdered-sugar coating, but he didn't want to hit a patch of black ice and slide into a ditch.

He turned onto Heddy Mountain Road, rolling in and out of the thick fog of the bottoms, then humped over to Chapel Road and booked it to Highway 70. A sheriff's pickup and cruiser shot past going in the opposite direction, blue lights flashing. He glanced in the rearview and held the speed limit all the way to Dogtrot Road, then turned off. He took a deep breath and let it out slow. Thank God. Almost home.

"Well, that was one goddammed fucking mess. Every fucking gomer and his brother showed up for the dance, tonight," he ranted as he swung the van onto Reevers Road and started up the hill to the compound. "And what the hell were you thinkin', Rad? Godamnit to hell." He shook his head. "Why'd ye have to go and get yourself killed?" He slammed a fist against the steering wheel. "Fuck!"

He pulled up in front of the house, shoved the shifter into park, shut the engine down and sat looking out over the hollow. The sky had begun to clear. Pinpricks of stars punctuated the bluish-black canvas of dead night. He tightened his grip on the wheel and bit his bottom lip until he tasted blood.

Fucking Cord, he thought. And that goddamned Lucas. Threw everything off. Could've swung it even with those DEA fucks showing up if it weren't for that ungrateful, stupid-ass hillbilly fuck.

He grinned now, remembering the boy's face as he'd turned and realized he'd been bushwacked. Thorn had fired off the first round, knocking the boy's shoulder half-back, throwing off his aim. The second bullet had hit him square in the chest. There'd be no more problems from that little shithead.

But Cord was something else.

He reviewed the night's events. Nothing directly implicating him. True, there was Beloit. Who, if he lived, might give testimony connecting him. But who'd believe some trouble-making hotrod wannabe outsider? Thorn could round up a dozen locals who'd vouch he'd spent the whole night at home throwing a big party.

But Cord. That bastard'd be down on him hard. Steady and mad, single-minded as a wild boar in rut. Well, there was only one way to stop a wild boar. Thorn nodded, stepped out of the van and walked quickly to the house. "A .44 magnum right between the eyes," he muttered.

26
Death's Harbor

Levon grabbed Eli's sleeve and yanked him from behind the boulder as Zippy's body bounced off a ledge and tumbled onto the Lookout parking lot thirty yards out. Levon had realized they were fucked when the DEA showed up. And now that they'd taken out Zippy, who'd at least offered them some cover, it was time to cut and run.

He'd picked The Lookout for the meet because there was an old forestry road leading down off the backside of the mountain. Sporadic gunfire popped behind them now as they stumbled and ran down the overgrown, steeply sloping track, skating over ice patches and wet leaves. They took one switchback, another, then veered off the road, sliding on backsides and hands down a slick-leaved bank to hit level bottom, where they waded a half-frozen creek. They scrambled up the opposite bank, where Sebastian waited with a couple of idling ATVs.

"Where's Zippy? Quentin?" he asked, looking from one to the other.

"Didn't make it," Levon snapped. He swung up behind Sebastian as Eli jumped on the other Rhino and they took off, bouncing and sliding down the trail. They came off the mountain, spinning a rooster-tail of mud and ice behind them and cut across a wide hollow that butted up to the French Broad. They followed the river shore for three miles to the ragged barbed-wire fence that marked the outlines of the Farm.

Eli wrenched the ATV sideways, skidding to a stop. He pulled out a fence post and moved it to one side while Sebastian and Levon drove through, and waited for him to follow them in after he set the post back in place. Five minutes later, they pulled up to the main house.

"What the fuck happened back there?" Sabastian demanded as they got off the mud and ice-encrusted vehicles. "Sounded like a war zone." He scowled, looking worried.

"A fucking set-up. DEA swarming on us." Levon paced across the yard and back, frozen grass crunching beneath his feet. "The Feds don't just show up on a whim. Those fuckhead Army dicks probably set 'em on us. Goddammit!" He glared at Eli, narrowing his eyes, and slapped the cap off his head. "Get rid of that fucking thing. You and your communist-socialist bullshit. What do you think this is, fucking Cuba, 1960?"

Eli glared back a split second, then bent and picked up the hat, brushing it off against his pant leg. "So what now?"

Levon clenched his jaw, staring out over the compound as if the future would unfold there on a giant screen. "They'll come after us, I reckon. But we won't go down easy." He looked back at Sebastian. "Get those ATVs stowed. Wake up the men. I'm calling a meeting, right now." He poked Eli's shoulder. "Go tell Maya to gather the women. Get them and the kids in the bunker. Then meet me back here in fifteen. We're gonna put this town on the map."

27

Into the Churn

Cord watched the bare, dark tree trunks rise in the headlight beams and advance like silent pickets beside the road. Only an hour away from sunrise, and looking up at the clearing skies of the false dawn he figured it'd be one of those hard, bright days of late fall. The kind where despite the sun's brilliant early luster, steel blue skies would weigh heavy and cold on the hills shouldering tight against the hollows. He thought about his son, barely ten years younger than Lucas, and prayed he'd never know the kind of hard scrabbling that bent a boy like Lucas down—twisted him out of shape, and then turned him to ways he'd someday curse. Ways no amount of tender mercies could reach in time to right him again.

Sam turned into a spot in front of the jail and yanked the gear lever into park. "Better get inside. Swany will call from the hospital." He unbuckled his belt and waited. "There weren't nothing you could've done. He was there by his own hand."

"Five men dead, three in the hospital, three escaped locals, and you say there ain't nothin' I could've done? Don't drop that horseshit on me, Sam. Hell, I had the whole goddamned mess misfigured from the beginning. Dammit!" Cord punched the dash, splitting the hard vinyl and a knuckle. "He was just a fuckin' kid." He grimaced, then pointed. "Get out."

Sam gaped. "What?"

"Get the hell out. I'm going for a drive."

"Sheriff. Don't do this. Those agents are on the way. We'll need to coordinate tomorrow's raid on the Farm."

"I don't give two shits about coordinating with those fucks. If they'd coordinated with us to begin with we wouldn't be in this mess. Now get the hell out and hold things down here until I get back."

"You can't do anything to him until we investigate what happened."

"I know who's to blame for what the hell happened tonight, and Thorn's not getting clear of it this time. Now get out!"

Sam stepped out of the truck and Cord slid behind the wheel, rolling the window down. "Don't worry. I won't kill him. Lowlife bastard ain't worth it."

He slammed into reverse, backed out and spun the tires, shifting back into drive. The truck hurtled over the river, headlights knifing through the pre-dawn darkness. An ash-gray haze floated above its surface and the powdered verges of its banks. His frustration, remorse and guilt over Lucas, combined with a loathing antipathy for all the repugnant, vile meanness of the world, burned in his gut. The top of his head felt cinched in a strap that grew tighter and tighter until it tinted everything red. Fueling a revulsion he hadn't known since he'd seen the dismembered and burned bodies of women and children lying in ditches alongside rough-cut mountain roads. Men with heads blasted apart, unidentifiable as anything human, and yet oh-so-human he still dreamed about them almost every night. As he drove, he tried to persuade himself the criminals he dealt with on a day-to-day basis were products of their upbringing and culture. That they too deserved the same recognition of human dignity, no matter their past misdeeds.

But tonight those thoughts kept getting buried beneath the stubborn, deep-rooted knowledge that came after all his years on the battlefield and his time on the streets dealing with malevolent thugs whose only moral compass seemed to point to green. Men who'd do anything, including killing or maiming those closest to them, just to grab more and more of the lucre that drove them. Their connections to any true humanity had somehow been severed. And consequently, all rights of consideration due a human being were also severed.

Fifteen minutes later, he pulled off the road and stopped at the bottom of the drive to Thorn's compound. He shifted the 250 into four-wheel drive, then laid the pedal down, still picking up speed as the heavy-duty grill smashed through the security gate.

In seconds, he was skidding to a stop ten yards from Thorn's front entrance. He unpinned his star, laid it on the dash, opened the glove box, pulled out a leather, lead-weighted sap and slid it in his back pocket. Then reached behind the seat for the thirty-five-pound Thunderbolt door ram Sam used for meth lab busts, pushed out of the truck and hit the ground running. He didn't pause at the filigreed oak double doors, swinging the ram back in a smooth motion and then flexing it forward with all the force of his upper arms. Splitting the center door support, driving the knob back like a grenade into the foyer as his left shoulder slammed the panel almost busting the doors off their hinges when he smashed through.

Thorn stood stopped in mid-stride, at the top of stairs that led down to the basement of the split-level. His eyes, hard as black opals, studied Cord. Not so much with surprise, but shrewd guile. The wheels clearly turning in his head as he started to reach for a large revolver stuck in his belt, decided against it, then turned instead and started back down the stairs.

Cord dashed across the foyer and halfway down the stairs, and dived onto Thorn, catching him just as he turned and grabbed a ball from the pool table. Cord drove an arm up between them to block the blow he knew was coming, but the back of his head still caught a glancing swipe, an audible crack. The jolt had probably split his scalp, but some switch had been flipped his his head, and he didn't feel it at all. His body was numb to pain, while everything around him vibrated with a hypersensory sheen.

He swung his right fist up, catching Thorn square in the chin, and followed it with a left hook to the kidneys that collapsed him to his knees. Cord grabbed his wrist and twisted hard, cracking bones, sending the blood-flecked cue ball clacking and rolling across the tile floor. He yanked him up by the collar and shortarmed a hard jab into his mouth, feeling through torn knuckles the teeth giving way behind Thorn's lips. He pulled him up again and slammed the fist into his cheek. A gash opened up under Thorn's left eye, blood smearing his face.

Suddenly, a sharp, blinding strike to the back of Cord's neck sent him to his knees, knocking him semi-consciousness for a moment before a kick to the ribs jolted him back.

He rolled onto his back, hobbling one leg of his new assailant in the crook of his arm, then rammed his boot hard up into the man's crotch. The man doubled over and fell back on his ass. Cord scrambled up, reached for the sap and swung it around and down on the man's raised arm as he tried to stand again. He jerked the arm back with a guttural grunt, dropping a bat. Cord swung again and again, thumping the man's legs and side, his ribs and back, until he lay at Cord's feet, curled into a ball of bruised, quivering flesh.

Cord turned back to Thorn, who'd pulled himself up and was staggering to the other side of the pool table, groping with his left hand for the hogleg in his belt. Cord angled around the corner of the table and swung the sap, the lead tip connecting just behind Thorn's ear. He crashed over a coffee table and onto his back, the handgun skittering away underneath the couch.

Cord stood over the unmoving body for a minute, breathing heavy. He glanced around, listening for others as the strange vibrating sheen of rage dissipated and his heart rate slowed. Then he knelt astride Thorn's body, yanked him up by his shirt and slapped him hard across the face. "Come on, you sonofabitch. You ain't gettin' off so easy. Open your fuckin' eyes!"

Thorn blinked one orb open and stared up blankly, as if trying to get his bearings. "What the fuck, Cord," he said finally, spitting out an ivory shard of tooth. "You put a goddamned whuppin' on me."

"Godammit." He bent down, inches from Thorn's face. "Why'd you have to shoot the boy?"

"I didn't know. I swear. All I knew was somebody was takin' shots at us. I come up behind him and when he turned, I'd already started squeezin' the trigger. You gotta believe me, Cord. I liked the kid."

"As long as you was gettin' something outta him. But no matter whether he lives or dies, you crossed a line. You saved my life once. This here? Me lettin' you live? Evens the debt up.

Cord shook him. Hard. "So listen good and know it sure! You're in the churn, now. And I'm gonna keep it spinning from here on out. Cause one thing's f'sure when it comes to dealing with low-down, mean thugs the likes of you. You're cocky. Think you're smarter than the rest of us. Hard truth is, you ain't. And one day, when you slip up, and you will. I'll be there." He let Thorn's head drop back to rap hard on the tile. Stood, brushed wood splinters off his jeans. He bent and picked up the .44. "I'll just take this for safekeeping. Maybe give you one bullet back, some day."

Cord crossed the room, stepping over the man he now recognized as John Quinn, a three-time loser whose family had once owned the largest tract of timber in Acre County. His father had sold off most of it to pay gambling debts. John's own vices leaned towards his father's, with a twist of perversion. He'd been released from Brushy Mountain three months back on a conviction for attempted murder, having almost killed a whore with a cattle prod, leaving her scarred, inside and out, in ways Cord could hardly stand to think about. He turned back to kick him once more for good measure. "Make sure you stay in the life, Quinn. It'll give me a good reason to do this again—only worse."

Outside, the false dawn was breaking purple and plum between white wisps of clouds. His shoulders sagged, suddenly heavy, as he tossed the ram onto the bed of the truck and slipped behind the wheel.

His head whanged. He winced when he touched the egg-shaped, gashed contusion. His fingers came away bloody. Cranking the engine, he wheeled around the circular drive, bumping over rattling remnants of security gate as he turned down the road back to town. Still an hour before sun-up, but enough light out to see the rim of the mountains looming dark above the hamlet.

The streets were empty except for a few early shift workers catching breakfast at Lily's. The steeple of First Presbyterian rose in the town center. His mother and father were buried in the graveyard that took up a block on the east side of the old church. What would they think about their little town now? Had it really changed so much, or had the evil that lurked here always been, only now more out in the open. Willing to proclaim its right to exist alongside the good and generous virtues that made up the bulk of its citizens?

How long would he be able to fight for those virtues, to face the malignant cruelty for which most didn't have the stomach, before he himself crossed that line and became as malevolent as the bitter, avaricious and vengeful? The ones he fought on a daily basis just to maintain a semblance of order which might allow the goodness to spread?

He pulled down Main and parked in the reserved space outside the office. Four black Suburban SUVs lined the street. DEA, no doubt. He slid Thorn's .44 into his coat, stepped out and crossed to the doors.

"Damn, son." Waddy grimaced at Cord as he passed through the gate. "You all right."

"Sure, Waddy. How 'bout call Doc and tell him to bring his bag."

"Will do."

Junior was standing behind Waddy. "Sorry to hear about Lucas, Cord." He shook his head. "He was a good boy. Wished I could of known him better at school."

"Yeah. Let's not give up. He's not gone, yet." Cord glanced at the two agents standing in the hallway in front of his office, but kept speaking to his deputy. "Heard you done good tonight. Hauled in a hundred and thirty-five gallons of honest-to-goodness 'shine whiskey. Thanks, son."

Junior ducked his head. "Yessir."

Sam strode to the front and took Cord's arm, walking him to the back wall in front of the map. "We brought in over six hundred gallons of whiskey, twenty pounds of meth, and locked up two runners. But them fellers." He jerked his chin at the agents. "Already startin' to raise hell about how we fucked up their sting. We took out five bad guys, arrested three. Trying now to sort out their allegiances. DEA's interviewing them. They lost one agent, another wounded. They want to move on the compound at sunrise. I told them they'd have to wait, talk to you. But they said it's outside our jurisdiction now." He studied Cord. "How's Thorn?"

"Alive. But he knows we're done with sparring." He pulled out the .44. "Check the ballistics against the bullets recovered from Lucas. But I don't think we'll get a match. Besides, think I pretty much broke every damn evidentiary rule to get it. But worth a try." He took a deep breath and let it out slowly.

Doc walked in. "What the hell, Cord! Told you I was runnin' out of room. Got so many bodies had to send some off to Newport General. Now you call me over here like I don't already have enough to do."

"Just got to look at a bump. Maybe throw a stitch or two in it."

"Sit down. Tilt your head down," Doc grumbled. He opened his bag, pulled out antiseptic wipes, and cleaned the gash. "Could use a few stitches. Need to shave it first."

"Goddammit, Doc!"

"Stings, huh?"

" Just bandage or stitch it, but get it done now!"

"Hold on, then." He quickly injected Novocain around the wound, pulled out his suture kit, and in a few minutes was snipping off the thread. "That oughta hold." He closed his bag, then looked around as he turned to leave. "Lucas's friend, Beloit? Barely hangin' on. Come over when you're done here. Do him good. Think he's takin' what happened to Lucas all on his own. Maybe you could share that load."

Cord nodded, a sick feeling twisting his stomach. "Will do."

He reached to touch his scalp, but Kirby slapped his hand off. "And keep your damn mitts off my good work." Doc turned and walked away.

"Good man." Sam tapped the corner of the desk, watching him leave. "We still have a few, Cord. Enough to keep the bad guys on their heels."

"Maybe." Cord stood and faced the others. "You men, listen up. Y'all really came through tonight. Thanks." He looked around at each and smiled. "I couldn't ask for better men willing to put their lives on the line for the good." He paused, thinking again about Lucas and Beloit, pushing back the lump rising in his throat. "But we still have unfinished business. So tie up your reports while I talk with our guests and I'll get back to you."

He walked down the hall to the waiting men in black tactical gear. "Sheriff Cord McCrae," he said. "Sorry for the loss of your men."

The taller of the two agents stepped up, jabbing a finger at Cord, ignoring the outstretched hand. "What the fuck were you doing out there tonight? And with a civilian! It took six months of operational surveillance to set up for this bust. And now, because of your fucking Hatfield and McCoy antics, we've probably lost our only opportunity to nail Levon Gladson without a major incident."

Cord's head throbbed, a bone-weary tiredness setting in from the long night. But now his heart began to race, the blood to rise hotly in his face. He reminded himself that these guys worked around the clock for months on end dealing with low-lifes most people would only recognize in nightmares. "Let's do this in my office, here." He stepped around them and opened the door.

Inside, Cord moved behind the desk and stood in front of his chair. "Now let me get this straight, agent—?"

"Special Agent Bob Murphy. This is Special Agent Kimmel."

Murphy was squared-shouldered, tall, mid-thirties with sandy-brown, close-cropped hair. His arms and chest had seen plenty of time on the free-weights.

"So, Special Agent, let me see if I understand the situation. You come into my county, don't inform us of your operation, set up a bust where you get caught in a crossfire with snipers raining down hell from above. Then when my men show up in pursuit of a suspect and end up in the middle of a federal operation gone bad, and we knock out the sharpshooters pinning you down, support you with fire and provide the medical personnel to save your sorry asses, you want to blame us for the fuck-up?" He leaned over the desk, glaring at Murphy. "And that young deputy, Lucas, who had more guts and smarts and heart than the two of you put together, he's up in ICU now from trying to save your asses. So get off that fucking high horse, dispense with the name callin', and get on with talking about what the hell you were doing out there."

Murphy glared, then nodded. "Sorry about the swipe at your office, Sheriff. Uncalled for." His eye twitched, and Cord wondered whether from embarrassment or irritation. "I don't want a turf war. We're on the same team."

"You ain't done much to convince me of such as yet." Cord straightened and scratched the scar above his brow. "Haven't even let us interview the men you arrested. So fill me in on what you know."

Murphy cleared his throat. He glanced at his stone-faced buddy, who nodded approval. "Our team's been keeping tabs on the Glad Earth Farm for six months. Ever since the big meth sweep that took out your last sheriff. Had a tip Gladson's group were tending large tracts of cannabis under the cover of thick timber just over the border in the Cherokee National Forest. But after months of helicopter flyovers and trying to infiltrate their group, we still hadn't been able to pinpoint the crop's location.

"We finally did get one man in. Quentin Mosely. He tipped us off to the meeting. Unfortunately, he's one of the good guys who went down in the crossfire tonight. Sorry we didn't coordinate with your office, now. But we weren't sure whether you'd cleaned up the internal corruption the old sheriff had left behind or just followed his lead.

"Anyhow, we were about to shut down the operation when a call came in from our office in Nashville, about some activity from a new group of wannabe Pablo Escobars. Made contact with a local vet living here."

Cord's mouth tightened. "Louis Pollard?"

"That's right." Murphy looked surprised. "We started monitoring their communications just last week. Weren't sure about the Glad Earth connection until our undercover got wind of it yesterday. Until then, we'd assumed the deal was between Pollard and those skinhead fucks locked up back there." He inclined his head toward the holding cells.

"Lou died Saturday night. Thought you were keepin' tabs."

"I said we were monitoring their communications. To be honest, we didn't have enough men on location to keep personal surveillance on all the operators." Murphy glanced at his partner and sighed. "It's been just the two of us and Quentin here for months. We didn't get a heads up on the meeting until Friday night. Spent most the next forty-eight hours coordinating logistics and personnel for tonight's bust."

Cord shook his head. "So much for cooperation. And what'd you learn from those creeps in back?"

"The Army's seen a rise in gang activity inside their units over the past few years. They've tried to handle it internally, with less than unqualified success. Some bad boys land back stateside, trained up in weapons and tactics, ready to take over new territory or grab it from the criminal douchebags already in operation. This gang out of Nashville was contacted by Pollard, who had a scheme to bring in heroin from Afghanistan. Not easy, but doable if you have access to military cargo flights in and out of the country. He told them he had a partner who'd take care of the distribution end. He and this partner wanted to arrange a meeting and deliver some sample product.

"Our man was wired up, so we planned to monitor that, pick up some intel that might lead to a bigger bust. Decided to move in when the meeting took a turn violent.

"Seems the bristle-heads weren't none too happy when the partner, who we now know was Gladson, showed up without the middleman, Pollard. We were afraid they'd draw down on each other. Our guy would end up in a shitstorm then. So we moved. If we hadn't gotten there when we did, bastards might've just blown each other apart."

Cord nodded and sat down. "Sounds like you'd have been better off at this point." He rubbed his nose with his thumb and sighed. "So, what's your next move?"

"We'll raid the compound at 0800 hours. An army of federal agents is converging on the highway about a mile from the farm now. Including the ATF. They might have their own arsenal up there. Levon may well put up a fight."

"Let me go with you." Cord leaned forward, hands flat on the desk. "I can talk to Levon. He's kinda crazy—but we have a relationship, of sorts. He may trust me enough to talk. Don't want to have another Waco, do we?"

Murphy studied him, frowning. "Fine. Come along. Maybe try to talk to sense into the prophet of doom. But if bullets start flying, stay out of the way. We know what we're doing, despite what you think about last night. Meet us at the rendezvous, 0730 hours."

Cord watched Murphy and his partner file out of the office, shutting the door behind them. He leaned back and looked out the window. The river reflected a slate-blue sky in the dim light, peeking over the ridge of the bluffs. He'd seen a thousand crisp, late-fall mornings like this. They carried both the fading hints of life-endowing summer days with the augury of dark, cold days ahead. He shivered at the thought, then punched the intercom. "Sam. In here."

Cord walked to the window and watched the river rubbing its back against the far shore until he heard Sam step into the office. He kept his eyes on the water as he told the deputy everything he'd learned from Agent Murphy. Then turned.

"In a couple hours, I'll need you to ride with me up the Glad Earth Farm compound. Our friends the Feds are planning a raid. But those three unsolved murders need to get solved before everything goes to shit up there and we lose our only chance to get answers."

He sat down again and leaned his elbows on the desktop. "So, let's review. Starting with Fred. Things ain't going well at the Pollard Farm after Katie dies. Fred's depressed. With the dry season last year, crops don't put out and bills are hitting hard. His farm's about to get foreclosed.

"So Lou joins the service to bring in a little cash, and gets shipped over to the desert. Falls in with some bad characters and schemes to bring heroin back Stateside to save the farm. Once home, he contacts Levon, who he knows already has a supply line set up for marijuana. Lou figures it'd be less dangerous than dealing with Thorn. Who gets wind of the plan from Eli. Who, according to Lucas, is now playing both sides, and maybe making a move for a coup at The Farm."

Sam frowned. "But Thorn ain't gonna sit back and let some low-lander come in and start a new operation." He tapped his knuckles against the desk, puzzling the pieces together. "He'd want to cut out the competition. Or move in and take over. But when he tries to talk Lou into pitching in with him instead of Levon, Lou refuses."

Cord nodded. "That's how I see it. So, when talking doesn't work, Thorn tries to intimidate Lou. Sends Webb out to throw a scare into him. But things go sideways when Lou ends up dead. Now Thorn's in trouble. He lost his connection to a new product line and he's implicated in murder."

"But old Levon's also caught in a cinch." Sam brightened, straightening. "Because now he's gotta figure out how to make the deal work with that gang out of Nashville, without Lou. Convince them of his bona fides. He knows Lou kept a record of his coordinates and heroin contacts, in the military and Afghanistan. So he sends his right-hand man, Eli, to toss the house, see if he can't turn 'em up."

"Right. But Eli, still playing both sides, tells Thorn. Who sends both him and Radley to the farmhouse."

Sam leaned forward. "How do you know it was Rad?"

"Because when he ended up on his back up on the Knob last tonight, I recognized those square-toed boots. The same boot prints we found at the farmhouse and at the compound arson scene, along with a Benchmade 500 knife. Same kind Webb testified Rad gave him to use on Lou."

"So, they killed Fred just trying to find those records."

Cord leaned back, biting his lip. "Probably thought Lou kept the info in his computer, which wasn't at the farmhouse, but in his backpack at the hospital. But Lou had written the coordinates and contacts in this-here book, instead." He curled his lip and grabbed the Moleskin off the cot. "Fred died for nothing. Even if they'd found Lou's tablet, they wouldn't have gotten anything useful."

Sam's look darkened. "We need to nail that fucking shit Thorn on this."

"Don't I know it. But he's wily as they come. Hell, I can't even pin Lucas's assault on him. Never got a clear look at him through the car windshield, and unless him or Beloit is able to testify. . . . " Cord rubbed his chin, feeling frustrated. "And he didn't pull the trigger on Fred. Don't think Rad did either. He was a mean sonofabitch, but his pappy and Fred were close. Rad's family ate plenty of suppers that would've been a lot thinner if not for Fred putting extra produce on their table lean times." Cord stood and walked to the window. "I'd bet my daddy's farm the round they pulled from Fred will mike a .357-diameter slug from the .38 Special I pulled off Eli when I arrested him."

Sam shook his head. "So what about the girl, Zoe?"

"Well, according to Doc, she was pregnant. And that boy you met at the Farm?"

"Highbeam?"

Cord smiled. "Right. Beam told Lucas that Lou was Zoe's boyfriend. Said they were planning to leave the farm and marry. Lou also knew about the Magdalene website. He'd just found out his cancer was terminal. But on the morning she was murdered, Beam saw them fighting over a purple ribbon necklace, just like one Sunny said Levon had given to her. So, we got motive pointing to Lou. A crime of passion."

Sam paced to the door and back. "I don't know. Lou was a good kid. Had a true heart before he got shipped to that shithole. Sure, something happened over there. But when he came back, didn't Ryanne say he'd gotten himself cleaned up? Off the smack." He stopped pacing and shook his head. "Come on, Cord. We both know the only reason he got mixed up with this gang was he couldn't see another way out for him and Fred. Can't say I agree with his methods." He scratched his head. "But if this deal had come through, he'd have been set. Farm out of foreclosure. Money to pay the hospital bills, set up a life for his kid. Maybe move his new wife, Zoe, and their baby in. I just don't see him doing her."

"No. Neither do I." Cord scratched the scar above his brow. "But I can see how the happy couple's plans wouldn't fit with Levon's designs for turning Zoe into a Magdalene. He'd not only be losing the money a gal like her could generate on that website. He'd also be losing one very sanctified piece of ass."

"Not to mention that Zoe knew about the site. She might've threatened to expose what he was doing with the other Magdalenes. That'd end his revenue stream, and bring down his entire little kingdom of heaven up there. Plenty of motive for murder. The classics: power, sex, money."

"I think you hit it, Samuel." Cord took a deep breath and sighed, shoulders again feeling heavier than they should. "We'll ride out in an hour. I got to try and talk some sense into Levon. Make sure he won't do anything stupid and get himself killed, if we're going to get any closure on this."

He dropped back heavily into the chair, leaned back and closed his eyes. "Wake me in thirty. Oh, yeah – and release Hawk. Almost forgot he was still locked up back there. Tell him he might could find a job with Thorn. I think the bastard's got a couple new openings."

Judy's voice buzzed over the intercom. "Wife on line two, Cord."

"Oh hell and damnation," he groaned. "Ain't got time for any goddamned toilets this morning. Tell her I'll call back as soon as I can." He punched the line dead and leaned back again, tired. Alone. Staring at the ceiling as some lines from an old bluegrass tune floated through his head:

I wandered again to my home in the mountains
where in youth's early dawn I was happy and free
I looked for my friends but I never could find them
I found they were all, rank strangers to me. . . .

28

Reading Currents

Maya sat at the loom studying the tapestry. The pattern was just starting to emerge. The golden grapes, the scrolled white vines trimmed in indigo, green leaves tinged peach. The blush rose-to-red background. She was excited Levon had finally taken notice. He'd been so distracted over the last few weeks he'd hardly noticed her handiwork. Macramé hangers filled with local plants she'd dug from the surrounding hills. Curtains from hand-woven fabrics. Soft, warm throws for the chilly mountain nights.

Maybe things will get back to normal soon, she thought, sliding the tapered wooden shuttle between the warp. She caught it on the other end, pulled the beater to tighten the weft, lifting and pressing her feet in set patterns over the treadles. Then she slid the shuttle back between the warp to the other side and repeated the process, changing only the sequence of the treadle rotation, following the hand-drawn, stenciled pattern copied from her college art book.

She swayed to the rhythm of the quiet, sauntering swish of treadles as she pressed her feet against the pedals, then lifted them between shuttling, hardly noting the firm easy pull of the beater that tightened the weave, the soft whir of the bobbin reeling from the shuttle as the patterns slowly appeared, the weft subtly insinuating itself into the warp, one fine thread at time, slowly bringing life to scenes and designs that were visually stirring, tangible. Unlike paintings or photographs, the three-dimensional quality of a tapestry highlighted the regularity of imperfection, in scale and depth and detail, creating a transformation that brought a scene quivering to life.

She thought again about Levon making love to her. It had been the first time in months he'd completely given himself over. How much of his new-found passion stemmed from Zoe's absence?

Suddenly the door burst open and Eli stomped in, bringing with him a gust of cold. "What the fuck, Maya? Still working on that thing when we need to be getting ready for the fucking apocalypse? What's wrong with you?" He walked over to the loom and pointed outside, glaring down at her. "The other women are gathering up the children and heading to the bunker. Pull your head out of your ass and forget about that fuckin' rag."

She pushed the beater away and spun on the bench. "I need to finish this! It's what Levon wants. A symbol of the good we represent."

He snorted.

"What? Are you still pissed off that your precious Zoe got herself drowned?"

His arm whipped out quick as a snake strike, and a biting slap burned across her cheek. "Dammit, woman. If that's the best you can do, just shut the fuck up!" He spun and paced to the desk. "You think this is about me? Or your goddamned emblem?" He crossed back to her, jabbing a finger in her face. "This is a lot bigger than any of us, Maya. It's the whole goddamned fucking ball of wax. We're about to lose it all unless we can stop those storm troopers from raiding this compound and dragging us all to jail. Those they don't shoot outright."

Maya stood unsteadily, hand to cheek, stunned. Eli had never struck her before. Even during the worst rages he'd always been respectful. "But why?" she gasped. "Why did you hit me?" Tears welled, streaking her cheeks. "I've always done everything I could to make you happy. I'm just trying to be a good wife for you and Levon. I don't understand."

"Of course you don't." He shook his head, looking disgusted and disappointed. "So caught up in trying to please Levon you've forgotten why we came here. To change this shithole world into something less ugly and rotten. Less filled with egotistical petty competition. So you spend all your energy the last few months trying to get Levon to pay attention to you. And in the process, you forget all your other responsibilities. Not just to me, but to the whole community."

He paused, then lowered his head and sighed. "Look. I—sorry, Maya. I shouldn't have hit you. It's just I think Levon's about to fuck us all. And I don't know what to do."

"What do you mean? I thought he had a plan."

"What? Posting sixty-five armed men ready to die for him along the property line, because we fucked up?" He shook his head. "He's forgotten the bigger picture. The long view. We're not ready yet, and we'll need those people around when we are." He paused, frowning as if studying the loom, but his gaze was distant. "But I can't see any other option right now. Besides, I'm as bad as he is."

She searched his face, puzzled. "What do you mean? You're not bad. Neither's Levon."

"Nothing." He waved a hand. "It doesn't matter, now. I've got to get back out there."

The front door opened, and Levon and Lilith stepped in. "What's going on?" Levon walked briskly to his desk. "We got an army converging out there. Those men ready, Eli?"

"Yeah. Posted like we planned. But we're lean on ammo. Can't drag this thing out too long."

Levon pulled his Glock from his holster, pulled the slide back and dropped it, loading a round. Then lifted his head, leveling his pale blue gaze at Eli. "Told you, it's under control. They're not gonna lay a siege on this compound. Not with the media attention they'd get today. This ain't 1993 and I ain't that crazy bastard Koresh. They're smarter now.

But anyhow, if they're not. . . ." He chuckled sardonically. "There'll be some surprises for them. Some of our boys are trained at planting IEDs. Fuckers'll have a minefield to cross before they even get close." He looked around. "Where's Sunny?"

"Securing the women and children in the bunker." Lilith stepped up beside him. "Should be here any minute."

"So just follow the plan, everyone. Now get downstairs. They'll be calling soon."

Maya stood, frowning. "Who?"

"The fucking Man, Maya. He always does. But all we got to do is stall them until our reinforcements get here. I put the call out to my buddies in the movement. Soon this place'll be crawling with anti-corporate anarchists and save-the-planet greenie utopians, complete with sympathetic media in tow.

"So get ready, girls and boys. We're about to put on a show."

29
Still the Rushing Waters

Cord and Sam arrived at the command post, parked outside a ring of black SUVs and unmarked cruisers, and headed for the rapid shelter the agents had erected beside the road. Agent Murphy had just finished dispatching the federal personnel. ATF tactical units, along with bulletproof-vested, shoulder-holstered DEA agents, most toting pump-action shotguns and automatic rifles, were purposefully striding toward their vehicles. Cord recognized the determination in narrowed eyes and the grim set of their lips. One of their own was dead, another badly wounded. They wouldn't be in the mood for reconciliation.

Nor could he blame them. Every day, good women and men lost their lives serving the public, upholding the law—for which they got little or no thanks. Made it hard to keep good people on the job, let alone fill the slots of those lost to sudden violence. So every one now headed for the compound would be figuring to honor his or her comrade's sacrifice by ensuring the perpetrators would be brought to justice.

But too often, on battlefields and the streets, Cord had seen such efforts trade justice for retaliation, or outright vengeance. And when that happened, innocents were almost always caught up in the crossfire.

Collateral damage, some called it; the euphemistic dodge now popular with the military brass. Cord hoped that mood hadn't taken over at the command center. A full-out assault on the compound would produce a senseless loss of lives, unless he could talk Levon into giving himself up.

He stepped into the shelter and tipped his hat. "Special Agent Murphy." He nodded at the agents. "Looks like you got a good handle on the operational side."

"Just ready to do what needs to be done." Murphy glanced past Cord to a couple of cruisers wheeling out onto the highway, then turned to a topo map on the laptop set on the hood of his SUV. "We've set up spotters along the perimeter of the compound. A patrol boat will be watching the river, and two larger units are posted at exit points to the south and east of the property. Here and here." He indicated points on the map. "The rest of the units are converging on the highway just below the main gate. We didn't have time to get the armored carrier. I'm hoping we won't need it. I don't want this to turn into a siege."

Cord nodded. "Makes two of us. A lot of good folks live on that compound. I don't believe most have any idea about what their leader's implicated himself in. They're young. Idealistic. Levon convinced them to come here to get away from what they see as growing intrusion into the lives of ordinary people. This kind of action will only convince them of that position.

"But Levon's probably desperate. Thinking this confrontation is his only option. Give me a chance to convince him otherwise."

Murphy shrugged. "That's why you're here. We've set up a direct line into the compound. Take as long as you need. My men are under orders to stand by until I give the signal. The show's yours, Sheriff. For now." He raised his head to look Cord straight in the eye. "I really do hope you can make this work."

"Me too."

But as they followed Murphy's SUV down the highway and up the muddied track, stopping about thirty yards from the gates of the compound, Cord wondered if he'd misjudged Levon from the start. His own reasoning and judgment hadn't been unerringly dependable over the past few days. He'd taken actions, with key pieces of the puzzle still missing, which had already led to Lucas's grievous wounding and possible death. Now he wondered what other pieces of Levon's story were still missing.

Agent Murphy approached the truck as Sam pulled behind the SUV and parked. He said, "We have a command post set up in the white van at the bottom of the drive there. Where you can make the call."

"On my way." Cord turned to Sam. "Go on. I'll catch up."

He found the card in his pocket, pulled out his cell and punched the numbers. The line rang twice then went to voice mail. "Dammit!" He waited for the prompt. "Sunny, listen. It's Cord. I only have a couple of seconds, but if you care about those men and women up there with you, please listen.

"They're getting ready to storm your compound. A lot of innocent folks will end up hurt or dead unless we can stop it. I'm gonna try to talk to Levon. Get him to resolve this peacefully. But I need you to do something first. I know you got a PA system set up there in the office. Please turn it on and let your people hear what I say to Levon. Trust me, Sunny. I don't want anyone getting hurt. But I need your help."

A minute later, Cord was in the command post. "Okay. She's all yours, Sheriff." Murphy handed him the phone.

In three rings, Levon picked up. "Glad Earth Farms. Where the people and the planet live as one. How can I help you?"

"Levon. Cord here."

"So they pulled in the local constabulary to talk down the religious nut running the farm. Probably don't know that you and I have absolutely nothing in common."

"I wouldn't say that, Levon. We both have strong convictions about right and wrong. We just disagree in principle."

"Not only disagree. I don't even recognize the basis for your positions. You've thrown in with the devil, and once you believe his lies, there's no seeing the truth of things."

"You may be right. I've been off on many of my assumptions as of late. But this here's a unique case. Ain't no lie to say that more than just you and me's involved."

"You got that right, buddy. A whole village here is ready to stand up to you and those men whose jackboots you're licking. Bet they're just itching to come up and end this little problem."

The agents standing close to Cord glanced at each other, frowning. Levon's voice was ringing out across the open fields of the compound. Sam panned a pair of field glasses over the open space in front of the main houses. He nudged Cord and handed him the binoculars. Several armed civilians standing sentinel around the perimeter of the compound were quizzically looking up, obviously taking in the exchange coming over the loudspeakers that ringed the outdoor sanctuary and stage. Cord smiled. Good work, Sunny.

He cleared his throat, but not too loud. "You got that wrong, Levon. Nobody here wants to see anyone else get hurt. Nobody else *has* been hurt, have they?"

"Hell no. All safe and sound here."

"So let me talk to them. A good-faith gesture before we start negotiating. Who's with you? Lilith? Eli? Put 'em on. Please."

"Yeah. They're here." Cord heard Levon fumble with the phone then click over to the speaker mode. "Say hello to Sheriff McCrae, Lilith."

"Hello, Cord." Her voice sounded tight, apprehensive.

"Lilith. Y'all hangin' in there all right?"

"We're fine. Just want you to leave us the fuck alone."

"Can't do that, darlin'. Your man's done gone and got y'all caught up in a fix."

"Come on, man." Sunny's voice broke in. "You're really gonna storm in here? Risk killing women and children over a few bales of reefer?"

"You think this is about y'all growing some weed? No, no. Levon's thrown in with some skinhead militant-types out of Nashville. Trying to smuggle in heroin for distribution. We've also got him for conspiracy to murder and attempted murder of a couple of DEA agents last night. And that's in addition to running an online operation that includes non-consenting women performing live sex acts. Did the Magdalenes know they were on Candid Camera when you were getting it on with them, Levon?"

"Shut the fuck up, you lying bastard." Levon's voice shook. Cord heard scuffling in the background.

Then Sunny, yelling. "Let him talk, Levon! Let him talk!"

"I ain't lying," Cord continued. "Just Google it. And we got those Nashville boys in custody. Already telling us all about your plans to bring that heroin in, Levon. Only they were wondering what you did with their partner, Lou. Were you in on getting him and his daddy killed? Or maybe you just wanted to snuff him for trying to run off with Zoe."

"Fuck you, Cord. I don't know what the fuck you—"

Suddenly the crack of two gunshots blasted through the receiver and across the fields from the loudspeakers.

"Let's move! Now, Move!" Murphy shouted over his radio. Cord and Sam sprinted ahead up the drive. They jumped the gate and rushed past the sentinels, who'd set their weapons on the grass and stood with hands above their heads. Cord reached the door of the main house just as Maya came rushing out, screaming.

"He's dead. He's dead!" She fell against Cord's chest. "Eli, Eli,, Eli. . . . Oh my God."

"Okay. Okay, Maya. Where are they?"

"Down in the safe room." She tried to push away, but he gripped her arms.

"Hold on now." He looked over his shoulder at Sam. "Stay here with her." The deputy nodded. Cord pulled his SIG and slipped into the house. "Sheriff McCrae! Put down your weapons."

"Down here, Sheriff."

Cord recognized the voice. "You okay, Sunny?"

"For now. But I could use some help."

Cord followed the voice to a set of stairs. At the bottom he found Levon lying crumpled beside a desk, and Lilith sitting in a pool of blood cradling his head in her lap. Sunny had Eli pinned against the wall in the far corner, one arm pulled up behind his back. A .38 Special lay next to them on the floor. Cord holstered his own weapon, stepped over, and pulled a kerchief from his back pocket. He picked up the revolver and slid it into his coat pocket. Then knelt beside Lilith, who was rocking from side to side, humming to herself.

"Let me check his pulse, Lil." He laid a couple fingers on Levon's neck for a beat he already knew wasn't there. Then stood and stepped over to Sunny and Eli, pulling out cuffs.

"Thanks, Sunny." He yanked Eli's other arm around and clicked the cuffs tight. "Figured Levon would keep the controls to those outdoor comm speakers close at hand. Glad you got my message. Prevented a lot of innocent blood from spilling today."

"Yeah." Sunny looked over at Levon. "But not everyone was innocent."

Cord took a deep breath, shaking his head. "No. Not everyone." He turned and yelled up the stairs, "All clear, Sam. Come on down. And bring Maya with you. There's one last piece of business to clear up."

In a few seconds, Sam was coming down the stairs, dragging Maya behind him. She was pleading, "Please. Please. Don't make me go back down there again. I can't stand to see him like that."

"This won't take long. Just need to clear up the matter of Zoe Chandler. Turn around, Eli. Take one last look at your handiwork." Cord spun him. "So. Why'd you shoot him, Eli? To save the commune?"

"He was fuckin' it all up." Eli spit across the room at Levon's dead body. "That country-ass freak was gonna get us all killed. And for what, a fucking drug bust?"

Cord nodded. "Yeah—what I was thinking too. No use giving up the whole farm for a lousy bust. But that ain't what got you worried—

was it? It wasn't till I mentioned Fred and Zoe that you got all riled. Ain't that right?"

Eli looked away. "I don't know what the fuck you're talking about."

"Come on. I got your gun right here. And we're going to match ballistics from it with the slugs we pulled out of Lou's daddy."

"Do what you want. I'm not saying a thing."

"My God, Eli!" Maya waggled her head, trying to pull loose from Sam's grip. "You killed Levon and that old man too?" She dropped to her knees. "I trusted you. Oh, my God! You slept with me after killing that poor old man! And Zoe, too? You fucking prick." She pointed at him, hands shaking. "He was the last person to see her. That's right. I saw her come in that day to finish that Magdalene tattoo. What did you do then, Eli? Lose your fucking temper and knock her around, like you did to me today? I found the blood on my shuttle and got rid of the fucking evidence because I was afraid someone would find it and think you'd hurt her."

"Shut the hell up, you stupid bitch. I don't know what the fuck you're talking about. I never even saw Zoe that day. I got here late but she never showed. Figured she'd changed her mind about the tattoo. Ask Lilith, she was there with me the whole time." He shook his head. "Hell, everyone knew she was getting ready to leave us because of that fuckin' Levon." He nodded at the body. "Bastard never could keep his dick in his pants. Especially around the young ones. So Zoe was going to run off. Ruin everything." He looked around the room. "Come on. Everyone in this room knows he killed her. Probably fucked her one last time before he did it."

"You asshole." Lilith looked up, eyes blazing. "You never understood. Never even got what he was trying to do here. His dreams were real, you fucking over-educated, pompous ass. He'd lived the kind of life a trust-fund prick like you could never understand. He knew what it was like to struggle. To get beaten down. He was trying to build a better world. To lead us back to Eden. Not a fucking poseur, like you."

She pulled Levon's head to her chest and sobbed. "Yeah, he needed women. So what? Lots of great men do. But he'd never murder anyone. Not Zoe, even though the bitch was about to stab him in the back. Yeah, we all knew she was going to leave. And on her way out, take this entire community down. He should've killed her. He should've! But he couldn't do it."

Lilith pulled his lifeless body closer and rocked it, sobbing. "So I did. For you, Levon. All for you. You were fucking mine. My hope, my light, my desire."

30
Roll on, Roll on

A dry cold wind whipped Cord's face as he made the turn at Sears Gully and jogged down the trail to the river. He'd awakened early, dressed in faded black sweats and thick knit cap before lacing up his Everlast trainers and walking to the barn. After warming up with a couple sets of push-ups and crunches, followed by fifteen minutes of jump rope, he'd put in a forty-five minute workout on the bag. Now, as he angled to the bank, dry, dead brambles snapping underfoot and snagging the seams of his pants, his breathing was steady, strong. But the strain of the last few days still clung like the sweat steaming off his body into the chill air.

It'd been five days since the raid on Glad Earth Farm. And five days since he'd found the note from Lucinda. Sam had dropped him off that evening around six. Almost thirty-six hours since he'd slept. And despite the success of the raid on the Farm and solving three murders, the last hours of processing paperwork, along with a nagging sense of guilt over Lucas and Beloit had left him drained and depressed. He'd just wanted to crawl into bed and sleep for a week.

Instead, he'd found an empty house and a note on the kitchen table.

Cord,

Blu and I left this morning to visit Beth. She said she mentioned it to you a couple of days ago. We might be gone a while. Please don't worry about us. We'll be fine. I just need some time away to figure things out. You're welcome to see Blu here whenever you like, but don't expect us home before Christmas. I still love you, Cord. But between your job, your guilt over what happened to me and Blu, and the drinking, I'm not so sure our lives can fit together anymore. Please, just give me some time to think and work it out.

Lucinda

He'd read through the note again, ears ringing, heart pounding. He reached for the phone and dialed her cell.

"Hello, you've reached Lucinda's mailbox. Please leave a message. I'll get back to you as soon as I can."

He'd hung up and dialed Beth's number.

"Hello?"

"Hey, Beth. It's Cord. Let me speak to Luce."

A pause. Then, "She said she can't talk to you now."

"Goddamn it, Beth! Put her on."

"No, Cord. Lucinda's a guest in my home. I won't force something on her she doesn't want. Now you just settle down and call back tomorrow. You two can work this out, but not now, in one night."

He'd paced the kitchen. "I don't understand. Why's she doing this?"

"Maybe that's the problem, bub. When you do understand, then there might be a chance of patching things up. Until then, just give her some space."

"But what about Blu? I need to see my boy, Beth."

"You'll see him. Don't worry. Now go on and get some rest. You've been at it hard the last few days. Look. . . I promise I'll do what I can from this end to smooth things out. I love you, cuz. Goodnight."

The phone clicked dead.

He'd slammed the receiver back into the cradle. "Goddammit to hell! What the fuck am I gonna do?" He paced across the room gripping his hair, and leaned against the sink, looking out into the twilight. A sudden gust of wind from the east rattled the window sash. The last of the rusted leaves that still stubbornly clung to the branches of the sassafras tree dropped and swirled out of sight, tumbling in the airstream. He slammed a hand on the counter, stomped out the back door to the barn, flung open the double doors, fired up the Mustang and shot out down the driveway. In fifteen minutes he'd caught the on-ramp to I-40, headed west.

Three hours later, he crossed the Cumberland River and pulled off the freeway onto the narrow, tree-lined streets of the Germantown neighborhood where Beth lived. He parked next to the curb in front of her renovated 1920s bungalow and sat for a few minutes watching the windows, trying to gather his thoughts.

He'd spent the last few hours reviewing his life with Lucinda. The years of struggle. The shifting balance of dreams deferred, waiting for the perfect time to start or end whatever was coming next. The slow but steady faucet-drip that turned the shiny surfaces dull, pitted, worn. All the broken promises, commitments, betrayals they'd somehow managed to ride out. Hanging on through the shifting currents. The flood of fears and heartaches. Navigating confusing headings and markers.

Yet they'd always landed, somehow, safely together again.

'Til now. He sat staring out into the darkness, realizing just how lost he was. His bearings were shifted and strange without Luce and Blu as star-points in the constellation of his life.

He slipped out of the car, stepped up the sidewalk to the door and knocked. Beth's shepherd, Tame, started barking, the sound muffled from inside the house. Followed by the click and clatter of paws on the tile of the foyer.

Beth cracked the door and smiled. "You're a sight, Cord. Had a feeling you might show up."

"I need to see her, Beth. Please."

"Is that Daddy?" Blu came running up behind Beth. She backed away and let him squeeze between her leg and the doorjamb to jump into his father's arms.

Cord caught him and held tight. "What's up, little man? Sure did miss you the last couple days."

"Yeah, me too. Look! Cousin Beth bought me this hoodie." He leaned back, showing off the Vanderbilt emblem on the front. "We're goin' to a game on Saturday. You comin'?"

He shrugged. "Maybe. Gotta get back home and take care of a few things, first. Just wanted to let you know I hadn't forgot about you." He glanced up and saw Lucinda watching them, a few feet behind Beth.

"Luce." He nodded, then set Blu down on the porch. "Can you give me and your momma a minute, son?"

"Sure. Beth rented *Horton Hears a Who*. We were almost to the end." He reached up to hug Cord's neck again. "Love you, Daddy." Then he turned and ran back down the hall into the house.

Beth leaned out and patted Cord's cheek. "So, I'll leave you two to talk. Hang in there, cuz." Then she followed the boy inside.

Except for the worry and sadness in her eyes, Lucinda's face still held the same composed, compassionate expression he'd fallen in love with all those years ago. He cleared his throat, then looked away. "I understand if you don't want to talk, Luce." He looked back at her, heart rising to block his throat. "But I—I just need you to know I love you more than anything. And I'll do whatever it takes to get you and Blu back home again."

She leaned against the doorjamb and sighed. "Cord, it's all just too complicated to talk about now." A breeze crossed the porch, setting the chimes hanging above the wicker rocker clashing and tinkling. "I love you, dearheart. Always have. It's just. . . I don't think either of us ever got past the guilt and hurt of losing our baby after that awful night when Frank tried to kill me."

"But I—"

She held up a hand. "Just listen. Please. It's like it cut us so deep and fast neither one of us knew it had changed us, permanently. We thought we could go on living like nothing had happened. That someday it'd be okay again." She bowed her head, pressing a hand over her mouth. A tear ran down a cheek, gleaming in the porch light. "But it doesn't work that way. And now, this much later, I have to figure out how to get through it and live my life again." She sniffed, wiping the tear away, and looked him in the eye. "And you do, too."

He reached out, touched her shoulder, and then pulled her to him. She leaned into his chest as he stroked her hair. "Okay," he said. "Okay, Luce. Take all the time you need. Just don't give up on us, yet." He lifted her chin and kissed her forehead. "I love you like no other. If there's anything I can do, just say it."

She looked up, shook her head, and touched the scar above his brow. "Nothing for now. Go home. Do your job. You're damned good at it. I'm gonna stay here for a time, see if I can't figure out what's best." She glanced over one shoulder back into the house. "You're a fine daddy. Blu needs that in his life. Just give me some time?"

He nodded and brushed her lips with his thumb. "I'll call you every day."

She smiled and nodded. Reached up and squeezed his hand. "Keep 'er straight, Sheriff McRae," she said, then stepped back into the house and shut the door.

The long, tubular chimes clanged again, reminding him of the first time they'd kissed outside her apartment, while a neighbor's chimes had tinkled and rung from a patio above. She'd looked up, grinned and recited, "On the Future how it tells of the rapture that impels to the swinging and the ringing of the bells, bells, bells." She'd stepped inside, and turned to look at him again. "Poe. Edgar Allan. Look it up." Then she'd winked and disappeared.

He had, and remembered now that the poem didn't end so well.

Back on I-40 East, he flipped on the radio and picked up a Nashville station playing John Prine's "Killing the Blues."

"Then you ask me
just to leave you,
to run out on my own
and get what I need to.
You want me to find
what I've already had.
Somebody said they saw me,
swinging the world by the tail
bouncing over a white cloud,
and killing the blues."

That's about right, he thought. Swinging the goddamned world by the tail—when all the times it was me gettin' swung.

He pulled into Falston around one a.m. and noticed the lights were still on over Doc Kirby's practice. He swung the Mustang into a space in front, parked and walked to the glass panel door. After Cord rapped a knuckle a couple of times against one pane, Doc swung the door open, squinting over half-frame reading glasses.

"What the hell you doin' here, Cord? Figured you'd be down for the count after fillin' up the jail and bouncing those agents outta here."

He shrugged. "Yeah, well. Lucinda left."

"Huh." Doc slowly nodded, then shrugged. "Well, come on in, son. Have a drink."

Cord followed him down the hall and up the stairs to his apartment.

276

Doc's place was a small four-room bachelor. A large front living room/study was lined with overflowing bookshelves. A dark mahogany desk set against one wall was piled with notebooks, an old, dusty portable Underwood typewriter, a large crystal ashtray, and a slew of brier pipes angling out of their stands. At the window overlooking the river, an old oak table hunched between two overstuffed leather chairs. Cord noticed a copy of William Gay's *Twilight* splayed open, spine up on the table. Beyond the front room was a kitchenette. Down a short hallway, a bedroom opposite the small bathroom.

"Have a seat." Doc motioned to one chair. "Ain't got none of that corn liquor ye like, though." He ambled to the kitchen, returning with a bottle and glasses. "But I just got a new case of Glenfiddich might do the trick." He sat down opposite Cord, poured two fingers in each glass, picked up the one closest and leaned back. "Wanna talk?"

Cord picked up the other, and sat silent for a minute, watching the moonlight waver and blink on the surface of the river. Finally he sighed, swigged down the shot, and set the glass back. "Not really. Think I'm past talkin'. Why don't I just listen while you pour us another and tell me something I don't already know."

Doc raised an eyebrow. "That bad?" He drained his own glass, filled both again. Pulled a pipe and a box of matches from the pocket of his robe, tamped in tobacco, and lit it. He squinted through the smoke, blew the match out, and dropped it in the ashtray stand beside him. "Think I'll just join you for a spell. All out of answers folks don't already know, tonight."

And there they'd sat, watching the river go by until the sun came up. Cord had finally dozed off—waking late the next afternoon sitting in the same chair, an old, striped wool blanket thrown over his chest.

Now, as he dug the toes of his trainers into the muddy incline, struggling up the bank, he also struggled to convince himself he'd been right. Just doing his job. The very thing he'd been elected to do: Uphold the law. Bring justice down on those who preyed on the innocents.

Eli had been charged with the murder of both Levon and Fred after ballistics matched the bullets from his .38 to the truncated-cone slugs found in both men. In addition, he was charged with intent to sell after two members of the militia gang identified him as the second man with Levon at the drug meeting. He was also charged with conspiracy to commit murder, since the round which killed DEA Agent Phil Hosford came from a 7.62 M110 sniper rifle used by the now-deceased Frank "Zippy" Johnson, a long-time member of The Farm. Finally, based on testimony from several Magdalenes, he'd been charged as co-conspirator, along with Lilith and several other Farm members, with unlawful sexual exploitation, illegal videotaping of sexual acts without consent, and other charges brought in under the RICO Act.

Lilith was also charged with Zoe's murder. According to her confession, when the girl showed up for her final tattooing appointment, Lilith had feared Zoe's questions might expose their online sex operation. So, she'd lured her down to the river, saying she wanted to talk in private about shutting down the website. Her choice of the weaving shuttle as murder weapon was mere convenience—it'd been lying there on the loom as they left the house. "It just felt right when I picked it up," she'd told Cord, smiling faintly.

So she'd slipped it in her pocket, and once they'd reached the riverbank and Zoe had turned to face her, she'd pulled it out and swung. The last thing Zoe must have seen before she stumbled over the bank's edge and fell into the rushing water was the enraged, pixie-ish face of Lilith. Maya, who would be charged as an accessory after the fact, had directed Cord's deputies to the ravine where she'd tossed the black-cherry shuttle. It matched the fruitwood splinter Doc had found embedded in Zoe's scalp.

Cord topped the crest and jogged along the bank. Below, the roiling dark water looked choleric from recent runoff, its pebbled, muddy shores littered with debris—waterlogged stumps and branches, twisted vines and briar bushes, planks, fencing posts, plastic bags, an old tire dangling a long strand of wire someone had probably used as a tree swing.

He imagined children's voices shrieking delight as they arced out over the rushing, cold water on hot summer days. He'd known that innocent joy himself once. Same as Lou and Webb and Lucas. They'd been baptized in the current of this river, its dangers and joys leaving a mark on each. He wondered now if he could've done more to prepare them for the rough waters they'd eventually encounter. He'd sure tried. Hunted deer, wild boar, squirrel and rabbit with them. Grilled a hundred messes of fish after long days spent trolling on the river. Fielded baseballs. Taught the importance of not just keeping an eye on the ball, but on the pitcher's eyes too, as he wound up. The importance of a good, sharp jab. Of how to land a combination and stay on the balls of their feet. Most of all, he'd tried to teach them to walk away from a fight. In short, he'd done everything he knew how to help pilot them through the hard currents and survive.

And for what, he wondered now. Clearly it hadn't been enough.

He glanced at the opposite shore, where the red-orange tint of morning sun was just filling the sky above town. The sheriff's office with its small jail around back still housed Webb Rasser, whose trial would start in a few weeks. He was charged with one killing and one count of conspiracy to commit murder. Cord had spent the previous evening going over the man's defense with Bob Crayton. He'd met with the DA's office to give a sworn statement about Webb's cooperation in the drug bust and the larger conspiracy. If Webb got a reduced sentence, Cord worried he'd just be back in front of the judge again a few years down the road—if he didn't end up dead first.

He crossed a foot bridge, turned east following the northward flow of the river, and looked up at the looming outline of Thorn's house stuck like a brown scab on the side of the mountain. He hadn't been able to convince Jake Harkell to roll over on Thorn, despite promises to reduce his charges of conspiracy and attempted murder after a round from his rifle had been matched with a bullet pulled from the wounded

DEA agent. Apparently Harkell would rather take his chances in a federal pen than deal with the renowned ire of Thorn Reevers. Beloit had also refused to testify, saying that it would be better to face legal consequences than to live in constant fear the rest of his life. Injuries to his arm and legs from the wreck had probably ended any hopes of racing professionally. Cord took pity on the boy and sent him back home with a promise to never set foot in Tennessee again—and figured he never would, unless it was at Bristol, on a race day, and he was on the track, driving.

Meanwhile, Lucas was still laid up in the hospital, a bullet lodged next to his heart. Doctors hoping he'd recover enough to stand the operation they weren't even sure they should try. Cord knew he'd never be able to prove Thorn had shot him. During the entire chase the night of the bust, he'd never gotten a good look at the figure riding shotgun in Beloit's car. He couldn't make a positive ID on Thorn, nor had they been able to tie him to any of the other crimes of the past week. But Thorn's violent ways would put him in Cord's crosshairs again. Probably soon. After the whipping he'd given the drug dealer in front of a subordinate, Thorn would be chomping at the bit for revenge. Only a matter of time. And Cord was good with that. It was personal between them, now. But God help Thorn if he ever threatened Lucinda or Blu. He hoped even a man as depraved as Thorn knew better, but wasn't altogether sure after the evil he'd done to Lucas.

He angled off the path and struck out across the bottoms towards Charlie Graff's farm. Charlie, the last surviving friend of Cord's father, Matthius, and a close friend to Fred, lifted his head from under the engine bib when Cord came huffing up beside him.

"Hey there." He grabbed a rag, wiped the greasy dirt from his hands and pushed the bill of his cap back, nodding at the tractor. "Damn filter's clogged. Reckon it needs changin' in these Farmalls more 'n ever ten years or so." He smirked at his joke.

Charlie was short and stocky, almost eighty, with a dark weathered complexion from spending most days outside. Those deep-set hazel eyes let you know he was smarter than he let on. In fact, just about the best man Cord had ever known.

"Need to get 'er workin'," Charlie added. "Gotta drag some deadfall up from the bottoms. Top of that big sycamore next to the crick split off last night." He tossed the soiled rag onto the seat and pulled a pack of Pall Malls from his shirt pocket, along with an old silver Zippo. He tapped one out, packed it against the back of the lighter, flipped that open and lit up. "So what can I do fer ye?"

"Stopped by to try and clear up a few questions about Lou."

"Damn shame." He shook his head and propped a foot on the tractor's running plate. "Heard about the troubles. Had a premonition somethin' bad was gonna happen to that boy."

"Why?"

"Well." He pinched a speck of tobacco off the tip of his tongue. "Fred been worried about Lou ever since he got back from fightin' them Afghanis. But the two of 'em got along all right. At least fer a time. Then the boy started sufferin' from somethin'. Weren't never sure what t'was. But he never did look right. Gettin' sick. Throwin' up. Skin turned yeller. And he was all figidy and irritable-like. Some days seemin' just fine. Others, he'd change of a sudden." He took a drag off the cigarette. "Hard t' figure. Went up t' the VA several times tryin' to figure it out. They didn't do a lot, 'cept give him a bunch of tests and some pills.

"Ol' Fred didn't say much, but I could see somethin' change in him, too. Losin' hope. Kept tellin' Lou he just needed t' get out and work some. Lay off seein' them no-counts down at the Rooster. Wished he'd of done it, Cord. I surely do." He shook his head and lowered his eyes, sighing.

He pinched the butt of the cigarette between thumb and forefinger, took another drag, then flicked it in the dirt. "Then Lou started seein' that girl. Zoe. Seemed real took by her. Not from around here, way he talked. Not that it mattered. Told Fred he was plannin' t' marry her. Then Fred fussed. Wanted Lou t' get straightened out 'fore he run off and get hitched. Said he weren't ready t' live with a woman. Wanted him to wait until he was feelin' better."

"Did they ever fight over her?"

"Hell. I don't know, Cord." Charlie rubbed the toe of his heavy tan work boot in the dirt. "Fred never said. But I think he'd of been happy, if Lou was." He paused, picked up a wrench and wiped it with another rag pulled from his back pocket. "Reckon things all went to hell when the youngsters called it off."

Cord frowned. "What do you mean?"

"Well, Lou come up here to see me the mornin' 'fore he got killed. He and that gal had got in a fight over her wearin' some damn necklace. Lou said, somethin' her old boyfriend had give her. I told him he was a damn fool. Iffen he loved the gal he oughter learn quick that a woman like decorations, and she can't abide petty jealousies. But he didn't listen, bein' in one of them fidgety moods. Stormed off yellin' somethin' about headin' over to the Rooster." He snapped his fingers. "Hang on a minute." He walked to his workbench and moved some tools around, then stepped back over to Cord. "Here." He handed over a thin gold band, a ring. "He tossed this on my workbench before he left. Ain't comin' back fer it now, I reckon."

Cord studied the ring, then tucked it under the knit cap for safe keeping. He sighed and glanced across the field at Fred's farm. It'd been in the family for five generations. Lou had been his only son. Probably nothing would've made Fred happier than for Lou to find someone who'd marry and live with him here. And nothing would've made him sadder than knowing his son had lost it all over his own stupid, jealous pride.

Charlie picked up the new filter and fiddled with it while he followed Cord's gaze down across the sloping field. "Reckon I'll run on out to the farm and cut their grass oncet I get that deadfall up," he murmured, half to himself, half to Cord. "See ye at the funeral?"

"I'll be there. How's the wife?"

"That Martha's fit as a boot on a baby. Lookin' forward t' the young'uns comin' up fer Thanksgiving. Ain't seed them grandkids in months."

Cord rummaged in the toolbox and handed him a flathead screwdriver. "Always good to get the brood together, I bet. Can't beat Martha's cookin'. Best pecan pie I ever tasted." He smiled. "Makes me happy just thinkin' about it."

"She ain't too bad at roastin' a turkey and slow-bakin' a ham, neither." Charlie grinned. "Only problem is, she don't know how to cook such as that fer just two. Onliest time I get t' eat good is when the young'uns come t' visit."

Cord shook his hand, patted his shoulder, and turned to leave. "Good seein' you again, Charlie. Give me a call sometime, we'll get some fishin' in."

"I'll do it."

Twenty minutes later, he was running across Collard's Creek Bridge. The cloud cover had cleared and the sun reflected sharply on the rolling, swirling surge. Many people had been lost in this river. Sometimes at work. Sometimes at play. Sometimes to the evil meanness that took over a man or woman when lust or greed drove them to change the course of life's current. To block, dam, or dredge it. To cut a new channel. Sometimes, somehow, they figured killing was the answer. And the river ended up as the repository, receiving death into its depths indifferently as it would anything else: unchanging in its steady, eternal course.

He slid down the bank, picked up a long, straight stick and began to etch the sandy slope.

Zoe Chandler
Born Dec 24, 1988
Died Nov 13, 2008
Neither shall there be mourning, nor crying,

nor pain anymore, for the former things have passed away.

He knelt to one knee beside the river. "I'll let your momma know you were good, he said. "But this just weren't a good place for a girl like you. I'm so sorry, Zoe. And for what it's worth, you don't have to hang around these hills now, like some do. Let yourself move on to whatever might be out there waiting. For the few good souls still left."

He was about to rise when, out of the corner of one eye, he caught a streak of purple rippling just under the surface. He stooped, cupping a hand under it. The purple ribbon had snagged on a twig, slowly waving like a flag in the current. Its wooden heart pendant was missing—probably swept off by the currents—if it even was the same ribbon.

Cord fished the ring out of his cap, slipped it over one end of the thin purple band, and tied the ends in a knot. He stood, pulling the cap down snug on his head. Then took one last look down at the river, wound up and tossed the necklace far out into the current. He watched it fly in an arc, splash in, and sink to the bottom. Then turned and walked away.

ACKNOWLEDGEMENTS

To all my family from the hills who kept me humble and straight no matter how far off track I stumbled along the way. There's not much I wouldn't give for another day spent with those who've gone on—and not many places I'd rather be than sitting on a porch up on the Appalachia Range early evening at end of day.

To my good friends John Erenberg, Scott Ethridge, Jim Everitt, Billy Haake, Robert Morris, Monte Runfola, Scott Rushing, Paul Shields, and Art Wrightson for teaching me the way of good stewardship to the land, family, and community.

To the boys on the mountain. Your stories remind me where I've been, who I am, and what I might do to pay the debt of gratitude I owe for another chance.

To Cheree, Isaac & Morgan Morris, and Steve, Mary Catherine & John Mousourakis, for putting up with all those hours and years when I was missing in action.

To Joe Stritmatter, and Sheriff Randall Tippins for their willingness to take time out of their busy duties to consult and advise. Hope I got it right—the way that serves your work well.

To Beverly Donofrio, Joni Saxon-Guisti, Robin Gunn, Lenore Hart, Craig and Judy Johnson, Matt Prickett, Jack Ramanos, Ron Rash who have served as my close readers, advisers and role models. Always good to get that push.

To all the folks at the Ossabaw Island Foundation. Your work helps writers and artists to remember what's important—nature's dark and silent ways.

And to the professionals at Northampton House Press. The gracious welcome from your patient and kind staff really made me feel a part of the family. Happy to join the team.

Finally, to Danelle Lejeune, whose faith and trust reminds me that I'm not half-crazy—or if I am—that I'm nevertheless fully loved.

Northampton House Press

Established in 2011, Northampton House Press publishes selected fiction, nonfiction, memoir, and poetry. Check out our list at www.northampton-house.com, and Like us on Facebook – "Northampton House Press" – as we showcase more innovative works from brilliant new talents.

Lightning Source UK Ltd.
Milton Keynes UK
UKHW012010100720
366354UK00002B/17/J